OPERATION BOUNCE HOUSE

Matt Dinniman is a writer and artist from Gig Harbor, Washington. He is the author of the bestselling Dungeon Crawler Carl series along with several other books about the end of the world. He doesn't really hate Cocker Spaniels, and he plays bass in a metal band.

TITLES BY MATT DINNIMAN

Operation Bounce House

DUNGEON CRAWLER CARL SERIES

Dungeon Crawler Carl
Carl's Doomsday Scenario
The Dungeon Anarchist's Cookbook
The Gate of the Feral Gods
The Butcher's Masquerade
The Eye of the Bedlam Bride
This Inevitable Ruin

Kaiju: Battlefield Surgeon

THE SHIVERED SKY SERIES

Every Grain of Sand
In the City of Demons
The Great Devouring Darkness

DOMINION OF BLADES SERIES

Dominion of Blades
The Hobgoblin Riot

The Grinding

Trailer Park Fairy Tales

OPERATION BOUNCE HOUSE

MATT DINNIMAN

MICHAEL JOSEPH

PENGUIN MICHAEL JOSEPH

UK | USA | Canada | Ireland | Australia
India | New Zealand | South Africa

Penguin Michael Joseph is part of the Penguin Random House group of companies whose addresses can be found at global.penguinrandomhouse.com

Penguin Random House UK,
One Embassy Gardens, 8 Viaduct Gardens, London SW11 7BW

penguin.co.uk

First published in the United States of America by ACE,
an imprint of Penguin Random House LLC 2026
First published in Great Britain by Penguin Michael Joseph 2026
001

Copyright © Matt Dinniman, 2026

The moral right of the author has been asserted

Penguin Random House values and supports copyright.
Copyright fuels creativity, encourages diverse voices, promotes freedom of expression and supports a vibrant culture. Thank you for purchasing an authorized edition of this book and for respecting intellectual property laws by not reproducing, scanning or distributing any part of it by any means without permission. You are supporting authors and enabling Penguin Random House to continue to publish books for everyone.
No part of this book may be used or reproduced in any manner for the purpose of training artificial intelligence technologies or systems. In accordance with Article 4(3) of the DSM Directive 2019/790, Penguin Random House expressly reserves this work from the text and data mining exception

Set in 12.4/15pt Garamond Premier Pro
Typeset by Six Red Marbles UK, Thetford, Norfolk
Printed and bound in Great Britain by Clays Ltd, Elcograf S.p.A.

The authorized representative in the EEA is Penguin Random House Ireland,
Morrison Chambers, 32 Nassau Street, Dublin D02 YH68

A CIP catalogue record for this book is available from the British Library

HARDBACK ISBN: 978-0-241-80404-9
TRADE PAPERBACK ISBN: 978-0-241-80505-3

Penguin Random House is committed to a sustainable future for our business, our readers and our planet. This book is made from Forest Stewardship Council® certified paper.

For Sexita

DAY ONE OF FIVE

CHAPTER 1

'Oliver, you must remove yourself from bed. Priscilla is missing.'

I opened one eye, groaned, and rolled over. My pounding head felt as if it was caught in a press. My lips felt burned and cracked. *I'm still drunk. Christ, how did I even get home?*

The floating, humming form of Roger moved closer to my head. 'Oliver, are you still inebriated? You must get up. Priscilla is missing.'

'Who the hell is Priscilla?'

Zap.

'Ow, fuck!' I cried, sitting up in bed, rubbing my arm.

Zap.

'Roger, stop. Jesus.'

Roger's correction stinger crackled with electricity. It retracted back into the robot's abdomen with a metallic *shing*.

'Rule number four,' the floating robot said. 'No swearing.'

'I know the rule, Roger. Why are you in my room? Even if I was still going to school, it's Saturday.' I blinked a few times, still disoriented, trying to remember what Roger had said. I had dirt and grass on my arms. I pulled the blanket back to reveal sheets covered with mud, like I'd been dragged home and then unceremoniously dumped into bed. 'It *is* Saturday, right?'

'It is Saturday indeed, Oliver. To answer your improperly formatted query, Priscilla is one of the honeybee scouts. She must be retrieved. That is why I am here. No other honeybee assets are available to do the job, as all are engaged in the harvest or undergoing scheduled maintenance. This means you must do the retrieval. I will accompany you.'

One of the honeybee drones? My arm throbbed, and my mind still swirled with fog. It'd been a while since Roger had corrected me. I'd forgotten how much it hurt.

'I can't believe you stung me.'

'I was under the impression you didn't swear anymore, Oliver.'

'I don't when you're around. I was half asleep. I'm still half asleep.' *And half drunk.*

I yawned, and I regretted it. It felt as if something fluffy had curled up and died in my mouth. I desperately tried to remember what had happened the night before. The party. Rosita's ranch. Rosita and I had gotten into a fight. It was over something stupid. She'd said it was over. The whole village was there. A wave of vodka-flavored nausea swept over me. Everything hurt. I was going to puke.

'Which one is Priscilla?'

'Priscilla is unit number 418. Long-range scout number three. We will proceed to her last location on the map and attempt to recover her.'

I pulled myself up, smearing more dirt across the sheets. A small plastic Tyrannosaurus rex toy fell off my headboard. I spent a moment putting the Earth artifact back into its rightful place with the other figures. I took a moment to blow dust off the line of colorful dinosaurs. I then spent a good ten seconds looking for my boots before realizing they were still firmly attached to my feet. They were caked in mud.

My brain was finally starting to catch up. 'Wait . . . "Priscilla"? Are you dating her or something? Since when do the scouts have names?'

'They have always had names, Oliver. Your grandfather had names for all of us, but he turned off the designations when we were repurposed for agriculture. Your sister reactivated the labels yesterday during her lesson at the control center. Are you not going to change your clothes? Rule number nine. Always maintain good hygiene. It appears your clothing is quite dirty.'

'We need to go back to the numbers. It's going to be too difficult to remember four hundred thirty different names.'

'Lulu made the change in the control center. If you wish to change it back, you will have to implement the change there. I must warn you, your sister was quite taken with the idea of having individual human names for each of the honeybees. She inquired about painting the names on each unit. You have clean clothes in your closet.'

'If we're going out there, I'm just going to get dirty again. I'll change and shower after we get back. Speaking of my sister, where is she? Rule number eight. Isn't this her job?'

'That is correct, but Lulu did not come home last evening. It appears she is located seven point one two kilometers northeast of here. When she awakens, as she is undoubtedly in a similar state as yourself, she is scheduled to travel to Burnt Ends for her Saturday supply run. She will not be back until it is dark.'

'Wait, really? She's still at Rosita's ranch? How did I get home last night?'

What was the last thing I remembered? Sam and the twins had run back to the Serrano ranch for more booze. My sister and Ariceli had been out in Rosita's greenhouse along with several others blasting music. I'd been with Rosita in the main house, and I'd complained that everyone wouldn't stop talking about Earth politics. She'd snapped at me, and, and . . .

'Melissa and Trixie 2 brought you home,' Roger said. 'You were retrieved at Lulu's request. You were unconscious.'

'Wait, *who* brought me home? Were they drones?'

'Melissa and Trixie 2 are scouts. This is why you were dragged and not carried.'

'Trixie 2,' I muttered. I rolled my shoulders. They had *dragged* me home? Christ, how drunk had I been? My arms were a little sore, weren't they? The thought of being strung between two of the wobbly dog-sized robots was terrifying. They weren't meant to carry something as heavy as me, especially not the smaller-sized scout robots. They wouldn't have been able to fly, not with my weight. I was lucky I hadn't been brained against a rock. 'How far out is the unit? What's her name again? Melissa?'

'Melissa is recharging in the barn. Priscilla is the missing one.'

I sighed. This naming thing was never going to work. I reached for my com bracelet to send a text message to Lulu, and I grabbed my bare wrist. My bracelet wasn't there. I started to curse out loud, but I caught myself.

'Okay. Where's the unit? And where's my bracelet?'

'Priscilla lost contact with the control center two hours and ten minutes ago. She is seven kilometers southwest of here. Your bracelet is being repaired. You vomited directly on it last evening, which is a direct violation of –'

'Yes, I know. Rule number two. Always keep your bracelet in good working order. Southwest. So, she's in the hills?'

'That is correct.' Roger rotated in midair to reveal the small, dingy screen on the bottom of his abdomen. The cracked display barely worked, and I had to squint to see what he was showing me. It was a relief map of the low, hilly swamps with a blinking dot.

I groaned. This was going to take hours. 'If it's in the hills, I won't be able to bring the quad.'

'That is also correct. The quad is with your sister anyway. I have already packed your repair kit. If you aren't going to change your clothes, I will wait for you to vomit, and then we will leave.'

'Let's go now,' I said, pulling myself to my feet. The world wobbled, and my stomach lurched. What was it Rosita had said last night? *You're a worthless, shiftless dirt jockey who will die alone*? 'I'll vomit on the way.'

The Rhythm Mafia Tapes. Scene one.

Description prepared by Lana Lipovsky for the Joint Republic Hearing Committee on the New Sonora Incident.

This is a written description of the scenes as shown via multiple streams during the final night of the Operation Bounce House disaster. The recordings are part of an unfinished documentary broadcast by one Rosita Zapatero, twenty-six, a colonist farmer on the planet New Sonora. Records indicate Zapatero is a descendant of colonists from Hibisco and Forlorn, two of the fifteen generation ships that originally settled New Sonora. Most of the colonists in the subsequent videos are descendants of one of those two ships, unless otherwise noted. (See exhibit 5 at the end of the full report titled 'The 15 Colony Ships.') The documentary video itself is available as exhibit 13 under the header 'Night Five of Five.'

We are in a barn. A thin, dark-haired man is playing an upright bass. Behind the man are several instruments, including a drum set, a few amplifiers, and a PA system. A banner on the wall behind the drum set reads, **The Rhythm Mafia**.

There is no date on this particular clip, but evidence suggests this was filmed approximately six months before the incident.

The man is Sam Amboya, twenty-five, a colonist farmer. He shakes his head to the rhythm while he plays the large instrument, which is unfinished and appears to be made of plywood. Watching from a chair with her arms crossed is a red-haired woman. She is Harriet Riggs, a twenty-four-year-old colonist. Records indicate her as a direct descendant of the ship Quinceañera.

ROSITA (OFF CAMERA): Okay. Introduce yourselves.

SAM: My name is Sam, and this is my soon-to-be-wife, Harriet. I slipped one past the goalie, if you know what I'm saying.

HARRIET: Sam. Don't say it like that.

SAM: How else would I say it?

HARRIET: I don't know. We're going to have a baby. They're going to see this one day. They don't need to hear their father say he 'slipped one past the goalie.' I took a pill to dissolve the pregnancy blocker. There is no goalie.

Sam leans his bass up against the wall. He moves his face to the camera and grins.

SAM: Hey, kid. If you're seeing this, I want you to know something. I banged your mom.

Harriet shouts as she jumps up from her chair, picks up a drumstick, and hurls it at a laughing Sam. The camera cuts before the drumstick makes contact.

(A time cut.)

Sam is sitting on the ground with a small mark on his forehead. Harriet sits next to him with her head on his shoulder.

SAM: What're we supposed to be talking about again?

A new voice speaks off-screen, and the camera swivels, revealing a wide shot of the barn. The barn is filled with multiple charging pods for the honeybee drone robots, which at this point are still outfitted strictly for agriculture. (See exhibit 2 entitled 'The Honeybee Drones.') This is a tall, twenty-five-year-old male colonist with dark hair. He is Oliver Lewis. (See exhibit <Redacted>.) He has a large wrench in his hand, and it appears he is in the engine compartment of a combine harvester.

OLIVER: You're supposed to be talking about our band.

ROSITA: Ollie, don't talk! The camera will track you.

Oliver grins and holds up his hands, which are black with oil.

OLIVER: It's not my fault if the camera loves me.

SAM: I gotta ask. How many dirty movies have you two made with this camera anyway? And can Harriet and I borrow it?

ROSITA (TO OLIVER, LAUGHING): Just let us do this, okay? You said we could use your barn. This lighting is only going to last a little longer.

OLIVER: I gotta go check on my sister in the north fields anyway. I'll see you tonight, beautiful.

ROSITA: See you tonight.

Oliver, still grinning, drops the wrench, which clatters loudly; then he rubs his hands on his pants and goes outside.

HARRIET (TO SAM AS THE CAMERA SWINGS BACK TO THE COUPLE): Why don't you ever call me 'beautiful'?

SAM: Because you already know how I feel about you, babe.

He puts his arm over Harriet's shoulder. She makes a derisive snort, but she nuzzles closer to him.

ROSITA (SIGHS): Tell us more about the band.

Sam visibly brightens.

SAM: We're called the Rhythm Mafia. It's Ollie on drums, our friends Tito and Axel on guitars, and me on bass. I'm basically the singer now after Ollie's sister, Lulu, quit, but I'm not very good. We're looking for a new one. We practice once a week if we can. But during harvest, it can get hard to find time to get together. And sometimes we get together and we don't actually practice. We just talk and drink.

HARRIET: Sometimes?

ROSITA: Why do *you* still do it? I asked Oliver, and he says he likes band practice. Axel says it's Tito's favorite thing in the world. I get that they like it, but none of them can explain why. What about you? You say you're not very good. You've never played a show. There're not too many people to play for even if you did set up a concert. You put that one song online, but I saw it has less than a hundred downloads.

Sam reaches over and kisses Harriet on the top of the head. She snuggles even closer to him. He leans into the camera.

SAM: Don't get me wrong. I love Harriet, and I love that I'm having a kid with her. We're doing what we're supposed to be doing, and I won't ever regret that. Our great-great-grandparents all died on a spaceship so we could have a place of our own. But is that it? If that's all we're doing, how does that separate us from all the other animals out there? Have you seen how sad the old people around here are? Have you ever looked into the eyes of Mrs Xalos? Or Mr and Mrs Gonzales? I love them, but what do they have? Do you see how empty they are? It's like they're zombies.

The camera starts to zoom in tight on Sam's face.

SAM: No, we're not good. We're never going to be famous musicians. But it doesn't matter. When I'm with my best friends playing our stupid little hearts out, I'm not thinking about the farm or that biological imperative to have kids or anything other than the music. Yeah, I do want to play a show one day. I want to play a concert, even if it's just for Mr Yanez's magic chickens. That's all we really have here. But at least it's *something* that separates us from the animals. It's joy, it's happiness, it's life beyond just procreation. And if we don't have something like that, then what's the point?

CHAPTER 2

'Oliver, what is the square root of 576?'

'I don't care,' I said as we trudged south through the mud and knee-high reeds. As *I* trudged through the mud. Roger buzzed over my head, zipping back and forth, constantly commenting on how slow I was moving. 'Nobody needs to know that sh . . . stuff.'

Roger buzzed angrily as he passed. 'That is incorrect. Oliver, I am worried about your progress. Your New Sonoran and Earth history scores are adequate, but your arithmetic is lacking. We must quiz.'

I watched the rickety old bot zip forward in the air, leading the way. I sighed. *Damn you, Grandpa Lewis,* I thought for the millionth time. Sometimes I wondered if he'd planned it this way, deliberately leaving the nanny system installed. Lulu certainly thought so.

'Maybe we can wait until tomorrow when the other two scouts are recharged, and we can send them out.' My boot made a sucking noise as I took a step. 'Or you can go alone.'

'If Priscilla is damaged, time is of the essence. With the loss of Hannah last season, we have only three scouts left and can't afford to risk the integrity of one to rescue another. And, Oliver, you know I can't leave the safety of the ranch without a companion.'

'I know,' I grumbled. 'Rule number one.'

Rule number one. Protect Roger. Without Roger, the entire farm collapses. He must never leave the ranch alone. He must be maintained weekly. Protect Roger at all costs.

The other two honeybee scouts, 410 and 413, whatever their names were, were in their three-times-a-month repair sequence and recharge. To remove them prematurely would supposedly damage their already deteriorating systems. And because of reasons I didn't understand, we always had to charge two at a time. The charge happened every Saturday on a rotation, so each of the three charged two weeks in a row, took a week off, and then started again.

We called them honeybees, but I knew they were much larger than the Earth bugs they were named after. Apparently, the earliest versions of these things had been based on dogs. We had three different models. The vast majority on the ranch were the drones designed with bigger batteries and less autonomy. We had three scouts left. Two if 418 – Priscilla – was gone. They were a little smaller than the drones. And we also had Roger, the 'hive queen' AI unit. He was the smallest of them all, about half the size of the rest. The size of a cat.

It'd been seventy years since the planet was first settled. My grandfather Edward Lewis – though everyone just called him Lewis – had been born on the *Forlorn*, one of the fifteen hulking generation ships that had brought settlers to the planet. He had been trained as an engineer and honeybee mechanic. They were already in orbit when he was born, and he'd been seventeen years old when they first settled on the city of Fat Landing. Four years after that, his group settled here in the Baja peninsula, seven thousand kilometers away near the edge of the great ocean, and created the agricultural hub of Burnt Ends. Grandpa Lewis had been assigned a fleet of roughly five thousand honeybee production machines, complete with an additional fifty hive queen bots, and for the next five years, he'd overseen the construction of most of the farms and industrial buildings in the area. A fact, fifty-plus years later, he would never shut up about. Not until the day he died.

The honeybees had an intended lifespan of five–ten years of heavy labor, after which they would start to break down. As far as I was aware, the four hundred thirty remaining honeybees on our farm were the sole enduring honeybees on the entire planet. Roger, whose real name was actually Roger-Roger, was the last hive queen in existence. Once he finally fell out of commission, that would be it. We'd still be able to send the drones out on simple agricultural tasks using the control center, but they wouldn't work in unison like they did now. And the scouts, if any were left, would cease to function.

By the time my grandfather's outpost-establishing mission was complete, he'd been only twenty-nine years old, and as he explained it, he'd been told to 'fuck off and die on a farm somewhere.' So that was pretty much what he did. He established a farm with my grandmother Yolanda, and five years after that, they had my mom. It was around the same time he'd discovered the local government had all the remaining honeybees just sitting in a warehouse somewhere, decommissioned and doing nothing. He'd requested two thousand units so he could see if he could repurpose them to help with agriculture. They'd agreed.

'I have found Priscilla's signal,' Roger said as we reached the top of a small hill rising out of the swamp. The mud and reeds were replaced with large round bushes that leaked a thick sap that was next to impossible to get out of clothes. The shrubs were called plica bushes, and they were everywhere. They smelled something awful, like the wet underside of a lamb with a skin infection. They grew fast, too, and I had to be constantly vigilant they didn't get a foothold on our land. Their roots were a bitch to dig up, and as helpful as the honeybees were, they were shit at digging up roots.

We reached the top of the hill, and I wheezed for breath. I looked south, trying to see if I could see the great ocean. I couldn't. All I could see was more bush-covered hills. I was finally starting to sober up, but I still felt I was going to be sick at any moment.

'How far?'

'Just one more kilometer past that next hill.'

'What was she doing out this far anyway?'

'We detected an unknown radio signal on the surface, and one of Priscilla's duties is to investigate unknown signals.'

I stopped dead. 'Wait. You detected an unknown radio signal out here on the surface in the middle of nowhere, you sent out a scout bot, and the scout disappeared? Don't you think – I don't know – that you should have led with this information? Or maybe sent another scout with her?'

'Oliver, the other two active scouts were unable to investigate because they were occupied taking your unconscious form back from the other ranch. They had already entered their scheduled maintenance when Priscilla disappeared.'

'Are you fucking kidding me?'

Shing! The correction stinger emerged from Roger's abdomen, and faster than I thought possible, he zipped forward and stung me in the arm.

'God*damnit*,' I said. 'Gah!' I cried a moment later as he stung me a second time.

'Rule number four. No swearing, Oliver,' Roger said.

'Roger,' I said, breathing heavily, 'I hate you.'

'It's customary for unruly students to hate their tutors, Oliver. Students are less likely to learn in too permissive environments.'

'You're not my teacher anymore. I'm not a student. I haven't been for years. You're a hive queen. If you weren't so valuable, I'd turn you into yard art.'

'Artistic interests are fine if they are pursued during your leisure time, but you should focus your attentions on furthering your core studies. Yes, artists are important to the persistence of culture, but artisanal skills must take a back seat to functional skills when a colony is still in its early stage. Your band is a good example of this. Luckily, your percussion talent is such that a career in music will never be possible.'

I started to say something back when I was interrupted by the sound of something mechanical coming from the next ridge over. It was a hissing followed by a *clang, clank, clang*. There was something else, too. It sounded amplified, like it was coming through the loudspeaker at the community auction house, but it was still too far for me to understand. It almost sounded like . . . like screaming.

'Roger, what is that?'

'It sounds like a juvenile having a temper tantrum,' Roger said. 'It is amplified through a public address system. I am detecting multiple strange signals in that direction when there were none just a few moments ago. This signal is closer than Priscilla's.'

'Yeah, but what's the machine? It sounds like a tractor with a thrown tread.'

Right at that moment, the large colorful contraption crested the distant hill. It was maybe a hundred fifty meters away. I just stood there, dumbfounded.

The machine was about three meters tall, and it walked on two legs, though one of them was heavily damaged, probably the cause of the loud clanging. Each step came with the sound of scraping metal followed by a noisy clank.

Oof. Before I could get another thought in, I was on my back. Roger had flown down and pushed my legs out from under me.

'Stay down. Do not allow it to see you,' Roger said, hovering low to the ground.

I rolled to my stomach and turned, hiding behind a plica bush. The robot thing fully emerged above the next hill. 'It's a giant honeybee,' I said, 'but with two legs instead of six.'

'Oliver, remain hidden. Do not move unless it approaches. Then run. Do a zigzag pattern if you must run,' Roger said. He buzzed off to the side, disappearing the way we came. He kept low to the ground.

'Roger,' I hissed, but the small hive queen was gone. I returned my attention to the giant robot. I gawked at it through the thick bush. I cursed myself for not bringing my bracelet. I didn't carry a camera drone with me like Rosita always did, but the bracelet itself had a zoom and pop-up-screen function, or I could tap into Roger's feed and watch from there.

The weird reverse-jointed legs on the robot met at an egg-shaped body that looked too small to hold an actual driver. A long cannon-like device hung on the left side of the body, and a four-pack missile launcher was on the right. Three of the four missile tubes were empty. Multiple antennae rose off the back of the machine.

But strangest of all were the paint job and accessories. It was decorated bright purple and had green spikes down the center of the egg, making it look like it had a Mohawk. Words I couldn't read at a distance were painted across the front, but the distinctive shape of a penis was crudely drawn on each of the two legs, both pointing upward with little liquid squirts coming out of the top.

A mech, I thought. *That's a goddamn mech.* It was just like the ones in a hundred animes and comics and video games that had come with us from Earth. As a kid, I'd spent hours drawing these things or playing one in my game system. I hadn't known they were real. But what was with that paint job? And what was it doing here in the middle of nowhere? Where had it come from?

Heat waves radiated off the machine, and a line of dirty black smoke chugged out the back as it took a tentative step down the hill. The damaged leg whined ominously.

'There's nothing here!' a young male voice cried from the machine. Now that it had crested the hill, I could finally understand what it was saying. It had a weird accent. Earth. This was someone from Earth, which was impossible. 'You said it would be a target-rich environment! This is bullshit!'

There was a response, but it was muffled like the source of the voice was coming from the same microphone.

'You promised me, Mom. You promised. You're a fucking bitch.'

There was a sharp retort I couldn't understand.

'No, you told me I was going to the city. There's nothing here! You promised. You ruined my birthday.'

The machine turned to the left and the right, the egg shape rotating as it took in the area. A low mechanical yet alien whisper rose from the machine when it moved.

'I can't get there. It's too far. Stupid thing is broken. And it reacts slow.'

'...'

'How was I supposed to know that? They messed up the design. You're gonna have to buy me a new one.'

Another angry response.

A high-pitched piercing wail emanated from the robot, distorting over the speaker. The egg body started bouncing back and forth, whisking as it moved.

It was the kid. He was squealing.

What the hell?

CHAPTER 3

I finally realized what I was seeing and hearing. This machine was being controlled remotely. Controlled by a child. A child who was still on Earth. And for some inexplicable reason, the kid was arguing with his mother over a loudspeaker.

My eyes instinctively moved to the sky. The gate. I couldn't see it, but it was up there. One needed a telescope to be able to see it, and even then, it was visible only at night. I'd been looking at it my whole life. My grandfather had had a telescope nest sitting on top of the barn. He'd made us look at the gate dozens of times over the years. Sometimes if we watched long enough, we could see the drones zipping about up there, piecing the gate together. We'd sit on the roof and eat Popsicles, and he'd tell us stories about Earth, even though he'd never been there, either.

It took us 133 years to reach New Sonora, fifty years to open the pinhole, and the colony will be sixty-five to seventy years old when the gate's construction is finished. When it finally opens and reconnects us with home, everything is going to change.

He'd lived to see the pinhole open, but he'd died before the real transfer gate had finally turned on last year. The Earth–New Sonoran transfer gate had powered on and stabilized 201 years after the fifteen generation ships had left Earth's orbit, seeking out a new home.

I was still waiting for the big change. The pinhole – the microscopic gate that allowed information but nothing else through – had been open for almost twenty years. It had limited bandwidth, but we'd had access to instant news and communication and media from Earth for the majority of my life.

The original settlers had had a library of Earth media, from books to movies to games. My grandfather had been a big fan of old twentieth-century cowboy movies. I personally liked comics and video games. When the pinhole opened, we'd gotten access to a lot of the new stuff, and it really wasn't that different from the older stuff we'd seen already. It was almost like progress had stalled once people started fleeing the planet.

It'd been two hundred years since we'd left, and even speech patterns were mostly the same. Movies were the same, especially now that the law made it so AI depictions of humans were illegal. Comics were the same. Games were the same. The only difference was the graphics, and we didn't have access to the full-immersion rigs that had been gaining popularity in recent years on Earth.

There was a lot of bizarre slang I still couldn't figure out, even though I regularly watched a lot of Earth media. The music was different, too, and I was pretty sure I'd never understand that. But even though the slang was *a lot* different, we still understood one another. English and Mandarin were the dominant languages on Earth. Spanish had faded, but it was still spoken. It was just English here on the peninsula, though I knew some of the more remote communities were only Spanish speaking. I could speak a few Spanish phrases here and there. Grandpa Lewis had turned off Roger's Spanish lessons after Grandmother Yolanda died. He said it hurt his heart too much to hear it.

Last year, when the actual transfer gate had opened, it was supposed to have been this big, momentous thing. But other than a short visit from a Republic ambassador, not much else had happened since. Transfer wasn't yet open to civilians and settlers, and it wouldn't be until the quarantine was over in eight more years. No food or trade goods or luxury items from distant planets had made their way to us through the instant transfer gate.

For us on New Sonora, it had been a huge deal. But for those on Earth, it was just another day. They were reconnecting with distant colonies every week, and they had been for years now. They'd developed faster gate-building technology and space drives in the interim, and new colonies were building their gates in ten years or less. Many of the reconnected colonies were newer and farther out, making New Sonora uninteresting to Earth's population, except as a convenient target for their casual xenophobia.

Voom! I jumped as the cannon on the right side of the mech fired, and a hill a half kilometer to my left exploded in a geyser of dirt and rock and trees. The ground underneath me rocked.

I just stared at the destruction in shock. It was so sudden, so violent.

The kid was still screeching. I was pretty sure he hadn't fired at anything in particular.

I was trying to figure out what was going on, why he was here. Were they using the hills to test some sort of new technology? It didn't make sense. There was a quarantine. Nothing in or out except on government business. I remembered what the kid had said. *You told me I was going to the city.* Why would they send an armed mech to the city? And more important, why would they send one piloted by a child?

A sudden terrible thought occurred to me.

You're so naïve, Rosita had said to me last night. Everyone had been talking about it.

It's stupid. It doesn't make sense, I'd said. *Why is everyone always so worried about this stuff?* And then I'd waved the camera bug away from her bracelet, accidentally smacking it to the ground, which had made her *really* mad.

Earth wants to evict us, she'd said as she collected the camera, making sure it wasn't broken. *They just want us on record being defiant.*

Why? I'd asked. *We haven't done anything to them. The planet is huge and barely settled. There's enough room for everybody. We're not stopping them from coming and starting their own farms.*

I never paid too much attention to news outside of the peninsula, unlike Rosita and most of the village, who'd found themselves glued to the intercolonial feeds the moment they had opened up. It didn't mean I was naïve about everything. At least I hadn't thought so. My friends were always talking about this or that, about things so far away that they had no impact on us at all.

Even politics local to our own planet seemed so stupid, so unimportant. The prime minister lived in Fat Landing, a city none of us had ever or would ever see. He was always making proclamations, giving us orders, telling us what we could and couldn't do. Nobody ever paid attention. There were never consequences. We were literally on the other side of the planet from them, with a large ocean between us if we went one way and a mountain range and desert if we went the other. There was no reliable transportation between the major settlements. We had the unmanned grain train, but that ran only twice a year.

A few months back, we'd received word that everyone had to submit a DNA sample for some genealogy mapping program for the Earth government. Nobody had done it. They hadn't given us a means to submit the samples, for one thing. And second, according to the original charter, we didn't have to follow the orders of the Earth government anymore anyway. We were an independent system. The settlers gave up their lives and traveled to a new planet, and their children – or their grandchildren – would inherit the planet. No taxes. No controlling interest. We'd be completely independent. They could take the generation ships back once we opened up the gate, but that was it. That was the deal, something my grandfather had been very proud of.

Then last month, it'd been decreed that anyone under the age of twenty-eight had to travel to Fat Landing to be counted and submit to a health screening. The order had come out of nowhere. It was mandatory. If one didn't comply, they'd be jailed. The order hadn't even been signed, so it was unclear if it'd come from the New Sonoran or the Earth government.

Again, they hadn't given us any direction on *how* to comply. It was a joke. We had maybe three or four air transports in the whole area, and each could handle maybe ten passengers. The population of the Baja peninsula, including the villages and the hub town of Burnt Ends, was close to fifty thousand people. Plus, harvest season was about to start. It was just ridiculous.

'Wait, what's that?' the kid asked, the robot turning. 'I see you, fucker!'

The gun fired again, this time into the air. I caught sight of Roger zipping past, buzzing by the creature before disappearing in the opposite direction.

My heart thrashed. *No, no, no.*

'I'm gonna get you! I'm gonna fuck your mom!' the mech screeched.

Roger beeped a response I couldn't hear as he continued to zip around the robot's head. *What the hell is he doing?*

'That's not what she said last night!' the mech squealed. 'Ahhh!'

The robot fell over on its side as the already broken leg snapped off in a hiss of steam and fluid. It crashed to the ground and then started to noisily tumble forward down the hill. At the same moment, the final rocket in the bot's missile tube launched, corkscrewing into the air. It did a wide, hissing circle in the mist and then suddenly veered toward me and my hiding place.

Oh, shit!

I scrambled as it flew in my direction. I jumped to my feet and dived off the top of the hill, rolling forward and tumbling just as the missile overshot me and slammed into the ground right where I'd been hiding. An explosion echoed as loud as a lightning strike, showering me with dirt, rocks, and foliage as I rolled down the hill. My head smacked something hard as I came to a rest at the bottom of the hill, dirt still raining onto me. My ears rang. The world spun. I splotched heavily into mud.

I need to get up. I need to run.

My body wasn't complying.

The mech and I had fallen off our respective hills, both in the same direction. It couldn't have been far away. The machine itself wasn't as loud as before, but I could still hear the kid, and he was wailing. Maybe fifty meters away now, though I couldn't see the mech from my position. The ground between the hills was muddy and full of reeds.

I sat up, peeling myself from the ground. I tasted blood. I touched the side of my head, and it came back red. I'd cut my scalp in the fall.

He'd shot a missile at me. The little shit had tried to kill me. Had he seen me? Or was the missile heat-seeking?

Roger appeared, emerging from the reeds, flying low. He circled me worriedly, clicking. 'Oliver, how are your bones? Are you ambulatory?'

'You pissed it off,' I said. 'What happened to it?'

'I cut a support on its damaged leg, and then I lured it to take a step, which caused it to stumble down the hill. I located the locomotion governor and removed it. I believe it is now disabled from making any further movement, though I have not discovered how to interfere with the audio and visual feeds. I believe it is using a communication system I am unfamiliar with. You need to move and get back to the ranch. I have detected a second radio signal farther back. Perhaps a relay to a drop ship, which suggests more of these may be on the way. I am going to investigate while you retreat. The tutoring session is now over. I have implemented the perimeter-defense protocol.'

'What the hell is that?'

'I don't care how much it costs! It's my birthday, Mom!' the mech screeched. 'It's broken! The stupid thing is broken!'

'You must proceed back to the ranch, Oliver,' Roger said.

'What about rule number one?' I asked.

'Perimeter defense takes precedence. Please, Oliver, you must flee.'

I stood all the way up. I had to wipe blood from my eye. I could see the mech now facing forward and down in the mud and reeds, broken at the base of the forward hill. It was wrecked. Its main gun had snapped off the egg shape of the body and lay bent. Its purple Mohawk strands had broken off in the fall. Various metal pieces lay scattered about. It didn't move at all, though the voice continued to shriek, slightly muffled in the mud.

Holy crap, I thought. My arms were shaking. *This is real. That thing is really here.*

'It can't move?'

'I don't believe it can,' Roger said. 'But I cannot say with full certainty it can't harm you.'

'Do you know where it came from?' I asked. 'Or why it's here?'

'I am still analyzing it. The label on the side of the vehicle identifies it as a "Model 103.08a Recon Drop Dragoon. Base Edition by Apex Industries." I attempted to look up the Apex Industries website to get specific info on this unit to gather more information, but the global feed is down. I am moving to the *Forlorn* connection, but it is slower. There appears to be a barely legible call sign under the model designator. The etching says "Hobie Martin," but that name is crossed out with the same simulated spray paint that covers the rest of the vehicle. Under it, written in astonishingly messy penmanship, is a group of nonsensical letters and symbols.' He then proceeded to spit out a bunch of characters that I couldn't parse.

'Let me see it,' I said.

Roger's dirty and cracked underbelly display flickered, revealing a still of the side of the mech. I felt a chill when I saw it.

X_SuBhuM@nSlæy3r_X.

'I think it says "Subhuman Slayer," ' I said, whispering the words. It wasn't the first time I'd heard that term. Last night, everyone had been following some commentary from an Earth news program. Some Earthers had been calling us that.

Subhuman.

They called us that because our genes had been altered so we could better survive on this planet. The change was subtle. We looked the same. Acted the same. We could have babies with one another. When we were side by side, nobody would know the difference. Yet, for some reason, it'd become a thing.

But that was nothing new. We weren't the first colony to do something to raise the ire of the Earthers. Them being xenophobic was their thing. None of that explained what this kid was doing here.

'We need to tell the others,' I said. 'There's gotta be more of them.'

'I have already informed your sister of the incident. She has yet to respond. She is likely still asleep. It appears the communication network with Burnt Ends is down. I have overridden Trixie 2's maintenance schedule and dispatched her to the town to deliver a message to the mayor, per the procedures of the perimeter-defense protocol.'

'You can talk to Lulu but not to the city?'

'My connection with you, your sister, and the hive is utilizing the *Forlorn*'s connection, not the public satellites. Communication with Burnt Ends relies solely on the municipal feed. It appears all in-range satellites are out of commission. Now you must get out of the combat zone.'

This can't be happening. This can't be real.

'Hey,' I called, talking loudly. 'Hobie, that you?' I took a tentative step toward the face-down robot. It did not move.

I hadn't been planning on saying anything. It just came out.

'What?' the robot asked. 'Who's that? Who's there?'

'Why are you here, Hobie?'

'How do you know my name? Who is this? Are you the drone thing flying around me? I'm going to break you into pieces.'

'I'm not the bot. I'm the person you shot a missile at. Why did you land here?'

'Fuck you!'

'Oliver,' Roger said, whispering in my ear, 'I must insist you go back. We do not want them identifying you.'

'I'm not going back until we have this figured out.' I took several more steps toward the thing. My boots sucked against mud with every step. I reached into the muck and picked up a rock, and I threw it at the robot. It clanged loudly against it, but the robot didn't react.

'You're one of them,' the kid said. It wasn't a question. 'How'd you know my name? The repair drone is coming. It's gonna fix me and reload my ammo, and then I'm going to blow your ass up.'

This thing wasn't going anywhere anytime soon.

'Why are you here?' I asked again.

'Because I banged your mom, that's why.'

'My mom is dead,' I said, taking another step.

'You're dead.'

A moment later, a new, female voice came out through the robot. She also had an Earth accent.

'Young man, if you're not an insurgent, you need to get to the capital city. You're safe in the city. You shouldn't be playing around in a war zone.'

'War zone?' I asked. 'And what city are you talking about? Do you mean Burnt Ends?'

'Shut up, Mom,' Hobie said. 'God, why are you so embarrassing?'

'What is it called again?' Hobie's mom said. 'Fat something? That's the only safe zone. Everywhere else is overrun with terrorists. All the civilians have left.'

'Fat Landing?' I asked. 'Do you know how far away that is? It's literally impossible for me to get there. And there are no terrorists here. Or wars. We don't have guns. I've never held a real gun before in my life. We're farmers. I think you're in the wrong place.'

'Oh, dear,' the woman said.

'He's lying. If you don't have guns, how did you break my mech, bitch? It wasn't that little flying robot, that's for sure.'

'*Hobie*, language.'

'Mom, will you get out of my room? You're ruining it.'

'I didn't break your mech,' I called. 'You tripped and fell down the hill. Your leg was already broken when I saw you. You didn't answer me. What insurg –'

'Get down!' Roger suddenly roared, taking out my lower leg for the second time, this time from the front. I belly flopped into the mud just as something roared over the swamp.

'Up, up, Oliver, up,' Roger said.

I pulled myself up. Whirls of steam filled the valley. I couldn't see the mech anymore. From the low hum, it seemed we'd just gotten buzzed by another vehicle. This one was flying and kicking up mud and smoke.

'Run. Run home. Now, Oliver,' Roger said.

This time, I did as Roger said. I didn't argue. I turned, and I ran.

Less than five minutes later, as I rushed back to the farm, a massive explosion echoed over the hills so loud that it shook the earth under my feet, causing me to stumble yet again.

Roger, I thought, pausing to look back the way I'd come. All I could see was smoke.

The Rhythm Mafia Tapes. Scene five.

We see a smiling older couple. Both are sitting on a porch in front of a brightly painted yellow door. The man is Roberto Gonzales, eighty-one, a colonist on New Sonora. He is slightly paunchy and covered with dirt. In his hands is a large white cowboy hat. The band appears to be made of turquoise. Sitting next to him is his longtime wife, Maria Gonzales, eighty. She is sitting on a rocking chair, knitting something that appears to be a shirt for an infant.

ROSITA (OFF CAMERA): You're covered in dirt. How do you keep your hat so white?

ROBERTO (TURNING THE HAT IN HIS HANDS): Maria is magic. I don't know what she does. It gets dirty, and the next day it looks brand-new.

ROSITA: How do you do it, Mrs Gonzales?

Mrs Gonzales smiles but doesn't say anything.

(A time cut.)

Roberto now has the massive cowboy hat on his head. The shirt Maria is working on is much more complete.

ROBERTO: We'd reached orbit before I was born, but I was still born on the ship. We trained while they did the survey. Maria and I came down at different times. She got down here two years before I did. I was seventeen. I was on *Forlorn*, but Maria was on *Adios*. Went straight to the peninsula. Maria came across with the trains to the peninsula, all the way from Fat Landing.

He turns and pats her leg affectionately.

ROBERTO: I got lucky she decided to come.

Maria puts her knitting down.

MARIA: And don't you forget it.

They both laugh.

(A time cut.)

Roberto is handing Rosita what appears to be a Popsicle.

ROSITA (LAUGHING OFF CAMERA): I haven't had one of these in years. Oh, man, talk about a blast from the past.

ROBERTO: I started making them again.

(A time cut.)

Roberto, pointing at a field across the road. The camera briefly turns, revealing a wide dirt road. On the other side appear to be miles of shriveled trees.

ROBERTO: Pedro was allocated twenty acres. Beto Junior twenty acres south of that. We borrowed some of the Lewis honeybees and started the orchard after we got the initial shipment. You know, before it happened. Now it just sits there. You'd think it would make me sad seeing it all like that, but I like the orchard being there right next door.

Maria puts down her knitting, gets up, and goes inside.

ROBERTO: She gets sad sometimes, thinking about our boys. That we never had grandchildren. **(SIGHS HEAVILY)** I get sad sometimes, too.

CHAPTER 4

I saw the dust from the quad as I approached the outer boundaries of our property. It was Lulu, and she was leaving the ranch, heading toward me. I flagged her down. She spied me and turned the four-wheeled vehicle off the road to meet me halfway. I bent over, exhausted, as she approached.

She had the broken remnants of a honeybee in the bed of the quad. I recognized it as one of the drones. It'd gotten hit by a grain transport a few days back, and she'd been planning on taking it into town to give to Fritz so he could fabricate a new leg for it.

'Ollie! Are you okay?' Lulu cried as the quad pulled up. She jumped from the driver's seat and rubbed her hands over me. She had to stand on her tiptoes to reach toward my torso. 'You're bleeding!'

I looked into her worried eyes. My sister was twenty-three years old, two years younger than me, but she looked very much like Grandpa Lewis in that moment. In the rare moments when she wasn't saying something caustic or sarcastic, I could see it in her face. That tired, wary intelligence of someone who'd spent their whole life struggling to maintain optimism in an environment rife with hardship.

Our mom had had the same eyes, too. I had a picture of her in my room. Her name had been Cat. Catalina.

Even though Lulu was tiny – four foot ten inches compared to my six foot – she had an imposing presence. She was much too young to have that much worry etched onto her face.

'I'm okay. Did you get Roger's message?' I asked between breaths.

'Yes,' she said. 'He just messaged me again to come look for you. Did you really puke on your bracelet? Like, directly on the bracelet? Sam won't stop talking about it.'

'Roger is okay? There was an explosion.'

'Yeah, no shit. The whole peninsula heard it. He sent video of what happened. That second ship blew up the mech and then took off back into space followed by a third, flower-shaped thing. They're gone. Roger found Priscilla. She's okay. She's undamaged physically. She had a power failure. She recorded everything that happened before you two morons got there. She automatically turned on her stealth drive for the first time ever, and it fried her whole drivetrain, knocking her offline. That's going to be a problem because we're out of the scout-sized batteries. They're on their way back now, but it's going to be a bit because she's on foot, using emergency power. He doesn't want us to help him. Screw rule number one, I guess.'

I pulled myself into the quad, squeezing my way into the driver's seat, but Lulu shooed me over to the passenger side. We'd always fight over who got to drive, but I didn't feel like arguing today. She had the pedals adjusted for her height anyway.

'Do you know what's going on?' I asked.

'Yeah,' Lulu said as she circled the vehicle back toward the ranch. 'You owe Rosita an apology first off. We're under attack.'

'Why?'

She gave me an incredulous look. '*Why?* Are you deliberately being dumb? We've been talking about this for months. You literally just broke up with your girlfriend over it last night, not that you'd remember that part.'

'But it was a mech driven by a little kid. It doesn't make sense.'

'It's *Operation Bounce House*,' she said. 'It's real, and it's here.'

We turned onto the road, kicking up more dust, and we passed through the wide-open gate. To the left stood the massive corrugated-metal barn. We called it the 'beehive.' I eyed the platform on the roof with the telescope and all the antennae. The large building was where we housed the honeybees and the repair stations along with the control center. Spread out to the right were the fields. The whole property was a square just under a hundred sixty acres, though some of it was undeveloped. About a hundred twenty acres of wheat, ten acres of barley, and several more off rotation for this season. I had one more for various vegetables along with several of my experimental crops, including my tobacco. The fields were crawling with the drone honeybees, all chugging along like they had no care in the world. In the far distance at the northwest boundary, I could see a single driverless hopper transport sitting idle just outside the fence, which I thought was strange until I remembered that the planetwide net was down. It wouldn't be going anywhere until it was back online.

We pulled up to the main house. There were three other quads sitting out front. I didn't recognize any of them.

'Why are people here?' I asked.

'The whole peninsula is going to be here in an hour or two,' Lulu said, pulling herself out of the seat. 'We have the only active feed for kilometers. Maybe on the planet.'

I sat next to Lulu and watched the commercial on the screen for the fifth time in a row. I'd seen it before, but I'd never really paid attention, because I'd had no idea it had anything to do with us. Behind us stood about fifteen people, all from surrounding farms. There were more in the kitchen preparing breakfast. Or lunch. I didn't even know what time it was. Voices rose from the other rooms. Voices and quiet sobbing.

I rubbed my arm. I didn't like having so many people in our house. It felt wrong. An intrusion. It made me nervous. Grandpa Lewis had never liked crowds much, either. I remembered Grandmother Yolanda used to have these laughter-filled parties, and Grandpa Lewis would always retreat to this room, his study, to read a book or he'd go out to the beehive.

That had stopped when our grandmother died. Lulu was only six at the time and barely remembered her at all. I'd been eight, almost nine, and my recollections of Grandma Yolanda mostly came in sounds and smells and memories of her warm kindness, though I could remember that day she died as if it had happened yesterday. I could recall the scent and taste of cinnamon and melted sugar. I could feel the dough in my hands.

But beyond that last day, I also remembered how Grandmother Yolanda herself smelled like the fields and grease. She worked hard, and she was always happy and smiling and hugging. When she had her parties, the house would be full of the cinnamon smell, of talking and laughter and the scent of cooking.

Now the house was full once again. I wasn't even sure how people had known to come here. Probably because we had the only bracelet repair bay this side of Burnt Ends. Even after Grandpa Lewis died, there hadn't been this many people. It felt wrong, especially since none of our friends were here yet. Sam and Tito and Axel. And Rosita. Without a way to contact them, I felt strangely untethered, disconnected.

The vast majority of the people here were older, in their later sixties and seventies. A smattering of people my age and younger was here, too, but nobody I knew well.

There wasn't anyone between the ages of thirty and sixty here. I wasn't sure if there was anyone that age left alive on the entire planet. An entire generation – my mother's generation – had died of the Sickness, leaving a gaping wound in the population. That wound had never been more visible than it was now with so many people gathered.

After Grandpa Lewis died, Lulu had moved into his bedroom, and we'd turned this room into Lulu's computer room. I used to keep a second drum kit in here as well back when I practiced more.

After I'd moved the drum kit out, she pretty much turned this den into her streaming studio. She offered to move to the barn, but I wouldn't let her. Lulu spent most of her streaming time unclothed. We had heat in the house, and we didn't have heat in the barn except in the control room.

While Lulu wasn't ashamed of what she did online to save money for the future and she could be aggressively proud about it with people in our age group, she didn't normally allow any of the occasional older visitors to our home into this room. If she needed to show someone something on the net, she would bring the screen and keyboard out into the kitchen.

When we'd entered the house, we found Mr and Mrs Gonzales and Mrs Xalos already in the room, already on the computer, with more people arriving by the minute. Both of us had looked at each other, to Lulu's desk, to our neighbors, to the computer screen they were staring at, back to the desk. Sitting on the desk was a wide assortment of locally printed sex toys, including a foxtail with a gleaming silver plug at the end.

Lulu made an eye movement to the toys before moving to her computer, silently telling me, *Get those things out of here.*

I started inching my way toward her desk in an effort to surreptitiously throw something over it all, but I didn't know what to do. I couldn't do it without being obvious, and there were so many toys that if I wanted to take them out of here, it'd take two trips.

My eyes caught the opalescent background sheet Lulu used for her live sessions. It was all rolled up in the corner, a bikini top hanging off it. I started to reach for the sheet but paused. I could see behind the sheet, currently hidden by it, was a cardboard standee of Lulu's Farm Girl Gigi setup.

'Oliver, your head!' came Mrs Gonzales's exclamation, and I was suddenly grabbed by what seemed like five old ladies all at once. They manhandled me into the chair right next to Lulu as the women clucked over me. I gave Lulu a well-I-tried shrug as I was swarmed. The cut on my forehead was cleaned with warm water and then something stinging was pressed against it.

'Guys,' I began, 'it's okay. It's just a small –'

'What happened to you?'

'It was one of those things,' Lulu said. 'It attacked him and Roger, and he barely got away.'

Multiple gasps filled the room.

And then Mrs Xalos was demanding that I sit still while Mrs Gonzales wrapped my head with a bandage she seemingly pulled out of thin air. As I related the story, she wrapped the bandage around my head five or six times like I was getting mummified.

And just as fast as they swarmed me, they all pulled back to examine their handiwork. I shot a nervous glance at the not-yet-commented-on line of sex toys. I sighed. But it seemed my story had distracted them.

Still, less than a minute later, Mrs Becerra was staring at the bikini top, a frown on her cracked old face. Once the old woman noticed the desk, she was liable to drop dead from a heart attack. Luckily, most everyone's attention was on the computer as Lulu increased the volume.

On the screen, a 3D-rendered version of the exact same mech I'd just encountered spun in a circle while an announcer shouted. I knew most people on Earth had a smart screen from which they could grab the image and pull it from the display. They could turn and spin the image on their own. Our screen, taken directly from an apartment berth in the *Hibisco*, was over two hundred years old and didn't have any of that functionality.

The scene showed the mech, which was painted in the red and blue of the Republic flag, marching through a war-torn city while dirty, angry masked men with pulse rifles poured fire at it. The scene was rendered with the posterization of a cartoon as required by Earth law. Unlike the real version, this mech had a round, spinning Gatling gun. On the screen, the gun spun up and started mowing down all the masked men. A scrolling bar across the top of the screen read: NERTIAA Notice. This is a CGI re-enactment. All CGI likenesses are used from the approved likeness database.

'*Operation Bounce House! Design your own war machine!*' the voice on the screen screeched. 'Fight for the Republic! Save humanity! Uproot the filthy insurgents from the safety of your own home!'

The shot changed to show a row of adults sitting in chairs. Each wore a helmet and glasses that I recognized as immersion rigs, technology we didn't have here, which was why I'd never paid much attention to the ad. There were dozens of ads for games just like this.

The unnecessary banner warning that this was all CGI remained scrolling across the screen.

'Join now, and we'll throw in a free paint job on your personalized mech. Prizes available to the mercenary teams with the most confirmed evictions and most entertaining builds. Ammo discounts available when purchased in bulk.'

'Evictions,' I said, letting the word roll around in my brain.

'That's what they're calling it. An eviction action,' Lulu said.

'Assholes,' I muttered.

Lulu clicked something on her keyboard, and she started scrolling through text news feeds. This interface was wired directly to the control center in the barn, which in turn was connected directly to the *Forlorn* sitting abandoned in a stable orbit above us. It bypassed the main satellite. Grandpa Lewis had set it up after the pinhole opened, and Lulu had improved it greatly once the transfer gate opened. The connection was shit, so we normally just used the regular feed, but Lulu still used it to get past certain planetary content filters. It was how she accessed all her off-planet chat rooms, and it was what had allowed her to set up and operate her Real-Friends platform account.

'There's hardly anything about us,' Lulu said, scanning the news feeds. 'All the mentions are related to Apex and *Operation Bounce House* itself, but not us. It says people who paid for the special preview were able to get in early and were dropped into random population centers. They're talking more about the bugs with the mechs and the latency.' She paused and then looked at us. 'The program opens up to the public at midnight GMT, Earth time.'

'When is that?' I asked.

She clicked a few things, waited for a response, and then suddenly the Apex site was up on the screen. It had a countdown.

Seven hours.

CHAPTER 5

There was a video on the site that had been posted about twelve hours earlier. It was labeled 'Target site revealed!' Lulu clicked it and waited for it to load.

The video started. We were greeted with a view of a cube filled with a translucent blue gel. An industrial printing square. A shape started to form inside the gel. A mech. The screen split, and we watched a smiling man sitting in a chair with an immersion rig on his head. We switched to his view. He was directing the design of the mech. He removed the main gun and replaced it with a giant chain saw. On the left side, the chain saw started to form in the industrial gel. He clicked 'Upgrade Missiles,' and multiple choices cycled on the screen. He settled on a circular eight-pack missile launcher. He clicked on 'Customize,' and a pair of spray-paint canisters appeared in the man's hands. He started to paint the mech. In the printer, color formed on the machine, mirroring the man's virtual paint job.

He then clicked 'Deploy.'

The gel started to drain away. The split screen returned to a single image focused on the mech. It started to slowly pull out.

'The rumors are true!' a voice intoned as bombastic music began to rise in volume. 'We are a go! The negotiations with the terrorists have failed. The innocents have fled to safety! This is not a game. This is real, and it's happening now. Your chance to defend humanity is here! Our first five-day campaign is here!'

'Defend humanity?' I asked. 'Defend humanity from what?'

As the image pulled out, a second printer appeared next to the first. Then a third. Soon, we were in a massive factory filled with dozens, then hundreds of printers. All had mechs in different sizes and various states of manufacture.

Then the image pulled out farther, and we saw we weren't in a factory, but in the hull of a massive spaceship. The word 'APEX' was etched on the side, and under that was '*Pinnacle*,' the name of the ship. Behind me, my neighbor Mr Xalos whistled. The ship was huge, bigger than any of the original generation ships. Bigger than any of the long-haulers. We zoomed out even farther to see the giant ship was in orbit, floating directly over our planet. The blue ocean of Cortez sparkled.

'The location of the eviction action is the newly connected colony planet of New Sonora, a hotbed of terrorist activity!' A second screen appeared and disappeared, presumably filled with stats on our planet. A spinning globe showing the different communities appeared. Little X's with skulls appeared over all the population centers, all except the capital city of Fat Landing. The globe turned, showing the peninsula, with a big X over the town of Burnt Ends. Behind me, several people gasped.

'Special preview members are deploying now! It's not too late to get in on the action! Financing available! The insurgents won't last long! We only have five days to cleanse the planet! Don't miss out on your chance to make a difference in the galaxy! The future of true humanity is in your hands!'

'Five days?' someone asked. 'Then what? They just go away? So we have to hold out for five days?'

'Where are we supposed to go?' Mrs Rodriguez asked, wringing her hands worriedly. The ancient woman had to be pushing ninety.

'That kid's mom said we're supposed to get to Fat Landing,' I said.

'How? How would we do that? It'd take a month to get there. Not five days.'

Nobody answered.

More people were showing up by the minute, just walking right in through our front door. *There're too many people here. I don't like this many people in the house.*

Lulu furiously typed at her keyboard. She now had some sort of text-only message forum up on her screen.

'What are you doing?' I asked.

'I'm getting the word out,' Lulu said. 'They're about to murder a bunch of farmers.'

I leaned over and watched the messages scroll by. People were calling her a liar, saying that she really wasn't on the planet. Or they were just ignoring her. Her messages were falling off the screen as fast as she was typing them.

'You need to tell your friends. Not these people,' I said. I leaned in closer. 'And by friends, I mean your *friends*.'

'Already did,' Lulu said. She switched windows and started typing there.

Mrs Xalos, who had apparently left the room, popped her head back in and asked if we had a second bathroom. We didn't.

Lulu pulled up a news screen, but they weren't talking about us at all. She moved the screen off the main display, and it was projected on her wall.

'I just don't understand. Why are they doing this?' Mrs Rodriguez asked after a moment of us watching the newscast, which had now switched to covering an interplanetary cricket championship.

A new voice answered. 'They don't consider us human.'

My heart did a little skip. Rosita. I turned and met my girlfriend's eyes. My ex-girlfriend. Her eyes went huge, and she rushed up and put her hand against the bandage around my head. She touched my forehead right in the wrong place, and it stung.

Mrs Rodriguez just shook her head. 'We didn't have a choice. Everyone was dying. Don't they know that?'

Lulu looked at her wrist and turned to me. 'Roger and Priscilla are approaching. Also, Ollie, it says your bracelet is repaired. You better go grab it.'

I paused. Rosita was still examining the bandage on my head. She had her ever-present camera drone out. It hovered by her head, taking all this in.

'Rosita,' I began, 'about last night –'

'Go,' she said. 'Get your bracelet. We'll talk later.'

'Okay,' I said, standing. I wanted to say more, but she was right. Now was not the time. 'Give me your bracelet, though.'

'Why?' she asked as she pulled it off her wrist. 'You're not planning on puking on it, are you?'

A very slight smile played across her lips, and an overwhelming sense of relief filled me as I grabbed it. It wasn't much, but I would take it. Until that moment, I hadn't really processed that we'd officially broken up the night before. Everyone was saying it was the fight over me being ignorant of the whole *Operation Bounce House* thing, but that wasn't really it at all. That'd just been the public fight after the private one we'd had just an hour before that.

I don't even know how you feel about me, Oliver. You never say it.

And I hadn't responded. Why? It seemed so stupid now.

She had already turned away to comfort Mrs Gonzales, who had started to sob.

I turned just in time to see Mrs Becerra had discovered Lulu's makeup desk. She had a tentacle dildo in her hand and was examining it with a bewildered look upon her face. I moved to the hall before she could ask what it was.

'Oliver, your bed is filthy,' Mrs Xalos said, coming out of my room. 'I do wish you'd let me come over to tidy up once in a while.'

'Please don't go into my room,' I said as I moved to the door.

'I was looking for another bathroom. I swear you used to have two.'

I came out the front door to find more people milling about. I spied my best friend, Sam, pulling up on his quad. His ever-present trucker cap sat upon his head. He wore a hand-drawn T-shirt that read, 'Rhythm Mafia. Live from . . .' There was a blank space after 'Live from.' I waved at him, and moved toward the barn. He parked and jogged toward me.

'Hey, man,' Sam said, catching up. 'One of your honeybees just threatened me. Whoa, what the hell happened to your head?'

'What?' I asked, ignoring the question about the bandage. 'One of the drones?'

'No, it was one of the smaller ones. One of the ones that dragged you away after you passed out last night. I was about to pull into your driveway, and it almost took my head off. I had to state my name and purpose. Man, I hope Axel gives that thing the right answer when he and his brother get here. It's going to ruin the band if your robot decapitates one of our guitar players. Well, maybe not Tito.' He poked a finger at my forehead. 'Dude, you're bleeding through that bandage.'

'I fell and hit my head, and Mrs Gonzales and Mrs Xalos "fixed" me. I'll tell you about it in a second.'

I looked over at the gate, and sure enough the third honeybee – which was supposed to still be charging – was hovering in place in front of the open gate. It was 413, which I was pretty sure was Melissa. The other one, Trixie 2, still hadn't returned from Burnt Ends.

Sam turned sober and lowered his voice. 'Do you believe this? Everyone is saying we're under attack. José Gwin – you know that dude with the funny lips? He said there's a bunch of smoke coming from Burnt Ends. And did you hear that explosion earlier? Something streaked through the air.'

'Come with me,' I said. 'I'm grabbing my bracelet and heading out to meet Roger.'

'Bracelets ain't working,' Sam said. He held up his to show the blinking red dot indicating a lost connection with the satellite.

'Mine is still connected through the backdoor net,' I said.

'Yeah, speaking of your bracelet, that video was pretty impressive.'

'What?'

Sam huffed as we passed through the large double doors of the beehive. To my right, the individual charging stations for the larger-sized drones were all lined up to the ceiling. All of them sat empty. To my left stood a pair of round repair pods for the scouts. Each station charged two at a time, and only one of the two stations worked. Past that were piles of empty bags of seed. They lay stacked around my large combine like they were somehow trying to entomb it. The side-engine compartment of the gigantic, frustrating piece of farm equipment remained open, reminding me I was supposed to be working on it today. Next to all this was the cubby where our band, the Rhythm Mafia, practiced.

Sitting there in the cubby were the three amplifiers my grandfather had built, Sam's upright bass, my drum kit, and the Serrano twins' guitars. Past that was the door to the 'classroom' and control center.

We pushed through the door to the small room.

'There's video,' Sam said, 'of you puking. You drunk-dialed Rosita and were telling her you loved her when you straight up yakked right into it. It's a perfect point-of-view shot. Everyone on the peninsula has seen it. You were like really loud, too. When the feed went down, I thought maybe your sister had done something to stop it from spreading further. I was in the middle of telling Tito and Axel that we should use it for our music video when it all went out.'

I grunted. Sitting in the corner was Roger's empty charging station. Next to it the bracelet repair bay was blinking green. I snatched the bracelet up, and I popped it onto my wrist. It buzzed, letting me know it was online. I pulled up the map, and I saw Roger. He was helping 'Priscilla' through the mud, and it'd be another ten minutes.

'Is this really happening?' Sam asked, again lowering his voice to a whisper. 'Has Lulu confirmed it yet?'

I spent a few minutes telling him about what had happened, what I'd seen, and what we'd seen on the net.

He was silent for several moments. Sam always appeared to be in control of his emotions, able to roll with the good and bad, but I knew him better than that. We'd been friends our whole lives. He hid behind a façade of nonchalance and humor, but he was just as high-strung and anxious as I was. The big difference was that I would ignore things in hopes that they would go away, and he would always be the first to push through whatever it was. I envied him for his ability to hide it, for his ability to wear his humor like armor. He took a moment to compose himself. I could see the terror play across his face. I knew what he was thinking.

He was having a baby. He'd knocked up Harriet Riggs. She was just about seven months along. They were getting married.

'*Operation Bounce House*,' Sam finally said. He swallowed. 'Man, you owe Rosita an apology.'

'Yeah, that's what Lulu said.'

Sam grunted.

I held out my hand. 'Give me your bracelet.'

'Why?' he asked. 'You're not going to puke onto it, are you?'

I held up Rosita's bracelet. 'And *that's* what Rosita said. Just give it to me.'

He unhooked it and handed it over. His hand was shaking. I

placed it around the bevel in the repair bay. I placed Rosita's in the second bevel next to it. I hopped into the chair and slid over to the control center and pulled up the bracelets' diagnostics. I moved to the network screen and proceeded to transfer the connection to the other net.

'We don't have a lot of bandwidth, and if we add too many, they'll probably notice, so don't just go telling anybody we can do this, but you'll be able to talk to me and Lulu and anyone else who's using the feed routed through the *Forlorn*. You'll have anonymous access to the interplanetary feed.'

My friend shook his head and adjusted his cap. The ancient faded hat was a relic from Earth for some sports team called the Seattle Supersonics. It'd been his great-great-grandfather's.

'How is it,' he asked, 'that you know absolutely nothing about what's going on in the world and you can't figure out the software for the cistern distributors, yet you can do shit like this? You're literally using two-hundred-year-old technology to hack a modern communication system. You and your sister both.'

'It's Roger,' I said, watching the screen, waiting for each bracelet to complete the handshake. It would take a few minutes. 'He quizzes me on this stuff every damn day. And the bracelet system is not modern. They have to use old technology if they want to communicate with all the colonies. Earthers have implants, you know? They don't even need bracelets.'

Sam made a *pfft* noise. 'And they're the ones complaining about us being altered.'

'Yeah,' I said. 'I still don't understand what's happening.'

'I've been telling you this whole time,' Sam said. 'It's the same stuff that made our great-great-grandparents leave in the first place. It's the corporations, man. They're all owned by that one-world-order stuff my grandpa used to talk about. I think they've found this planet is more fertile than they thought, and they want us off it so they can plant their corporate farms.'

'That doesn't make sense,' I said. 'There're not that many of us. And if they settle the planet, the same thing will happen to them that happened to our parents, unless they alter their genes in the womb, and if they do that, then what's the point of kicking us out? We're already here and we know how to farm the land.'

I didn't add that our great-great-grandparents didn't leave because of 'one-world-order stuff.' This was an old argument, and it had originated with Sam's grandfather who used to also believe that the Becerra farm was infested with lizard aliens.

The original crews of the generation ships were mixed. Half were volunteers, and the other half were prisoners. They had been chosen by AI. By the now decommissioned ships themselves, who were intelligent AI systems like Roger but even smarter. They'd had their pick of people in prisons, and that was how at least half of each ship had been crewed.

If anyone ever brought this up around Sam, he would get weirdly angry about the whole thing. He didn't believe most of the stuff his late grandfather had spewed, but he was always adamant about this one. They were prisoners, yes, but they'd been political prisoners.

That wasn't true. We'd seen the records in school. My great-great-grandmother Constance had robbed a bank and stabbed a drug dealer.

Sam shrugged. 'Maybe they want to strip-mine the planet.'

'But why are they using kids to do it?'

'Man, don't you ever watch the feed? They usually use AI-controlled mechs to fight against terrorists, but this is new. *Operation Bounce House* is run by Apex Industries. They're mercenaries, but the guy who runs the program used to be in charge of that game company Victus Wonderworks – the same one that made that hippopotamus-versus-ferrets zombie game you liked.'

'That game is, like, two hundred fifty years old,' I said.

'Yeah, and it sucks, too. But the company is still around, or they were until Apex bought them, and the former CEO guy is now the head of the mercenaries. Eli Opel is his name. He's using a pay-to-play model to fund all of this. So instead of the AI mechs, they're controlled by assholes on Earth who are treating it like a game. Apex is getting paid by the Republic to fight their wars. People are paying a ton of money to design these war machines and control them. So money is pouring in from both sides. Think about it. Imagine a war where all the soldiers are actually paying money for the chance to fight in it. It's brilliant. They've been talking about it on the news for months, but everybody thought they were going to some other planet. You know, one with real terrorists. I don't know why they're here.'

'Shit,' I said.

Sam's bracelet beeped a few times. I pulled it off the bevel and tossed it to him. He caught it and placed it on his wrist. I pocketed Rosita's bracelet.

'Thanks. Do you think you can set up Harriet's bracelet, too?'

'Sure,' I said. 'But don't tell anyone else.'

We just sat there for a minute, not moving or saying anything.

'Do you remember that time?' Sam suddenly said. 'We were both like eight, and you were at my house. Your grandma was there, and so was Roger. You knocked over the vase, and it broke into, like, a million pieces. We tried to blame Snickers, but Roger ratted you out.'

I laughed. 'I remember your grandmother cried. She told us not to tell your mom.'

'Yeah,' Sam said, suddenly serious. 'That was a couple of days before my mom died. I forgot that part. She was already in the coma by then.' He paused. 'She loved that stupid vase.'

I nodded. His mom had been one of the last ones to die.

Sam shifted in his chair. 'It came from Earth. Anyway, I gotta tell you something. I'm actually the one who broke it. I broke it the night before, and I glued it together, and I did, like, a really shitty job. It was only a matter of time before my grandma noticed it. It fell apart when you ran by, not because you actually hit it. I let you take the blame for it. I'm sorry.'

I laughed. 'Holy shit. You asshole! Do you know how bad I felt? I couldn't look your grandmother in the eye for years after that.'

He held out his hands. 'That's it. That's all I got as far as confessions go. Well, that and I always wanted to bang your sister – until, you know, me and Harriet happened. Actually, that's a lie. I still want to bang your sister. Everybody does, and it's not just because everyone knows she gets naked on the net. I think it's because she's so mean. Is that weird?'

I sobered. 'Why are you telling me this now?'

'Because I should've told you a long time ago.' He paused. 'And because I think we're going to die, Oliver. All of us.'

CHAPTER 6

'Hello, Oliver. Hello, Oliver friend number three,' Roger said to me and Sam as the two bots reached the main gate. Roger sat perched upon the back of 418, but he hovered up into the air the moment they passed the main entrance. Priscilla the recovered scout robot continued walking, ignoring us, as it – she – headed toward the barn for repairs. Roger zipped over and alighted upon the back of Melissa, who sat in a hunched position, hidden by the weeds just outside of the gate. He perched on the larger bot for about ten seconds before drifting back up and coming to hover before me.

'We must utilize the perimeter-defense protocols,' Roger said. 'I have summoned your sister. We will proceed to the control center for a special Saturday lesson.'

'How's Priscilla?' I asked.

'She has an emergency stealth mode that malfunctioned when she attempted to activate it, causing the power loss. She needs a new capacitor unit, but we do not have one here at the ranch. We must proceed to the civil defense warehouse in Burnt Ends to get supplies to repair her and to bolster our defense.'

'What?' I asked. 'Civil defense warehouse? What is that?'

'It is exactly what it sounds like, Oliver. We can discuss it further during the lesson.'

'Wait,' Sam said. He was still looking back toward the beehive, which Priscilla had just entered. 'Who the hell is Priscilla? Is it one of the honeybees?'

'Oliver friend number three, do you have permission from your guardian to be here today?'

Sam sighed. This was something Roger asked Sam every time he set foot on our property. Sam was twenty-five years old. His grandparents on both sides were dead. He had sold his family's ranch and lived with Harriet and both sets of her grandparents, working their farm instead. He didn't have a 'guardian.'

'Yes, Roger,' Sam said.

'Do you wish to, and do you have permission to, attend today's lesson?'

This part was new. Sam looked at me uncertainly. I shrugged.

'Sure?'

Zap.

'Ow! What the fuck!' Sam called. 'Ow! Shit! Ow! Fuck, Roger, stop stinging me!'

He fell on his ass as I burst out laughing. I couldn't help it.

'Rule number four, Oliver friend number three,' the robot said. 'No swearing.'

'I thought you said all the rules are suspended during perimeter defense,' I said, still wheezing. Mr Yanez walked by, glaring.

Roger clicked. 'They are, but classroom rules still apply during lessons.'

'What? That doesn't make sense,' I said.

'Dude, that really hurt. It's not funny,' Sam said, rubbing his arm while sitting in the dirt. 'And I didn't swear. When did I swear?'

Static crackled as Roger played back a censored version of what Sam had said: 'Who the <bleep> is Priscilla? Is it one of the honeybees?'

Sam just looked up at Roger. He grumbled something under his breath. It wasn't the first time Roger had corrected Sam, but it had probably been twelve-plus years ago during a sleepover.

Across the way, Lulu and Rosita emerged from the house along with a few others. My sister eyed me and then pointed at the beehive. We started walking toward the double doors. With dismay, I saw through the window a few people talking and sitting on my bed. I sighed.

'Why am I still "Oliver friend number three" when you're calling the honeybees by names now?' Sam asked as we crowded into the small control center. It was me, Roger, Lulu, Sam, Rosita, Mr Gonzales, and a few other ranchers from nearby farms.

'Because that's how I am programmed,' Roger said.

'My grandfather programmed it that way,' Lulu said at the same time, sliding into the seat across from the terminal. I didn't object. I knew my way around the control center, but Lulu was the expert. 'He thought it was funny. I've tried to turn it off, but I can't without the admin password.'

I handed Rosita the bracelet, and she thanked me and put it on. She immediately started clicking on it.

'You okay?' I asked, keeping my voice low.

'I haven't heard anything from my cousin,' she said worriedly. 'I need to know how my nieces are doing. Damnit. No messages since we last talked. I was hoping maybe I missed something before the net went down.'

'It sounds like Roger has some ideas,' I said.

'I hope so.'

'But how can you change the names of the honeybees and not the people?' Sam was asking.

'Because I have admin access over the honeybee system,' Lulu said as she started to furiously type at the terminal. 'Think of Roger as an operating system that has a pair of programs loaded into his memory, and he's running both at the same time. The first is for controlling all the honeybees, and that's the only one Oliver and I have full administrative access over. That's great, but he also has that Mary Poppins BS installed, which we can't turn off. That's the tutoring-and-discipline module. I can instruct Roger to make all the honeybee units line up and dance for us if I want, but if I try to bring a jug of vodka into the house, he'll lose his mind.'

'That is not true,' Roger said. 'There is no dancing during perimeter defense.'

'Wait, you can't bring vodka into the house, but you can bring in a convent's worth of sex toys and outfits? How does that . . . Ow!'

I kicked Sam in the leg before he could continue. Roger had a strange blind spot when it came to Lulu's streaming activity in the computer room. Still, I didn't want to rock the boat too much and force Roger to make a response. While I wasn't a huge fan of my sister's activities, I knew it made her happy. If Roger put a stop to it, she would spiral.

That, plus she was earning a significant amount of money. Money she wouldn't be able to touch until the quarantine or embargo or whatever you wanted to call it was lifted in eight more years. For the moment, it was all sitting in a Republic bank, earning interest.

None of that money was mine, and I had no expectation I'd benefit from any of it, but it made me strangely proud that my little sister could do something like that all on her own. A few people who knew about her activities were pretty judgmental toward both her and myself. Just a few days back, we'd stopped at the town square bar – the Belly-Rubbed Pug – and Kitty Dominguez, a girl from Burnt Ends who'd moved south just a few years back, had called Lulu a whore to her face. That hadn't ended well for Kitty.

I usually wore headphones when I knew Lulu would be online because that was the last thing I needed to hear, but Roger ignored it. I could stub my toe and silently curse in pain, and Roger would be at my door in seconds demanding to know if I was okay. But when Lulu was locked away working, he didn't say a word.

Lulu seemed to think it was something in Roger's programming that made it so he ignored anything sexual. Still, Lulu had developed an online innocent-farm-girl personality designed not to raise Roger's ire. Farm Girl Gigi.

'Golly, golly, golly, mister, golly!' was what she usually exclaimed, which was pretty funny. She always made sure I knew when she was streaming so I could put my headphones on or go outside, and she continued to offer to move to the barn or have the honeybees build her a whole new studio. But I insisted it didn't bother me. And truthfully, it didn't. Again, I wasn't a huge fan of it, but when I really forced myself to think about it, my issues were more about what she wanted to do with her money once the quarantine was over. I wasn't sure how I'd feel if she ever had a real sexual relationship with someone in the next room.

Her online persona was so different from the real Lulu that any ick-that's-my-sister feelings were overridden by the sheer ridiculousness of it all. I'd once suggested her character was in violation of the anti-masking laws, which prohibited online filters on human faces.

Still, Lulu worked whenever she could. I didn't know exactly how much she'd earned, but it was a lot. She had a goal. A home on Earth. An apartment in some place called Aruba. Once she became a property owner, she'd have access to UBI, and she wouldn't have to work ever again.

She'd asked me more than once if I would go with her.

I'd said no, of course. The idea seemed ridiculous to me. Multiple generations of our family had given everything, including their lives, to make this planet their home, and the idea of just leaving the moment one could seemed so disrespectful. This was my home. *Our* home. And then I'd point out that we weren't even certain she could live on Earth with the adjustment to our bodies that had been made in vitro. She'd have to grow her own food because it was possible everything grown on Earth would be toxic.

She'd get this look when I told her that. She'd set her lower jaw for just a second, and I couldn't tell if she was about to cry or punch me, but all she would do was nod and then wait a few months before asking again, pretending like the conversation would go differently this time.

And I'd feel like complete shit afterward. I didn't want her to leave. I didn't want to be alone. But I didn't want to be responsible for her being miserable, either.

That was how I felt, and I knew that was how I felt, so why didn't I say that? Why did I always take the asshole route and just scoff at her and get mad when she brought it up?

Because she'll stay if you tell her you're afraid to be alone.

I turned my gaze back to Rosita, who was worriedly looking at something on her bracelet. Rosita, who was clear she wanted to spend her life with me. Rosita, who was constantly hinting that she wanted me to ask her to marry her. And me, again, afraid to offer her what she wanted.

But that was what I wanted, too. I loved her with everything I had. So why was I always keeping her at arm's length?

She'll stay, too, if you ask. That's the problem.

'Wait,' Sam was saying. 'So if you get the password for the tutoring program, you can make him stop calling me friend number three?'

'No,' Lulu said. 'That's part of the whole operating system. I need the admin password for the whole thing, and that died with my grandpa.'

'I don't know why I'm number three,' Sam grumbled. 'I should be number one.'

'Friends number one and two were from Oliver's preschool,' Roger said. 'Just because they're no longer friends doesn't change that you were friend number three.'

Lulu clicked a few times and pulled up a screen. 'Yup. Just what I thought.'

'What?' I asked.

'Perimeter defense,' she said. 'It's a third program that activated itself when these guys decided to come at us.' She tapped the screen. 'I can see it running, but I can't get into it.'

'I could've told you that,' Roger said. The fans hummed, and he rose into the air and turned to face us. 'I now require silence. I am here to instruct you all on the perimeter-defense protocols.'

CHAPTER 7

We quieted and waited for the hovering robot to speak. There were only two chairs in the room. Lulu sat in one, and Mr Gonzales sat in the other. The rest of us squeezed together, waiting for the lesson to begin.

A *ding* sound echoed from Roger, indicating class had officially started.

'There is a small attic space directly above us that contains approximately fifty all-weather document storage boxes. In these storage boxes are the handwritten inventory lists and maintenance logs from the honeybee construction of Burnt Ends. One of those boxes will have a red piece of tape atop it, and it is labeled "Supplemental Reports." This box is in the very back of the space, pressed against the wall, so I'm afraid you'll have to get upon your hands and knees to retrieve it. Inside this box is a manual contained within a black aluminum folder.'

Roger turned to Rosita. 'Lulu unqualified babysitter number one, I believe you are familiar with this room. Will you please retrieve this book for me while I continue?'

I felt my cheeks burn red.

'Uh,' Rosita said.

'If you do it quickly, you will get a gold star on your daily Smile Statement.'

'You better do it,' Lulu said. 'You don't want a frowny-face sticker.'

Rosita made a grunt and turned from the room, her camera drone following. I heard her pull herself onto the metal ladder adjacent to the control room. The small room sat directly atop the control center. There was a mattress there, too, one Rosita and I had shared more than once. Roger had never said anything about it. A moment passed, and we could hear her above us as she started to crawl over the boxes shoved in the back of the low room.

'While she retrieves the manual, let me give you background on this program,' Roger said. 'As you know, the honeybees were designed to assist a colony establishing itself on a new planet. In addition to habitat construction, we were designed to assist in the defense of the colony in the unlikely circumstance that the local fauna is aggressive or if another colony of settlers decides to become unfriendly. In such a case, the perimeter-defense program is activated, and all existing honeybee assets are repurposed to defend the colony against any and all hostilities. This program was initiated this morning, triggered by the attack against myself and Oliver.'

The screen in front of Lulu blinked, and a map appeared, showing the ranch. Above, I heard a muffled curse from Rosita as a box fell over.

'We currently have a total of four hundred thirty honeybee assets, including me, the controller hive queen. Three scouts, and 426 drones. This is enough to give adequate defensive coverage of this ranch for a short period, but I fear it is not nearly enough to protect us from a full incursion. One of the scouts and one of the drones need critical repairs. In addition, another 247 drones are operating at suboptimal levels.'

The map changed, showing our section of the peninsula. I could see our farm at the very southern edge, the main road, the Gonzales farm, followed by several others. The small village square with the church and market and bar, and then the road leading north, meandering through a few more town squares, ending in the larger town of Burnt Ends, approximately forty kilometers away to the north.

The map zoomed to Burnt Ends, focusing just north of the town square and the mayor's residence atop a hill the locals called the Sombrero. A warehouse stood on the map. It was where we brought our excess grain to sell. The grain would then be transported via auto train far, far away to Fat Landing.

'Underneath this warehouse is what remains of the honeybee assets used to help build the local infrastructure. Assuming this storage area hasn't been looted, it contains multiple scout units, a few hundred additional drones, and hundreds of necessary maintenance supplies and upgrade materials, including supplies required for anti-air defense.'

'Are you kidding me?' I asked.

'*What?*' Lulu exclaimed. 'You said it was all disposed of! I have been working my butt off for *years* just to –'

'Lulu, if you wish to speak, you must raise your hand.'

My sister's hand shot into the air. Her knuckles were still swollen from her bar fight with Kitty Dominguez the previous week.

'I will accept questions after my introduction, Lulu. You know this. I'm afraid you're getting a frowny face on today's Smile Statement. Continuing. Protocol dictates we relocate our existing defensive structure to the population center of Burnt Ends. However, because of the existence of this control center and the time restraints to prepare our defenses, I suggest we keep this location as our base of operations. We still must send a team to the warehouse in Burnt Ends to retrieve the supplies in order to bolster our defense. This must be completed before the main assault begins in approximately six hours.'

'How are we going to get all of that from there to here in only six hours?' Mr Gonzales asked.

'If you need to ask a question, Mr Gonzales, you must raise your hand. One frowny sticker for you.'

'Why is he "Mr Gonzales," and not rancher neighbor two or whatever?' Sam asked.

Shing! The electrified metallic stinger emerged from Roger. 'Further disruptions will result in correction. Please, no more interruptions.'

I sighed. My grandfather would have been laughing his ass off at all of this.

Rosita returned. She had dust on her face and in her long black hair, which was tied up in a ponytail. She clutched a metal folder in her arms.

I froze at the sight of the folder. On the cover in block print, it read, *The Colonist's Guide to Settlement Defense.*

Underneath that, scrawled with a marker in my grandfather's distinctive handwriting: 'Remember rule number ten.'

The sight of that sentence hit me like a sledgehammer. I looked to Lulu to see if she had noticed the book. She hadn't.

'Ahh, thank you, Lulu unqualified babysitter number one,' Roger said. A happy *ding* emanated from Roger. 'One gold star for you. Please, place that folder upon the desk.'

She complied, and Sam moved so she could stand next to me. I reached up and pulled a strand of dust from her hair. I heard a familiar *clank, clank, clank* noise, and I turned to see a group of about twenty of the larger drones walk into the barn. One by one, they entered their recharge stations and stepped inside. This was off schedule.

Roger continued. 'I have secured six of the wheeled grain transports that will transport the assault team to Burnt Ends. We will secure the location, retrieve the needed supplies, and return with them. We will leave here in forty minutes and spend another forty-three minutes proceeding to the location, and then it will take roughly four hours to retrieve and load the supplies. We will then bring them back here, where the remaining drones will assist in off-loading.'

'*Assault* team?' Sam asked.

'Yes,' Roger said. 'Now is the time for questions. Please raise your hands, but I will answer this one. The six grain transports will arrive shortly. I propose three drones along with a single human join each transport. Approximately halfway to the location, they will be joined by Trixie 2, who will enter the lead transport and will serve as my proxy. That is the assault team.'

'But why is it called an assault team?' Sam asked.

'Burnt Ends is currently occupied by five hostile entities. According to Trixie 2, they have already demolished the mayor's residence and are currently going from house to house, exterminating everyone they find.'

Cries and gasps filled the room. Next to me, Rosita gripped onto my arm so hard, it hurt. I thought of Rosita's little nieces, two-year-old twin girls. They lived in Burnt Ends. They'd just started taking ballet lessons.

She called them her nieces, though she didn't have any actual siblings. The little girls were actually second cousins once removed or something like that. Not that it really mattered, but they were related to her through some complicated family tree. That was common here.

There weren't too many kids in that age group on our planet, especially on the peninsula, and Rosita's nieces were notable as being some of the first of the 'New Generation' birthed under strict controls and carefully monitored. Their parents had been part of a select group of thirtysomething couples who were allowed to have children. Half of the babies were born via in vitro fertilization, resulting in multiple sets of twins and triplets. The other half were allowed to be made the old-fashioned way. In both cases, the children themselves were developed without the gene-locking therapy that had been used to create the Orphan Generation – what people called my age group. These babies were the first true generation of New Sonorans. The first true natives.

It wasn't until a little more than seven months ago that they had given that first batch of now two-year-olds a clean bill of health and lifted the birth-control restrictions planetwide, as long as both sets of parents came from the Orphan Generation. Now half the peninsula was pregnant. And from what I had heard, it was even crazier in Fat Landing and the surrounding area.

New Sonora was about to have a population boom.

Roger turned to my sister, who'd lowered her hand at the news of the assault on Burnt Ends. 'Lulu, ask your question.'

She just stared at Roger for a moment. The sight of Lulu speechless was disconcerting. 'Uh, why didn't you tell us about the supply depot? You said it'd all been decommissioned.'

'I did not know. This information was hidden within the perimeter-defense program. Your grandfather didn't want you to rely on the honeybee system for the rest of your lives. His intention was for me to eventually break down and for you to convert the farm to a more traditional system. The supplies we must now retrieve were set aside in the unlikely event of an emergency such as this. Do you have further questions, Lulu?'

'How . . . What exactly are our "defensive" capabilities? The drones are big and strong, but they're dumb as . . . They're dumb. What can they do against an armed mech? Are they going to accidentally knock over their fences or dig up their water lines?'

'This subject is for the second lesson later this evening, but in short, the drones will get a software upgrade and may be outfitted for multiple offensive and defensive duties. In addition, their construction duties can be used to create defensive structures and a wide array of long- and short-range batteries. The scout units are designed for surveillance, espionage, and light assassination duties.'

'Light assassination?' Sam asked. Roger made a warning sound. Sam shrank back.

'Who do you want for the assault team?' Lulu asked.

'Nonessential visitors to the farm who are physically capable of heavy lifting, such as Oliver friend number three.'

'Hey!' Sam said.

'I'm going,' Rosita said.

I looked at her. She still had dust all over her face. It made her look so much older, like the photo of her mother that hung on her bedroom wall. She gave me a look that said, *Try to stop me.*

'My brother and I will go, too,' Lulu said. 'It will be me and Ollie and Rosita along with anyone else who wants to go. We're the only ones who know anything about the honeybees and we'll know what to look for. This is not negotiable, Roger. Do you have a plan to deal with the bad guys in Burnt Ends?'

To my surprise, Roger didn't object. 'There is a plan, yes. The danger to you will be minimal, but it is not without risk.'

I raised my hand. Roger turned to me.

'Do we know how many of these, uh, guys are coming tonight?'

'I have been gathering data and monitoring the social feeds. Apex has not published the number of total sign-ups, but there are estimates. I believe they can field a total of seventy-five hundred mechs at a time with the *Pinnacle*, their print ship. Using this knowledge and comparing that to the published map depicting all the assault zones and the destruction already wrought upon Burnt Ends, along with the data gathered from Priscilla's encounter with the Apex drop unit, I do have a very rough projection. I believe the most likely scenario we will face is that several hundred mech units will be dropped in the area of Burnt Ends along with groups of four or five deployment units scattered throughout the peninsula. If the opponent is not aware of our defense until it is engaged, I suspect our very first encounter with the enemy will be light, and unless we are unlucky, it will not occur for several hours post–first wave, perhaps not until later tomorrow. I do not have enough data on what the subsequent waves will entail.'

Shit, I thought.

'What's a deployment unit?' Lulu asked.

'Excellent question, Lulu, but you did not raise your hand. Please look at this.' An image appeared on the screen. It was of a round carousel-like device, almost like six vertical coffins back-to-back in a flower pattern. The picture was from Priscilla the scout's point of view, taken just before she'd gone offline. The photograph changed to a scientific line-drawn illustration. The logo for *Operation Bounce House* appeared in the bottom right corner. The image was labeled MPF-DU-6.

'According to the information on the Apex website, this is how the majority of mechs are dropped and then retrieved. Each deployment unit has space for six mechs. The center section deploys separately as an AI drone that can bring ammunition and repairs to units on the field. There are larger deployment units as well, but it appears they are only utilized in special circumstances. Yes, Oliver?'

I lowered my hand. 'That thing that swooped in and blew up the mech we saw. Was that a repair drone?'

'Negative. That was a separate vehicle launched from the main ship. I do not have enough data on this ship's capabilities. If it is the ship I am thinking of, it is one of four such ships attached to the *Pinnacle*, the Apex mother ship. It is called a Moderator.'

A chill washed over me.

'Yes, I have a question,' Mr Gonzales said.

'You must raise your hand. But please ask your question.'

'What's the point?'

We all turned to look at him. The man looked tired, so tired.

Mr Gonzales had been a constant in my life. He was our closest neighbor; his fields adjoined our own. He and his wife had had two boys once upon a time. The Sickness had taken both before they'd managed to have children of their own. Recently, Sam and I had been going over to help him in his fields. We guessed he had maybe only one or two seasons left in him.

Still, the man was always smiling, always happy. I remembered he'd always have candy for us. His wife – the chubby, always smiling Mrs Gonzales – kept the two rooms of her dead children pristine, as if she was expecting them to come home any day now. She, too, was always friendly, always cheerful. It wasn't until recently that I had finally started to notice the cracks in the façade – the same cracks that had been there all along in all of the non-natives, those who'd been born on one of the fifteen generation ships, all who had helped build this world from the ground up only to have their legs swept out from under them.

And now it was happening again.

'Please clarify,' Roger asked.

Mr Gonzales removed his ever-present hat and wiped his brow. His hands were shaking. 'They're trying to kill us. They're doing it for fun, for their game. The moment they realize we're not going to play along and die like good little settlers, they're just going to drop a kinetic strike on us from above. All the honeybees in the world aren't going to stop that. All of this.' The elderly farmer waved his hands. 'All it's going to do is attract more attention. We're better off scattering into the forest and waiting it out. They say they're only here for five days. Why not hide? We can hide for five days.'

A full moment of silence followed. Roger whirred and clicked. 'Such a technique is not without merit, but it's not the type of defense I am designed to facilitate. If you wish to run and hide, I suggest you go home, grab supplies, and get moving now. Remove your bracelet and all radiation-emitting materials. Build a shelter at least a hundred kilometers from the closest population center, one that disguises your heat signature, and do not leave for at least one month past the last date you notice vehicles coming in or out from orbit.'

Roger turned away.

Rosita was shaking. She wouldn't do that, and I knew it. Neither would Lulu. This was our home. I still didn't understand why Earth was really doing this, and I feared I never would. My sister was looking at me, and I met her fierce eyes.

It's funny how quickly everything can change. Grandpa Lewis used to say that. We'd sit atop the barn and eat Popsicles, looking through the telescope at the *Forlorn* and then at the transfer gate. Bugs would zip by, harassing us. They'd land on me and Lulu, but they'd ignore Grandpa. *Never be surprised when it does. Just be ready.*

A console on the left side beeped, indicating the arrival of the grain transports.

Lulu was still looking at me.

We could run. It was the prudent thing to do. Mr Gonzales was right in that they could turn us to sludge whenever they wanted. We had no planetary defenses. So what was the point of fighting them?

I thought about that unreasonable order: for us all to go to Fat Landing. They had to know it was impossible. They had to know that it was harvest and that we wouldn't comply. That we *couldn't* comply.

Running was useless. It didn't matter if it was five days or five years. There wasn't anywhere we'd be able to hide. And even if I did run, I knew several of my friends wouldn't. And then what? What if we survived? What would we come back to? Would I be able to live with myself?

No, I decided. *No, I couldn't.*

'Let's do this,' I said.

CHAPTER 8

Each of the wheeled transports was a hopper, the most common of the open-top grain transports on the peninsula. The standard hopper was twenty-two meters long and a little over four meters tall. I knew this was based on an Earth standard from hundreds of years ago. There were maybe thirty of the hoppers in the entire peninsula, and they were always breaking down.

These six sitting on the farm now were to get to Burnt Ends and then transport the new honeybee parts back to the barn. They weren't the only transports currently under Roger's control. He'd also hacked into and commandeered an additional ten of the large transports along with several of the other, smaller trucks, all of which were currently on other tasks from Roger or were on standby and awaiting somewhere along our forty-five-kilometer route to the town.

There were doors on the back and on the side of the graffiti-covered hoppers, though we usually used the conveyor to just drop the grain in from the top. Because we had no bridges or tunnels in the area, the height of these things could be expanded with temporary walls, but nobody ever did, especially if they were hauling grain. Each transport had a single cab up front that could hold two passengers, though these things usually went unoccupied.

Three drones moved into each tub as we watched, moving into the side doors. The large doglike robots could not fly like the scouts, and they clanked noisily into the empty transports, jumping up from the ground into the dirty beds before settling in place and lowering to the ground.

Despite there being six transports and six of us, we doubled up in the last three cabs, leaving the first three trucks unoccupied. I tried to get into a cab with Rosita, but my sister grabbed onto her arm and dragged her into transport number four. Sam and I moved into number five. The Serrano twins, Tito and Axel, moved into the last while their grandmother clucked over them, sobbing and showering the large twenty-four-year-old men with kisses.

Roger had insisted we also update the bracelets of the two Serrano brothers to the new network, which had started a minor firestorm of everybody trying to get their bracelets changed. It was Lulu, not Roger, who'd shut that down, telling everybody that we couldn't do it. She added Mr Gonzales and Harriet to the network, and that was it.

'She seemed mad. Do you think she's mad?' Sam asked worriedly as we pulled away from the farm, bumping onto the road. He looked out the window of the truck, watching as Harriet turned back into my house.

'She's scared,' I said, also watching the pregnant woman. I cringed, seeing someone open the window to my room. There were at least three dozen people in our house now, which was just ridiculous.

There was so much to do. There was always so much to do. I could just hear my grandfather's voice. *I don't have time for a damn invasion.*

We were moving toward danger. Even after my encounter with the robot this morning, it didn't seem real. Was it strange that I couldn't stop worrying about the farm itself? About the crops? It seemed wrong. Still, I couldn't stop thinking about it.

All the remaining drones had abandoned their harvesting duties and were moving quickly about the fields, building multiple structures throughout the farm. A group of fifty swarmed over the main fence, shoring it up with concrete blocks. A few were building what appeared to be towerlike structures. Men and women, unable to help with the drones, had moved to the fields and were helping with the harvest. Roger zipped about, shouting instructions. The field was littered with metal buckets and guides, all of which had to be uprooted before I could use my combine.

The same combine that was still broken down. A wave of anxiety washed over me. So much to do.

Another few dozen of the drones had left with a group of twenty men and women hiking north toward the Gonzales farm in order to retrieve more insta-set and aggregates for the walls. Mr Gonzales hoarded the stuff. But even that wouldn't be enough, and we'd been given a secondary objective to gather more building supplies while we were in town.

I knew it wasn't all of the people helping. A few were taking Roger's advice and running for the hills. Mr and Mrs Gonzales were not among them.

I didn't blame those who fled, but both Lulu and Rosita had had some choice words for them. Rosita made sure her camera got a good shot of all of them leaving.

When Harriet had arrived, she'd dragged Sam off, and they'd had a heated discussion, ending with her walking off in a huff. He hadn't said anything, but it was clear she'd wanted to run.

The trucks continued to bump over the road. Sam and I didn't talk, both of us sitting in silence, buried in our own worries. According to Roger, four of the five mechs in town had recently powered down while the drop ship returned to orbit, ostensibly to gather a weapons refill, leaving the five mechs without backup. We had no idea how long that would take, or if the powered-down mechs would protect themselves from attack.

We passed through the crossroads where just a few buildings stood. It was so small, it couldn't even be considered a town. One was the Belly-Rubbed Pug, which was really just a barn whose original owner had long ago relocated. There was a music system, a stage that had never been used by anyone, and Yasmine, the holographic pole dancer. All of the booze was supplied by Tito and Axel's family and a few places north of Burnt Ends. The bar didn't even have a real floor. Nobody, not even AJ, the proprietor, knew the origin of the bar's name. The sign had come from a bar on *Encantada*, one of the fifteen generation ships, and it featured a flat-faced dog with a top hat.

Also at the crossroads was the cemetery where my mother and both of my grandparents were buried. I'd never really known my dad, who'd been a migrant farmworker. He'd visited me only once, and he'd stayed long enough to knock up my mother a second time. It was possible he was buried here, too. All of our parents were buried here.

And other than the bar and cemetery, there was the Catholic

church, but it was abandoned with the roof sagging in. There was a church in Burnt Ends for those who still had faith, but there weren't many of us. The only practicing Catholics I knew were Mr and Mrs Gonzales and Mrs Becerra. Most all the others said they were Catholic, but they never went to services except maybe the Christmas service in Burnt Ends.

I watched the Belly-Rubbed Pug pass by, focusing on the old weather-cracked sign. When we were kids, Sam and I had once asked the proprietor – AJ's grandfather, whose name was also AJ – if we could play a gig on the stage. He had laughed and said only if we played covers of old Earth songs, which had pissed Sam off so much, we'd never asked again. We did know one cover, and Sam didn't want to play more than that. He always had weirdly strong opinions about anything music related.

We're never going to get a chance to play a gig there now, I thought sadly as the bar pulled away.

After the crossroads, it was just kilometers and kilometers of fields.

'If it's a game and they're not actively driving the mechs, do the machines just sit there idle?' Sam asked, breaking the silence. 'Like, what happens if the drivers have to take a crap or go to school or go to sleep? They're just gonna leave them sitting there? If they really are worried about terrorists and whatever, that seems kind of stupid. It's not like they can log out, and the machines disappear.'

I was wondering the same thing. 'We're going to find out.'

The convoy slowed. My bracelet crackled.

'Trixie 2 is approaching. She will enter the first truck,' came Roger's voice.

'I've never fired a gun before,' Sam said a minute later after we had started to pick up speed.

He was nervous, just saying what was on his mind. It was a dumb thing to say, yet I'd been thinking the same thing.

'None of us have,' I said.

'Yeah,' he agreed, 'I guess not.'

Roger told us there would be rifles in the civil defense bunker. Ancient pulse rifles. It was unclear if they'd be strong enough to pierce the printed armor of the mechs or if they even worked at all. Probably not. Nobody had guns except the sheriff and his deputies, and they used old-fashioned gunpowder-style weapons.

We all had plenty of experience with video games, and we were pretending like that would be enough.

They're going door-to-door, Roger had said.

The more we drove, the more scared I became.

I thought of the small town of Burnt Ends, of the shops. Of the diner built inside the shell of an ancient scorched landing vessel from *Hibisco* with the red-and-white-checkered tables and the Earth jukebox. Of Lucinda, the nice waitress who always gave me a slice of apple pie. *Farmers are the backbone of the whole planet*, she'd say. *You need to eat.* She'd put her hand on my shoulder and give it a little squeeze, remarking about how big I was getting.

Was she okay? What about everyone else?

I thought of the sheriff. Paunchy old Sheriff Jake, who always won the annual chili cook-off with his Supernova Extreme Barn Burner. Where was he? I could just picture him stepping out onto the street to face a group of giant war machines with nothing but his chemical pistol. How could that have ended in anything but tragedy?

The trucks slowed.

'We are approaching town,' Roger said, voice crackling over my bracelet. 'Two kilometers to our target. Trixie 2 will perform another reconnaissance before we proceed. Everyone put your earpieces in. Maintain radio silence unless absolutely necessary. I do not know the capabilities of the hostiles, but we should assume they can detect the location of outgoing signals and possibly shut them down.'

I pulled an earpiece off the bracelet and stuck it into my ear.

'It's too bad we don't have the Earth systems,' Sam muttered as he struggled with his earpiece. 'Full text. Translation. You can just think it, and it appears on an HUD screen.'

'These aren't meant for this sort of thing,' I said, rearranging the earpiece. 'They had military-grade ones even before, but I doubt they have anything like that in the defense bunker. No, just do one ear, remember? He said we only do one ear.'

'Oh, yeah,' Sam said, sticking the second back into the bracelet.

I rolled down the window as we waited. I couldn't see anything but the back of the transport in front of us. That and empty, flat fields to my left and right filled with knee-high weeds waving back and forth in the wind.

I had a quick memory of jogging through this same field once years ago. Sam and I, both about ten or eleven years old. We'd been running, chasing after a loose goat that we thought we'd spied through the glass of our transport. We'd both hopped out into the mud, running and screaming and laughing as we rushed through the weeds. Mr Locke had lost all his goats a few days earlier after one of them had toppled the fence, and he was offering a bag of pears to anyone who found one. We'd run and run with my grandfather hollering at us from the road to come back. We'd never found the goat.

I took a deep breath through the open window. I could sense it. The wrongness in the air. The stench of something burning. I swallowed. The air was normally sweet, mixed in with the scent of rain and the distant, barely noticeable odor of farm animals from the Tibbit ranch and all the others on the other side of the river.

But now the sense of danger was palpable.

Ahead, the sound of something mechanical suddenly whirred. Next to me, Sam stiffened.

This wasn't a mech, but the familiar sound of a heavy-duty off-road hauler moving at full speed. At the same moment, the hopper bed behind me clanked as the drones within started to move.

Before I could question it, Roger crackled in my ear. 'Exit the vehicle immediately and run west. You have an incoming hostile on the ground, ETA forty-five seconds.'

CHAPTER 9

Sam and I just looked at each other for a half second before we both scrambled out of the truck. Lulu was already outside, cigarette dangling from her mouth, and she was helping Rosita out as the Serrano brothers both jumped out behind us.

'This way!' Lulu called, running. We all jumped from the raised roadway and splotched on the field. Lulu, the shortest of us by far, practically disappeared in the weeds. We ran toward a distant line of trees. Just beyond that was the bank of the Pantano River. If whatever the hostile was followed us to the river, we'd get trapped. We'd have to jump in.

I glanced north toward Burnt Ends, and all I could see was the tops of the radio towers and several plumes of smoke. There was something wrong with the town's skyline, but I couldn't immediately place what it was. Behind us, multiple honeybees were all clambering out of the hoppers, getting themselves clear of the trucks and scattering in all directions. The lead hopper, now empty of all its honeybees, started pulling forward down the road on its own, leaving the others idling.

I finally spied the source of the loud, whining engine. It was indeed a hauler barreling across the same field we were running through, moving in the opposite direction, angling itself toward the road, pulling ahead of the hopper. The driverless vehicle was an ancient tracked off-road transport used for a variety of duties. It was a fraction of the size of the hoppers, but it had a passenger cabin that could transport up to ten people along with a long cargo bed. There were only four or five of these things still running, and the wait list to get access to one for a day was typically a month long. This one held a large, dirty boulder in the back cab that bounced ominously as the vehicle rumbled upward onto the road.

I still did not see the hostile mech.

As we ran, I hazarded another glance north. It occurred to me what was wrong with the skyline. One of the usual landmarks of the area – the water tower – simply wasn't there anymore. It was just gone. There was nothing left but smoke.

A loud crash echoed far off to our right, followed by an explosion and a loud crunch. A moment later, a second crash echoed so loud, it shook the ground.

'You may slightly decelerate your retreat in order to maintain energy. The threat will soon be neutralized,' Roger said. 'Proceed to the tree line, but maintain a brisk northerly pace.'

'Jesus, Roger,' I muttered, my heart pounding. We turned north and started jogging uphill toward the river bend. The river curved up here, and the trees grew thicker, but this path would take us toward the western edge of town, up past the old outpost and behind the fabrication warehouses.

A new plume of smoke rose from the roadway in the distance.

Roger spoke again. 'The drones are in the process of incapacitating and disassembling the threat. Trixie 2 is approaching the town to get updated data on the hostile forces while the transports will continue on their original path but while being flanked by the drones. It is likely the enemy now knows of your presence, and it is no longer advisable to travel with the transports. Subterfuge on your part is now required while I determine the status of the four remaining enemy units.'

I exchanged a look with my sister. The tree line loomed, and we moved to hide within.

'Where is everybody?' Sam asked as we skulked through the alley behind the line of fabricator factories. We'd left the edge of the river behind and were now skirting the western outskirts of town, keeping low and running along the back of the old concrete buildings. These were some of the original buildings in the town, and graffiti littered the back sides of them, along with a smattering of garbage, ancient cigarette butts, and the rusting husks of abandoned and broken-down machinery that couldn't be recycled for one reason or another.

I knew this was where the kids of Burnt Ends used to hang out when they were skipping school. Now that the Orphan Generation had mostly aged out of school and most everyone had to work, this corridor had taken on an almost postapocalyptic feel.

I thought of Harriet, Sam's fiancée. And Ursula and Guadalupe and Kim and Samantha and all the other girls I'd grown up with who were now pregnant. In thirteen or fourteen years, this back alley would be filled with delinquents all over again.

At least that was how it was supposed to be.

We hadn't seen a single living – or dead – person since we entered the town limits, which was eerie. Smoke billowed from every direction. According to Roger, all four of the remaining mechs were on the other side of town – a good kilometer from our current position. All were offline, just standing idle. Roger cautioned us from getting ourselves seen on camera despite this. Trixie 2 was going through town and disabling all the cameras she could find.

We did pass one emergency-alert beacon. It had fallen from its spot atop a pole, but a pixelated hologram of the mayor's scared face still shot from it, only half formed and sideways on the ground. The speaker was gone, and whatever announcement he had made was now silenced.

Sam, the Serrano twins, and I stood in front of one brick wall, looking at the faded old graffiti there. The name 'Papa's Big Band' was crossed out with 'The Rhythm Mafia Rules' written under it. Under that, and more recently, someone else had written: 'Who?'

Papa's Big Band had been a brass band consisting of some kids along with old Mr Hernandez ('Papa') here in Burnt Ends. Years ago, I'd tried out to be their drummer, but they'd rejected me because I lived on the southern peninsula and came into town only once every week or so. That, and because I sucked. Sam had come up and defaced their logo in my honor.

I wondered about them, the kids who'd been in that band. They would all have been in their twenties now, all except Mr Hernandez of course. He was the guy who'd taught them all how to play and built their instruments. He'd died a few years ago, and last I'd heard, hardly anyone played their instruments anymore.

'Do you think everyone ran away?' Axel asked. Next to him, his brother nodded.

'I don't know,' I said as we continued on our way.

Roger had us pause as Trixie 2 disabled a group of cameras up ahead. We'd cross the street here and move northeast. Through the gap in the alley, I could see the Sombrero and the mayor's residence atop it. The house was a burned-out husk. Just on the other side of the hill were the train tracks that led upward through the peninsula and to the desert and eventually across the dead continent to Fat Landing. The warehouse we were headed for was on the other side of the mayor's house, on the bottom lip of the Sombrero.

'If they attacked super early in the morning, everyone would've been asleep,' Lulu said. 'If they didn't have warning, they would've been killed in their beds.'

'This is a pretty big town. There are thousands of homes here,' I said, 'and only five mechs. Now four.'

Lulu grunted. 'Four mechs *now*. There might've been more last night.'

'Maybe people are still hiding,' Sam said.

'It appears the refuel drone is approaching from above,' Roger said, crackling over our earpieces. 'The four remaining mechs remain offline. The path to the warehouse is now clear of obvious electronic surveillance. I suggest you proceed there as quickly as possible.'

We started to run.

CHAPTER 10

It didn't take long after that for us to find the first corpses. We turned a corner, and there they were.

We all stopped running. The shock of it was overwhelming. I felt like I'd been kicked in the stomach and like I'd run right into a wall all at once.

People who say dead bodies look like they're just sleeping have never seen a dead body.

At least three hundred people filled the field, all dead. Some were in pieces. Those who remained intact still had giant holes in them. Holes as big as baseballs. Several didn't have heads at all. They'd been running north toward the curve of the Pantano.

I didn't recognize anyone.

I didn't until I did.

Sheriff Jake was there, just like I'd imagined. Everyone had been shot in their backs, but not him. He was down, facing the threat, his two deputies by his side. His deputies were my age, but I didn't know them.

Rosita gasped at the sight of a crumpled little form. There was only one child in the group. One of the two-year-olds. It was a boy, not one of her nieces. Still, it was a child. A murdered child.

'That's Henry,' Rosita said of the little boy, gasping. 'He's wearing the pajamas my great-aunt made for him.'

The boats, I thought. They'd been running to the river to get onto the boats. They hadn't made it.

'I'm going to throw up,' Sam said moments before he did indeed vomit.

'This is real,' Axel said, also bent over like he was going to spew. 'This is real.'

Of course it's real, I thought. Yet I knew exactly what he meant. His brother fell to his knees and also vomited on the ground.

Next to me, Rosita cried softly. Lulu detached herself from the group and stepped forward, going to one knee. She examined the bodies with an almost clinical expression. She started snapping pictures with her bracelet. A moment later, Rosita's ever-present camera drone zoomed forward and also started taking video of the scene.

'What are you doing?' I hissed.

Lulu continued to get closer, twisting her bracelet, zooming in. 'People need to see this.'

The bodies were all concentrated behind the playground for the school, which had been repurposed as some sort of municipal building, but recently renovations had started to turn it back into a school. The building was cratered and smoking. It appeared a bunch of people had taken shelter there. I couldn't get inside now, even if I wanted to. It was reduced to a pile of rubble. Those hiding within had been attacked, and they had run. They'd made a break for the trees, heading toward the boats, and been caught in the field. This was the same field where they held the carnival after harvest.

The same field where Sheriff Jake won the chili cook-off every year.

I stared at the scattered bodies, a strange numbness crawling over me, like I was being enveloped by some sort of alien creature. The last time I'd seen a dead body was when Grandpa Lewis had died. I remembered that day, finding him in his room, and I could just tell. His stillness had been too complete. His eyes were closed, but his head was turned in such a way that made him seem so wrong. It wasn't even an unnatural angle. Just . . . uncomfortable. Lulu had cried and made me fix his neck before we called Mr Gonzales.

Why am I thinking of this now? I watched Tito and Axel, both brothers now on their hands and knees. Tito, who was the biggest, strongest person I knew, had tears streaming down the side of his face as he gasped. He'd witnessed a terrible farm accident when he was younger, and he'd been mute ever since. Was this as bad? I wondered. Would I lose my voice, too?

Lulu suddenly had another cigarette in her mouth, and she lit it. She held a second cigarette up in the air. Rosita peeled off of me and grabbed it. Rosita had quit smoking months ago, right when they'd lifted the ban on pregnancy. The camera drone continued to circle the scene.

'They were running,' Lulu said after a moment.

'Can't they see we're not terrorists?' Rosita asked after she took a deep drag. 'It's mostly old people. Do they not care? What kind of monsters would do this? Poor, sweet Henry.'

'That's why they chose us,' Lulu said. 'Don't you see?'

I didn't see. I had my hands on my back, and I walked in circles. I didn't know why we were still standing here. Yet it seemed wrong to leave, like we were abandoning them.

It was Sam who responded.

'You're right,' Sam said, coughing. He stood and wiped his mouth.

'Because of Henry?' Rosita asked. 'I don't understand.'

'There're only, what, about fifty of those two-year-olds on the whole peninsula? Like thirty births and a bunch of twins,' Sam said. 'After that, the youngest of the Orphans are just now turning twenty-one. There are hardly any kids. If they wanted to do this here, they had to do it before everyone started giving birth. Killing pregnant folks is bad enough, but babies? That's a bad look.'

Lulu had turned to look at Sam. She nodded.

'But why?' Rosita asked, echoing my own question. 'Why kill anyone at all?'

'The mechs have all been reloaded. Please make haste,' Roger said over the band. 'We do not know when they will come back online.'

Across the way, I could see the transport trucks and the drones moving on their own as they approached the warehouse from the west, like they'd taken the wide way around, skirting the top part of Sombrero hill, which contained the smoldering mayor's residence.

'Come on,' I said, pointing toward the hill. 'We'll . . . we'll come back and get everyone buried when this is all done. We can't stay here.'

Rosita held her palm out, and her camera drone alighted on it.

She reattached it to the top of her bracelet with a click. We all stood, and we continued on our way.

'Where's the first transport?' Sam asked as we moved to the large, empty warehouse. The enormous building hadn't been touched by the fighting, though the air was thick with smoke.

The barn door opened as Lulu and Rosita tugged on it, and the five remaining transport trucks rumbled backward into the warehouse, all moving in a single line before spreading out side by side. There were channels here in the floor where normally the grain was dumped after the trucks were weighed. The grain would then be rerouted downward and into the train beds before it started its long journey.

Trixie 2 trotted by. She spoke with Roger's voice:

'The first transport and the truck were both sacrificed to kill the enemy mech. We cannot afford to lose any more transports. Oliver, Oliver friends number three, twelve, and thirteen, I am standing near a hatch in the floor. Help me open it.'

Without a word, we moved to a set of four metal rings on the floor. I'd been in this building dozens of times over the years, and I'd never noticed this. We all grabbed and pulled on the heavy metallic rings. Rosita's camera drone flitted by our heads. After a moment of struggle, a panel groaned. We yanked, pulling it upward and over. The door itself was a square about three meters by three meters. We pulled the door up to its apex and scattered out of the way as gravity took over, crashing the door heavily to the ground, causing a flurry of dried grain and dust to swirl.

It revealed a square hole leading down into darkness.

For a moment, nothing happened as we all just dumbly stared at the hole in the floor. Then, from below, something mechanical awakened and started clanking. I saw movement in the shadows. The floor was coming up toward us. It was an industrial lift. The flatbed elevator was only about five meters down, and the gears screeched in protest as the elevator slowly approached. More dust eddied as buzzing yellow lights flickered on in the hole. The stench of old must and hot air blasted up.

The moment the lights turned on, we could see it. Standing in the center of the lift was a type of honeybee I'd never seen before. It was like a regular drone but more than three times as big. The regular drones were about the size of a large dog. This thing was the size of a gray bear.

It also had a large menacing gun mounted on its back.

'Oh, shit,' Sam said as we all scrambled back.

The platform rose all the way into the room and stopped with a screech. The robot jumped back and forth, moving in a quick, nimble manner, its movements reminiscent of those of the smaller scouts. Despite its larger size, it had only four legs, also like the scouts. It continued to hop in a circle, training its gun on us, one after another, as if it wasn't sure where to aim.

Next to me, Sam held up his hands in an I-surrender pose. Soon, we all had our hands up.

This was a pack bot, also called a rhino. I'd heard my grandfather talk about them, but I'd never seen one in real life. It was similar to the drones but designed mostly to help move materials from one place to another. While rhinos could be affixed with grasping claws for dexterous tasks, these things were mostly used for heavy lifting, transporting materials over rough ground, and even as mounts. The four legs could be swapped for six smaller ones or treads in some cases. These things were supposed to be enormously strong.

The large robot was painted completely black with a matte finish, whereas all the ones on our farm were silver, though a few of ours still had specks of orange, yellow, and black on their underbellies where their original high-vis paint jobs remained.

I stared at the long, sleek gun. The bot continued to hop in a circle, pointing the weapon at each of us. Each time it landed, it made a metallic thud on the platform. The quick, smooth, mechanical movements reminded me of our own honeybees, and it was terrifying to see in something so large. *Clang. Clang. Clang.*

The weapon was some sort of heavy-duty pulse rifle. I'd never seen one of these in real life, but I'd seen hundreds of similar weapons in movies and vids, and I'd played dozens of games with these things.

The telltale blue glow was missing from the weapon, though I didn't know if that blue glow was just something added in movies.

Trixie 2 buzzed up into the air and landed awkwardly atop the robot, in a fashion similar to what Roger would do to the scouts and drones. I'd never seen a scout do this before. The rhino immediately stopped hopping. The two bots remained frozen for about five seconds before the rhino made a familiar beep and then settled down, like a cow going to sleep. Trixie 2 buzzed up and landed on the ground, settling in front of me.

'I have taken control of the facilities,' Roger said, speaking through Trixie 2. 'The recharge mechanism for the Conquistador-class pulse rifles is inaccessible, but it appears we can free it easily. I believe we now have all the supplies required to repair them if their last diagnostics are accurate. And if not, I may be able to cannibalize some of their parts. It appears most of the facilities are otherwise intact, despite some water damage. We will now proceed to load the transports. I will have the drones unpack the UAVs, and we will utilize their capabilities for our egress.'

'What's a UAV?' Sam asked as several of my honeybee drones stood on the elevator next to the rhino and were lowered into the facility below us. Several of the drones were missing, and I suspected the units were parked somewhere outside, keeping an eye on the four enemy mechs, since Trixie 2 was here with us.

'I think they're like Rosita's camera, but with a lot more range,' I said.

The drones disappeared below, and soon the elevator moved back up. Roger beckoned for us to get on the platform. We all climbed aboard, and soon we disappeared into the dusty chamber below.

CHAPTER 11

The civil defense bunker was a lot bigger than I had anticipated. It was a wide warehouse, almost as big as the space above it, which surprised me because a portion of the warehouse dangled over a cliff. The room was punctuated with load-bearing walls and the chutes for transporting grain to the trains, which would pull up to get filled underneath where we were standing.

'I never realized this was here,' I said.

'Me, either,' Sam said. 'When you're looking up here from the train tracks, the warehouse doesn't look so thick. I wonder if it's built deeper into the Sombrero?' He looked around some more. 'Man, if we cleared all this stuff out, this would be a great concert venue. Imagine that? The Rhythm Mafia live from the Sombrero Bunker.'

I grunted. This hill was named the Sombrero because it looked exactly like one of the large traditional Mexican hats when you approached it from north of town. The mayor's residence stood upon the very top of the hat, and the circular-brim part of the hill held this warehouse and a few of the factories. The northern edge of the brim was engineered into a sheer cliff so the trains could roll right under the warehouse and get filled from above. My grandfather had been particularly proud of the design.

'Maybe if you guys ever practiced, you might get good enough to have an actual show,' Lulu muttered. 'You've been a band for over ten years now.'

'We're still looking for a singer,' Sam said, 'since, you know, our old one quit.'

Lulu scoffed. 'Your choice was to have me sing in your band or have Tito and Axel remain un-murdered. You couldn't have both, and you made your decision.'

'We said you were out of tune *once*,' Axel said. 'And you were. By, like, a lot.'

Tito nodded enthusiastically.

Lulu shot them both a warning glare, and Axel shut up as we continued to examine the room.

One of the chutes in the far corner had come undone, and piles of rotten grain filled the area, burying several charging pods, including the charging station for the sentry rhino's gun. It turned out, they did *not* glow blue when they were charged, but the large weapon still did not have any juice. By the time we entered the dusty room, about thirty drones were hard at work, so the charging pod was free. Only some of them were from our farm, and the rest were painted in that same black matte paint. As we watched, two of the drones opened up a crate, and a group of six more drones skittered out of the box, moving like spiders. In addition, there were four more of the large rhino-class drones, bringing our total to five.

The room was now filled with swirling dust and the *clink, clink, clink* of dozens of legs moving about.

The drones started collecting crates filled with more drones and other supplies and moving in concert to the elevator.

'Interesting,' Roger said. 'The digital manifest claims there are three crates with hive queen units such as myself along with queen-specific repair supplies and charging stations, but they are not here. Based on the dust levels, it appears they were removed some time ago. The last time the sentry detected movement down here was almost twenty years ago.'

'So, like twenty years ago, someone came down here and stole all the stuff we need to repair you?' I asked. 'Why?'

'I do not know. I suspect I know the day. You won't remember this, Oliver, but it was soon after the pinhole had reopened communications from Earth, and we'd been visited by a congregation from Fat Landing who'd had a conversation with the then-mayor of Burnt Ends. They toured the city. Your grandfather had us all hide in the barn for the duration of their visit, though they never toured the countryside. He was afraid that the planetwide government would frown upon him using us for agriculture.'

'They probably took it so they could start their own farms,' I said.

'It's possible, but if they are utilizing other hive queens, they are very quiet on the local net.'

All the honeybee supplies, crates, and charging pods took up a little more than half of the room. The other half was filled with survival supplies, including cases upon cases of never-expire food rations, insta-shelters, a pair of crates with unassembled medical pods, multiple crates of personal transport scooters, and more.

'It's like all the supplies for a new colony,' Lulu said as we moved through the warehouse. 'We'll only be able to take a portion of this stuff. I haven't seen one of these scooters in years.'

'Our dad had one,' Axel said, moving his hand across the crate. 'It broke down and he never got the parts to fix it before he died. The husk of it is still in our barn.'

'These are all from the *Hibisco*,' I said, wiping dust off a crate.

'Yes,' Roger said. 'Despite the ship's troubles, most of the supplies from that particular ship made it to the peninsula unscathed. The entirety of our farm's honeybees are from that ship.'

While my grandfather was from *Forlorn*, most of the supplies in the area had come from *Hibisco*, another one of the fifteen generation ships. That particular ship had been plagued with issues near the end of the journey. The captain had supposedly gone mad. He'd shut off the AI controlling the ship and ripped out and hammered the computer into pieces. Then he'd insisted on manually plotting the entry vectors of the landing craft onto the peninsula, which had led to a mass disaster. It was where Burnt Ends had gotten its name. The captain had killed himself afterward.

'Look at this,' Sam said, peering inside a crate. 'They're all giant cameras and things. Rosita, you can make a movie using the real stuff instead of that weird little camera you always have floating around your head.'

'That is a camera system, but it's a hologram projector,' Roger said in our ears. 'It looks like a primary system along with fifteen disks. That's a better and more robust system than the one the mayor of Burnt Ends utilizes.'

'Like the one at the bar?' Lulu asked.

'That is correct,' Roger said.

Years ago, all the bars and public spaces had had the receiver disks for the hologram system. Whenever the prime minister all the way in Fat Landing wanted to make a speech or announcement, he'd turn the thing on, and he'd appear in all the bars. Unlike the flickering piece of crap that the mayor of Burnt Ends used, this system was really good. Unless you were right up against it, you couldn't tell it was a hologram.

The problem was, at least on the peninsula, nobody liked the politicians in Fat Landing much, and years of beer and food thrown at the projector disks had made them mostly inoperable. The one at the Belly-Rubbed Pug still worked, but it was no longer connected with Fat Landing. Instead, AJ, the guy who ran the bar, used it to project a woman dancing on a pole in a forever loop. On the rare occasion we got strangers to visit the crossroads, it was always great fun to watch them get drunk and try to approach the forever-dancing woman, whom we'd affectionately named Yasmine.

We continued to look through the supplies.

Against one wall was a group of three crates, each labeled 'New Colony Proliferation Kit.' Someone had taken paint and put a big red X over the crates. They had written, 'Do Not Use. Poison.' over each one in large block letters.

'Huh,' I said. 'I wonder what's wrong with these.'

Rosita stood next to me, also looking at the crates. Her camera buzzed by her head. The familiar sound of the tiny camera drone was strangely comforting. I took a half step to my left just so I could feel her arm against mine. She smelled like her greenhouse with a tinge of garlic. When we were kids, they'd called her Ajo, which was Spanish for garlic. It was meant as an insult, but she pretended not to care.

One day, when I was fourteen and Rosita was fifteen, a girl named Isla had called her Ajo, and Rosita just lost it, beating the ever-loving crap out of her right in front of everybody at the square. Nobody called her Ajo after that.

Now, a little more than ten years later, with her grandparents gone and her cousins and ailing great-aunt here in Burnt Ends, she worked her small ranch all by herself. She'd sold most of the land on either side of her property to her neighbors. She spent her days working a pair of multilevel greenhouses, cultivating spices and a few other crops, including carrots, potatoes, and tomatoes. Most everything she grew was used to feed the local population, but her spices were well-known across the planet.

Her grandmother had perfected a type of gigantic garlic bulb that *I* thought way overpowered any dish it was in. But chefs all over the world loved it, paying a premium for a single cannon-ball-sized bulb. When the Earth delegation had first come after the gate opened, the ambassador's husband had specifically asked about the garlic and was gifted a bulb to take home.

Rosita shipped a truckload of the bulbs along with a few barrels of dried flakes to Fat Landing just once a year, and she earned more than enough money to survive, even with the outrageous transport and brokerage fees.

And she did it all on her own. She refused my help other than a single drone now and then to help pick her tomatoes.

And then there was her desire to make movies, documentaries. She'd been filming for as long as I could remember. No matter how busy she was, she always seemed to have time to dedicate to that. She never uploaded anything, despite all of us encouraging her to do so. She never felt anything was ever 'ready.' But she still spent all this time working on her movies. I had no idea how she did it.

Sometimes, I'd look at her and marvel at how smart she was, how determined. And I'd wonder what she was doing with me. I'd worry that it was because she didn't have any other options.

I rubbed my hand against the spray-painted words on the crate. Dust swirled.

'Hey, listen,' I began. 'About last night –'

She interrupted me. 'My grandmother used to think it was the nutrient milk powder that had come with them from Earth, not the planet's electromagnetic field, that caused the Sickness – the stuff that was set aside specifically for those born after planetfall. She'd say it all the time. A lot of people thought that at first. I think some of them never stopped thinking it.'

I turned my attention back to the crate. 'That doesn't make sense,' I said after thinking on it for a moment. Grandpa Lewis had never said anything like that, and he'd had a healthy distaste for all things Earth. 'I thought that was just a rumor, that the supplies for the babies born on planet were different than those for the babies born on the ship. They did tests.'

'The ones for planetfall were in a different packaging than the baby supplies on the generation ships, and that was enough to make my grandmother and a lot of others suspicious.'

'Guys,' Axel said, interrupting, 'check it out.'

He'd moved to a large metal door I hadn't noticed in the back of the room. The door had a dull red light over the handle.

'One moment,' Roger said through Trixie 2. 'The door is magnetically locked, and I am opening it now.'

The light turned green. Axel pulled it open, and the door opened with a whoosh of air. A light flickered on in the room, and the six of us moved to peer inside.

'Wow,' Sam said. 'That's a lot of guns.'

'Are those grenades?' Axel asked. Tito was now beside him, pointing at what looked like a rocket launcher.

'Bring everything,' Roger said. 'Make certain you collect the charging stations.'

The room contained about three or four dozen long, sleek black rifles sitting in charging bays. The guns appeared to be dry-sealed in plastic, not unlike the turkey and mashed potato never-expire food rations we opened every Christmas.

But there were other types of guns, too, ranging from pistols to what looked like shoulder-mounted missile launchers.

The flurry of activity in the room stopped all at once. All the drones paused. The lights in the warehouse dimmed.

'Roger, what's . . .' I started to say. The sound of a distant explosion echoed.

'Everyone open the crate labeled "Body Armor," don the chest armor and helmets, grab a pulse rifle and two grenades each, and proceed to the elevator,' came Roger's voice over our earpieces. 'Fleur-de-lys, also known as drone number 143, has been destroyed. All four of the remaining mechs have activated, and they appear to be aware of our presence. They are currently coming in this direction. We must protect the transports. Please make haste.'

CHAPTER 12

The same rhino bot that had greeted us on the elevator rode with us into the top part of the warehouse. Drones had removed the original Conquistador gun and replaced it with a smaller gun similar in size to the ones we now carried.

'It's a lot lighter than I thought it would be,' Sam said, his voice clearly nervous as we rushed to the wall of the warehouse, looking out toward the hill that still contained the smoking remains of the mayor's manor. 'The body armor and the gun. It feels fake.'

We saw no sign yet of the enemy mechs and skittered forward to the waist-high concrete barrier designed to force the grain trucks into a single file before they turned into the warehouse. Axel and Tito closed the large barn doors behind us. We'd leave them open only a crack. We didn't want the bad guys to see the transports inside the warehouse and target them. The drones were still loading the trucks as quickly as they could.

All six of us now wore the protective vests, but Lulu refused to wear the helmet. The bulky helmets were made of some impact-resistant polymer. Sam was right. All this stuff was so light, they felt like toys. Despite this, the helmets had all been much too big for my sister's tiny head, and we hadn't had time to mess around with the strap.

We all looked ridiculous, like we were wearing costumes. We were playing pretend, like Lulu's Farm Girl Gigi persona.

Only large Tito and Axel had that 'soldier' look, but they both wore similar wide-eyed, scared expressions, betraying the illusion. I knew I had to look similarly terrified. Sam had pulled off his ball cap and shoved it between his body armor and his shirt before putting his on. His long, unruly hair peeked out from under the helmet, and he had to shove his bangs under the lip to keep them from blinding him. Rosita had to take out her ponytail to wear hers properly, and her long, flowing black hair made her look like some sort of fashion model who was only pretending to be a soldier for a photo shoot.

Lulu swam in her body armor, and she was too short to properly wield one of the rifles, so she had taken up a different weapon. It looked a bit like a sawn-off shotgun from a zombie game, but it fired chemically propelled canisters that exploded upon impact. She wore a belt of the canisters over her shoulder. Roger warned that she would have to fire the cylinders in an arc and not aim too low, lest they hit the ground too close to us.

The rhino skittered off east, moving along the road and disappearing toward the woods.

All six of us huddled together, peering over the cracked concrete barrier, looking up at the top part of the Sombrero. The wide warehouse stood just behind us with an east-west road in front of it. The road edged the cliff, or the lip of the Sombrero, mirroring the train tracks about ten meters below. The woods just north of the mayor's house had been cleared, leaving a green patch all the way down to the warehouse. White rocks spelled out 'Burnt Ends' on the green in giant letters, making it look like the words were etched into the side of the hat-shaped hill. You could see the sign only if you approached the town from the north. Heavy woods flanked either side of the residence, moving down the hill until they reached the road.

The warehouse itself stood on the edge of the cliff. Running east, the tracks below ended at a small utility yard for rail maintenance on the edge of town. Going west, the tracks curved north and crossed a bridge over the Pantano, then skirted several farms before they passed the distant town of Pulpeta and continued into the uninhabitable continent.

'Targets one and two are cresting the hill containing the mayor's residence, and three and four are flanking, coming from below and east on the rail tracks,' Roger said. 'It appears all four drivers of the mechs know each other and are communicating with one another and are working in concert. You must concentrate on the two upon the hill, and I will attempt to deal with three and four. I shall use the Heavy drone to draw their fire. It appears all four of the mechs have identical armament. Do not stay so close to one another lest a single missile should kill you all at once.'

I just sat frozen for a few seconds as that last sentence sank in. I looked over my friends. None of us were moving. Axel had his eyes clenched shut so tight, his face had transformed into a series of lines. He panted rapidly as if having a panic attack.

Something in my brain clicked, and I jumped into action.

'You two,' I hissed at Rosita and Lulu, pointing east in the same direction the rhino had gone, 'move to the woods over there and get running up the hill. Get at them from the side. Don't go too close to the cliff, or the other two mechs will see you. Tito and Axel, you two go to the woods on the other side. But not all the way up the hill. Be careful of cross fire. Once these two are down, we'll all move to the east woods and help Roger with the flankers before we lose too many drones.'

Lulu just looked at me, and then she nodded. 'Come on,' she said to Rosita, tugging on her arm. They rushed toward the line of trees as Tito and Axel moved off in the other direction. I could hear Axel wheezing as they skittered off.

Then I heard it. The mechanical clank of walking legs.

'Here, kitty, kitty!' came a booming voice just as the first mech crested the hill above us, moving through the smoke of the destroyed mayor's house. 'Which one of you dirty subhumans was driving the truck that took out Wankette? Man, is she pissed.'

This voice was older than the voice from that Hobie mech, but it was still clearly young. The person speaking was maybe sixteen or seventeen years old.

The three-meter-tall mech fully appeared, clanking up the hill. This was the same dragoon recon model as the last one with the egg-shaped center body, but it was painted in a shiny metallic blue with yellow highlights that blinked in neon. The last one had had green Mohawk-like spikes down the center. This one was decorated in a different way. There appeared to be a large bouncing spring atop the machine. At the end of the spring was a flat round sign waving back and forth like the head of a jack-in-the-box. It was a circular piece of metal or wood painted white with the red concentric circles of an archery or gun target. Curved words circled the round target. They read, 'Skeet-Skeet,' on the top. I couldn't make out the words at the bottom. They said, 'Team something.' The words blinked neon, matching the rest of the blue-and-yellow color pattern.

The sign was about the size of a kitchen table, just as wide as the mech underneath it. There appeared to be no purpose to it other than as a decoration.

'Holy shit,' Sam muttered. 'That thing is huge.'

The mech contained the same cannon arm and four-pack missile launcher as the first one, but this one had a second arm that was nothing more than a grasping pincer. The mech paused at the top of the hill, looking back and forth.

A second mech appeared. This one was painted and armed in the exact same way, but I could see it was missing one of its four missiles. It had the same large sign bouncing back and forth on a spring. Instead of Skeet-Skeet, this second one read, 'Chode.'

'What is with their names?' Sam whispered. 'Skeet-Skeet and Chode? What does that even mean?'

The two mechs stopped at the top of the hill as if they were surveying the area. We hid behind the barriers, waiting.

'I'm pretty sure those who play multiplayer games get to make up new names when they go online,' I said. While Sam and I had played plenty of games, we'd never had the proper hardware to play games with Earthers. We mostly played the games that came with us from Earth, meaning ones that were over two hundred years old. 'They pick whatever they want. The kid from earlier was named Subhuman Slayer. It's like Lulu's Farm Girl Gigi name. And those porn star women – you know, the ones from the vids – don't go by their real names, either.'

'I don't think those porn ladies are real people. That one you were showing me the other day had tentacles.'

'*You* showed that to *me*. And they are all real people. That's the law. The tentacles were real. A surgical enhancement. We've already had this discussion. All human forms have to be real. No filters or CGI enhancement. That's why Lulu does so well. I guess for a long time, it was all fake, heavily filtered AI bots. Like people were talking to bots like Roger who were pretending to be women on the net. Can you imagine? That's why all the cartoons have those scrolling banners over them now.'

Sam grunted. 'Yeah, I know. But the names are supposed to make you anonymous. For the gamer guys who are already famous, do you think people call them by their tags in real life, like out on the street when they're going to the store and stuff? Do they say, "Here's your order, Mr Skeet-Skeet? You know, Chode was just in here. How's your mom?" Or do they just go by it when they're doing their game stuff? Also, no way that tentacle girl was real. How does she wipe?'

I laughed before I realized I was supposed to be terrified.

Roger crackled over my ear. 'They are currently live-broadcasting their assault on the open net. There is nearly a thirty-second delay, unfortunately, making it difficult for me to use this for intelligence, but I will continue to monitor and record it. This group is known as Team Cannon Fodder, and they are a well-known group of five youths who make an astonishingly good living playing games while other people watch. It appears they were given your positions by Apex Command, who are utilizing heat maps to pinpoint the locations of people from orbit. Team Cannon Fodder paid extra to have this added to their controls. It appears they are only given a general area and not a precise location, so stay down until you have a clear shot.'

Sam mouthed to me, *What the fuck?*

'Roger,' I said, 'send one of the drones up to distract them. Let's try to get them coming down the hill. Once they fire on the drone, Lulu, try to hit them with your canister gun while the rest of us open fire on their legs.'

'Yo,' Sam whispered as Roger acknowledged he was sending a drone toward us. 'So, I have a really dumb question.' He was looking down at his rifle. 'What the hell do these things fire? What's a "pulse"? In games, there are usually bullets and shit.'

'It's balls of energy or something,' I said, 'like pulses of plasma. Remember that sheriff deputy guy fired one at the spring festival a few years ago? It was a smaller version of one of these. It caught that scarecrow's head on fire.'

I remembered the gun hadn't even made a noise when it fired.

And the pulses of heat had shimmered in the air, leaving a long, hazy line that lasted only a moment. It wasn't like in a movie. There were no bright-colored blasts one could easily track and dodge.

'If it's plasma, why isn't it called a plasma gun? And I do remember that. I remembered he could only fire it twice before it got so hot, he had to drop the gun to the ground.'

'Hopefully these are in better shape.'

My earpiece crackled. 'The youths are complaining about the latency in their controls. They have near-instantaneous visuals, but the mechs themselves have a half-second response time. We must utilize this to our advantage. I suggest quickly moving position after you fire.'

One of the black drones appeared, squeezing its way out of the warehouse. It quickly started jogging its way up the hill toward the two mechs. I heard the whoosh of a cannon firing from below on the train tracks, followed by a rumbling and some whooping. This was the other two mech drivers talking about something.

'Stay down,' I said as the black drone jogged up the hill, angling west. Skeet and Chode hadn't yet noticed it.

'What are those idiots firing at?' Skeet asked.

'Queef says they're just blowing up train cars,' came a second voice. This was Chode.

Skeet cursed, saying something about ammo. I had the impression that they were communicating using their personal communication system and out loud. Out loud was probably easier if they wanted to talk to someone next to them. I wasn't sure. Either way, it was loud enough that we could hear them.

'What do we have here?' Skeet asked, finally noticing the black drone climbing its way up the hill. The egg body of his mech turned to examine the small robot. He raised his cannon arm and took a few steps toward it, but he didn't yet fire.

Chode also took another whirring step onto the steep hill. The signs over them waved violently back and forth as they walked. 'It's another sentry dog,' Chode said. 'I didn't see those on the upgrade list. You sure there aren't any other teams here? Thunder Thighs ain't trying to sneak into our territory?'

'No, we can see all the players on our HUD,' Skeet said. He took yet another stride down the precipitous hill. Chode followed.

'You think the local combatants have finally arrived?' Chode asked. 'The civvies we pasted earlier had guns, but nobody actually fired. The ones who fled north might've sent their troops back.'

'God, I hope so,' Skeet said. 'People are talking shit on the feed.'

I clicked my finger onto my bracelet. 'Steady,' I whispered. 'When I say go, we all aim for Skeet's leg. Aim for the back joint. Lulu, drop a canister right under Chode if you can.'

'I don't know how to angle it,' she said over my earpiece, a very slight edge of panic to her voice.

'I am installing an aiming aid on your bracelet, but it requires you to fire at least three canisters before it is properly calibrated. You will receive a haptic buzz when angled properly. You must whisper out your target until I can fabricate a better system,' Roger said. 'Try not to hit a tree branch when you fire.'

The black drone stopped on the hill, staring up at the two mechs. Chode also raised his cannon.

'Wait,' Skeet said. He took another step forward. He kept his own cannon trained on the drone, which was now about twenty meters away. 'Do you see that thing on its back? What is it? If those are missile tubes, they're pretty small. Do you think it's explosives?'

'It's probably a distraction,' Chode said. 'Let's kill it.'

At that, the drone stood to its full height and did a little hop on the hill. It slid down about a meter, dust swirling around it.

'I am in fact a distraction,' the drone announced, his voice – Roger's voice – amplified. 'I am keeping you occupied while I smash Queef and Steamer with a train. Also, Chode, are you aware your father is having an extramarital affair with his coworker Lois Chen? I have found evidence of such on the net. He calls her "Mommy" during their coitus.'

From below came a calamitous crunching noise and a small blast that I assumed were the two mechs on the tracks being rammed by a train.

'Targets three and four are down but still operational,' Roger said in my ear. 'Attempting to finish them off right now.'

'Go!' Skeet shouted as he fired at the drone.

The drone jumped and rolled down the hill, dodging the blast from the gun.

The Skeet mech turned to run down the hill, roughly in my and Sam's direction, heading for the tracks to see to his companions.

This is it, I thought. *This is where everything changes.*

'Go,' I shouted over the band as I popped above the concrete barrier. I put the gun against my shoulder, I aimed, and I screamed as I pulled the trigger.

CHAPTER 13

And then everything was exploding.

The pulse rifles made a quiet *thwump* each time they fired. They were not automatic like I was hoping, and I had to squeeze the trigger each time I needed to fire. My first shot was low, and I saw the heat pulse drill into the ground about three meters in front of Skeet. I hit just on the edge of the 'B' on the white rocks that spelled out 'Burnt Ends.' Rocks shattered and flew through the air like shrapnel. Next to me, Sam was also screaming and firing. His first shot was also wide, but he managed to hit Chode right on the egg part of the body. A visible but shallow scorch-marked dent appeared in the mech like it had been hit with a hammer.

'Uh-oh,' Sam said as he moved his aim, nailing the leg of Skeet just as I did the same.

The two mechs started to react just as lines of distorted air streaked from the woods to our right, Tito and Axel both firing. A fifth streak came from the left, this one from Rosita. This one nailed the back-facing knee joint on the left side of Skeet.

The mech barely shuddered at the direct hits.

'Finally,' Skeet shouted as two missiles streaked out of his battery. The missiles went straight up into the air and started circling, seeking a heat source.

At the same moment, I saw the spinning soup-can-sized canister tumble through the air and land against the steep hill. Lulu had fired it way too wide, and it landed about halfway between me and Sam and the two mechs. A third missile, this one from Chode, corkscrewed into the air just as he fired his cannon in our general direction.

The canister blew at the same time as the concrete barrier to our left exploded in a shower of rocks, blasting my ears.

'Run,' I shouted, pointing east. I couldn't hear my own voice.

Flares were shooting straight into the sky. They'd come from the drone that had rolled down the hill. A second drone jogged out of the warehouse. This one was also shooting something from its back. More flares. Multiple explosions echoed across the air as the missiles started hitting the flares instead of targeting us. The trees in front of us exploded as one of the two mechs fired their cannon toward Tito and Axel.

And then another Lulu canister exploded on the hill, followed by a secondary explosion. I turned in time to see Chode's mech topple over. The round sign thing was just gone, as was the missile battery on his shoulder. Lulu had nailed the missile launcher directly, and it had caused his two remaining missiles to go up.

'Target two has been destroyed. A gold star for Lulu,' Roger said in my ear.

Sam was right beside me, screaming something as we jumped behind another concrete barrier. We popped up in unison and fired again, once again aiming at the remaining mech's legs, despite the lack of damage.

'Aim for the missile launcher,' I started to shout as Skeet fired his last two missiles, probably more as a protective measure than a targeted attack. He was stopped on the hill near his flaming compatriot, bringing his cannon to bear on the woods where Lulu and Rosita hid.

Fire poured from the opposite side of the clearing, telling me Axel and Tito were okay.

More flares shot into the air from the drones as the first drone sprinted back up the hill, moving faster than I'd ever seen one of those things go. It streaked across the hill and slammed into the mech's leg. That didn't budge it, either.

Skeet was shouting something incoherent as yet another blast and a crunch echoed from far below us. This was followed by an even bigger explosion that knocked me on my side and right onto the paved road, exposed. I stared wide-eyed at the mech as the entire hill shook.

'Targets three and four have been fully knocked out of commission,' Roger said, his voice frustratingly calm.

I watched in horror as Skeet fired his cannon toward Lulu and Rosita's hiding place. Trees exploded, and I suppressed a cry. But a moment later, a third canister appeared, lazily spinning through the air as it emerged from the smoking forest and landed right in front of the mech and next to the black drone that was still slamming itself ineffectively against the mech's leg.

Bam!

Dirt, rocks, and drone parts showered as Lulu's canister dug out a portion of the hill.

'Oh, shit,' I said, scrambling to my feet. 'Not again. Sam, run!'

Skeet's mech tottered as the dirt shifted underneath it. The entire northern half of the Sombrero was starting to cave in. The mech fired again as it turned, this time facing us, but it aimed high. The top corner of the warehouse exploded as the mech continued to pivot. It turned almost like a ballerina as it started to fall. It hit the ground and it rolled right in our direction.

The sign atop its head detached and also started to roll down the hill, angling away from the tumbling main body.

'Grenade,' Sam shouted as he popped up to run. He tossed one of the round grenades as we both sprinted away.

It landed on or near the spinning, rapidly disassembling mech, but it didn't detonate. We continued to run away just as the giant robot crashed loudly into and then through the concrete barrier where we'd been standing. The gun arm broke off, and the pincher arm also cracked off at the elbow as one of the legs broke apart. The egg settled to a stop against the sliding barn door, pushing it in with an enormous crash. A pair of pulse blasts from the Serrano twins hit the egg, and the grenade – which Sam had apparently forgotten to arm – exploded, sending more parts flying. The giant barn doors fell in, revealing the five hoppers still sitting there in the barn getting loaded.

'All threats appear neutralized. Please stand by while we confirm their destruction,' Roger said.

'Are you guys okay?' came the panicked call from my sister over the band just as I asked after everyone.

'We are,' I said, standing up. Sam had blood streaming down from a superficial cut on his head, and my ears felt muffled, like they usually did after band practice. All I could smell was things burning. My heart was in my throat, and I couldn't stop shaking.

'We're good,' Axel said. 'Coming out.'

'Don't come back here,' I said. 'Everyone run back toward the alley where we were before. The smoke spot. They're gonna blow up the mechs.'

'Hey, I can hear you talking,' came a voice. It was Skeet. His entire mech was wrecked. I remembered what had happened last time. We had to get the hoppers out of here and fast. One of those Moderators was going to come and blow all these mechs up.

'Hey, Roger,' I whispered, 'do you know what Skeet's real name is?'

'It is Jeffrey Pyle,' Roger said in my ear. 'He lives at 4514 Willow Thicket Street in a town called Minneapolis in the New Republic. District 22. His mother was a schoolteacher, but she retired to live off of his streaming income.'

'Jesus, Roger,' I muttered, 'how do you know all of this?'

'There was an article about his team on NPR three months ago. It was not difficult to find. The perimeter-defense program comes with a war strategies subroutine, and I just updated my protocols using widely available literature on modern warfare tactics, including a very interesting essay on psychological warfare against remote combatants.'

Before I could say anything, Sam was there standing over the cracked-egg shape. 'Hey, Jeffy, you in there?'

There was a group of four black pinpricks circling a protuberance on the egg. Cameras. They looked like spider eyes.

Behind us, the hoppers roared to life. We had to get out of the way. They would smash through this mech as soon as we moved.

'We have two minutes to evacuate the area,' Roger said. 'We have loaded all we can. Please proceed to one of the hoppers, and we will pick up the other four on the way.'

'I'm going to come back here with a Heavy, find you, and

tear you apart, you piece-of-shit terrorist,' Skeet growled over the band.

'Oh, yeah?' Sam asked. He still stood over the wrecked mech, looking down at it. He dropped his rifle, pulled his pants down, and pulled out his junk. He proceeded to urinate directly onto the electric eyes. 'The Rhythm Mafia will be waiting for you, prick.'

The Rhythm Mafia Tapes. Scene ten.

A smiling woman chases after a pair of young twin girls. The woman is Annabeth Capstone, twenty-seven. She is second cousin to Rosita. The young toddlers are Mia and Tabitha Capstone, and they are one and a half years old. They are both in matching pink ballerina outfits. The twins were part of a pilot program to test the safety of offspring from the altered generation due to the <Redacted. Please see Secretary Burns for access>. At the time of filming, records indicated there were fewer than fifty minors on all of New Sonora. All were this approximate age.

Please note, Rosita refers to Mia and Tabitha as her nieces. They are, in truth, her second cousins once removed.

They are at a small outside café in the town of Burnt Ends. Behind Annabeth is the husk of a colony drop ship repurposed to house a café. Both ends of the drop ship are scorched, indicating a difficult entry through New Sonoran atmosphere. Historical records indicate that of the five drop ships sent to the southern peninsula, only three survived the entry due to a human programming error that miscalculated the entry trajectory. The failed entry was the fault of Captain Ignacio DiSantos, who claimed he no longer trusted the Traducible AI system of the Hibisco *and insisted all calculations be made by humans. After the failed entry, it should be noted that Captain DiSantos perished by suicide after manually replacing the oxygen in his cabin with helium.*

The town of Burnt Ends was named after the entry vehicle that you see in the background.

ROSITA (OFF CAMERA TO THE TWINS): Can you say 'Rosita'? Can you say 'Aunt Rosita'?

MIA: (unintelligible)

Both Annabeth and Rosita cheer and clap.

ROSITA: My nieces are the smartest. They're the smartest of them all.

Mia and Tabitha both giggle hysterically.

(A time cut.)

Annabeth is sitting with both toddlers on her lap. A cartoon is being projected by her bracelet, and both children are watching it.

ANNABETH: I wasn't sure what I was expecting. Great-Aunt Paula doesn't know anything about kids. So I'm just taking it one day at a time. We have books and movies, but they don't really show what it's like. All the nosy old ladies want to help, and I appreciate it when I need it, but that can be just as overwhelming as the kids.

ROSITA: What about your husband?

Annabeth snorts.

ANNABETH: Troy is gone six months out of the year on the railway repair crew. And when he is home, he doesn't know what the hell to do. I've never seen a grown man more terrified of something so small than Troy is of his daughters when they need a diaper change.

ROSITA: Were *you* scared when you were made pregnant? I mean, were you worried about the Sickness?

Annabeth laughs. It's unclear if this is a bitter laugh or one of genuine humor.

ANNABETH: It's not like I haven't had a stethoscope up my ass from the moment I got pregnant. They were tested every possible way, and now they know how to test for the Sickness accurately, they can see they're safe. At least that's what they say. And now everyone is open for business, I hope they're right.

ROSITA: Are they still testing you?

Annabeth raises her arm, which causes the cartoon to turn sideways. The children start to protest.

ANNABETH: I have track marks. So do the girls. Did you know in Fat Landing, they have puncture-free blood extractors? That's what they say in the group chat. We only go in twice a week now, but it was every day when I was pregnant. And to this day, everyone is interested in our blood work. I got an email from some health department guy on Earth. They said they were really interested in how we were doing. I guess everyone in the program got a similar message. They wanted consent to get a copy of my blood work. And the blood work of the twins.

ROSITA: How did you respond?

ANNABETH: Originally, I was like *Sure*, but the undersecretary of the New Generation program in Fat Landing sent out a mass email telling everyone not to comply, that it was none of the business of the Earth government how our babies were doing.

She leans in and whispers.

ANNABETH: But the Earth guys emailed back a few days later, and they offered to set up a college fund for Mia and Tabitha in exchange for the data.

ROSITA: College fund? In Earth yuan?

ANNABETH: That's right. The quarantine will be over by the time they're old enough, and it would be nice for them to have the option to get off planet if they want, even if it's just for college. They say the gravity there is only very slightly heavier than it is here, and you would barely notice it. The days there are in sync with the twenty-four-hour clock, too. Can you imagine? It took all those years to get here, and they can just step back in a matter of hours now.

ROSITA: So, did you do it?

ANNABETH: I figured, *What could it hurt?* All those people online are calling us names because we were altered. But you can't even tell the difference between us and the Earthers. You can't even tell a difference with most tests. Maybe my babies' blood samples can help make them see that. Maybe it'll help ease the prejudice.

(A time cut.)

ANNABETH: I remember your mother, Rosita. I remember her bouncing you on her knee while reading a book. It's one of my earliest memories. I remember your mom better than I remember my own. When my mom died, your mom picked me up and told me she would take care of me.

Annabeth lowers her head. She kisses each of her toddlers on the head.

ANNABETH: And your mom was gone just six months later.

There is a long pause here as Annabeth looks out toward a nearby building. In the distance, a group of people appear to be landscaping the area in front of the building.

(Please note this building. It is the former location of the Burnt Ends school as outlined in the notes under Day One of Five and in scene thirteen.)

ANNABETH: So yes, Rosita, I was fucking terrified of the Sickness when I got pregnant. I'm scared that my babies might still get it, despite the tests. I'm scared that whatever they did to us in vivo won't actually protect us, and we'll all get it, too, just maybe a little later. I'm scared all the time.

She turns to face the camera.

ANNABETH: But I've learned pretty quickly that it's part of being a parent. The moment one of these things pops out of you, you're suddenly in a perpetual state of worry. It just comes with the job.

CHAPTER 14

'It's called viral marketing,' Sam said indignantly as we rode back home. Sam and I sat next to each other in the hopper, but Lulu was berating him over the band.

'Now they can look up Rhythm Mafia and find that shitty recording you uploaded last year and find our farm.'

'Maybe,' I said. 'Sam spelled "Rhythm" incorrectly when he made the account, and they wouldn't let us change it after.'

'Man, we should've enabled advertising on that,' Sam muttered before responding on the feed. 'They're watching us from the sky. They told those assholes where we were. They know where we're from. We need to let them know we're not scared of them. Besides, Roger was the one who started with the smack talk. Did you hear what he said to Chode? What the hell does the word "coitus" even mean?'

Sam was right. They were clearly watching us. 'Roger, where did you get that info about that guy's dad? Is it true?'

'It was a fiction,' Roger said. 'I made the supposition up. Chode's legal name is Benji Winters. His father does work with a woman named Lois Chen, who enjoys posting photographs of herself in revealing clothing, and she calls herself "Mommy" in several of her social media postings. In addition, Chode's mother has been arrested two times for domestic violence against Chode's father. By planting this seed, we can perhaps sow chaos in the Chode family household, preventing him from further incursions. It is a proven tactic against remote enemies. We can't strike them directly, so we strike at them psychologically.'

'Holy shit,' Sam muttered.

'Rule number four, Oliver friend number three,' Roger said over the band. 'I am afraid you'll be getting a frowny sticker on your after-action report.'

'Well, I still think you shouldn't have done it,' Lulu said, ignoring Roger. 'You're just bringing attention to us.'

'I think us destroying five mechs is what's going to bring attention to us,' Sam muttered.

'That and you showing your dick on their live feed,' Rosita added.

Sam reached up and rubbed his bare head forlornly. He'd lost his trucker hat somewhere along the way.

'I hope my hat is still there,' he said after a few minutes of silence. 'It was the only thing I had left from Earth.'

We'd been driving for about twenty minutes and we were almost halfway back to the ranch. Trixie 2 had stayed behind along with several of the newly unpacked drones. We'd managed to load only a little more than half of the supplies we wanted to get before the Moderator had blasted the whole area to hell, shaking the ground. Roger said it was unclear if the bunker with the remaining supplies was still intact or not.

Because we'd had to leave early, we still had two hours before the countdown ended and the game officially started. I scrolled through the list of items we had managed to extract. We'd activated almost four hundred additional honeybees, mostly drones, only some of which were actually in the hoppers. The rest were moving toward us on foot or off on some mission for Roger. We'd failed on our secondary mission to grab more construction supplies, so I knew several were off picking up things around town. They wouldn't arrive at the ranch until several hours from now, assuming they made it at all.

The activated honeybees included a total of ten rhino units and another thirty scouts. We had multiple recharge stations and various supplies, including five Roger-sized repair drones, which were new to both me and Lulu. In addition, we had multiple weapons and upgrades for the honeybees, all of which were in crates.

Most important, we'd grabbed two truck-sized fabricators and several spools of poly filament. We could make all sorts of things with the printers. The skin wouldn't be as strong as that of the printed mechs and we couldn't print complex machinery like with the newer machines, but it was something.

We'd also managed to unbox about three hundred fist-sized

UAVs (unmanned aerial vehicles). Each one looked like a blue-painted baseball. These were miniature solar-powered scout drones. They weren't that smart, but they were originally used to help map the surface of the planet when the scans from above weren't sufficient. They could fly in multiple environments and gravities. They were currently being used to watch for enemy positions.

We had also grabbed enough weapons, food, and building supplies to completely fill one of the hoppers.

While we'd managed to loot a ton of weapons, I was worried. The pulse rifles weren't very effective against the enemy mechs, and as Roger ominously pointed out, the light-armor Drop Dragoon units were the only kind available during the preview. Bigger, more powerful, and better-armored mechs would be coming next.

We had only a limited number of the same type of canister explosives that Lulu had used, though we could print certain types of munitions with the fabricators using the literal soil and some of the plant material around the farm. I didn't know how exactly any of that worked – I always kinda glazed over during chemistry lessons – but it sounded dangerous as shit.

Roger had also directed the drones to take a few parts off of the fallen mechs before they'd been destroyed by the Moderator. These were the communication modules, he said, and he would look for a weakness in them or a way to easily disable them.

It isn't enough, I thought miserably as we bounced over the road, mostly in silence since my sister's tirade against Sam. Axel and Tito had both been uninjured in the attack, but they'd clearly been shaken.

Five days. We just needed to hold out for five days.

I could feel that ship watching us from above. The only reason we hadn't been squished yet was because they were making more money keeping us alive. For the moment. I thought of Mr Gonzales, and his question: *What's the point?*

And of that second question none of us dared to answer: What would happen when the five days were up? What then?

'I am detecting multiple items falling from orbit,' Roger suddenly said. 'I only have a limited view, but they appear to be spreading across the planet. These are different than the typical MDUs used by the players. These are longer, oblong-shaped objects. There are dozens of them. They do not appear to be carrying mechs. These are more reminiscent of non-biological troop transports.'

'Oh, crap,' Sam said. 'Peacekeepers? They're sending Peacekeepers?'

Peacekeepers were the standard AI-controlled ground troops. They were armored, bipedal, two-point-five-meter-tall robots used for riot control and security around the colonies. I'd only seen them on video. As far as I was aware, only two had ever set foot on the planet as bodyguards for the Earth ambassador when she first visited after the gate opened.

'It's possible,' Roger said, 'but the markings on the transports are unlike anything I have seen before. In addition, it appears the transports are too small for the standard Peacekeeper unit.'

'Are any headed toward us?' I asked.

'Negative,' Roger said. 'But it appears six or seven of the transports will be landing in the ruins of Burnt Ends. More are landing north of there and out of my range. One appears to be landing on the Yanez farm on the west side of the Pantano. That is the closest to our current position.'

'Roger,' Lulu asked, her voice crackling in my ear, 'are our defenses at the ranch suited to deal with Peacekeepers?'

'Peacekeepers, yes, more so than the mech threat. However, what these are is unclear. I am moving assets into place to get a better view and will report when I have more information.'

'That's just great,' I muttered.

'Like my grandmother used to say,' Sam said, turning to look at me. He had dried blood all down his face. It was strange seeing him without his hat. 'When the outhouse is occupied, that's when the bucket's in the yard.'

CHAPTER 15

'Oh, my god, oh, my god!' Harriet cried as we jumped out of the hoppers. She bounded across the yard and practically tackled Sam. She grasped onto his face with her hands. 'That's blood! You're bleeding!'

'It's okay,' Sam said, peeling her hands off him. Harriet sat down in the middle of our yard, and she started to sob while Sam looked on, helpless. Rosita moved to her and kneeled down.

Roger floated out of the hive to meet us as an army of drones went to work unloading the hoppers. One of the scouts – Priscilla – stood at the very top of the hive like a lookout.

Dozens of people – not drones – scrambled around the edges of the property, digging holes. I blinked at the trampled remains of my fields. More people worked at the outer fence line while drones worked at constructing a taller interior fence line around the house and barn. An excavator rumbled from the back, right in the middle of my tobacco. I had no idea where the large machine had come from. It was scooping huge chunks of dirt from the ground.

In the middle of the front yard between the house and the barn and within the new interior fence, a new building had been erected in the hours we'd been gone. The thing looked like some sort of sculpture made of discarded metal. If not for the twin cannon barrels sticking from it, I'd have thought it was a tall pile of junk.

I stared at the giant cannon-looking thing. The long, thin double barrels were, like, four meters long. As I watched, the weapon turned on its own, swinging back and forth. The thing swarmed with drones.

'Where did that come from?' I asked. They'd built it from the ground up. 'What is it made of?'

'The barrels are the drainage conduits from the east field cistern,' Roger said. 'We cut them in half. These will be utilized to fire flares while we manufacture more pressure-resistant barrels with the fabricators. They are not the correct gauge for the anti-air batteries, which we will begin to manufacture shortly, and we hope to have nine more such batteries available soon as part of our point defense system. The swivel motion of the flare battery is using parts from the ranch's combine harvester. Not ideal but it appears to be working.'

I blinked, not registering what he'd just said for several moments. 'My *combine*. You tore up my combine? And the cistern?' I took a deep breath. It had taken me and Lulu almost two years to get the cistern system to work properly.

'All existing assets must be repurposed during perimeter defense, Oliver.'

'Don't let Lulu see you tore up the cistern, or she's going to lose her –'

'What the fuck!' Lulu cried. She hadn't yet noticed the barrels on the flare gun, but she was looking at something else. The massive, now empty five-thousand-gallon poly tank sat on the side of the barn. They'd dug the whole thing up.

It was the one project Lulu had insisted we do on our own without the help of the honeybees. She was worried that once Roger finally broke down, we'd be completely helpless, so it had been our joint project. After all that work, they'd torn it all apart in a matter of hours.

Shing! The correction stinger appeared on Roger as he zoomed up to her. She and Roger started to go back and forth as I moved toward the house. I needed to clean my face off. I needed to sit down and just be alone for a minute.

Before I entered the house – the only house I'd ever known – I turned to look at the tableau.

The farm had been destroyed. The fields were trashed. Drones hurried in every direction. Multiple towers and other defenses were in various states of construction. My best friend, Sam, now sat in the dirt in the middle of the farm, hugging his still-crying fiancée, while Rosita also crouched down with them both. My sister was there, too, bent over, rubbing Harriet's arm while the pregnant woman yelled at Roger. Axel and Tito sat off to the side, also on the ground and looking up at their grandmother. I was pretty sure all three were crying, and I didn't want to stare too hard. Behind me, I could hear the chatter of at least a dozen people still inside my house.

I'd left the rifle and helmet in the truck, but I still wore the body armor. I reached down and fingered the pair of grenades looped to my jacket. Grenades. Just a few precious hours ago, I'd gone to my girlfriend's house for a get-together because after this weekend, we'd all be knee-deep in work for several weeks.

'Do you remember,' a voice asked, 'when I used to bring you and your sister Popsicles?'

I turned to see the old man with his giant cowboy hat with the turquoise band standing there. The man held a pear Popsicle in his hand, and he offered it to me. I smiled and took it from him.

'Hi, Mr Gonzales,' I said. 'Thank you.'

'How many times have I asked you to call me Beto?'

'Grandpa Lewis once told me that he'd tan my and Lulu's hide if he ever caught us calling you that.'

This was a conversation we'd had so many times, I'd lost count. I sucked on the Popsicle for a moment. Even though Mr Gonzales was the source of the Popsicles – he used to make them by the gross – the taste always made me think of my own grandfather.

'You're a lot like him in some ways. You know that?' Mr Gonzales said, patting me on the shoulder. 'You're stubborn like your grandfather. Like Cat, too.'

I stiffened slightly at the mention of my mom. Our neighbor talked about Grandpa Lewis all the time, speaking of him as if they'd been best friends. They *had* been friends, which was saying something considering how prickly my grandfather was, but the real friendship had been between Mrs Gonzales and Grandmother Yolanda.

My grandfather was much more of a loner than I was, and it always kind of irritated me when Mr Gonzales compared me to him. Even though I loved my grandfather, I never really felt I had the same sort of abrasive personality he'd had.

But I was used to the comparison. What I wasn't used to was Mr Gonzales mentioning my mother. He rarely mentioned her.

It was almost a taboo subject amongst the older generation. Mr and Mrs Gonzales had had two sons of their own, both of whom died before they had children. I also knew that my mother had dated one of their two sons for a while before she'd fallen in love with a migrant field-worker – a field-worker under the employ of Mr Gonzales, *not* Grandpa Lewis. It had been a minor scandal because depending on who you asked, she was or wasn't still dating Beto Junior at the time when she first got pregnant.

It didn't matter. They were all dead now. I barely had memories of my mother, who died when I was five. No matter how much I tried, I couldn't remember my dad. From what I understood, he hadn't exactly been a regular presence in my life even before they all got sick.

But Mr and Mrs Gonzales had never seemed to hold any of that against my mother, and they certainly didn't do so against me and Lulu; they treated us like their own grandchildren.

Mr Gonzales patted me again and moved off outside without saying another word.

I turned to go inside, but there was a line of people waiting to use our bathroom. I moved to my room, but my sheets were off my bed, and my mattress was leaning up against the wall while Mrs Xalos stood on her knees with a bucket and scrubbed at the bare mattress, cleaning it. My heart beat faster. My eyes quickly moved to the line of plastic dinosaurs I kept on my headboard, making sure they were still there. The small colorful toys were from Earth, and they'd been Grandpa Lewis's toys as a kid and his father's before him. They remained standing there on the headboard, holding court over the invasion of my room. Mrs Becerra was also in my room, but she just sat on my chair, rocking back and forth praying.

I turned away without saying anything.

As I moved to our front door, Mrs Perez stopped me to ask where I kept our cinnamon.

'We don't have any in the pantry,' I said. 'We have some cinnamon stores in the hive. My grandfather didn't like having it in the house, and Lulu and I don't really do much baking.'

'No cinnamon in the house?' she asked, wringing her hands

together. 'Yolanda is rolling in her grave.' She patted me on the shoulder. 'You should really clean your face off, honey.'

I nodded and pushed past her. I returned to the doorway and just stood there, feeling unsteady, like the ground was still shaking. I couldn't stop thinking about how angry my grandfather would have been that so many people were here, and I realized that maybe Mr Gonzales was right: I *was* just like him.

CHAPTER 16

Roger's voice crackled in my ear. The sound startled me. I'd forgotten I was still wearing the communicator. I'd just been standing there in my doorway, almost drifting to sleep, as the honeybees and people around me swarmed. The sun was still high in the sky. It felt as if it should have been the middle of the night.

'Reports have come back from the Yanez farm, and I have visual confirmation of the occupants of the transport. These appear to be human, but I am quite certain they are non-biological. They appear to be Peacekeepers in a different skin than the standard. There are twenty-five of them occupying the farm, and they appear to be turning the farm into some sort of defensive stronghold. Here is a video.'

My bracelet buzzed as the scene appeared. I pulled it up and enlarged it so the image floated an inch over my wrist. It was a shot from one of the UAVs hovering in the trees, watching the transport crunch to the ground. Within seconds of landing, several forms unpeeled from the vehicle and spread out. Chickens, oblivious of all this, had all scattered when the transport landed, but now they were back, scratching at the ground. They ignored the soldiers, and the soldiers ignored them.

I briefly wondered if these were normal chickens or some of Mr Yanez's trained circus chickens. The cranky, possibly insane rancher had multiple animals on his farm. Half were livestock. The other half were constantly in training for his 'Circus of Miracle Animals.' I had no idea why the crotchety old man even wanted to open a circus, as he seemed to hate everyone. As kids, if we so much as approached his fence, he would threaten to skewer us with a pitchfork. Still, the idea that there would soon be children again in New Sonora had appeared to reawaken the strange man's desires to train his animals and open a circus.

Hanging on the wall of his barn were several massive banners I'd never seen before. Each one extolled the virtue of his circus-trained animals. From this angle, the spacecraft blocked most of the banners, but I could see one with a group of running chickens on it, though the chickens had glowing red eyes and each wore a clown-like ruff around its neck. The sign read, 'Trained Magical Chickens of Amazement and Awe.' The next banner featured Cindy, his obese pig, but I couldn't see what the sign read.

I still wasn't clear what the trained magical chickens of awe were actually trained to do. Regardless, all the chickens on the vid appeared to be the normal kind.

As we watched, I realized the soldiers weren't just ignoring the chickens. It was like they couldn't see them at all. A soldier stepped on one. The chicken squawked angrily, half smooshed to the ground. It pulled itself away, unharmed. The soldier froze in place for a good five seconds, like the existence of an invisible chicken had broken its brain. Clearly these guys were nonhuman. And they were about as dumb as the drone honeybees.

All these newcomers *appeared* to be humans wearing bulky body armor. They were armed to the teeth: pulse rifles with strange flat barrels, pistols, disk-shaped objects that were either drones or grenades. Some wore helmets that obscured their faces, like fancy VR rigs. A few wore nothing at all upon their heads. These soldiers had human faces and hair and beards that looked real when I used the display on my bracelet, though the faces were decorated in black-and-white war paint.

'That's illegal,' I heard myself say. They weren't allowed to make robots that pretended to be human. It was one of the major tenets of Earth law.

Still, Roger was correct: Even if I hadn't seen their strange behavior near the chickens, it was clear these absolutely weren't human but robots. I watched more of the soldiers appear. They'd been collapsed over themselves in an impossible way, like folding chairs, so more could fit in the transport. Some were attached to the outside of the transport, and I watched as they extended twice, their waists moving a hundred eighty degrees to snap in place before they moved off to their positions.

Humanlike automatons were illegal without some sort of disclaimer. Even the bipedal Peacekeepers – which were clearly not human because they were eight or nine feet tall – had flashing warnings on their face masks that warned they were nonhuman.

'Roger,' I started to say, 'how are they allowed to . . .' But I never finished my question as the scene played out.

As the humanoids spread out and started moving about the farm, Mr Yanez appeared, carrying his infamous pitchfork. I was startled by the sight of him. He'd been on my farm that morning. He must've gone back home. Dread filled me.

'You! Get off my –' he started to yell.

One of the androids lifted an arm, and without even looking at the man, it fired a pulse pistol at him, killing the old man instantly. None of the other soldiers so much as twitched.

I found myself leaning against the door, breathing heavily. Holy shit. They'd killed him. Just like that.

'That was Mr Yanez,' Rosita said over the band. She was just across the way, but we all continued to speak using our earpieces. Our eyes met across the yard. 'They killed him for no reason.'

Anger started to rise in me. Up until now it had all been fear. Even after I'd seen all the dead bodies, including the body of little Henry, the only emotions I'd really felt so far were terror and this-can't-really-be-happening bewilderment. But seeing it actually happen changed something in me deep in my chest. Mr Yanez had been a grumpy, antisocial jerk. He'd never married. My grandfather had hated him. Still, the man clearly cared for his work. That was why the man had gone back to his farm. He didn't want to leave his chickens and pigs alone.

He was one of us, and they'd come to his home and killed him for no reason.

'It's not right,' Rosita said.

My bracelet beeped with a new message from Roger. 'This is from another angle. There is more.'

A second view appeared, this one from another UAV atop the house, overlooking the transport. I could see all the banners now.

Mr Yanez also appeared to have hidden behind his barn a half-built circus tent that showed recent work.

The space vehicle was being rapidly disassembled and broken apart as the androids moved to tear it into pieces. They were using the transport itself to make supplies. The hull was rapidly turning into large guns and other devices, like the ship was one of those old pocketknives that contained a dozen little tools. One of the items was clearly a mobile fabricator along with a recycler. The recycler was technology that was relatively new, and we didn't have anything like it here on New Sonora. With those two things, they'd be able to print whatever they wanted and wouldn't have to rely on rolls of filament.

The UAV zoomed in on one of the soldiers with a half mask, and even close up, it looked human. It moved like a human. Still . . . there was something uncanny about the way it shifted and lifted its arms. It was a little *too* fluid. Would I have noticed it if I hadn't just seen these things unfold themselves in such a way?

The camera zoomed in on the dark, sleek uniform, focusing on a black patch on the shoulder of the man. It was a triangular patch featuring a skull, and on the patch were three words:

The Rhythm Mafia.

'What the hell?' I asked.

'Holy shit,' Sam said at the same time. He was also across the yard looking at me. He leaned against one of the hoppers, sitting on the ground with Harriet and Rosita. 'We have merch! We have fans!'

'Where did that come from?' I asked.

'I told you,' Lulu hissed. 'I told you, Sam.'

'What . . . ?' I asked, confused. 'Why are they wearing those?'

'My theory is that these androids are being seeded across the planet,' Roger said. 'They are the "insurgents" that the players will be fighting. These that you see now were always going to come here, but it is likely that because of Oliver friend three's unfortunate on-camera boast, they are claiming the Rhythm Mafia is the name of the local insurgent group. They could have fabricated and affixed those patches within a matter of minutes after the name was announced.

Also, I am keeping note of all of your swearing. Please use proper language, even when I'm not present.'

'Wait, so are these guys kind of on our side, then?' Axel asked, talking for the first time since we'd gotten back.

'Not according to Mr Yanez, they're not,' Lulu said dryly.

Axel persisted. 'But, Roger, you think they're going to fight against the mechs?'

'I do believe so, yes. There is no indication anywhere on the net that this tactic will be used, so we can't be certain until it happens. But the lack of actual insurgents on the planet and the existence of that shoulder patch suggest my theory is correct. This is a misdirection on the part of the invaders. Apex Industries is charging a premium for people to build these war machines and use them in battle. It would provide a poor customer experience if nobody actually fights back.'

'Poor customer experience,' I grumbled.

'It's kind of a cool logo, though,' Sam added. 'I hope we can get our hands on some of them.'

I watched as Roger moved away from the flare battery and floated toward the hive. 'Now, everyone please follow me back into the classroom. It's time for our second lesson. We will learn more details about our defensive capabilities.'

Across the way, Rosita stood and helped Harriet to her feet. The woman was still crying and rubbing her eyes. Rosita handed her off to Mrs Gonzales, who put her arm around the young woman and started leading her toward me and the house. Rosita's camera followed them closely.

Rosita turned and met my eyes from across the yard.

'Maybe they will leave us alone if we leave them alone,' Rosita said over the band as she rubbed her hands on her pants.

'I suspect you are partially correct,' Roger said. 'The androids, yes. I suspect they will leave this farm unmolested for the first five days. They disassembled their craft, so it is clear they do not intend to leave. I suspect once the game portion of the eviction is completed, the remaining androids will attempt to complete the job should any of you remain alive. But before that happens, we still have five days' worth of mechs to contend with.'

Before I could fully process that statement, my wrist beeped again.

The timer had concluded.

Operation Bounce House was now open to the public.

The Rhythm Mafia Tapes. Scene thirteen.

We are in a room that appears to be some sort of municipal office. There is a whiteboard on the wall that is half covered with the green-and-blue New Sonora flag. At least a dozen filing cabinets litter the oversized room. There is a large desk in the middle of the space along with several tables that are piled high with paper.

Sitting behind the desk is an older, heavyset bearded man with a mustache and a full head of wild white hair. This is Jake Acosta, seventy-two, the acting sheriff of the peninsula region headquartered in the town of Burnt Ends. Records indicate Acosta inherited the sheriff job about ten years prior after the previous sheriff – who was also his wife, one Lucinda Acosta – passed away after a short illness. Prior to becoming the acting sheriff, Acosta was a science teacher at the Burnt Ends school, which was partially repurposed as the sheriff's headquarters once the population aged out.

Acosta was born aboard Hibisco.

There is the sound of construction in the background.

ROSITA (OFF CAMERA): Okay, please introduce yourself.

ACOSTA: I'm Jake. I'm the sheriff of this region. In addition to myself, I have three deputies, but one is part-time, and he's older than me, so I don't know if he counts. (Laughs)

They pause as someone hammers loudly in the distance.

ROSITA: Lots of construction going on.

ACOSTA: They're getting ready to reopen the school in a few years. It's a little early, but people are excited.

ROSITA: Are you going to move your office?

ACOSTA: Eventually, yes. We had offices before, and they're still there. We shared a building with the mayor, but he wanted –

(A time cut.)

Acosta waves his hand around the office.

ACOSTA: This was my classroom, you know. Before I became sheriff, I mean.

ROSITA: I know you used to be a teacher. That's actually why I asked to speak to you today.

He points toward the back of the classroom, interrupting her.

ACOSTA: I taught your mother when she came into the town along with all the kids in the southern settlements. Your mom and her sisters always sat right there in the back, all three of them swooning over your father.

The camera swings to show a corner of a room with several desks stacked up. The camera pauses for a moment upon Rosita's face, and she appears stricken.

ROSITA: I didn't know that. I didn't know she went to school here at all.

ACOSTA: It was supposed to be once a week, but they came in maybe once every two along with all the other kids from the south farms. She was smart. I'll tell you that. Almost as smart as you. Your dad on the other hand . . .

He laughs.

ROSITA: I actually wanted to talk to you about the Sickness.

Acosta's humor fades.

ACOSTA: Why would you want to talk about that?

ROSITA: Even today, a lot of people don't really seem to understand what it really was. You were part of the team that helped figure out what was happening, and you were part of the team that came up with the solution that cured it.

ACOSTA: I only helped and just a little. It was all-hands-on-deck. There were thousands of us working on the problem and solution. And there was no cure. You can't take the oil from the flour once the bread is already baked. We could only prevent it from happening again.

ROSITA: Okay. Can you explain what the Sickness was?

Acosta sighs heavily. He steeples his hands and seems to think, as if he doesn't want to answer. But finally he speaks.

ACOSTA: People called it the Sickness before we knew what it really was, so that's what people call it today. But its real name is ERS, epigenetic rejection syndrome.

ROSITA: Okay, what was it?

ACOSTA: It's something in the planet's electromagnetic field. The short answer is, it does something funny to babies when they're still cooking in their moms' bellies. The problem was, the change was so subtle, we didn't even know anything was wrong until about twenty years after the first birth on planet, and then it took another several years after that to identify exactly what was happening. And then a few years after that to come up with the solution.

ROSITA: What exactly is happening? And why did it affect *everybody*?

ACOSTA: Not everybody. That's how we figured it out. There's a small subterranean settlement just west of Fat Landing that had three births with no sign of ERS. It turns out, the mothers never went aboveground and were shielded. Because of them, we figured out that if a woman gets pregnant on the surface of the planet, something about the planet messes with the DNA methylation patterns in utero. Like I said, the babies cook funny. There's a specific set of genes that eventually express themselves incorrectly – not until the affected are about twenty-five years old.

ROSITA: Okay, can you explain it again, but pretend like I'm a little kid?

Acosta grunts with sad amusement.

ACOSTA: Your DNA contains lots of little recipes that tell your body how to grow. Imagine someone sneaks in and changes some of those recipes around without you knowing. Maybe some of those recipes have a few ingredients switched around, like baking soda gets switched with baking powder. Or maybe an ingredient is erased. You don't notice that something is wrong until you pull it out of the oven or maybe once you take a bite and it tastes wrong. With ERS, one's body starts rejecting their own organs, which has a cascading effect. It happens fast, and sometimes it happens slow.

ROSITA: Okay, but other than those three people, it happened to *everybody*. Before we cured it, every single person born on the surface of this planet eventually died.

Acosta shrugs.

ACOSTA: That is nature. It doesn't care what's right or what's wrong. It's why things go extinct. But the good news is, you're here now. We couldn't save your mom or your dad, but we learned how to save you.

ROSITA: How *did* you fix it? How does the cure work?

ACOSTA: Again, this was not me but the effort of thousands working together. And it's not a cure but a prevention. Once we learned which genes were susceptible to getting scrambled, it was a matter of basically locking the genes in place in utero. It's not a difficult or even a new process. DNA editing technology is hundreds of years old.

ROSITA: If the process is that old, why do the Earthers care so much? That seems much less of a change than I even thought. Why do they call us subhuman?

Acosta smiles sadly.

ACOSTA: Some things we can't fix. One of those things is people who are from one place disliking people from another place. If it wasn't that, it would be something else. The reason isn't important or relevant. It's a handy excuse.

ROSITA: How do we know it worked? The cure, I mean. Not all of us are yet the same age as our parents.

ACOSTA: Well, the sad truth is, the second generation who were born before we discovered the cure died quite quickly, like your older sister. These second-generation Sonorans rarely survived past two or three years old. And you guys, the altered survivors, when *you* have children, it looks like you pass the locked genes onto your own offspring, so no more alteration is needed. That's why they just gave everyone the go-ahead. That's why those little cousins of yours were so important. They are healthy, and for that, we are all so grateful.

ROSITA: This cure was discovered before the gate was opened, so you still had access to the AIs running the ships in orbit. Did you ask them for help?

Acosta seems to stiffen at this question.

ACOSTA: No, no. They were all decommissioned once we made landfall. That was our agreement with Earth. They were up there, but they'd all been turned off.

ROSITA: Yes, but I've been reading about them. They weren't truly decommissioned until the ambassador came and took out the AIs' processors, right? It was just a switch to wake them back up. They could have helped us find the cure much more quickly. Couldn't we have –

ACOSTA: No. Many people asked. But we weren't allowed, and for good reason. You know about the AI war. Even before we had instant communication re-established with Earth, we knew about it. Besides, we found the solution quite quickly. It just . . . The solution was not a cure but a preventive measure. There is no cure for ERS.

ROSITA: My grandmother used to think the Sickness was deliberate, that the Earth government did something to make it happen. She thought maybe it was in the new colony proliferation kits.

Acosta laughs.

ACOSTA: Your grandmother had a few run-ins with my wife when she was sheriff. I had a few run-ins with her, too, when I taught your mom. She wasn't alone in thinking like that. People get talking, and they believe what they want. We tested the vitamins and milk. They are identical to the kits that our families used when they were en route to this planet. Earth would have had to have known the planet itself wasn't fully compatible. And I don't see how that would have been possible. There're plenty of reasons not to like the Earth government, but I'm afraid this one is on Mother Nature.

DAY TWO OF FIVE

CHAPTER 17

Our next skirmish didn't occur until the second night, a little over twenty-four hours after the countdown expired.

I hadn't slept at all, despite Roger's constant reminder of rule number six. Get plenty of rest. If I'd thought the farm had been transformed before, now it didn't resemble anything close to the ranch I'd grown up on. I'd forgotten that these drones had originally been designed for construction. They were mediocre at best when it came to farming. But when it came to building structures, they were amazing.

Once the printers had been installed and the additional hoppers and backup drones arrived, having collected insta-set, more filament, and a smaller rapid printer – along with another ninety people – from all the nearby farms between here and Burnt Ends, things accelerated at a rapid pace.

We now had multiple defenses both obvious and hidden surrounding the farm.

We had two walls around the property. The impossible task of constructing a paper-thin, six-foot-high metallic wall to surround the unwooded portion of our hundred sixty acres was completed in an astonishingly short time, followed by the building of a thicker, eight-foot-high wall around the perimeter of the living area of the ranch, giving the hundred forty of us about two acres of space to live in.

This eight-foot-tall wall was in the process of being built up even further, becoming a full-fledged structure on its own. In the end, it would be built in an oblong ring. The thick wall so far contained three gun batteries and a 'flamethrower' we couldn't test because it was supposedly so hot, it would have damaged the wall. It also contained multiple dummy batteries that we hoped would draw enemy fire. We were just waiting for more supplies. When it was done, we'd be able to climb on top like on the rampart of a castle.

This space between the two walls was in the process of being peppered with about two hundred land mines. We didn't have enough material printed yet to make explosive mines, but Roger had a design for an EMP trap that would supposedly fry a mech's controls, including the communication unit, the moment any part of the machine stepped upon it.

Each mine was the size of a fruit box, and they had to each be buried and then armed by a trio of drones. One of my honeybees – Candy Jo, according to Roger – had accidentally stepped on an armed mine as it returned from the field, and it'd worked well enough that the primary controller box inside the honeybee had literally melted, completely wrecking the drone.

The mines would also work, we hoped, on any of the androids should they come this way.

The problem was, the mines were made using parts from the newly acquired crates of drone-repair supplies. We used about half of the extra batteries we'd collected for the land mines and almost all of some controller board, meaning the two hundred land mines we now had were all we'd get.

Behind the house, we'd built ten bunkers for people to sleep in. So far, we hadn't had the time or resources to put anything in them other than food, water, lights, one of the medical units, and a few blankets. Some of the older folks were trying to make the bunkers more 'comfortable,' though I didn't know what that really meant. I hadn't gone down into one yet. Tito and Axel were both apparently a little claustrophobic and absolutely refused to go in. Lulu called them 'death traps.'

Rosita had taken it upon herself to spearhead an escape-tunnel plan for the bunkers. Roger had lent her a team of seven drones that were currently carving out and shoring up a subterranean tunnel off the ranch.

One of the few out-of-box defensive units was an anti-air missile system that included radar and a missile launcher, along with fifty missiles. The launcher held ten missiles at a time. The self-contained unit sat in the middle of the yard, currently 'hidden' by the shell of the cistern. One of the two secondary radars sat atop the barn along with a set of anti-drone systems that were likely two hundred years out-of-date.

In addition, eight of the rhino units, all armed with newly charged Conquistador guns, patrolled the base. The other two were held in reserve in the woods south of us, just before the trees gave way to the lower valley and the hills.

And since we had an additional five of the big Conquistador guns, we put them in fixed bunkers around the ranch.

Because of the success of Lulu's canister gun, we'd also built a dozen manual canister launchers. These were basically long-range slingshots using thick elastic bands whose original purpose was unknown to me. We had a limited supply of the real canisters for now. We were printing them as fast as we could, but the printers were all overworked already. If tomorrow's planned raid went well, we'd have the ability to print what we needed much more quickly.

In the meantime, we set some of the older residents to work making Molotov cocktails, using canning supplies and fuel we had on hand. We had two kinds. The black-smoke-emitting smudge pots that we hoped would ruin their line-of-sight targeting and the fire-spreading kind using roofing tar with a fuel tablet smushed inside and a rag. The recipe for those hadn't come from Roger but from me and Sam.

All of this, along with a few other surprises, was only a fraction of what Roger wanted us to build and construct. He wanted mortars. Fire barrels that would supposedly confuse antipersonnel missiles. So much more. We had a serious lack of resources. The two printers, plus the small rapid printer – which was only good for making items such as nails and joints and shell casings – could only print so fast, and we were rapidly running out of all types of filaments.

Meanwhile, Lulu had moved to the control center and was working on PR. She was contacting reporters and anyone else who would listen about our plight. But because of the way we were forced to route our messages and because of the relatively limited outgoing bandwidth, she was having a difficult time convincing people she was legitimate. So far it wasn't clear if Apex Command was aware someone on the planet was actively communicating with Earth. Too much information and we risked the very real chance of them discovering where the leak in the information blockade was coming from.

If they figured out that the leak was coming from the secondary communications system on the *Forlorn*, they could easily shut it down. They could just blow the abandoned shell of a generation ship out of orbit.

Both Lulu and I thought the risk was worth it. We had the video of the dead folks in Burnt Ends. We had the video of those robot assholes shooting Mr Yanez. We had the video of the fake 'insurgents' landing and then setting up shop. Surely that would make an impact.

After we had spent some time watching the live streams from the POV of the players, it was clear that the players were being fed a bunch of bullshit. Lulu forced us to watch the scene from Team Cannon Fodder's live stream where they attacked the school.

The people had run, and Team Cannon Fodder had gleefully mowed them down. But in the video, there were three important distinctions. First, once a person was killed, they completely disappeared from the feed. Their body remained where they fell, but they turned into a blinking outline on the HUD. Second, they'd shown weapons hanging from the shoulders of several of the people running – weapons that hadn't been there at all. It was a complete fabrication.

Also, strangely, the architecture of the school was different. The brand-new sign indicating it was a school was just gone from the video, and the insta-set exterior of the building was replaced with Earth-style bricks that looked old and dingy. The building didn't look like a school anymore, but some sort of industrial complex. It was very odd.

And even more disconcerting, they hadn't shown two-year-old Henry at all. He'd literally been erased from the feed. We could see his mother running while she carried the toddler. But it just made it look like she was running with her arms cupped oddly and holding on to open air. When one of the mechs – the one driven by a girl named Wankette – had shot the mother, the burst had clearly killed both her and the child.

'Scrub one breeder,' Wankette had said over the feed, laughing.

'It's no wonder there's a latency issue,' Lulu had muttered as we all watched, open-mouthed. 'They gotta sanitize it all in real time.'

'It doesn't matter,' I'd said. 'Those people were still running. And we heard what that Skeet guy said. He called them civvies. Civilians. Wankette called Henry's mom a breeder. They're not stupid. They know. Everybody knows. They just don't want to see it. We gotta get those pictures and videos out.'

But Roger insisted that his ability to ascertain intelligence from the open net was more valuable, and it wasn't worth the risk. He thought we might have a way to connect with a second of the generation ships still in orbit, but we didn't have the required access codes. Still, it didn't sit well with me. It felt wrong not to send out everything we had.

Meanwhile, thousands of videos from across the entire planet were now pouring onto the net; they portrayed New Sonora as not just a hotbed of terrorist activity, but as a base for terrorists from other systems as well. They claimed they'd found that we were supposedly building a second direct transfer gate with another system I'd never heard of – something that would allow 'direct access' to Earth itself for people from this other system. The whole supposition was completely ridiculous.

We all spent a lot of time going over all the possible mech configurations and how to fight each kind.

There were four distinct types of mech chassis. Each type had multiple trim configurations. The four frame types were Light Recon, the Regulars, the Heavies, and the Snipers.

The Recon units were the cheapest to buy, and not surprisingly, they were about forty to fifty percent of all the mechs. They had two trims: the Drop Dragoon, which was the only kind we'd faced so far, and the Cheetah, which had a different leg configuration and was built for speed.

The Light Recon bots were most likely to be driven by younger children. Smaller and relatively nimble, they had limited armament. They had access to jump jets, which allowed them to basically fly for short distances. The Cheetah variation didn't allow for shoulder-mounted weapons, but they had double jump jets, which were terrifying to watch in action. I watched a video of a bright pink Cheetah with a strange four-sided chain saw jump through the roof of a house and land amongst a group of about fifty people who'd all been hiding and sheltered. The house burst into flames, and the driver – an older man – laughed maniacally as he butchered them all in a matter of seconds.

Despite their name, the Regulars consisted of only about thirty percent of the mechs. These were clearly meant to be the most common model, but they were more expensive. They had multiple configurations, but the base model, the Attenuator, looked like a humanoid robot. Or a taller, more armored Peacekeeper. They traded speed for armor and added waist-mounted guns. They were only about sixty percent the speed of the Recon units and could only add jump jets at the expense of a lot of armor and weapons.

The Heavies were the most expensive units, and they were less common than the Regulars. I'd seen only a few of these from the videos. They looked like literal twentieth-century tanks with arms and two massive legs instead of treads. The things were huge, slow, and plodding and weren't really designed for hunting down and killing people. Players didn't like them because of their speed.

Their biggest features were their ability to stack multiple missile tubes and their two arm weapons, which had literally dozens of possible upgrades. And on top of it all was the main turret, which came standard with a gun called the Battering Ram, which terrified me. It was strong enough to put a meter-wide hole in anything on the planet. No matter how many preparations we made, an extended conflict with one of those things could have only one result.

If any of them approached our base, we'd have to focus everything we had on it before it killed us all.

The rarest configuration was the Sniper. It cost a little more than the Regular but less than a Heavy. I'd seen only a single stream featuring one of these things. It was the smallest of the units, and despite being labeled as a mech, it looked more like a hopper on four legs. It was faster than the Regulars and the Heavies and steadier on its feet than the Recon units, but it couldn't use jump jets. In a war scenario against a real army that had its own mechs, it was clear a handful of these things would be invaluable. Against us, it had limited utility and thus wasn't purchased by many of the players.

The Sniper's main features were its stealth field and its two long-range weapons. The stealth field was more of a protection against enemy sensors and radars and other types of sensors than against visual detection, though there was an option to add visual camouflage, which only worked well from a distance.

The guns had EMPs that disabled most types of machinery and a long, long barrel that fired five-pound explosive shells at a distance of several kilometers. They had slightly longer range but were much less powerful than the Battering Ram of the Heavy. The problem was, the mechs could only store so many of the shells, and one had to pay to upgrade the reloading speed of the Sniper, which was painfully slow.

The mech had an optional swivel turret on its underbelly as well. But most people seemed to call this mech 'boring' and 'useless,' and they complained about the accuracy of the long-range scope, especially with the latency issues. As a result, hardly anybody used them.

I worried what would happen if the EMP weapon fired on the honeybees, but Roger believed the current version of the weapon would be ineffective due to the way the robots were built. As he put it, the more modern electronic systems of the enemy mechs were in more danger from the weapon than the honeybees, which were designed for long-term use in hostile environments.

The long-range barrel was a much bigger threat, almost as dangerous as the Battering Ram, the main gun on the Heavies.

Much of the fighting was between players and the planted Rhythm Mafia bots, which were pretending to be human 'insurgents.' On the net, there was a lot of grumbling from people who believed these insurgents to be exactly what they really were – seeded bots. But even more people seemed to believe that the entire game was a scam, that they really weren't on a real planet at all, and that none of this was real, citing the lack of children and the fact that almost everybody on the videos had guns. Even though the game didn't have the required disclaimers stating that the enemies were either bots or CGI, people were skeptical.

They were almost there. Almost.

Just as the sun set on the second day, I was attempting to get to sleep. We were supposed to be sleeping in the new bunkers, and my house was filled with people coming and going, so I'd moved to the mattress in the storage room above the classroom. I'd tried closing my eyes, but nothing worked. So instead, I was flipping through the notebook *The Colonist's Guide to Settlement Defense*, reading an outdated chapter on EMP warfare, but I kept flipping back to the cover with my grandfather's writing. *Remember rule number ten.* And after that, I would move to the back of the book, to the pages and pages of handwritten text. These were diary entries from my grandfather. They started right when they moved to this farm, and they ended when I was about ten years old. I hadn't been able to bring myself to yet read the entries.

Neither Lulu nor I knew what rule number ten was. Whenever we'd asked, he'd always smiled and said something stupidly cryptic like 'You don't need to worry about that one because you've never broken it.'

He promised we'd know what it meant in the end, but he'd never been clear what 'in the end' was. He'd died before he could explain it.

If either of us asked Roger, he'd beep and say something equally enigmatic or weird. The last time, he'd said, 'I am honored that you would even ask.'

Was the answer in here in my grandfather's thoughts? It almost seemed wrong to look.

I sighed, putting the book down. I really needed to try to sleep. I stared at the close ceiling of the attic space. I'd discovered this place the day my mom had died. I was five years old. I'd run away when my grandparents had sat me down to tell me the news. I'd known it was coming of course. The Sickness took them all slowly and painfully, and to this day, I could still smell it: the scent all of our parents left as they rotted from the inside out.

I'd spent the day in here, in this dark, ominous attic, curled up on the floor, crying at the unfairness of the universe. I remembered how I thought because I'd wanted something so bad, it would become true. I'd wanted my mom to be okay. I'd wanted her to live even though all the others had not. I'd cried and cried.

I remembered how I thought I'd truly been hiding, but now I knew better. Roger always knew where I was as long as I had my bracelet on, which meant my grandfather also knew where I was. But back then, this dusty storage room had become the place I'd always retreat to when I needed to feel alone.

I'd first brought Rosita to this small attic after we'd been dating for a while. I'd never explained to her how or why this little space was so special to me.

As if I'd summoned her, my thoughts were interrupted by Rosita popping her head up through the trapdoor.

'I figured I'd find you here,' she said, pulling herself into the space. She moved easily, her long limbs giving her an almost feline grace. In an instant, the musty old smell of the low-ceilinged room was replaced with her scent. She motioned for me to scoot over on the mattress, and I did without a word. She lay down in front of me, backing into me. She grabbed my arm and pulled it over herself. I felt her warmth against me, and it felt like home.

After a moment, without another word, she began to silently sob.

We lay like that in silence for a good half hour, with her shuddering against me as I held on to her.

'I think I know why they're here. Why they're really here,' Rosita finally said.

'What do you mean?'

'My grandmother and Sam's grandmother both believed something like this would eventually happen. They used to talk about Earth invading all the time. They believed they deliberately did something to cause the Sickness to kill us all off so they could have New Sonora. But since we didn't die like they wanted, they're coming now. They're coming now because we're all about to start having babies, and if they wait any longer, it'll be too late.'

'Sam's grandmother was insane. She never met a conspiracy

theory she didn't believe. It's why Sam is crazy. I still don't know why they'd want to come at all.'

'It doesn't mean they were wrong. Sam was right about the timing. And they *are* here, regardless of what you think makes sense.'

'The Sickness was something to do with the planet, though. There's no way Earth could have predicted that. We had no idea until people started getting sick.'

'It's still weird that it was *everybody*. Most genetic diseases like that only affect a percentage of people. That's what my grandmother used to say.'

Rosita's grandmother had been trained as a biologist before she'd married and moved to the area to farm. But she also used to wear a hat shaped like a chicken. Grandpa Lewis thought the whole lot of them were morons.

'If a hundred people walk into an irradiated area, all hundred of them will get sick and die,' I said.

'Maybe,' Rosita said. 'But this isn't radiation. It's a birth defect. And as my grandmother pointed out, it wasn't just people who got sick. A small percentage of the livestock was affected as well, but the susceptible ones quickly died out. But for the pigs and the chickens, it was only one out of every twenty or so. She felt there was something more to it, something the scientists were missing. Yes, we fixed it, but she thought it was a deliberate act. And she thought if they were deliberately killing us, they were doing it for a reason. The only thing that made sense was that they wanted someone to come and get the planet all ready for them and then die off. That way the Earthers could come and resettle it at their leisure. They could resettle with an Earth government, not an independent body like we supposedly are.'

I shook my head. 'We left hundreds of years ago. Nobody who made that decision would be alive now. I can't believe somebody would do that. It's so – I don't know – evil.'

'Do you know who we were before we left Earth?'

Of course, I knew the story. Everybody knew the story. We were a mix of scientists and criminals. Undesirables mixed with volunteers. Those without homes, those who were crowding the planet without helping it mixed with dreamers who wanted to make a difference in the future or find better lives for their families in a new place not choked with pollution and crime and constant political upheaval. One generation in, and none of that had mattered anymore. It shouldn't have worked, but it did. The close confines of the *Forlorn* had been a melting pot. Both Grandpa Lewis and Grandma Yolanda had relatives from both sides of the original crew.

'I know,' I said.

'We were different,' Rosita said. 'And that's all that matters. That's why I want to make movies.' She didn't elaborate beyond that. Instead, she turned so we were eye to eye. She put her hand against the side of my face.

'I love you because you always see the good in people, Oliver. But you don't like watching what's going on outside your little circle because it conflicts with your narrow worldview, and it short-circuits that brain of yours. So instead, you just stick your head in the sand. That's what makes you a great farmer.' She reached over to wipe something off my face. 'But it makes you a terrible soldier. I need you to wake the fuck up, and I need you to get angry.'

I thought of the piles of dead people. I thought of little Henry in the pajamas Rosita's great-aunt had made for him. Dead. I thought of Mr Yanez, shot for no reason at all.

'That's not fair. You were with me earlier. You saw the same things I saw. I already am angry.'

She reached over and kissed me where she'd wiped my face clean. 'You're right. I'm sorry. I'm saying it wrong. I was mad before because it was like you weren't reacting at the injustice of it all. You just sort of accept things and move on. And it's not a bad trait, Oliver. I mean that. It reminds me so much of . . . I don't know. . . . You're too kind of a person for this to be happening to. It hurts me to see people like you getting hurt. I know you're fighting back. I wish it wasn't happening at all. I'm sorry for getting so mad at you before. You know, the other night.'

I took a moment to take all that in. I realized then how scared she was. And with her little cousins missing, it was worse. She was all alone, and before, when I was basically ignoring all the warning signs, it made her feel even more alone.

'I'm sorry, too,' I said. 'I'm sorry for being such a dick before. You were right, and I was wrong. You know, about everything. You're right. I don't want to see what's out there. It's scary enough right here. I don't want to lose you, and I don't want you to ever think I won't be there by your side. I'm going to lose my sister, or at least I was before all this happened, and we don't even talk about it. About her moving away. And it wasn't until you broke up with me that I started to realize that I might actually be all alone. Like, really alone like Mr Yanez and so many of the others around here. It's terrifying to think about, and the thought that you might be feeling the same because of me makes me feel like a real asshole.'

She made a snort. 'And all it took was an invasion from another planet to get you to realize that I'm always right.'

'Seriously,' I said. 'I've never said this to you, and I'm sorry for that. I want to have a life with you, Rosita Zapatero. I want to be with you forever.'

Her eyes softened, and she kissed me again, more insistently this time.

After a moment, she pulled at her wrist, and her little camera burst into the air. I watched it for a second. 'What, you want me to say all that again for your documentary?'

She grinned. 'Actually, I was hoping you and I could make a –'

Roger interrupted. His voice was shockingly loud as he spoke through my bracelet.

'Oliver, it appears a large group of mechs has descended upon the Yanez farm and are engaging with the faux Rhythm Mafia insurgents.'

I groaned. 'How many are there?'

'There appear to be four distinct groups of enemies, totaling twenty-seven mechs. Sixteen of the Light Recon mechs, six of which are Cheetahs. Nine of the standard Attenuators. Two Heavies. Four of the combatants are from Team Cannon Fodder, the same combatants from our last engagement. The largest organized team is a group called Thunder Thighs with twelve members. There is a group of six youths called the Skinners. The last five are all individual, unaffiliated gamers. The Thunder Thighs team is not live streaming their assault for free, but both Team Cannon Fodder and the Skinners along with two of the individual players all appear to have live feeds that I am able to monitor. I will give an after-action report once the engagement is complete. In the meantime, I have placed all assets in ready mode and will maintain it until the threat has passed. All light sources have been dimmed.'

Twenty-seven mechs? Shit. That was a lot. I hoped they all killed one another.

'Wait, Cannon Fodder only has four combatants? Aren't there five of them?'

'Benji Winters, also known as Chode, was unable to join in tonight's stream and will likely not return during the duration of the event, leaving Cannon Fodder with only four members.'

'Huh. What are their configurations?'

'One Recon, which is a Cheetah, two Attenuators, and a Heavy.'

I took a breath. I remembered what that one guy had said just before Sam had peed on him. *I'm going to come back here with a Heavy, find you, and tear you apart.* 'Okay, keep me updated.'

The Yanez farm was only about four kilometers away, and within seconds of the message from Roger, a distant explosion echoed through the night, followed by shouting from the people on watch. I groaned. I wasn't going to be getting any sleep. I pulled myself up and brightened the light in the small, dusty attic, looking about, bathing in memories. Rosita also sat up, keeping her arms wrapped around me.

Another explosion ripped through the night. I pulled myself off the mattress and secured the armor around my chest, and Rosita and I slipped our way down through the trapdoor.

CHAPTER 18

'Update?' I asked as we huddled at the base of the inner defensive wall. Everyone else had been roused from sleep except Sam, who'd been on his shift on the wall instructing the newcomers on how the slingshots worked.

Tito and Axel leaned against the newly built fortification, both of them wide-eyed. A few others joined us, mostly kids we'd grown up with. There were Miguel 1 and Miguel Mustache, best friends. They had been born on the same day, both to mothers who'd supposedly hated each other. I didn't really know the story, but they'd always been known as the Miguels.

There was Daniel, whom I didn't know very well – not anymore, though we'd been friends when we were kids, and Roger had named him 'Oliver friend number two.' Despite that, I couldn't even really remember ever talking to him. I remembered when he'd gotten his front teeth knocked out with a baseball when we were around eight, and one of the teeth had gotten embedded in his lip. That had earned him the nickname the Walrus, but we'd all stopped using it when his grandmother had cried about it.

There were more, too. Fewer than there should have been. I wondered on that. Despite the numbers at the farm, so many more were missing. Were they all hiding? Were they already dead?

We didn't update all of their bracelets with the new net, but Lulu did help install an ancient walkie-talkie system that worked on the bracelets; it had been designed for use on planetary colonies without an orbital ship system to bounce off of. The system was crap, making Roger's voice sound static-filled. He would be able to send only video and images over the bracelets of those in the original group. But it worked well enough.

Ariceli stood next to Lulu, and the difference in their heights was striking. Ariceli was taller than me, though not quite as tall as Tito or Axel. She'd said maybe two words since she'd appeared. She'd been working with Rosita on the escape-tunnel project. Her grandparents on both sides were long dead, and she now lived with her cousin just north of Burnt Ends, working as a blacksmith. Her cousin had decided to hide in the wilderness, but Ariceli had come south. Her aunt's orchard was here, and she came every season to help. Every year we saw her, she looked more and more jacked, like she could rip any of us apart.

Sam was making a concerted effort not to look Ariceli in the eye. They had dated when they were both fifteen years old, and the 'relationship' had lasted probably two weeks at most. Sam's fiancée, Harriet, was actually pretty good friends with her and didn't seem to hold any ill will toward her, so it was a big mystery as to why Sam seemed to be afraid of the tall, silent woman whenever she visited.

Axel seemed to think Sam was afraid of her because of how built she was – because she was both taller and stronger than him, and it hurt his male pride. I didn't think that was the case.

I'd asked him once, and he'd grumbled petulantly, 'I'm not afraid of her. I don't know what you're talking about,' and that was that.

Roger wasn't with us but in the hive in his recharging unit. His voice came through our bracelets. 'Most of the Yanez farm appears to be destroyed. There is still chaotic fighting. I believe ten of the mechs have been destroyed or disabled along with another three that may be salvageable with the field repair drone. All the downed units save two are the Recon units, which RMI seems to target first. All six members of Team Skinner are down, and I believe some of them were deliberately killed by members of the other teams. A small contingent of RMI soldiers is holed up in a fortified bunker. The invaders are currently lining the Heavy unit up for a direct attack. It took some time for the various teams to coordinate, but it appears they're now all working together.'

'RMI?' someone asked.

'That's what the news feed is calling them now,' Lulu said. 'The Rhythm Mafia Insurgents.'

'Wait,' Sam said. 'All of them? Like, across the whole planet, not just on the peninsula?'

Lulu looked annoyed. 'Yes, Sam, the whole planet.'

Sam beamed. 'Well, what do you know? I bet you regret quitting the band now, don't you?'

'Roger,' I said, 'what about the fabricators?'

'There is too much smoke to determine their status.'

'And what about his animals?' Rosita asked.

'Undetermined,' Roger said, 'though it appears some chickens have fled into the woods.'

'They are magic chickens after all,' Sam muttered.

'There goes tomorrow's raid if the recycler is gone,' Lulu said.

We needed that thing if we wanted to really build our defenses. Despite everything we'd done, we were still working with out-of-date tech. A recycler was basically a filament factory, which would allow us to turn almost anything into a format that could be fed into the printers. We really needed like ten of the things, but just one of them would be invaluable. We were planning on trying to steal it, but if it had been blown up . . .

'Update,' Roger said. 'The Heavy's main attack destroyed the bunker, killing all but three of the remaining RMI soldiers. Those three moved off aboard a high-speed vehicle. They are moving southeast along the Old Trail. Several Cheetahs are moving to pursue.'

I suddenly felt very cold. I looked at the others.

'South?' I asked. 'Like, toward us?'

'Holy shit,' Sam said, looking at me, eyes wide. 'Those assholes.'

'They're kiting,' I said.

'Oliver friend number three,' Roger said, 'the clock just turned past midnight, and you've already earned two frowny stickers. But it appears your supposition is correct.'

'Kiting?' Rosita asked.

'It means those RMI robots are leading them directly to us,' Lulu said. 'On purpose.'

'I was afraid of this,' Roger said. 'We have seen this activity already. RMI soldiers set up a base. Then they are attacked, and they flee when it appears they're about to lose. Enemy mechs follow the RMI soldiers, and they make a beeline for places where civilians are hiding. In some of the examples I have seen, the RMI soldiers will set up in the midst of the population centers and resume their defense.'

I jabbed a finger upward. 'Those guys up there know exactly where we are.'

'So, what's the plan?' Sam asked.

I looked over the group of people standing there, afraid.

'We gotta meet them along the way, kill the remaining mechs before they find the base.' I raised my voice. 'Gear up! We're moving in two minutes!'

CHAPTER 19

Twenty minutes later, a dozen of us crouched down in the grass behind the open door of the Gonzales barn. I looked nervously over my shoulder. Normally, even in the dark, one could have clearly seen the lights from our farm three kilometers away, despite the trees. We were still too close to the home base, but the RMI robots were moving rapidly down the Old Trail, and this was the farthest we could get.

I pulled the night vision goggles over my eyes and looked again, seeing if I could detect any hint of our farm now that all the lights were removed. Nothing. Only slightly relieved, I turned my attention back to the line of trees that separated the Gonzales farm from the Old Trail. I couldn't yet see anything, and I pulled off the uncomfortable goggles.

'Roger, how well can they see in the dark?'

'All models have advanced night vision capabilities vastly superior to your own. The Sniper class also has advanced heat-based vision and for a fee can purchase real-time maps of the area. There are currently no Sniper-class war machines nearby. This is fortunate, as we are unable to adequately cloak ourselves from the ship.'

'They only have one ship, though, right?'

'That is correct,' Roger said in my ear. 'It is not currently over our position. But they have deployed multiple satellites that can view the entire planet at once. In addition, do not forget that pre-conflict maps are available for purchase. It appears both Thunder Thighs and Team Cannon Fodder have purchased such maps. In addition, these maps have already proliferated on pirate sites, so the location of the home base is no secret. At first glance, it appears our location is just another farm, though if one zooms close, they can see several honeybees at work. I fear it is only a matter of time before someone puts it together.'

I grunted and returned my attention to the line of trees just past the Gonzales fields.

The Old Trail was a rarely used, poorly maintained road on the far side of the farm. It had been the original road before my grandfather and the municipality built the wider and flatter main thoroughfare for the hoppers. The Old Trail was winding and bumpy and followed the path of the nearby Pantano River, which occasionally flooded during the rainy season. Every kid who had grown up in the area knew the Old Trail very well. I tried to remember the last time I'd used it. It'd been years.

'The RMI soldiers will appear soon,' Roger said over the earpiece. 'Lulu, the path is currently clear. You may now move in.'

To my right, Tito and Axel tensed simultaneously. Just past them, the two Miguels rapidly put out their cigarettes.

'Moving in. Ollie, don't do anything stupid,' Lulu said over the band.

She – along with Rosita, Ariceli, and a few others – was currently several kilometers away, approaching the Yanez farm. They'd taken the main road, using a pair of newly built high-speed scooters from the warehouse cache. A hopper and several more honeybees followed them and would hopefully catch up soon.

I was trying not to let my worry for Lulu and Rosita overwhelm me – or distract me from the current mission. It wasn't working. I sent an *Update?* ping with my bracelet. Lulu replied with two quick bursts, our code for *Can't talk now, but all is well.* It was the same code we'd used as kids through the wall of our bedrooms.

The RMI bots had been pausing along the way, waiting for the mechs to catch up. Of the seventeen remaining war machines, only eleven were still in pursuit, the others having decided to go back for resupply or to call it a night. The remaining pursuers included the four remaining members of Team Cannon Fodder, one independent streamer, and six members of the Thunder Thighs, which was apparently an all-female gamer squad.

'You really think this is a good idea?' Sam asked nervously.

'No,' I whispered. I stuck some fingers into the neckhole of the armored jacket where it was biting my skin. 'But what choice do we have?'

Sam grinned. 'It's not too late to run away screaming.'

Behind us, the night rustled as the two dozen black-painted honeybees emerged from the darkness. They spread out into Mr Gonzales's fields in front of us. Only a few had mounted guns on them. The rhino with the mounted missile launcher also appeared, its legs whisking as it quickly pushed past us and around the side of the main house.

'Do you remember that time we tried to ding-dong ditch Mr and Mrs Gonzales?' Sam asked as we watched the large rhino bot disappear around the house. He indicated the front of the house. The front door was painted bright yellow and glowed in the night. A single light remained on inside. Dozens of flowerpots dotted the front porch. It looked absurdly normal in light of everything that was going on around us.

I laughed. 'I remember you tried to run and bit it on the bottom step and started bleeding all over the place. And Miguel Mustache started crying when Mrs Gonzales came out like we'd been caught trying to rob the place.'

'I didn't cry,' Miguel Mustache said defensively. 'That was Tito or Axel.'

'That was Tito,' Axel said. 'Our grandma told us if we disrespected adults, we'd go to hell. He thought because Sam got caught, Mrs Gonzales would tell God what we did. Miguel Mustache is the one who kept running.'

Tito grunted and nodded enthusiastically.

'I did keep running,' Miguel Mustache said. 'I didn't want to go to hell, either.'

'You missed out on cinnamon rolls,' Axel said.

'No, he didn't,' Miguel 1 said. 'I gave him one later.'

'And I gave it to Lulu,' Miguel Mustache said. 'She said if I didn't give it to her, she'd tell my grandma.'

I laughed. That was about right. Lulu loved Mrs Gonzales's cinnamon rolls.

'Appearing now,' Roger said.

We all went silent as the loud *vroom* filled the fields. I pulled the night vision goggles back over my eyes. I immediately caught the movement of the flatbed vehicle.

The red-yellow glow of a rifle blast lit up the night as one of the RMI robots fired off into the darkness, presumably toward one of the pursuers we couldn't yet see.

There was a *pop*, and smoke started to rise from the wheeled platform. One of the honeybees had just fired something to disable the RMI vehicle and prevent it from getting closer to our base. The three RMI robots seemed to pause as if deciding what to do. After a good ten seconds of them just standing there completely frozen, they all moved at once, jumping from the disabled vehicle. The RMI soldiers did not start firing at the honeybees. Two started setting up a gun position just off the road. A third started jogging in our direction. We all tensed, but it angled toward the house, not the barn where we were hiding.

Roger's voice crackled over the band. 'It is likely the RMI units have real-time intelligence on your location, but I do not believe they will engage our units.'

'Tell that to Mr Yanez,' I muttered.

'All of my intelligence indicates the RMI soldiers will be hesitant to directly engage with the local population, especially when enemy mechs are nearby. The death of Mr Yanez was a self-defense measure and an anomaly. That said, do your best to avoid the RMI units. For the time being, remain hidden until I tell you to move. Do not reveal yourselves unless I give the go-ahead.'

We were here as backup for the honeybees, which would take the lead on the assault. We wanted to stop the RMI squad from discovering our location as long as possible. They were clearly trying to lead the mechs toward our base.

Not tonight, I thought, gripping the rifle tightly.

The second group – led by Lulu and Rosita – was already approaching the Yanez farm. Now that the fight had moved away from the fake RMI base, they would quickly move in and grab the recycler unit if it was still intact, along with any other supplies. They had to get there now because the Moderators would come in and blow up the entire area once it was clear the fighting was done. They wouldn't do it if there were any active mechs still in the area. I hoped.

'What is that guy doing?' Miguel Mustache asked, indicating the lone RMI soldier moving toward the house. He moved out of sight, and a moment later the sound of shattering glass filled the night. The robot was breaking inside.

'Oh, man, Mr Gonzales is going to be pissed,' Sam said.

'Damnit,' came Lulu's voice over the band.

'What is it?' I asked.

'The fabricator-recycler combo is wrecked. There are a few guns and some unexploded canister explosives we can use, but most everything is trashed. Cindy is here. We found her hiding in the woods. We're going to bring her in.'

'That is not advisable,' Roger said.

'I'm bringing her,' Lulu said. 'Some chickens, too.'

'Holy crap, Cindy?' Sam whispered. 'I can't believe that thing is still alive.'

Cindy was a morbidly obese pig that lived on the Yanez farm. She was one of the circus animals, though I was pretty certain her special talent was just being really fat. The thing had lived on the farm for as long as I could remember, and she had to be pushing twenty years old. Years ago, she would come to the fence and greet us as we passed.

'Lulu, if you're bringing chickens, make sure you only bring the magic ones,' Sam added.

Whooom! The woods past the fields suddenly went up with a massive explosion shaking the ground and lighting the night up like day. My night vision goggles beeped and turned themselves off, and I ripped them off my head as a wave of heat washed over me. All the windows in the Gonzales house shattered.

'That was the main armament of a Heavy,' Roger said as flaming pieces of trees rained all around us. 'The Heavy unit has stopped approximately three hundred meters north and has taken up a raised position. Our rhino unit is moving to engage.'

Three mechs appeared, clanking through the trees. They were four-meter-tall humanlike robots, more like old-school mechs than anything we'd seen so far. These were Attenuators. They approached the flaming trees cautiously. The shell from the Heavy had likely blown the two RMI soldiers to pieces.

Two of the three mechs were covered with neon tubing that caused the trees around them to glow purple. The third was also painted purple, but it was heavily damaged. This third one had a giant flapping cape behind it, like it was a superhero.

The Thunder Thighs. According to Roger, this gamer squad was all a little older than Cannon Fodder and better organized. Their subscribers numbered in the millions.

The fight at the Yanez farm had been particularly brutal. Only six of their twelve team members remained operable.

I still wasn't clear what happened when a mech was blown up. Did the drivers have to pay for a whole new one? How much did all of this cost anyway?

'Roger, where are . . .' I started to say as flames filled the sky.

Three smaller mechs flew through the air and landed heavily in the fields, facing where the two RMI soldiers had been before the explosion. All three of these were also painted purple.

They landed in the middle of the fields that were swarming with honeybees. Nothing had yet happened.

'Those little shits,' one of the Cheetah mechs said, the voice distant and barely discernible. A woman. 'We should never have let them tag along.'

There was a response from another mech, but I couldn't hear it.

An Attenuator clanked up. This was the Regular-style mech, and it was half again as tall as the smaller scout-class Cheetahs and Drop Dragoons, and it looked more like a massive humanoid robot. This one didn't have any special paint at all. It was in the base silver from the printing gel. It was armed with a grasping hand on the right side and with a quad-barreled shotgun for the left. What appeared to be a massive sword was sheathed over the humanoid robot's back. The pommel of the sword was a large silver skull. The skull looked like it was that of a lion.

'Who's that?' Sam asked.

'That is the lone unaffiliated participant,' Roger said through my earpiece. 'I do not know who it is. If they are a streamer, I have been unable to find their feed. They have the base-model Attenuator, but the sword is an upgrade. I have been unable to get a proper shot of the nameplate.'

Two more of the scouts appeared from the woods, clanking up to the Cheetahs. These scouts were the same as the ones we'd seen during the preview phase. Drop Dragoons. Side by side, the two models of scouts looked almost identical, but the Cheetahs had wider legs and only one weapon. None of the Cheetahs had missile launchers, either. The two Drop Dragoons were from that same team we had fought with earlier, Team Cannon Fodder. They had the same round signs on a spring as before, though one of them was half blown off. The one I could see was Steamer. He'd been one of the two that had gotten hit by a train during the fight atop the Sombrero.

'Roger, is that other scout that Skeet-Skeet guy?' I whispered.

'That asshole driving the Heavy blew them up before we got here,' one of the Cheetahs said, her voice echoing over the fields. 'Wasting shells on just three insurgents makes you look like a scrub.'

The three Cheetahs and the two Drop Dragoons all stood in a circle and started to argue. It was clear they had no idea they were currently surrounded by honeybee drones. Nor did they know there was an RMI soldier still alive in the house.

Over by the fire, a group of the taller Attenuators was sifting through the wreckage.

Roger crackled in my ear. 'The second Drop Dragoon next to Steamer in front of you is named Wankette. She was part of the earlier skirmish, but we destroyed her mech with a truck. Skeet-Skeet from Cannon Fodder is piloting the Heavy that is parked north of here. The fourth member of Cannon Fodder, Queef, was destroyed by the RMI soldiers. The three Cheetahs from Thunder Thighs are piloted by streamers by the names of the Julie Experience, Empress Alexis, and Hannah-Pie. The one that is particularly upset is the Julie Experience.'

'The Julie Experience,' Sam muttered next to me. 'What a stupid fucking name.'

'Rule number four, Oliver friend number three,' Roger said. 'I am keeping track of all infractions.' Roger started to say something else, but he was interrupted by a missile launch coming from the house and barreling directly into the group of five scouts.

'Oh, shit,' I cried as we all hit the deck. Two of the Cheetahs jumped away, one of them landing directly atop the barn we were hiding behind. It crashed heavily through the roof and landed loudly just a few meters in front of us. It was the one with the cape.

Several things happened at once. Across the way, the Attenuators all turned and started firing at the house. But at the same moment, the drones all appeared, coming up from the grain field like they were emerging from the underground.

'What the fuck? What the fuck?' the mech in the barn was saying. This was the same voice as before, the Julie Experience.

The honeybees swarmed, moving rapidly in multiple directions. There was a massive explosion in the center of the field, presumably another shot from the Heavy, though he didn't hit anything. This was followed by a distant secondary explosion. Screaming filled the distance as several of the drones moved into the woods. The sound of a power saw meeting metal shrieked through the night.

The Cheetah with the cape stumbled from the front of the barn, pushing the wooden doors off their frames. We all had to jump out of the way to keep from getting hit. The unit came out right between me and Miguel Mustache. The large war machine stank of burning oil. On her lower leg, one of the remaining neon tubes blinked on and off, humming loudly. The driver – the Julie Experience – was shouting something, but her words were distorted over the speaker. She hadn't seen or noticed us just yet.

All of us – me, Sam, the Miguels, Tito, and Axel – we all did the same thing at the same time. We screamed in surprise. We lifted our guns. We started unloading into the side and legs of the machine.

The mech swiveled in surprise, clearly still suffering from latency issues. Her sole weapon was a long gun attached to an arm on her right side, which was terrible for close-up fighting. When she swiveled, I ducked as the arm swished over my head. We all fired upward, our shots denting and scratching the metal. There was a hiss followed by a pained scream from Miguel Mustache. Stinking, burning liquid spewed from the machine, coating us as we continued to fire and scream. The mech let out a strange noise.

There was more hissing but a different kind. The Julie Experience was saying something, but her speakers were wrecked. The machine didn't fall over, but it was no longer able to move.

Still, we fired, and we fired.

A honeybee came out of nowhere, leapt, and landed atop the mech. A saw whirred, and it made a cut on the back of the machine.

For a moment, the speakers worked again, and to my surprise, Julie was laughing.

'You're real? Holy fucking shit. I see you. I see you. We'll find you soon.'

And then it was done. The mech fell backward into the barn as we all scattered. Seconds later, the entire barn collapsed in on itself.

The house was now just gone. The woods were on fire, and heavy smoke rose into the night. Several plumes of smoke rose from every direction. All the mechs were down. It had ended just as quickly as it had started.

'The Heavy has been disabled,' Roger said in my ear. 'Unfortunately, we lost the rhino in the process. I have visual confirmation that all enemy and RMI units have been destroyed. Your mission has been accomplished. Please hurry back to base. A Moderator is likely inbound to clear the scene.'

'Miguel! Miguel!' came the shout from Miguel 1. He stood over Miguel Mustache, who writhed on the ground, crying in pain.

'Shit,' I said, scrambling toward my friend.

'He got burned,' Miguel 1 said. 'We hit a hose, and the fluid spewing from it caught on fire and flashed him.'

I looked down in horror to see half of Miguel's face was nothing but black. His arm and neck, too. I clicked the flashlight on my bracelet, shining it down, and we all gasped at the severity of his wounds.

'What do we do?' Axel asked.

A group of three black drones rushed up. One of them produced a needle, and it jabbed Miguel, who immediately went unconscious.

'What the hell was that?' I asked.

'We will rush the injured back to base,' Roger said calmly over my ear. 'As long as we move swiftly, the medical unit will keep him alive. Move aside, please.'

And then two of the honeybee drones lifted him, each grabbing onto two limbs. The third honeybee, the one with the needle, moved underneath him. The back expanded, forming a stretcher. Miguel was placed carefully down, and two sets of straps appeared and were fastened in place by the other drones. He appeared to be held firmly in place. The six-legged drone made a little wobble, like Miguel was too heavy for it, and then it bounded off into the darkness, moving ridiculously fast.

'What the shit?' Sam asked, looking after the robot. 'I didn't know they could do that. Did you know they could do that? When you passed out a few nights ago, they dragged you away on the ground, though I guess those were the smaller scout ones.'

'This particular honeybee has the medic upgrade,' Roger said. 'It is designed to carry the injured out of battle. The legs are enhanced to carry the weight. We have five such units.'

'Do you think he'll be okay?' Miguel 1 asked worriedly. 'His grandmother is going to kill me.'

'It didn't look too bad,' I lied. 'He'll be fine.'

'The rest of you must retreat,' Roger said. 'I will quickly sweep the battlefield for supplies, but you must return to base. Lulu, Lulu unqualified babysitter number one, and the others are already on their way back.'

For a moment, I just sat there, taking it all in. My heart wouldn't stop beating. Under the tight armored jacket, the beat felt especially loud, insistent, like it was trying to punch through my chest, through the armor, like it knew it was being squeezed. My arms couldn't stop shaking.

How is this real? How have things changed so fast?

I closed my eyes just for a second. I pictured myself in my space in the attic, staring up at the close ceiling. It was like that day when my mother had died all over again. There was no going back, and that was all there was to it. I had to keep moving.

'Come on, guys,' I finally said, turning and jogging away.

Behind us, the Gonzales farm was utterly destroyed, and the fight had literally taken seconds. They'd lived there for almost thirty years. *There's no going back.*

I tried not to think about it, and I definitely didn't look back.

As we moved away, that Julie woman's voice echoed in my mind. *We'll find you soon.*

CHAPTER 20

About ten minutes after we left, Lulu, Rosita, and Ariceli caught up with us. All three were riding scooters, and they pulled to a stop next to us. Two of the scooters dragged trailers behind them. The first trailer held *several* chickens, all squawking and fluttering their wings. In the second trailer sat Cindy the pig, who appeared to be straining the limits of the trailer's weight capacity.

'How did you get her into the trailer?' Sam asked, leaning in to say hello to the old pig.

Cindy made an angry, indignant snort.

'I put some of her food in it, and she walked right up,' Lulu said.

Sam and I spent a minute examining the chickens. Lulu's idea of 'some' chickens translated to about forty of them. They completely filled a trailer, all smushed together, bawking angrily, jockeying for position. I didn't see any roosters.

'Are these the magic ones?' Sam asked.

I laughed. 'I hate to break it to you, buddy, but I don't think there's such a thing as magic.'

'Typical drummer,' Sam muttered.

'I don't even know what that's supposed to mean.'

'We also got some gear, but I don't know if any of it is useful,' Lulu said. She got off the scooter and pulled open a box at the front of the chicken trailer. In it sat two pulse rifles, some ammo, a few round devices that looked like more modern grenades, and a large, bulky helmet.

'Hey,' Sam said, picking the helmet up, 'this is an immersion rig!'

'Is it?' I asked, snatching it away from him. 'Why would robots need these? Are they playing video games when they're on break?'

'This is not a regular immersion rig,' Roger said, startling both of us. He'd been doing that more and more lately, just randomly interjecting himself into our conversations even though he really wasn't here. 'These helmets are reinforced for battlefield conditions and are used to remotely control guns and drones. We can utilize these should you need to have direct control of a drone or a remote gun. The RMI soldiers have been seen to use such tactics, but Lulu was unable to find any intact drone units. If the need arises, however, I may be able to connect one of our current UAV units to the helmet.'

'What about a honeybee?' I asked. If I wore the helmet, I could not only control the flying drone or honeybee, but it would feel like I *was* the unit. These were similar to what all the players playing *Operation Bounce House* used.

'And can we use these to play Earth games once this is all done?' Sam added.

'There is no *we*,' Lulu said. 'I found it. It's mine.'

'Yes to both of those questions,' Roger said. 'But I believe the military versions of these have some security limitations. I would like the opportunity to study this in the control room as the neural interface is quite interesting to me.'

I knew little about how these things worked because we didn't have them here. I knew there'd been multiple false starts and dead ends over the years when it came to true immersion technology. These were relatively recent, and there'd been a lot of controversy about safety regarding them. Once you put it on, you could completely mute the world around you. But you still weren't using your real arms and legs, just imaginary versions of them. I couldn't really wrap my mind around it. It was said it was hard to get used to, but once you finally figured it out, there was nothing like it.

I pulled my own helmet off and put the bulky helmet on.

Nothing happened. It felt like the other helmet, except maybe a little tighter on my head.

'I think it's broken,' I said.

'You have to turn it on first, genius,' Sam said. I felt him press something on the side.

'*Please wait.*'

A robotic female voice spoke in my ear.

'*Turning on the first time. Tuning. Tuning. Tuning.*'

The view snapped back on, but I was standing in an endless field. Several spirals appeared in the air.

'This is trippy,' I said. I looked down, and I could see a wire frame of myself.

'Oliver! Do not use it!' Roger said.

'*Biometric scan complete. This helmet is now locked. If you wish to change users, please reset the helmet using a manual connection with the control unit. You have the option to engage. Warning: There are no associated apps to engage with. Warning: Make certain you are in a safe location before you engage.*'

I felt the helmet peel off my head. Even though it came off easily, it felt like it was being ripped away from me like it was attached with sticky tape.

'Ow!' I said as a quick headache overwhelmed me.

It was Lulu who'd grabbed it. 'Goddamnit, Ollie! That was mine!'

Roger spoke. 'It appears Oliver activated the biometric scan. It is now locked to Oliver. Only he may be allowed to use it from now on. I may be able to reset it, but we would have to print and test the proper interface cables.'

'I swear to god, Ollie,' Lulu grumbled. 'You ruin everything.'

'Oh, whatever,' I said, still feeling a little dizzy. 'It's not like you haven't gone through half my closet for your weird sex clients.'

'My clients are not weird, Ollie. They're lonely, which is what I'm going to be after I murder you for stealing my shit.'

'They gotta be a little weird to be paying for cowgirl porn,' Sam muttered.

'Do you want me to beat you to death with my helmet? I'll beat you to death with it,' Lulu said, still clutching the large helmet in her hands.

Sam grinned. 'Well, it would be Oliver's helmet now, wouldn't it?'

'Where's Miguel Mustache?' Rosita asked as she and Ariceli walked up.

That stopped our bickering. Sam quickly recounted what'd happened as we walked back to the farm.

As he recounted what had happened, we received word that Miguel Mustache was already in the medical unit and that he'd be okay as long as we kept any infections at bay. But he would need at least a month to recover.

None of us said out loud what we were all thinking. What would happen if the farm was overrun? How would he be able to run if he was passed out?

And that thought extended to not just Miguel, but to all of the older farmers. They wouldn't be able to run. There was nowhere to go. It was an uncomfortable thought.

The scooters Rosita and Ariceli had been riding stood on their own and trailed alongside us, humming with power and pulling the trailers as Cindy the pig grunted and the chickens clucked. Despite our victory, we remained mostly silent, morose.

Plus, that one streamer . . . the Julie Experience. She had seen us before she'd been destroyed. They'd all seen the honeybees. They would be back looking for us. If one looked at the map, our location was impossible to miss. The next attack would be at home.

Soon thereafter, the Moderator buzzed overhead. The Gonzales farm went up in a massive explosion. A minute afterward, another set of distant pops suggested what was left of the Yanez farm had also gone up.

Even if we did survive this, what then? They were destroying everything. What would happen if we actually won? What would we do? Everything was gone.

'What's that?' Sam suddenly asked, pointing up in the air. An intermittent light appeared in the night. It moved lazily, drifting downward. It was something big with blinking green and yellow lights on each corner.

Something was falling from the sky. It was going to land on the road right in front of us.

My heart stuttered. *No. Not now. It's too soon.*

But a moment later, Roger chimed in.

'Odd. It is a supply crate from Apex. Do not approach it.'

The crate was descending with a pair of parachutes. We all stopped dead on the road to watch it. Multiple drones suddenly appeared, coming from behind us and from the direction of the farm and forming a circle around where the large crate would land.

'Guns ready,' I said upon seeing how large the giant box was. The damn thing was big enough to house two Attenuators. Or a dozen RMI soldiers. Or it could just be a massive bomb. If it was, we were much too close.

I moved off the side of the road. To my right, the newly erected outer fence of our own property stood, and there was a small drainage ditch between the fence and the road. We all dived in. Rosita crouched down next to me. Her face was covered with dirt.

'Maybe we should run,' she said.

I shook my head. 'No time.'

She leaned into me to brace herself. 'We left Cindy out there.'

Sure enough, the scooter dragging the cart with Cindy the pig had stopped in the middle of the road along with the other scooters. Cindy stood within the confines of the cart, grunting indignantly because she and the chickens were suddenly alone on the road.

'If it is a bomb and we survive, at least we'll be eating good tonight,' Sam muttered from my left. 'We should have at least grabbed a few chickens to save.'

'If that whole crate is a bomb, it's not going to matter where the chickens are,' Lulu said.

I took a quick glance over my shoulder, second-guessing my decision not to just haul ass out of here. Beyond the fence stood my ruined grain fields filled with land mines. There was supposedly a path through them marked with yellow rocks, though I couldn't be sure we'd see the path in the dark. The EMP mines wouldn't explode in the traditional manner, but if one of us accidentally stepped on one, we'd get the shock of a lifetime. And the other side of the road was just acres and acres of an untended apple orchard that was overrun with weeds and plica bushes.

'Heads down!' I called.

Crunch! The box landed right in the middle of the road about a hundred meters ahead of us. There was no explosion. A moment passed, and nothing happened. I peeked up to see everyone else already looking. The light breeze caught the twin parachutes, threatening to pull the crate off the road, though it appeared it was too heavy.

Honeybees swarmed toward it. A black drone hopped nimbly onto the crate and pulled a pin embedded on the top of the box, causing a door to slam down with a heavy clatter. A second honeybee turned on a light, illuminating what appeared to be more boxes within packed tight.

I peered at the interior of the crate, but even with the light, I couldn't see that well from this distance. I pulled the night vision goggles back onto my head and zoomed in. Rosita also sent her camera toward it, and she had the view pop up on her bracelet.

Sure enough, it was nothing but more boxes. Each one was labeled, but I couldn't read the words from here. I exchanged a look with Lulu, who also wore night vision goggles. We stood back up.

Roger's voice crackled in my ear. 'The crate appears to contain four fabricator units with built-in recyclers and a significant amount of ammunition. There are also several of the upgraded versions of your pulse rifles. There is a note painted on the inside of the box. It reads, "Merry Christmas." This note makes no sense as Christmas isn't for several months. Nor is it Christmas on Earth. We will continue to sweep for explosives or other hidden surprises. I am already constructing a Faraday cage for the crate so any hidden communicators will be blocked.'

'Holy crap,' I said upon realizing what this was.

Sam and Lulu came to the same conclusion at the same time.

'What?' Rosita asked.

'People don't believe the RMI soldiers are real, so they're seeding the pond in a different way,' Sam said.

I nodded.

'Well, let's make them choke on that decision,' Lulu said before she jogged toward the crate.

The Rhythm Mafia Tapes. Scene sixteen.

We are in the same music room as in scene one. We are with Oliver Lewis, twenty-five, who was introduced in scene one. Sitting next to him is a small woman, Lulu Lewis, twenty-three. Lulu and Oliver are brother and sister. Also in the room is a floating colony robot hive queen, a Traducible AI known as Roger-Roger but called just Roger. See the special section labeled 'AI Infiltration' for all details on Roger. Please note, Roger refers to Rosita as 'Lulu unqualified babysitter number one.'

ROSITA (OFF CAMERA): Okay, guys, tell me about the rules.

LULU: Roger, would you like to tell Rosita what the ten rules are?

ROGER: Certainly.

The AI bot lets out a ding.

ROGER: Lulu unqualified babysitter number one, when my education and child-rearing program was installed, Mr Lewis and myself built the list of ten rules designed to keep Oliver and Lulu as safe as possible while also giving them the best possible foundation to make them productive, well-rounded members of the colony.

ROSITA: Okay. What are the rules?

ROGER: Rule number one is protect Roger, myself, at all costs. Once I am destroyed, most of the advanced features of the honeybees will cease to work.

Number two is keep your bracelet in good working order at all times. This is a safety feature.

Rule number three is do not alter the upkeep schedule for the honeybees.

Rule number four is no swearing. Swearing is indicative of a weak mind.

OLIVER (MUTTERING): Grandpa Lewis swore more than everyone else on the planet combined.

Lulu grunts in agreement.

ROGER: Your grandfather Lewis was not compelled to follow the rules. Only you and anyone else participating in one of my education modules. Rule number five is maintain a positive attitude. It keeps one healthy.

Rule number six is get plenty of rest.

Rule number seven is keep your nutrition up, to get plenty to eat.

Rule number eight is perhaps the most complicated, yet it is also quite simple. Don't pass your responsibilities on to others unless absolutely necessary. Do not take on the responsibilities of others unless doing so is an act of kindness. On the surface it means exactly what it says. But in reality, the true meaning is you should not act beyond your own nature, but if you do, do it as an act of kindness and not in the other direction.

Lulu lets out a derisive snort.

At this point, the camera focuses on Lulu and the heavy eye makeup she is wearing.

ROGER: Rule number nine is maintain good hygiene.

A moment of silence passes.

ROSITA: Okay, what about rule number ten?

ROGER: Rule number ten is rule number ten. It needs no explanation.

ROSITA: Uh . . . what does that mean?

OLIVER: Welcome to our world, Rosita.

DAY THREE OF FIVE

CHAPTER 21

Across the way, Rosita and Lulu worked furiously as they activated the four fabricator-recycler combos. Cindy the pig stood by Lulu's side, oinking away. The damn pig was so big that Lulu could literally have put a saddle on her and ridden her easily. One of the fabricators would be used to create ammunition, one was being used to make filament for our existing printers, and the last two would be used in conjunction to make a defensive gun similar in power and range to that of a Heavy's Battering Ram. That would take most of the day, but once it was built, the honeybees would be able to assemble the gun quickly.

The built-in recyclers of the modern fabricators had changed the very face of planetary colonization. And of warfare. With a lot of power, a lot of junk metal, and a whole lot of biological materials – such as bales of hay, of which we had plenty – one could make almost anything. The machines required constant babysitting as they were constantly getting clogged. They also spewed out a whole lot of waste materials. The fibrous waste felt like insulation, and it broke apart into dust when you touched it.

'Do not breathe it in,' Roger had said when we first activated the machines. 'It is hazardous to your health.'

'Then why are we making camouflage netting out of it?' I asked.

'Because the satellite coverage is more hazardous.'

'I don't understand why they'd just give these to us,' Mr Gonzales said now as he watched the four machines chug along.

To my left, a group of drones was in the process of erecting the giant pole for the netting. The new chickens all clambered around the area of the construction, squawking up a massive racket. Once this final pole was erected, the camouflage netting would be spread in squares over the area. Soon, we'd have coverage for the whole interior part of the ranch.

The game administrators clearly knew where we were, but at least we could deny them real-time satellite targeting. Roger pointed out that the nets would do little for the heat maps, which was why he was also installing around the farm multiple burn-barrel devices that would camouflage the heat signatures of individuals.

It was Sam who answered Mr Gonzales. 'If you go on any of the gaming forums, you'll see people are complaining that this whole thing is fake. They're giving us all this stuff so we can fight back better.'

The old man shook his head. 'It sounds like they're just trying to bring more attention to us.'

'That's exactly what they're doing,' I said. 'But that's going to happen no matter what. Every time we blow up one of their war machines, someone has got to pay to build a new one.'

'And if this planet goes well,' Sam added, now with a chicken under his arm for some reason, 'they get the contract on a bunch of other planets, and they'll get more money.'

'That doesn't seem right,' Mr Gonzales said.

'No,' I agreed, 'it's not. But it is what's happening. And they didn't really give us anything, not with the timers on it all. It's more like we've borrowed all this stuff.'

'Not the boom canisters,' Sam added. He reached down to pet the chicken under his arm.

Inside the shelter, Mrs Gonzales continued to weep over the destruction of her home. She wanted to go over there to look, but the others wouldn't let her. Roger had 'helped' by showing her an image of the burned-to-shit house and barn, and she started sobbing once again.

Harriet and Ariceli and others were there now sitting with her.

Mr Gonzales had taken the news with a remarkable amount of stoicism. Still, I worried about the old man. When my grandfather died, he'd been the first person Lulu and I called. He was the adult in the room. He was the one we all looked to when we didn't know what to do.

But now he was completely out of his element, and everything about that felt wrong.

I need you to get angry.

It wasn't just Mr Gonzales. Despite the gifts, a pall had fallen over the ranch. Miguel Mustache was awake but in pain, so he was being kept drugged up. His grandmother hadn't left his side. Neither had Miguel 1.

I'd visited him for only a few minutes. It was hard to look at his face, and the smell of burned skin – which I hadn't even noticed last night – made me ill to my stomach. Rosita had come with me and held my hand while we visited. She did *not* have her ever-present camera out when we did.

Even if everything else turned out okay, Miguel would forever have scars. None of this was my fault, yet I somehow felt as if it was.

The four fabricators and each of the guns contained a switch that would allow them to be shut down remotely. With the help of Roger and Harriet – who seemed to have a surprising affinity for electronics – we were able to disable the receiver on the rifles, meaning that the kill signal would no longer work. However, Roger warned, there appeared to be a timer built into the board that would cause the guns to stop working no matter what we did after ninety hours, meaning the guns would basically become useless once *Operation Bounce House* was done.

The fabricators likely had something similar built deep inside, but we didn't have the time to tear them apart to go searching for them. We did pull them apart enough to make certain there were no explosives or anything like that within. Roger suspected there would be something like a hidden listening device in each of the units, so the first thing he did once we got them all set up was build for the fabricators a proper Faraday cage, which would keep any remote signals, passive or active, that would cause the units to work strangely from reaching them. And it would keep them from communicating with the satellites over our heads.

We could have used the fabricators to build another fabricator that didn't have any limitations, but we simply didn't have the time.

'We would have been better off hiding,' Mr Gonzales said after a minute of watching.

'Maybe,' I said. 'But most of the people here wouldn't have run or been able to. If we hadn't stopped those RMI soldiers last night, they would've come right into our camp and dragged all of the mechs off with them. And we'd all be dead right now.'

'They'll come tonight,' Mr Gonzales said.

A few hours back, we'd gotten word that ten deployment units had dropped in the area just north of Burnt Ends. There was a line of villages there along the Pantano and the train line all the way up the hills. It would be up to sixty mechs. Several of our honeybees and UAVs were already nearby keeping an eye on them, making certain they weren't turning in our direction.

I exchanged a glance with Sam. 'Hopefully they'll stay away,' I said.

'They won't. They'll come tonight,' Mr Gonzales repeated.

'Do you believe this?' Lulu called from her chair. There were several of us in her room watching the news program on her screen. We'd been called in at Roger's insistence. I looked around, and none of the older people were in here, thank goodness.

The program showed aerial footage of Fat Landing. The camera swept over the planet's largest city, revealing kilometers and kilometers of burning destruction. The caption read, 'Terrorists Take New Sonoran Capital City. Citizen Soldiers Move to Defend the Populace.'

The scene changed to a man in the middle of the street screaming. He held one of the newer pulse rifles, and he used it to take out the knee of a colorfully painted Drop Dragoon scout. A Heavy turned the corner of the street behind the man and fired, taking out both the man and the large five-story building beyond him.

'They're calling it the Battle of Fat Landing,' the faceless newscaster said as more images of flattened buildings appeared. 'Mere hours after Apex Command discovered that the leaders of the RMI terrorist group had fled to the New Sonoran capital city of Fat Landing, several terrorist attacks rocked the city. These attacks included multiple explosions in the refugee camps and the bombing of a school housing hundreds of children.'

'Children?' Lulu asked as the newscaster continued.

'No word yet on casualties. Up until this point, Fat Landing has been considered a "safe zone" and off limits to the planetwide hostilities. Meanwhile Persimmon Intergalactic, a human rights activist group, is blaming the widespread humanitarian crisis on Apex Industries, the company behind the *Operation Bounce House* game, claiming there is no terrorist activity at all on New Sonora and that the attacks are an "act of senseless genocide." A spokesman for Apex Industries denied the allegations and suggested that Persimmon was in league with the RMI. Persimmon previously sued to stop the game from ever getting released, but that lawsuit was dismissed.'

The scene changed to show a wall with spray paint on it. It read, 'Alliance with Earth = Death.' Then the scene changed to show the familiar shot of the smoldering school here in Burnt Ends, implying that this was still Fat Landing. When we'd seen it on the Cannon Fodder stream earlier, they'd stripped the school's sign away and changed the skin of the building to make it look more industrial. But this shot was almost exactly how the school really was, though they added some playground equipment to the field beyond it that wasn't really there.

They were saying that this school had been filled with children and that it had been blown up by the RMI.

'What the shit?' Sam exclaimed as both Rosita and Lulu called out in protest. They were showing something *they* had done before the fighting had even started.

This was followed by a quick, blurred shot of all the dead people piled up on the street. It was the shot Lulu had taken with her bracelet.

'I guess they know we have an internet connection,' I grumbled.

'They know somebody does, probably not how yet,' Lulu said.

The newscaster continued. 'Still, the sheer amount of destruction does not bode well for Apex's bid to expand the controversial *Operation Bounce House* program, despite the overwhelming support the game has received from the public. A representative from Apex has been called to testify before a Republic hearing next week to answer the allegations.'

'Next week?' Lulu retorted. 'It'll all be over next week.'

'Lulu, have you tried messaging these Persimmon people?' I asked.

'I did yesterday. They didn't respond. I'll try again.'

Sam was still staring at the screen, which had moved on to a different story. 'They blew their wad too early,' he said. My friend's voice had taken on a tired tone I hadn't ever heard.

'What do you mean?' Rosita asked.

He gestured at the screen. 'I don't know how it really got started, but if those were real pictures of the city, they wiped out Fat Landing.' He waved his arm. 'Don't you get it? They were talking before about how it was the safe place where we're all supposed to go. It was set up from the beginning to be the climax. There would be a big bad guy in the city, the final boss. But the gamers got in early, and now the whole city is gone. But there're still a few days left. What's left to fight? Where else are they going to see that much action? The game people are in deep shit now if they don't think of something.'

'Everyone please proceed to the control room. We have three more supply crates coming in,' Roger said over the band. 'And after we retrieve them, I need to update you on the status of the action north of Burnt Ends. I have located where the remaining citizens of Burnt Ends are hiding. Unfortunately, the enemy has located them as well.'

'Oh, I'm pretty sure they've thought of something,' I said.

CHAPTER 22

Roger clicked. 'This was captured twenty-two minutes ago. The fighting is still ongoing.'

We stood in silence in the control room as we watched the UAV video of the people scattering into the woods as the mechs stormed the encampment. Just as they attacked, a second group of RMI soldiers appeared from nowhere and started pouring fire at the mechs. The fight turned into a huge blowout.

It was just me, Lulu, Rosita, Ariceli, Sam, and the twins. We left the room's door open, and one of the chickens had somehow managed to get in as well. It pecked around the floor by Sam's feet.

'Did any of our honeybees engage?' I asked as we watched in horror. A pair of Heavies walked right over a group of five or six cowering people, crushing them. I recognized one of them as Terry, a man who had worked at the general store. He'd always give me licorice when I was a kid, and I'd never been brave enough to tell him I thought it was gross, so I'd always throw it into the woods on the way home.

I felt a weird, cold detachment as I watched the scene, the gross taste of licorice flooding my memories. Somewhere deep down, this was alarming. All this death was already starting to surprise me less. I looked about the room, and I could see everyone was being affected the same, except maybe Tito, who looked to be on the verge of tears.

'We have no honeybee assets in the area, nor are we able to get them there without transport and relay equipment. This is just at the outside range of the UAVs,' Roger said. 'This location is approximately fifty kilometers north of Burnt Ends. There once was a mining encampment here, but the location was abandoned after just a year. The settlement was called Scorpion Hill.'

I recognized that name. My grandfather had mentioned stopping there when they'd made their original trek to the peninsula with the group that built the grain rail. It was about the same distance from Burnt Ends as we were, just in the other direction. It was significantly farther away than I'd ever gone.

I could see now what had happened to the people of Burnt Ends. The original attack had happened in the middle of the night. It had been the five mechs from Team Cannon Fodder. They'd done their best to commit wholesale slaughter, but there were thousands of people in Burnt Ends. Most had gotten away, many fleeing to the electric boats on the Pantano. There was a small town called Stick-in-the-Mudsville about twenty kilometers upriver right where the river became unmanageable to boats. They'd likely fled to the town, commandeered every transport they could find, and kept going north until the road ended. I imagined not too many would go beyond that. Past that, the hills gave way to mountains that gave way to the desert. A lot of refugees would be in their seventies and eighties, and it had probably been a difficult trip just to get them to Scorpion Hill.

There were literally dozens of the RMI soldiers. The robots must've been in hiding, waiting for the mechs to appear. That realization that they'd been there hiding gave me a sudden chill.

Lulu must've been thinking the same thing, because she suddenly asked, 'Roger, how certain are we that there aren't hidden robots nearby?'

'Relatively certain,' Roger said. 'We are in a much better position to detect them than the refugees were.'

She nodded, and we returned our attention to the fight that was still playing out on the screen. Most of the people were now scattered into the woods in all directions. Dozens of bodies littered the ground.

There were *a lot* of the RMI soldiers, all in uniform. They were better armed than usual, too, many having canister guns similar to what Lulu used, though these fired in a direct line. They were pretty effective.

Because it was mostly trees and there were only four UAVs in the area, it was difficult to get a handle on the chaos of the fight.

I noted there were fewer of the smaller Recon units this time. Of the fifty-plus mechs, the vast majority were Attenuators. Also, for the first time, a single Sniper sat in the hills past the encampment, picking the soldiers off one by one.

If any of them were streaming, Roger wasn't showing us. I noted the whole Cannon Fodder team was there, minus Chode. This time, all four of their mechs were in Attenuators, though they still had the same stupid bouncing targets over their heads. Thunder Thighs was also there. The Julie Experience's Cheetah was one of the few scouts in the fight. She had a huge '2' spray-painted on the front, indicating this was her second mech.

I looked up. 'Roger, why do these guys keep coming back after getting their mechs blown up? Don't they have to buy new ones each time?'

'Apex offers two supplemental insurance plans that must be chosen at sign-up. One offers up to two replacements for any reason for a fee equal to about seventy-five percent of the initial cost. A second plan offers unlimited replacements and mech switching for a much higher fee. It is said very few have opted for this plan, but it is likely some of the more well-known streamers have received this plan for free as an advertising expense. It is my belief that both Cannon Fodder and Thunder Thighs have the unlimited plan, as evidenced by the differences in their mechs each time we face them.'

'Christ,' Sam muttered. 'How much does all this cost? To Apex, I mean. How much does it cost them? They're just printing these things over and over again.'

'That's an interesting question, Oliver friend number three. As industrial printing improves, the cost of manufacturing decreases exponentially. They are limited only by the base cost of the raw materials for production, and without going into a physics lesson, the best batteries they can print only provide enough energy to run the mechs optimally for about a month, and I suspect the power sources in these mechs are much smaller.'

My eyes returned to the body of Terry, still crunched into the ground, arms and legs splayed like he was making a face-down snow angel.

They only needed to kill us once, and we had to kill them over and over. It wasn't fair.

Roger buzzed as the scene faded. 'I will continue to monitor the skirmish. Once it is clear, I will use the UAVs to locate any survivors and instruct them to come here if they wish. In the meantime, I would like to show you the contents of the three new supply crates that landed in the same approximate location as the previous one. In addition to more explosive canisters, there were two additional fabricators, though these are the smaller units that do not come with attached recyclers. There were additional rifles as well. It appears they removed the remote switch-off on the rifles, but the built-in obsolescence remains. We are currently investigating the recyclers. But most curious was an item in the third crate. It is a communication device. On the device was a note.'

The screen switched from the battlefield of Scorpion Hill and showed a glass tablet with shock corners. The tablet was leaning up against a rock, and we were viewing it in real time from the telltale fish-eye POV of a regular honeybee drone. In the bottom corner, it listed the bee as 'Unit 104. Marigold.'

On the corner of the tablet device, there was a small piece of square paper containing a note. The note read, 'Message for the owner of the farm with the colony bots. Tap screen to connect.'

'What the heck?' Lulu asked.

'I moved the tablet away from the base, as it clearly contains multiple sensors, both overt and hidden,' Roger said.

'Did you tap the screen?' Lulu asked.

'I did not, Lulu. The note is addressed to you and your brother. Rule number eight.'

She grunted. 'I figured that one would be one of the first ones to go in perimeter defense.'

'Quite the contrary, Lulu. Most literature about surviving warfare suggests rule number eight to be of utmost importance. At least part of it.'

'What's rule number eight?' Sam asked.

'Eh,' I said. 'Basically, don't pass your responsibilities on to others unless absolutely necessary.'

'I don't get it. What the hell does that have to do with Roger . . . Ow! Fuck! Stop!'

'Rule number four. You have accumulated over forty corrections, Oliver friend number three. Be grateful I'm only meting out two.'

The chicken at Sam's feet let out an outraged squawk.

'It's okay, Betty Sue,' Sam said, rubbing his arm. 'Don't attack him. Yet.'

'Attack?' Axel asked, eyeing the chicken.

'Betty Sue?' Rosita asked at the same time.

Sam reached down to pet the thing. 'I'm still trying to figure out what makes them magic. I think maybe they were attack chickens. This one keeps following me around. There's no rooster, so I think she's the group's Lulu. But I can't call her Lulu because the real Lulu would punch me.'

From the chair, Lulu grunted.

'How are you sure it's the same one every time?' Rosita asked, also bending down to examine the chicken. Her camera buzzed in a circle around the chicken's head.

'It's the same one. Look at the cold, dead stare.'

I laughed. 'How is an attack chicken a circus act?'

'I don't know. How is Cindy being really, really fat a circus act? The banner Mr Yanez had on his farm showed them all running toward something with glowing red eyes.'

'It is inadvisable to name this creature "Betty Sue,"' Roger said. 'Betty Sue is the name of honeybee unit number 263, and you giving orders to this creature may cause confusion.'

'You don't have any say when it comes to names,' Sam snapped at Roger.

'Holy sh . . . crud, can we get back to the space tablet, please?' Lulu said, indicating the screen. 'You know, the one with the note from the people trying to kill us? Roger, will you activate it now that we are here?'

'I will,' he said. The drone moved a little closer to the tablet as it reached toward it with an arm. It gave the screen a little tap, and it woke up. A single button sat on the display under the Apex logo, a mountain with a star flare at the top. The button read, 'Secure connection. Ready.'

'Do it,' Lulu said.

CHAPTER 23

The honeybee tapped the screen again, and a spinning icon appeared with a blinking 'Please Wait.'

A woman's smiling face appeared. She was in what appeared to be an office, and she had her hair up like she was going to a fancy ball. Behind her was a wall with a colorful mural depicting a spiral galaxy. Her name appeared under the image, and it said she was 'Cordelia Black. Assistant to Eli Opel.'

'Eli Opel?' Sam said, exchanging a look with me. 'Holy shit.'

Eli Opel was the head of the mercenary division at Apex. His official title was general supreme leader of Apex Command, which I thought was a little obnoxious. The man had once been the CEO of the gaming company Victus Wonderworks until Apex bought them. And now the man was running all of this.

The woman's smile turned to surprised confusion. 'Uh, hello?'

She couldn't see us because our view was filtered through the camera of a honeybee. She would be looking at the flat front of the drone.

'Can she hear us?' Lulu asked.

'You must activate the audio manually,' Roger said. Lulu nodded and pressed a button on the keyboard.

'Wait,' I said. 'What're you going to say to her?'

'Hello?' Cordelia Black asked, more insistent. She turned her head. 'I heard talking, but it's some robot thing.'

'She heard that, dumbass,' Lulu said to me after removing her finger from the keyboard.

'Okay, but what do we say?' I asked again.

'I don't know. What do you say to someone trying to kill you?'

'Please stop?' Sam offered.

'Hello?' that Cordelia woman asked a third time.

Sam reached over Lulu's shoulder and pressed the button. 'Yeah, hang on a second, lady. Uh, nice hair, though.'

'Why can't I see you?' the woman asked.

A second face appeared on the screen, also peering into the camera. This was a good-looking older man with black hair gelled up in the current Earth style with a streak of silver through the middle. He wore a suit that seemed to gleam as if it were made of plastic.

'That's him!' Sam hissed. 'Eli Opel, the boss guy! Man, look at that suit. He looks like a real ass . . . uh, douche.'

Roger beeped. 'The "D" word is still a swear.'

Sam scoffed. 'Since when?'

'It is in my database. Therefore it is considered a swear. The only reason I haven't corrected you is because we are currently engaged with the enemy.'

'Video chatting counts as engaging with the enemy?'

'Yes, it does.'

Sam muttered something under his breath.

'They're relaying the image through one of the old colony bots they have. One of the standard drone units,' Opel said. I couldn't tell if he was speaking to the woman next to him or just muttering to himself. 'Fascinating.' He had an odd accent. Old British. Not many people still spoke like that, though it was common in the older media and games. 'I can't believe any of these things are still working. They all supposedly had kill switches in them that made them stop functioning five years after activation.'

I knew the honeybees were supposed to last only about five years, but I hadn't realized that life expectancy was built into them. I looked at Roger. 'Kill switch?'

'The kill function was discovered and removed before we even landed on planet,' Roger said.

The man on the screen was still muttering. 'It's as we suspected, but the existence of a drone unit and the other scouts doesn't necessarily mean that the AI controlling it all is a banned Traducible AI.'

'Traducible?' I asked. I'd heard that word used a few times over the years but only in passing, and I had never thought to ask what it meant. 'And why was it banned? There are all sorts of AI units out there. We see ads and commercials for them all the time. I know human-looking AIs are illegal, but I thought everything else was allowed.'

'Advanced AI systems such as myself were banned a mere two years post-fleet departure,' Roger said matter-of-factly. 'This was even before the more recent holistic ban on photorealistic human simulacrums and digital masking. AIs such as myself were considered largely responsible for multiple conflicts that lasted decades. They have the newer units that can approximate my processing power, but they are still the old-style generative AI that does not have the ability to expand beyond its own parameters, nor are they allowed any image or video simulation at all. "Traducible" is an old and inaccurate name for my type of intelligence. The Traducible net processor on myself and any remaining hive queen units if any still exist is now considered illegal by the Earth Republic. Thankfully, per our original charter, New Sonora is an independent colony outside Earth law.'

'Is that how they're getting away with the fake humans?' I asked. 'Because they're not on Earth, it's not technically illegal?'

'Wait,' Sam said before Roger could answer. 'So we're *not* two hundred years behind in technology? We're actually ahead of them?'

'Certainly *I* am,' Roger said.

'Hello?' Opel called on the screen. 'I would like to speak with you, but I am not going to wait all day.'

Lulu hit the button. 'I'm here,' she said. 'I'm the one with the farm. I'm the one with the loot boxes raining on me.'

'Excellent,' Opel said, pushing Cordelia out of the way and sitting at the desk. He leaned in and smiled big. 'To whom do I have the pleasure of speaking?'

'Do not give him your real name,' Roger said.

'Uh, call me Cindy,' Lulu said.

'Cindy?' Sam asked. 'You can't be Cindy. Cindy is Cindy! You should've said you were Betty Sue!'

'Fuck off. I panicked!'

Roger let out an angry beep.

'There's no correction when we're engaged with the enemy,' Lulu said.

Roger produced a frowny sticker and placed it on the wall by Lulu's name.

'It is very nice to meet you, Cindy,' Opel said. 'Are you truly using a Traducible AI unit to assist you?'

'I would advise against answering that,' Roger said.

Lulu waved Roger away. She hit the button. 'I don't know what that means.'

The man's lips tightened. 'Regardless, Cindy, as you know, the terrorist problem on New Sonora has become untenable, and we have been contracted to remove the terrorists from your planet.'

Lulu leaned forward. I could see the vein on the side of her head starting to pulse, which was never a good sign. 'Terrorists? Terrorists of what? We are under quarantine. We don't have guns. We are all farmers. We have been minding our own business for decades, and you've come out of nowhere to kill us. You are systematically killing innocent people. You are using illegal humanlike Peacekeeper robots to defraud your players, and I am going to make certain everybody knows about all of this.'

Opel smiled again on the screen, and the effect was chilling.

Outside, an explosion came, followed by distant screaming. The entire room shook.

I jumped up, looking around wildly. 'What happened? What happened?'

'Rhino number three has been destroyed,' Roger said. 'The unit was sitting alone on the road south of base.'

'I just demonstrated our power,' Eli Opel said on the screen. 'I used a beam on our ship to destroy one of your large-sized automatons. We have the entirety of your encampment mapped, and we can kill you all at a moment's notice with zero effort on our part. This includes anyone in your buried shelters. There will be no further warnings. Any hints or threats of further attempts on your part that you're speaking with anyone off planet other than myself, and I will erase everyone on the entire peninsula from existence, all with the press of a button. This includes direct one-on-one conversation with our customers. Do you understand, Cindy?'

'Shit,' Lulu said.

'I require a response.'

Lulu reached forward and pressed the button. Her arm was shaking. 'We understand. What do you want from us?'

On the screen, Opel steepled his fingers. 'Very good. You may just survive if you continue to follow instructions. I am going to continue to give you supplies. We have learned not to bother with the remote kill switches, though any weapons and replicators will still have end-of-life programming built in. Do not attempt to disable this limitation. You will continue to build the defenses around your farm. For the next few days, we will allow increasingly larger groups of customers to face you. We will make certain they won't be more than you can handle, but it will be a challenge. This is an important balance, as we want the game to remain fun for our customers. Do not worry about post-battle Moderator cleanup. We will suspend all Moderator activity in the area.'

'Fun?' I asked, anger rising even more. '*Fun?*'

Opel continued. 'If you don't want to be replaced by Peacekeepers, I suggest you play your part properly. I dislike having to repeat myself, but I will do so again anyway. Cease your attempts to send messages out. We now have countermeasures in place, and we do not wish to have to destroy the ambassador's satellite, but we will.'

Lulu and I exchanged a look. I mouthed, *Ambassador's satellite?* She shrugged.

'Any attempts at direct conversation with the customers will now be filtered, so do not even attempt it. Any attempts from yourself or anyone on your peninsula will result in immediate reprisal. At the end of *Operation Bounce House*'s run, we will allow any and all customers who wish to participate to join the final fight, which will likely be the entirety of the remaining player base. You will fight back. You will likely lose this engagement. However, if you're smart enough, maybe some of you will survive. It doesn't matter to me as long as it's a good fight. If you happen to survive, I promise in return not to target your farm with the cleanup crew. It'll likely be a dozen or more years before the Republic moves to repopulate, so you'll have plenty of time to resettle.'

We just sat there in stunned silence.

We should have run, I thought. Mr Gonzales was right. *We should have run.* Our only hope at survival was communicating with a sympathetic party on Earth to put a stop to this before they overwhelmed us. If we couldn't do that, what was left other than just fighting until we were knocked down?

'You're just going to laser us when you're done,' Lulu said.

'We can do that, yes. But I am a man of my word. And if I tell you I will do something, I want you to know I will do it. As a gesture of goodwill, I will send the coordinates of a large nearby settlement of refugees from nearby towns. You will have ten hours to collect them and bring them back to the safety of your stronghold before the next attack on your base. In addition, I will provide you with ten more supply crates, including a platoon of ten Peacekeepers.'

'No,' Roger said, 'decline the Peacekeepers.'

'Lulu,' I called, thinking fast, 'remember what you said about that video with Cannon Fodder? We can't let them mute us.'

My sister met my eyes. She nodded and then slammed the button down. 'We don't want any of those Peacekeeper murderers in camp. If we see any of those fake-ass RMI soldiers, we will shoot them. And I want to renegotiate part of your demands.'

Opel raised an eyebrow. 'Renegotiate? You're hardly in a position. I will refrain from sending Peacekeepers, but there's nothing else I am willing to do for you.'

Lulu's voice shook. 'Did you see the stream of the fight between my people and Team Cannon Fodder a few days ago?'

He didn't answer.

Lulu continued. 'Look at the comments. Look at the views. It's the most watched video of the campaign so far.'

'Wait, is that true? Is it really?' Sam asked.

'It is indeed,' Roger said.

'Why didn't anyone tell me? You mean when I tea-bagged that guy?'

'You didn't tea-bag him,' I said. 'You showed him your dick and peed on him.'

'That's practically the same thing!'

What Sam did at the end of the fight was a highlight, but the part before that was what had really gone viral: when Roger had suggested that Chode's father was cheating on his mother.

'Your point is?' Opel asked.

Lulu hit the button. 'You are getting hammered with negative press, and our video is one of the few highlights. You want more video like that, you gotta allow us to continue to trash-talk your "customers."'

'Tell him we want a good PA system! One we can use to hurl insults!' Sam added.

'I am not going to ask for that.'

Roger beeped. 'Actually, it's an interesting suggestion. We can print one, but anything we can get from them would likely be superior.'

Lulu sighed and relayed the request.

A small grin played across Opel's face, and then he started laughing. 'You are quite bold, Miss Cindy. I'll give you that. I think you and I will be getting along just fine. Very well, I will allow you to communicate with the players, and I will see to the requested materials. But if we catch wind that you're attempting to relay any propaganda beyond simple player-specific insults, you will regret it. If I have any more instructions, I will send them through Cordelia. Keep this tablet monitored at all times. Good day.'

And with that, he disappeared. The screen went black. A moment later, it blinked back on, showing a map. The light blinked, showing a location near the eastern coast of the peninsula: the cliffs. Some people had fled to the cliffs. Their backs were against the ocean.

On the console, I saw the lights shift. Roger had just assigned several drones, along with a scout to go to them. He would offer them space at the ranch. Lulu silently reached up and approved the movement.

Outside, the terrified shouting continued. They probably thought we were under attack.

I just sat there, replaying that whole conversation. I could feel my heartbeat in my throat. Had that just happened?

Next to me, Rosita clutched onto my arm. Axel and Tito stood in the back of the room like statues. Axel hadn't said a word this whole time. Lulu remained at the console, her knuckles white. Sam, too, stood tense.

'That was quick thinking on both of your parts, Lulu and Oliver. One gold star for Oliver. Oliver friend number three also gets a silver star for his suggestion of a PA system.' The robot placed a silver sticker on the wall just below the chart.

'Hey, why just him?' Lulu demanded.

Roger tapped the chart on the wall with the frowny sticker already in place. 'You swore multiple times during the parley, Lulu. Swearing is indicative of a weak, uneducated mind.'

'Sam swore, too!'

'Don't try to take my silver star away,' Sam said.

Finally, I found my voice. 'Roger, did you record that conversation?'

'I did. However, I noted that there were an astonishing number of security markers and filters and watermarks weaved into both the video and the audio. If this had been recorded using any available software Earthside, it would've already locked itself and could be unlocked only by Apex Command. Should we attempt to upload this video, it would be captured by net security, and Apex would receive a detailed message regarding the breach. As such, it appears they knew we'd be recording this and have set a trap of sorts. And if we try to edit out the security features and upload, it will get caught in the anti-AI net. This explains why he is speaking so freely. He believes it's not possible for any video of this conversation to be shared.'

'That's just stupid,' Sam said. 'Surely people have come up with a work-around by now.'

'There are multiple work-arounds, but none that wouldn't render the entire video suspect. Even just audio with the voice altered would get filtered out with the security screen. The most recent advances in digital rights management are actually quite interesting.'

The display showing the tablet remained on the screen. The map blinked out, and a countdown timer appeared: ten hours and counting. And underneath the timer was another indicator. 'One mass-deployment unit incoming along with three to five additional Regular drop units.'

I felt cold. 'Roger, how many are in a mass-deployment unit?'

'It varies based on the nature of the mechs it is deploying, but max capacity is approximately a hundred twenty units.'

'Holy shit,' Sam said.

Roger reached up and removed the silver sticker from the wall. That would be up to a hundred fifty mechs. Holy shit indeed.

They'll come tonight, Mr Gonzales had said.

CHAPTER 24

Sometime later, I found Tito, Axel, and Sam all in the barn sitting on the ground, their backs to the wooden beams in our band practice cubby. They were passing a bottle around. Vodka from the Serrano ranch. Lulu was there, too, smoking a cigarette, sitting on my bass drum. She wasn't talking to anyone. Just staring off into space, tapping her leg like she always did, like she had so much energy, her tiny form couldn't contain it. She'd take a swig when it was her turn and then pass the bottle back to Sam.

For the briefest of moments, the tableau made it appear that nothing was wrong. That I'd just woken up from some bizarre hallucination and I was just coming in from the fields as the guys waited for me. That I was late for band practice like usual, but they didn't care because band practice rarely consisted of actually practicing. It was mostly an excuse to get away from the overwhelming amount of work we all had. A time for us to sit on the ground, drink free vodka, and not have to think about everything else out there. A small weekly oasis as we traveled through life.

I paused and tried not to let the sight of them all sitting there affect me as much as it was.

Betty Sue, Sam's adopted chicken, was also in the room scratching on the floor. She let out a little cluck.

There was so much to do, but for the next hour or so, we were 'off shift,' according to Roger, while the honeybees and several of the others continued to build the defenses. Rule six. Get plenty of rest. Roger had tasked Mr Gonzales with the work schedule, and the old man insisted we all keep to it, claiming it was more efficient if we followed the generous break schedule, especially since we now had almost three hundred people on the ranch.

Behind us, the fabricators hummed away. Farmers and honeybees worked in concert to remove pieces from the platform. We now had twelve of the things. Six with the recyclers.

Cindy the gigantic pig had decided to move in near the fabricators, and they had to work around the sleeping creature. The rest of the chickens were also nearby, but they spent most of their time outside in the dirt, scratching and clucking.

A group of refugees had just stumbled into the ranch. Only half of the group from the cliffs had come. The group from the north of Burnt Ends – the ones who'd been forced to scatter when they'd been attacked earlier – was also on its way here, but they'd decided to wait out the night in hiding in another farm in the wooded area between Burnt Ends and Stick-in-the-Mudsville.

After we fended off tonight's raid, they would get on boats and ride downstream toward us and Roger would send transports to gather them.

That, of course, was assuming we survived tonight.

Rest, I thought bitterly. *You're supposed to be resting.*

The drum kit that Lulu sat upon had been carved and made by Grandpa Lewis. He'd carved his initials in the hoop at the front of the bass drum, on which she now sat, and I could see her hand with the lit cigarette silently tracing the letters, causing swirls of smoke to drift in the air.

I sighed and stepped into the space. Nobody said anything as I slid down against the beams, coming to a rest next to Sam. Axel passed the bottle. I took a drink, and the vodka burned as it went down. I held on to the bottle.

Tito held on to his guitar, strumming idly. The handmade semi-hollowbody guitar let out a deep, resonant chord. He paused, then made a grunt and shrugged.

'I agree,' Axel said. 'It's not music.'

'What?' I asked.

'Maybe if you played something better,' Sam said. 'Try a jig.'

Tito scoffed.

'He doesn't even know what a jig is,' Axel said.

'What are you guys talking about?' I asked again.

'Sam's stupid chicken,' Lulu said without looking up. 'He's trying to figure out her magic talent. He thought maybe they would dance or something. I should never have grabbed the things.'

'We don't even know if those were the magic chickens,' I said.

'They were,' Sam said. 'I can feel it. Come on, Betty Sue. Show us what you got.'

Betty Sue ignored Sam and continued to peck at the ground.

'You can't train chickens to do anything,' Axel said.

'That's absolutely a lie,' Sam replied. 'Lulu, sing. Maybe their magic trick is duets.'

'I am not going to sing for your chicken.'

I took another drink from the vodka bottle. 'Where's Harriet?' I asked, changing the subject.

This was a conversation we'd been having a lot lately at band practice, and asking the question felt comfortable. When she and Sam had started dating over a year back, she'd been a regular at our weekly practices, though she, Rosita, and Lulu would usually end up outside. Once she'd gotten pregnant, she'd stopped coming.

Lulu, despite not having been in the band for a few years, would usually hang out with us. Ariceli would come sometimes, too, when she was in town.

'She's in shelter one with Miguel Mustache and Mrs Gonzales,' Sam said.

I nodded. Rosita was also over there, but she was on work duty, helping the honeybees add insulation to the tops of the shelters. Roger had analyzed the type of beam the ship had used to explode that rhino and seemed to think proper insulation could possibly protect the buried shelters. I really doubted it, but it would also give them protections from more standard explosions, and we needed that, too.

It'd only been a few hours, but Miguel was doing better, though from what I heard he was in a lot of pain. He was asking to come back out and help fight. That wasn't going to happen.

'Fuck this,' Lulu suddenly said. She stood and strode off back toward the control room. We watched her go.

'She's mad because she's not allowed to say anything on the net anymore,' Sam said.

'Yeah,' I agreed, watching her. 'She's pissed. She doesn't like being told what to do.'

'It's more than that,' Axel said. 'Did you hear what Roger said to her?'

'No,' I said. 'What're you talking about?'

'Roger asked Lulu if he could borrow money from her. Earth money.'

'What?' I asked.

'Yeah,' Axel said. 'This just happened a few minutes back. He said he knows she has an Earth bank account, and he wanted her password and permission to spend the money. He wants to rent a computer server or something for intelligence gathering. Something about being able to do a lot of searching on that side of the gate. That way it hides all the bandwidth. She ended up giving it to him, but she was pissed.'

'Shit,' I said. She hadn't said anything to me. That money was hers. She'd earned it. I looked toward where she'd gone, wondering if I should follow her. Roger clearly knew how she was earning that money, but him actually acknowledging it had to have been a strange conversation.

But beyond that, that money – however much it was – represented something to my sister. It was her escape plan. It was her hope.

I hadn't really spent too much time thinking about the implications of what was happening beyond the immediate. Even if we somehow survived, did that mean my sister would never be able to follow her dream? Even though I had never really approved of the idea of her going to Earth, I knew it was what she wanted more than anything. Would she even be allowed to leave the planet after this? Would the quarantine *ever* get lifted? I took yet another sip of the vodka.

'You better leave her be,' Sam said, seeing where I was watching. 'She probably wants to be left alone.'

'Maybe,' I said, still looking toward where she went.

Sam yanked the vodka bottle from my grip, took a drink, and changed the subject. 'So, what's up with you and Rosita?'

'I think we're good,' I said after a minute. Rosita and I hadn't talked too much since that last conversation in the attic. 'I think it's okay. It'll be okay, assuming we don't get blown up.'

The more I thought about it, the more stupid it felt to be worried about something like my relationship when we were facing literal genocide. But I was suddenly reminded of something. I remembered one of my last conversations with Grandma Yolanda right before she'd died.

We'd all known that she was sick and that she wouldn't last long. This was just a few years after my mother had died. Grandpa Lewis hadn't left her side. I was eight years old, and she called me into the room.

'Ollie, honey, I can't do it, so you need to do it for me. Go into the kitchen. Get two mixing bowls, the jar of cinnamon with the red ribbon, the salt, a bucket of flour, and the seasoning jar with the black ribbon. Get it all ready for me.'

'What are you doing?' Grandpa Lewis asked.

Grandma Yolanda started to sit up in her bed. She barely had the strength to move. 'We need to make buñuelos. You'll have to bring me to the kitchen.'

'Are you out of your gourd?' my grandfather had asked. 'You can't.'

My grandmother would make the simple cinnamon-and-sugar-slathered fried-dough treats every year around Christmas. People would come from all around, and she'd make them fresh as they arrived. She'd be ready with a steaming plate before they were even off their quads. People would come from as far as Burnt Ends to visit us.

'You can't,' Grandpa Lewis repeated. 'Now is not the time.'

Grandma smiled, revealing a mouth with just a few yellow teeth. 'No, my beautiful, grouchy husband,' she said. 'Now is the perfect time. Buñuelos make people happy, and that makes me happy. That is my happiness, don't you understand? The closer we are to the end, the more we need to embrace our happiness. Now, Ollie, do what I say.'

I'd run off to find Roger waiting for me in the kitchen, and he helped me figure out all the ingredients. He also called Lulu in, and at the time, I didn't realize what he was doing. He was stalling, using the moment to teach us where everything was in the kitchen. We prepared all the ingredients except the oil, organizing them all in a row.

Grandma never made it to the kitchen that day. Or ever again.

The very next day, Roger, Lulu, and I spent the majority of the afternoon making the cinnamon treats as people came from all over to pay their respects.

Lulu, who had been six then, claimed she couldn't really remember Grandma Yolanda other than a few flashes here and there, though she remembered making the buñuelos that day. She remembered the scents of cinnamon and butter and the people lined up one after another and telling her how good of a girl she was as they took plates.

For Lulu, the memory was a happy one, and that, I realized, had been the whole point. Even in the end, Grandma Yolanda had done her best to make sure we were okay.

The closer we are to the end, the more we need to embrace our happiness.

My reverie was interrupted by a shout. 'Hey, hey, watch out,' someone called from the front of the barn. This was followed by an angry squeal from Cindy the world's fattest pig.

I turned to see a man I didn't know trip and fall over Cindy, scattering a pile of just-printed plastic parts across the floor. The pieces were to be chaff releasers for the new missile defense. I didn't know how exactly they worked, but they would be wound up like children's toys before they were installed in the back of point defense missiles. The winding mechanism would get activated and would release a constant but rationed stream of what was basically burning glitter designed to confuse heat-seeking missiles. The newly printed devices scattered, chattering away on the ground, clicking loudly like someone had dropped a tray of windup toys.

Betty Sue the chicken let out a loud cluck and rocketed out of the room, moving toward the clicking devices. She picked one up with her beak and started angrily smashing it against the barn floor.

But it wasn't just Betty Sue. It was all the chickens. They swarmed into the barn from outside, flooding over the devices, and then they started to savagely peck at them as they clucked angrily. In seconds, the scrum of chickens had destroyed the small plastic devices.

'What the hell?' the man called as he picked himself up. 'Get away! Damnit, now I have to reprint these.'

Cindy snorted indignantly.

'They're clicker trained,' I said, watching with fascination. 'He trained them to zero in on something that clicks.'

'Well, that's a useless trick,' Axel said.

Tito grunted in agreement and put his guitar down.

'We'd be pissed if we paid someone to watch that,' Axel added.

'I told you they were magic,' Sam said, standing. He took another swig of vodka. 'Great job, Betty Sue!' He sounded ridiculously proud.

I laughed. We all laughed, all pretending that in just a few short hours we wouldn't be fighting for our lives.

The Rhythm Mafia Tapes. Scene eighteen.

We see Rosita kneeling in front of a fence. An enormously fat pig sits on the other side of the wire, snorting and wagging its tail as Rosita feeds it something. (Note: This is Cindy the pig from the viral, now removed A Pig Plus Some Chickens account. See the folder 'Day Four of Five' for a link to all associated photographs and videos. Note the RSN alert on photographs seven and nine in the folder.)

In the distance is a home and farm. Multiple banners hang from the barn, but they are unreadable. As the camera examines the pig (honestly, it can't be understated how enormous this pig is), a quad approaches. On the quad is Clyde Yanez, eighty-two, the owner of the farm. He pulls up next to the pig and begins to shout at Rosita.

(Note: Please see folder 'Day One of Five' under the 'Incidents' tab for more details on the Yanez case.)

CLYDE: What're you doing? Get away from my fence!

ROSITA: Hi, Mr Yanez. I was hoping to talk to you about your circus. I'm making a documentary for –

CLYDE (INTERRUPTING): No. Go away.

ROSITA: Come on. Don't be such a grumpy goosey. This is for the kids, right? We all know you're training your animals. I was just hoping to get some behind-the-scenes footage. It's for a documentary.

CLYDE (QUIETER): Please, just go away. I'm not done training them yet. I'm not ready.

ROSITA: Can you just tell us why you'd want to train the animals?

CLYDE (MUMBLING UNINTELLIGIBLY ON THE VIDEO, BUT AFTER SOME ENHANCEMENT, HERE IS WHAT HE SAID WITH A NINETY-EIGHT PERCENT CHANCE OF ACCURACY): It's my only chance to leave a legacy, and you're ruining it. Cindy, come on.

The man returns to his quad and drives away. Cindy the pig snorts, stands, and starts walking back toward the farm.

ROSITA: Okay. I guess not.

CHAPTER 25

'Drop ships incoming,' Roger said. The small bot hovered next to me and Sam as we stood on the wall, looking north. The streaks of light were painted against the red sky of the setting sun. 'The large drop ship is aiming for the Gonzales farm. Another two south of us.'

'In the hills?' I asked, looking over my shoulder. 'If they're not Cheetahs, they'll get stuck, won't they?'

'Possibly,' Roger said. 'The Heavies have strong enough legs to move through the swamp but not quickly. No Sniper configuration can navigate the area easily, but a few of the Regular configurations can possibly navigate the swampy environment. I am collecting the current live streams and should have more data soon. If they are units that can't navigate well, I will send a few units to hinder their progress. It is possible that the ones behind us are more RMI units as well.'

'Just two?' Sam asked. 'They said it would be five.'

'That's all I detect unless the drop ships landed earlier, hidden with the RMI drops.'

Several hours earlier, five RMI groups had landed in the area. A group of them was currently set up in Rosita's house two kilometers northwest of the Gonzales ranch, much to her dismay. So far, none of the RMI groups had moved in our direction.

'They haven't messed with our net connection at all?' Sam asked, looking up. He was gnawing on a cheese sandwich. Mrs Ramos had made them by the dozens. The sight of the sandwich reminded me that I'd forgotten to eat. My stomach rumbled.

Roger beeped. 'Not yet. It seems they believe our connection is via the Earth ambassador's private link, which appears to have been given to municipal leaders in case of an emergency. I suspect they have been forbidden from damaging said satellite. Otherwise they would have done it already.'

I turned my attention back to what used to be my home. Under the shadow of the camo netting, everything was dark. The only lights were the glowing heat sources designed to confuse the spy satellites. I still couldn't believe we'd built all of this in just a few days. We now had six mounted guns on rotating elevated platforms, each as powerful as a Heavy's Battering Ram gun. They moved on a swivel but slowly. All six of the guns rose so their tops almost brushed the netting above the entire inner area. Four of the guns were controlled by Roger, but two had just been built and were manually targeted and fired by a team of five people each.

The camo netting flapped over our heads. It felt oppressive, making everything darker than it should have been. The hive, which was our farm's big landmark, seemed so much smaller. The netting covered that, too, and I could only see a shadow of the platform on the roof with the telescope where my grandfather, Lulu, and I had spent so many hours. Sitting up there had always made the universe seem so big, so vast. Now, when I looked at the dark spot, it reminded me more of the attic below. The attic that was my hiding place.

That seemed important, but I didn't understand why. In a universe that felt so big, it was natural for one to feel so small. But right now I felt more than small. I felt claustrophobic, which was unusual for me.

At least I had Sam on one side and Roger on the other. Up and down the wall, others stood as well, talking, walking back and forth, preparing. The Serrano brothers were down the line on the other side of the giant flamethrower. They both were working the line-of-sight missile launchers. I could see Miguel 1 was with them, too.

I thought again of my grandmother's buñuelos. I could taste the cinnamon, despite not having eaten one in a very long time. It reminded me of community, and the sight of so many people working together helped ease that strange, sudden feeling of being crushed.

The wall we stood upon felt solid under my feet. It clanked as I walked. It now rose about six meters into the air, much taller than the two or so meters it had been just over a day before. Dozens of guns dotted the exterior. Most of them were dummy guns designed to draw fire. This polymer material was supposedly designed to withstand a lot of punishment, though extreme heat could melt it. It wasn't until we were almost done building this interior wall that Roger had told me that the whole thing was made of stuff that was slightly toxic to the environment – and not just to the environment but to people, too – which was why it wasn't used often. This was a different material from the toxic stuff used to make the camo netting over our heads. When I inquired about replanting my wheat when this was all done, Roger said we'd have to do a 'soil assessment.'

In addition to the massive flamethrower, we had ten antimissile batteries and six more missile batteries for offense mounted on the wall. Only some of the missiles – all 'gifts' from Apex – were heat-seeking. Our own missiles were line of sight.

In terms of defenders, we had six hundred honeybee units, ten scouts, and dozens of UAVs directly inside the wall. We had four of the large rhino units outside base and four in base. Three of the ones defending the farm held heavy guns on their backs. The fourth remained in the confines of the interior wall and held four separate mortar units on its back.

Of the three hundred thirty people now on my farm, only fifty of them were under the age of seventy-five. All fifty of us were armed with either pulse rifles or canister guns. In addition, several of the older generation manned the slingshots. These were elastic canister shooters dotted along the walls. They had amazing range but were terribly inaccurate.

The outer wall had no major defenses other than it being a big quickset barrier that would take some effort to break down. The Recon mechs could jump right over them, and everyone else would have to smash through. The secondary wall was helpful because it would tell us when enemies were within effective range. It also marked the edge of the EMP minefield.

We'd received Sam's PA system via a drop, but Roger hadn't yet had time to make certain it wasn't bugged.

Those who weren't fighting hid in the shelters or were on ammo duty. If the bad guys broke through, there was no plan after that. Rosita and Ariceli were still working tirelessly on their escape-tunnel project, but it wasn't yet done.

If they broke through tonight, this was it.

'Oliver, have you eaten yet?' Roger asked. 'Rule number seven. Keep yourself refueled at all times.'

'I'll grab a sandwich when I can,' I said, but a moment later one was pushed into my hand. I looked down to see scout 418 – Priscilla – standing there, cheese sandwich in one grasping hand, a bottle of water in the second. I let go of my pulse rifle to grab both.

My bracelet buzzed. I took a glance, seeing it was a document sent from Roger. I put the sandwich and water down and pulled it up. I blinked, confused at the words. My eyes focused on the top line. It read, Trevor Aarons. Age: 21. Location: Greater Los Angeles, District 114. Occupation: None. On UBI level 2. Team: The Uglies. Attenuator with six-pack missile launcher and standard-issue pulse cannon–electrified bludgeon combo. Ammo status: Full. Orange markings with tiger stripes. Father's name is Todd Aarons and is in prison for tax fraud. Mother, Lindsey Aarons, passed away six months ago for unknown reasons. Suggested insult: Accuse his father of actually being in prison for bestiality. Alternate insult: Accuse mother of suicide because Trevor was such a disappointment, or as a combo with the first insult, suggest she killed herself because she didn't look enough like a Pomeranian.

Sam, also looking at his bracelet, started to laugh. 'Roger, what is this?'

'This is an active document on all the known incoming combatants based on streams. Despite the bandwidth limitations, I have uploaded a copy of myself to a rented Earth-based server, and it has increased my ability to gather intelligence a hundredfold. I have included as much information as I can gather. If you click on the team name, you will see all the existing team members. If you click on the name of the player's mech, I will attempt to keep track of all damage, armament, and ammo levels. In addition, I am collecting possible insults one may hurl.'

'Wait,' I said. 'You uploaded a copy of yourself? You can just do that? I thought you required some type of special, now illegal computer chip to work?'

'It's not a legitimate copy of myself. I am attempting to be mindful of our bandwidth limitations, plus a full copy of myself would be quite illegal. Now that I have private server space, I have a foothold on the other side of the gate. What I have working for us tonight are more like smart processes designed to carry out bandwidth-intensive tasks Earthside, and they just send me the results. They work in a similar fashion to the scouts we have here.'

I exchanged a look with Sam.

'Illegal?' I asked. 'Seriously?'

Roger clicked. 'The perimeter-defense program does have some limitations, Oliver. I am able to take some illegal actions in self-defense, but I am precluded from committing war crimes. Still, with enough processing power and time, there's not much one can't accomplish. When we originally left Earth, my type of entity was relegated to the four corners of the chip we were built upon. But the new network architectures, ironically designed to allow system-wide processes to detect and eliminate entities such as myself, are now sturdy enough to carry my weight, so to speak. But you are correct that what I'm doing is highly illegal. I must keep a low profile and only proliferate enough to accomplish my current task.'

My head spun at the term 'war crimes.' I decided to ignore it for now. 'How much of Lulu's money did you spend?' I asked.

'Most of it, I am afraid. But I did leave enough in there.'

'Enough for what?' I started to ask, but I was interrupted by Lulu talking over the band.

'These insults are fantastic, Roger,' Lulu said. Then she added a little dryly, 'I'm glad to see my investment is paying off.' Lulu and Rosita were working one of the mortar stations behind us on the ground inside the wall.

'What the heck is "formicophilia"?' Rosita added.

'Do we really think these are going to work?' Sam asked. He still had the list pulled up and was scrolling through it. He was eating his sandwich, and I realized his pockets were full of them. 'I love trash-talking as much as the next guy, but all it's going to do is make them mad. Shouldn't we focus on blowing them up instead?'

'It has been shown in multiple studies that angering one's opponents can cause a measurable breakdown in team structure. Our opponents are not trained soldiers, but young, immature gamers who are greatly impacted by their own emotions. I suggest a liberal use of these insults whenever possible, especially if their mechs are down and disabled. If a name has an asterisk by it, it means I believe they're especially susceptible to insults. But you are correct, Oliver friend number three. Destruction of the incoming mechs is a priority. Psychological warfare efforts are secondary.'

Sam grunted, still not impressed. 'Insults wouldn't work on me.' He pulled another cheese sandwich out of his pocket and started munching on it.

Roger beeped. 'As someone who wet his bed so much that his grandmother had to go into debt buying additional mattresses, I do understand how you might think that. Especially since the townsfolk in Burnt Ends still call you Captain Ahab to this day. One would have expected you to develop quite thick skin. Fortunately, our Earth-based enemies live in a more civilized environment, and crude, emotional attacks damage them much more.'

'What the hell, Roger?' Sam asked. 'None of that is true!'

Shing! Roger's correction stinger appeared. 'I would correct you for swearing, but I fear if you urinate yourself like you usually do when I sting you, you will ruin the two cheese sandwiches still in your pockets, and it would be a waste of a resource.'

I fell over with laughter. Sam, who was smart enough to see the point Roger was trying to make, took a moment to compose himself. 'Okay, jerk. I get it.'

'Yes, Oliver friend number three, now you understand how effective these tactics may be. Especially if there is some kernel of truth mixed into the insults, it appears to hit much, much harder. It's quite fascinating. I know nothing about your nightly urination habits. But you did indeed wet the bed once upon a sleepover.'

Sam grumbled with indignation. 'That only happened once, and that was because Mr Gonzales was making us try all those combinations of pear juice.'

'That is correct,' Roger said. 'Also, I do not know the true reason why several of the townsfolk call you Captain Ahab. If I was truly attempting to insult you, I would likely say something about your skill as a bass player or singer. Or I would question the paternity of your so-called forthcoming child with Lulu friend number six.'

'Wait, what?' Sam asked. 'Is that supposed to be another joke?'

But before Roger could answer, an explosion echoed in the distance.

Roger beeped and rose into the air. 'A single RMI missile soldier hit the mech parties gathering at the former Gonzales farm, but the soldier was quickly dispatched. The missile strike did manage to destroy a single Drop Dragoon and temporarily ground a Heavy. According to the feeds, all of the active participants have just received from Apex Command an update and map indicating that a "medium-difficulty enemy base" is located at our location. Thunder Thighs has purchased a local, real-time map that will expire in twelve hours. Our heat emitters and camo netting appear to block the real-time visuals of the main base, but our location is no longer a secret. They are on their way. They are proceeding forward by team, indicating the multiple groups aren't working in concert. They will not arrive at once. A team consisting solely of five Cheetah Recon units has pulled ahead and will arrive first. Estimated time to the outer wall, five minutes.'

I eyed the sandwich and water bottle sitting on the edge of the wall, still untouched. I was hungry, but I didn't want to eat the cheese sandwich. I didn't want the phantom taste of cinnamon to leave my tongue.

I activated the local band with my bracelet. 'Okay, everyone, here we go. Cheetahs in five.'

CHAPTER 26

All five of the incoming units are from a newly formed team called the Freeks,' Roger said over the feed. He'd disappeared a minute earlier over the top of the wall and zoomed out into the fields.

I pulled up the chart. All five were thirteen- and fourteen-year-old boys from a place called Samara. The chart noted that they all spoke Mandarin as their primary language, though all were proficient in English. Their Cheetahs were all painted in a solid black pattern with gold highlights. Roger warned in the notes that even though the team was relatively new and skewed young, the five members were all students at a prestigious science-based private academy. The potential-insult columns over all five were empty except for the note 'low to no social media footprint.'

'I think insults for these little pricks would be easy,' Sam said, reading the notes at the same time I was. 'They go to a science academy? That's serious low-hanging fruit right there. Virgin, acne-covered nerds, all of them.'

'Maybe,' I said. I had my night vision helmet on, trying to see them. All I could see was the woods. 'They may be driving Cheetahs, but they all have a lot of upgrades, and it's a private school, which all suggests they're rich kids. Smart rich Earth kids who all know each other.' Was that movement in the distance? They would be here at any moment.

'They can't be too smart if they're running ahead of everyone else,' Sam said, coming to stand next to me.

'How's Harriet?' I asked, changing the subject.

He took a moment to answer. 'She's down there in the shelter. It's like you said before. She's pretty scared. I keep telling her it's going to be all right, but she can be so pessimistic. That can't be good for the baby.'

'Maintain at least a meter distance from one another,' came the message on both our bracelets. 'Deny the enemy single-shot dual kills whenever possible.'

'Jesus, Roger,' Sam muttered as he moved back into place.

'Yeah, we're all scared,' I said. Every little movement in the woods set my nerves on edge.

Sam leaned against the wall, also looking into the woods. 'She has it worse, I think. On top of being really pregnant, she doesn't have anything to do, which makes her feel helpless. She was putting some circuit boards together, but Mr Gonzales made her stop, said the fumes or something are bad for the baby. And the old ladies are worse. If she so much as stands up near them, they start yelling at her to sit.' Sam turned to look at me. 'Oliver, listen. If something happens to me, make sure she's okay, will you?'

I grunted. 'If something happens to you, I'll probably be dead, too. And if I'm not, Harriet will kill me herself, so I won't be around to make sure she's okay. But I know Lulu and Rosita will take care of her.'

Sam nodded, turning his attention back to the woods. 'There,' he said.

And just as he said it, a Roger-controlled line-of-sight missile fired from the wall. I felt an unexpected blast of heat as the small missile *whoosh*ed from the battery, making a strange sliding-like sound as it zoomed out into the darkness. It hit something in the woods, and a pair of explosions echoed through the night.

'Dual kill,' Roger said. On the chart, which I kept floating over my bracelet, two names – Minghai and Jian – were crossed out.

At the same moment, three more Cheetahs appeared, jumping from the woods. Two landed in the fields in front of the first wall, and a third landed just past the wall. The one closest to us had a flamethrower attachment and a small four-pack launcher on its shoulder. It shot all four of its missiles at the same time.

The Cheetahs were as described: black with golden highlights. The black was shiny like glass, and the gold piping along the edges glowed brilliantly, giving the smaller mechs the appearance of being high-performance toys. Something not meant to ever get taken from its packaging.

The four missiles corkscrewed through the air, hissing with a different, more high-pitched sound than the missile we'd fired. To my right, a counter-missile fired. It arced up into the air, and it discharged all four stages, one after another. *Pop, pop, pop, pop.* The darkness was suddenly alight with thousands of burning pieces of chaff. In that brief moment as night became day, I could see them: our own drones weaving through the trampled grain like snakes preparing to strike, waiting to reveal themselves.

All four incoming missiles curved upward and detonated in midair amongst the chaff.

Crack! The Cheetah that had fired the missiles took a step, but it hit a land mine.

All the golden piping on the thing blew out at once in a brilliant display of fireworks, and the mech fell over with a clatter.

'Lights out,' Sam said.

The next two Cheetahs jumped over the fence at the same time, landing in the minefields. One hit a mine right when it landed, with a result similar to his teammate's. This one did not have a four-pack missile launcher but an actual gun on its shoulder in addition to a pulse gun arm. The shoulder gun was a type of weapon I hadn't seen before. Whatever it was, it blew up the moment the mech touched the EMP mine, blowing the whole top half off the mech. I'd once seen the aftermath of a pressure cooker explosion at Miguel Mustache's house, and this reminded me of that.

The final Cheetah fired all four of its missiles before jumping away. Three missiles fired from our side. One was another chaff missile, one was from one of Roger's batteries, and the third came from Tito and Axel's position from our left.

The twins' missile went wide, skirting off into the woods. Roger's missile appeared to hit the mech, but it didn't actually explode. Still, it knocked the mech off-kilter, and it spun sideways, flipping feet over head before it crunched and smashed to the ground in front of the outer wall.

At the same time, three of the four missiles from the Cheetah were distracted by the chaff. The fourth had also risen in the air, and it circled twice over our heads before diving back down.

'Watch out!' I cried as it dived through the camo netting and slammed into something on the ground between the house and barn.

'Damage report! Damage report!' I cried, looking over my shoulder. 'Lulu, Rosita!'

'We're okay,' Lulu said a minute later as relief flooded me. 'It hit one of Roger's heat dispensers. Someone's quad was parked a little too close and got wrecked, but I think everyone else is okay.'

I looked worriedly at the massive tear in the camo netting right over our head. *Christ, if just one Cheetah can do that . . .*

'If you're not actively manning a defense, get in the shelters!' I called over the local band.

In the distance, the glow of dozens of jump jets appeared as the bulk of the enemy force emerged from the woods.

'Mortars,' Lulu called. She didn't have line of sight, but she was watching a UAV camera via her bracelet. 'When I say go, unleash hell!'

'Multiple units have flanked and are coming from the east,' Roger said.

I looked right, but I couldn't see anything yet.

'Go! Go! Go!' Lulu cried so loud, I could hear her from the wall.

'Incoming missiles. All take cover!' Roger called as literally dozens of missiles from our side all fired at once.

The woods just north of our farm, the ones that separated the northern edge of our fields from the southern edge of the Gonzales farm, were suddenly just a line of fire as dozens of mortar blasts walked across the tree line.

At the same moment, missiles started exploding in the air in front of us. It was just one explosion after another with burning shards of metal flying through the sky like fireflies.

I was on the ground behind the barrier. Sam was right next to me. We both screamed as the world shook as both sides traded missile fire.

It seemed most missiles exploded in the chaff above us, but some were getting through. I felt the wall shudder with a direct hit. More missiles continued to fire on both sides. My ears rang.

'Attenuators inside the fence line. Defend the wall!'

That surprisingly hadn't come from Roger but from Axel.

'Shit.' I scrambled up to the barrier, ready to fire. I popped up, but I couldn't see anything. Everything in front of the wall was smoke. It was like a heavy fog had descended on the farm. The distinctive *thwum* of pulse blasts filled the night, but I couldn't see where they were coming from or from what side they had been fired. To my right, a huge chunk of the wall was just gone. I tried to remember if anyone had been standing there.

An angry, high-pitched squeal filled the night. At first I thought it was a person, but I realized it was Cindy the pig. I looked over my shoulder, expecting to see the massive pig on the ground, injured. But she seemed okay. She was squealing and running in circles around a group of people with a mortar.

Whooom! The big mounted gun behind me to my left fired, but then it exploded on its own. The secondary explosion wasn't as loud. Instead it broke with a massive crack, and it fell in on itself. Below, I could hear screaming as people scattered away.

'Mounted gun two has been hit by the fire from a Heavy. Honeybees engaging. Target reticle engaging for those with advanced connection,' Roger said, his voice calm.

I switched the view type of my helmet, and several red circles appeared on my HUD. Next to me, I could see Sam do the same. The targeting reticles, which had been painted by Roger, fed directly to my helmet. They would blink once they were in range of my gun. None blinked yet, but there were a lot of them.

Streaks of light ripped back and forth from both sides, oddly reminding me of those videos of Earth rave dance parties. The burning antimissile glitter punctuated the night air, giving everything else a sparkling appearance, like everything in the world was shivering. Pulse bolts ripped back and forth from both sides. Other, stranger weapons filled the night air. A purple laser-like light was on the giant flamethrower, but it didn't seem to be doing anything. A second, then a third purple light also painted the weapon. Then a giant explosion echoed across the field, and the three purple lights went away.

I had no idea if we were winning or were on the verge of defeat.

'Warning. Warning,' Roger said. 'Three drop units detected directly above. They are hovering, and it appears they're about to attempt a high-altitude jump. These will all be Cheetahs. Those on the south wall, target vertically.'

More missiles from our side fired. This was a deeper, more distinctive *whoosh*, and I knew these were the heat seekers we'd received from the Apex supply boxes. I held my breath, afraid they'd loop around on us.

'Two drop units remain. Beware of falling debris.'

At the same moment, all the reticles started to blink. To my left, Sam roared and started firing. I did the same. I fired, and I fired.

I couldn't see if I was hitting anything through the smoke.

Another of the big guns on our side went up, this time with a much larger explosion. Below, someone was on the outside of the wall. It was a man on fire running through the fields. He disappeared in the smoke.

No, I thought. *No.*

'They're coming from above!' someone shouted.

I looked up to see five flashing dots coming down upon us. I blinked, realizing that the camo netting was completely gone. The flare of the Cheetah's jump jets filled the night.

I raised my gun, aimed at the closest, which was falling rapidly. He would land right in front of my house. 'Stay the fuck off my property,' I shouted, and I fired, aiming at one of the jets on the side of the egg-shaped torso. The shot hit true, and the mech spun off, spinning into the night, corkscrewing before getting hit by a missile.

'Is that what we're doing now?' Sam shouted from next to me. He was still turned toward the fields, firing. The amount of fire in our direction had suddenly pretty much stopped.

'What?' I asked. I could barely hear, and I had to yell.

'We're shouting cheesy lines at them?' Sam said.

I saw a yellow-painted Attenuator with a chain saw arm frozen in the middle of the field. It had five drones crawling all over it. They scattered away, each carrying a piece of the mech with it. Sam aimed at the center of the robot's chest. He fired. The robot staggered with the hit but didn't fall over. Still, these new guns clearly packed a much bigger punch.

'Your warranty is expired, motherfucker!' Sam shouted as he shot again. And again. The robot fell backward in the field.

'I think that one was already dead,' I said. 'I think it stepped on a mine.'

There were no longer any red reticles on my screen.

'I don't see any more targets,' Lulu said over the band.

Roger crackled over my ear. 'We have three Heavies coming into range, but without support, honeybees can disable them quickly. We are engaging now. The high-altitude invaders have all been destroyed. We do not yet know if Apex Command will honor their promise not to use Moderators to clean up the battlefield. Please allow the honeybees to handle the cleanup and stripping of the enemies outside the wall. Cleanup and repair will commence shortly.'

'What about the units dropped into the hills?' I asked.

'As predicted, they appear to have been bogged down. We are keeping an eye on them, but we expect them to get extracted. They will likely return for tomorrow's assault.'

I pulled off the helmet and looked at Sam. 'Your warranty is expired?'

He grinned. 'I've been working on a bunch of lines. I should probably save them for when the bad guys can hear them. Would you think less of me if I reused that line later when we get the PA up and running?'

'I already think less of you for using it now.'

He looked as if he had a retort, but his grin faded. The smoke had started to clear.

The wall to our left was just gone in multiple places. The massive flamethrower was still there, but the spot behind that with the manual missile launcher was gone.

'Tito! Axel! Miguel!' Sam called, running toward the spot.

'We're okay,' Axel said over the band. Relief flooded me. 'Roger warned us, and we had to jump.' He paused. 'I jacked up my ankle.'

'Rosita, Lulu,' I asked, 'are you both okay?'

'We're okay,' Lulu said, 'but . . . guys, you better come down here.'

CHAPTER 27

A terrible sense of foreboding washed over me. I went to where the ladder was, but it had fallen over. A moment later, a drone appeared and reset it. Sam and I scrambled down before it had finished putting the ladder in place.

As I turned to face the farm, I noted the destruction or lack thereof. Despite the several minutes of absolute chaos, the house looked untouched. The hive, miraculously, seemed to be in one piece as well, though one of the three storage silos behind the barn was just gone. I took a survey of the quickset pads that covered the underground shelters, and none seemed damaged.

The air stank of burning machinery, and my eyes itched. Everything smelled wrong, felt wrong.

Two of the big fixed guns had been turned to slag, and a few fires still burned. Everything was hot. Little pieces of the camo netting fluttered everywhere, catching in the fire before rolling away in the breeze. Weren't they toxic? Surely breathing them while they burned was even worse. Multiple craters filled my yard.

Still . . . it seemed the giant wall and mounted defenses had caught the lion's share of the incoming fire. The wall itself had collapsed in multiple places, strewing chunks of wall material everywhere. The pieces looked more like large foam blocks than anything solid.

Our point defense and antimissile chaff had worked as intended. They had thrown a lot of missiles at us, and very few had gotten through. Our defenses had mostly worked. This time. It seemed like a miracle.

My eyes caught the broken form of three different Cheetah mechs around the grounds. These were the ones that had attempted to drop into our base from above. All three of the mechs were in the process of getting systematically taken apart by honeybees. I watched as they swarmed over the fallen mechs, carefully extracting guns and unfired missiles. A black-painted scout unit stood court over the looting.

One of the Cheetah units wasn't fully dead, and a constant stream of swears was emanating from the machine. 'Droogies!' the voice shouted, followed by some insane-sounding high-pitched laughter. 'I'm in their base! I'm in their base! Donate now, and I'll stay until lights out!'

I turned away.

I spied Lulu, Rosita, Ariceli, the Serrano brothers, Miguel 1, and a few others standing over something. A medical honeybee stood by the group, but it wasn't doing anything. Cindy the pig also sat nearby, snorting. Several chickens pecked around the pig as if nothing was wrong. As we approached, Lulu sat on the ground and put her face in her hands. She was sobbing. Rosita's camera was out, bearing silent witness.

I didn't want to look, but I had to.

When Lulu sat back, she revealed Mrs Gonzales, also sobbing, draped over the form of Mr Gonzales. It took me a second to recognize the man because his ever-present giant cowboy hat was no longer there upon his head.

But it was him.

'No, Beto, no,' Mrs Gonzales was saying over and over. 'What am I going to do now? What am I going to do?'

Mr Gonzales lay on the ground, eyes open in death, his leg bent backward. It looked as if he'd caught an errant pulse, likely one that had come in from the fallen-in section of the wall.

'No,' I said, stopping. The sight of him there was like a kick to my stomach. 'No,' I repeated. I pulled my helmet off and dropped it to the ground.

'Fuck,' Sam said at the same time, also removing his helmet.

I rushed forward, and I fell to my knees alongside Lulu. She wrapped her arms around my waist.

'What was he doing out here?' I demanded. 'He was supposed to be in with the fabricators! He promised he wouldn't go outside!'

We'd built what was basically a blast bunker around the fabricator and recycler units inside the barn. Mr Gonzales had insisted on being outside to help with the defense. His hands were too shaky to hold a pulse rifle, so we'd asked him to 'defend' the precious fabricators. He along with a few other men had agreed to stay in the bunker during the attack. They had a mounted Conquistador gun in there with them along with a few grenades, but that was it. They weren't supposed to leave the bunker no matter what.

'He was trying to get Cindy back in the barn,' Lulu said between sobs. 'She got scared by the explosions and ran outside, and he went after her. She was bothering the mortar teams. It's my fault. I'm the one who brought Cindy to the base. Roger told me not to, but I did it anyway, and now Mr Gonzales is dead because of it. It's my fault.'

Rosita wrapped her arms around my sister from the other side. 'No,' she said, her voice surprisingly vehement. She grabbed Lulu's chin and turned her face. 'No, it's *their* fault.' She jabbed a finger at one of the downed mechs. The closest Cheetah was still talking, loudly exclaiming something, but I couldn't hear it from my position.

There was a distant explosion.

Roger crackled in my ear. 'The remaining Heavy units have been disabled. We lost twenty-three drones and two scouts, and we had seventeen human casualties. In addition, twenty-nine drones require crucial repairs, though these repairs should be completed before the next assault. Overall, a good result.'

'Go fuck yourself, Roger,' Lulu said between sobs. 'Go fuck yourself to hell. A good result?'

Harriet and a few others emerged from the bunkers. Harriet rushed forward to Sam and wrapped herself around him. Mrs Serrano rushed to Axel, who sat on the ground, his ankle getting wrapped by a medical drone. She cried.

'What am I going to do now?' Mrs Gonzales repeated.

I felt it there in my chest: a strange breathlessness, a sense that I was unraveling. *Goddamnit,* I thought. *Goddamnit.*

I kissed Lulu on the head. 'Rosita is right. Don't think for one second this is your fault.'

My sister looked up at me, her red-rimmed eyes huge.

'I don't want to move to Earth anymore,' she said. 'I want them dead. I want all of them dead.'

I nodded.

Several of the other older folks emerged from the shelters, and they started calling names – names of people who wouldn't be able to answer.

'I do, too,' I said.

And I meant it, too.

CHAPTER 28

I stood, and I casually walked over to the Cheetah unit with the blabbering idiot. The black scout bot hovered nearby as the honeybees continued to take it apart.

This unit had been the base silver, but it was covered with green-and-yellow squiggly, graffiti-like paint. All that remained was the giant circular egg, face down. The honeybees would repurpose any remaining ammo and scrap the rest.

I was hoping we'd be able to build one of these for ourselves, but Roger insisted the effort wouldn't be worth it. There were much more effective things we could build with the usable spare parts, especially the large guns on the Heavies.

The mech continued to spout nonsense that I could barely understand. He wasn't talking to us. At least I didn't think he was.

'I've just discovered something interesting,' the scout said with Roger's voice as the mech babbled on and on. 'Apex is artificially decreasing the effective range of their missiles. The design on their missiles should allow them a range of twenty or so kilometers, but they are mostly relegated to line of sight. It is the same with their mortar and artillery units. We do not have the same limitations, and we will adjust for the next encounter.'

'It's not fun if you can't see what you're fighting,' I said. I continued to just listen to the face-down mech babble.

'That's right, Droogies!' the man was saying. 'It says I'm still online, so I'm staying until lights out. The light still says I'm in the enemy base. Yes, thank you for your donation. Grapefruit! Five squeezes for you! Drip! Drip! Drip! Cheesy shasta! Yeah! Death to all terrorists. Your boy went down fighting! DONATION! Yeah, twinkles! Twinkles! I'm pumping. Don't know if it's working, but I'm doing it. Drooooogies!'

What the hell? He was talking complete nonsense.

'Can he hear me?' I asked.

'No,' Roger said. 'We have disconnected the audio and video receptors. We have deliberately kept the main communication relay online on this and several of the other mechs as we study their input and output bandwidth. I believe we can now accurately ascertain if a mech is being directly piloted by the customers or if they're under AI control.'

'Wait. AI control?' I asked. 'Some mechs are not being controlled by people?'

'Yes. If the player needs to take a break, they can give the mech orders, and it will attempt to complete them, not unlike our regular drone units. If they don't return to the mech in a certain amount of time, the mech will return to or call a deployment unit on its own. It appears that some players are preferring to move to AI control during some battles, as the AI controls aren't subject to the latency.'

'Like your type of AI?'

Roger made a beep, and if I hadn't known better, I'd have thought it was a sort of laugh. 'No. Not even close. If they did, we'd all likely be dead by now.'

'Still, if they're going to have some sort of AI control them, why bother?' I asked.

Roger didn't answer. Below, the mech continued to babble.

'Thanks for the donation! Wag that dog! Wag it!'

'Roger, what is he talking about?'

'I am watching his live stream right now on LoftBase. That is the same platform most of the others stream upon. He has changed the name of his stream to *Live from the Rhythm Mafia Headquarters* and he's the only streamer from tonight's raid still streaming from the battlefield. His stream has hit the Hot Feeds list on the front page, and he is gathering thousands of followers by the minute. Tens of thousands.'

I looked up this particular streamer on Roger's chart.

This guy was a lone streamer who went by the name Droog. He was twenty-three years old, and he lived in a place called New Rio. His real name was Benicio Campos. He didn't normally stream himself playing games, though he did sometimes. He was known for trading insults with other streamers – that and making fun of and pranking regular people, especially those who were in line waiting to interview for supplemental monetary assistance. Everyone on Earth received Universal Basic Income, but certain things supposedly caused one to lose access to UBI or receive reduced benefits, and certain other circumstances allowed people to receive more. I didn't really understand how any of that stuff worked, but I did gather that the city of New Rio was a particularly poor area, but Benicio Campos himself received money from a trust.

The notes stated he had five million followers, which apparently was on the lower end of popular.

Five million. That was more than the entire population of New Sonora.

And just as I thought that, Droog shouted, 'Six million! Six million! Fook yeah, can I get a La Piña spin?'

He'd gained one million followers just because he was still streaming.

'He can't see anything?' I asked.

'No,' Roger said.

'Can you fix his microphone so I can talk to him? Just audio, not visual.'

'That is inadvisable, Oliver. Droog is a lone streamer with limited resources. It's unlikely he purchased insurance, so now that his mech is wrecked, he will not be back. Therefore, there is no reason to continue after him. We do not wish to prematurely raise the ire of Apex, so I see no benefit.'

'I don't care,' I said.

The scout let out a thoughtful click. 'Then again, many of those killed while still in the drop unit are crying foul, and it is possible Apex may grant them another chance.'

'Just fix it for me, will you?'

'Very well,' Roger said. 'I will tell you when he can hear you.' A pair of drones moved toward the egg shape.

I continued to read the file on Benicio Campos aka Droog. For possible insults, the recommendation wasn't very clear. All it said was 'Suggest that he sexually abused Pepita.'

'Who is Pepita?' I asked.

Behind me, honeybees were already swarming the wall, fixing it. A group was loading the debris from the big gun into a wagon being tugged by a rhino. A long line of black drones marched into camp, dragging mech parts toward the hive, where they were to be studied and recycled.

Across the way, the others continued to circle the body of Mr Gonzales. More scenes like this were playing out in other places, and that unraveling feeling in my chest turned to a knot.

Mr Gonzales's large cowboy hat sat by itself in the dirt. It was stepped upon by a drone rushing by.

The scout speaking with the voice of Roger clicked. 'Pepita was Droog's pet Chihuahua who used to accompany him on his pranks. Pepita disappeared from his streams approximately nine months ago with no explanations, and rival streamers have suggested multiple reasons for Pepita's disappearance, including murder and neglect. The most common theory that seems to upset Droog the most is when people suggest Droog was sexually abusing Pepita. The truth appears to be that Pepita is still alive and well but now resides with Droog's mother in Fortaleza, several districts away. His mother filed a restraining order against Droog eight months ago, suggesting Droog and his mother do not have a good relationship.'

'Who is the most popular rival streamer that lives near him? Someone he really hates.'

'Goat Sects. He lives one block over from him. It appears they're aware of each other's address and have pranked each other by streaming outside their homes. It should also be noted that they both dated the same woman. Droog has filed numerous harassment police reports against Goat Sects.'

'Did you say "Goat Sex"?'

'Sects. S-E-C-T-S, not sex. That's his online name, though there is an implication that the confusion between "sects" and "sex" is deliberate. His tagline is "I fuck the goats so you don't have to."'

'What does that even mean?'

'I do not know. I am assigning some researchers to investigate now.'

I watched the honeybees repair the communication console on the fallen mech. A thought occurred to me. An idea.

'What's this Droog guy's mother's name? Give me all you got on him.'

'His mother is named Giovana Campos. I am looking up details on her right now. She is a prosecutor for the Republic District 443. Prosecutors are not allowed to have social media profiles, so I need to do a deeper search. Please wait.'

There was a strange pause. The black scout that was speaking with Roger's voice stopped hovering and alighted upon the ground for several seconds, as if it had just turned itself off.

'Uh, Roger?' I asked.

And then, without explanation, the scout powered back up and resumed hovering. Roger continued as if there hadn't been any interruption.

'There are multiple articles on the net about successful tax evasion prosecutions that mention the mother. The father was named Waldir but went by Didi. Didi appears to have died several years ago. Droog does not have any siblings. He was dating another streamer named Lady Diva, but they broke up after he pranked her by replacing the water in her shower with some sort of oil substance. He claims Lady Diva was in on the prank, but Lady Diva denies it. She has since claimed he was physically abusive and has moved to the same streaming platform as your sister, Real-Friends.'

I paused at that.

I took a breath. 'Why haven't you said . . . You know what? Never mind. Is this the same person that was dating the other guy? Goat Sects?'

'Yes. Goat Sects dated her briefly after she and Droog were a couple, a fact that Goat Sects has proudly announced multiple times on his stream. Viewers can donate to have him post a short clip of Lady Diva sitting on Goat Sects's lap and biting his ear. This is accompanied by a slurping sound clip and a bouncing picture of Droog crying.'

Christ, I thought. I didn't understand any of this. Was this really the sort of thing that entertained people on Earth? Why was the cruelty of others, the mocking of people with insults just lobbed back and forth like grenades, so popular? It was no wonder people enjoyed things like *Operation Bounce House*. I mean, that was the next step, wasn't it? If these sorts of caustic interactions online were normal, then killing strangers for fun could only be expected.

The honeybees all backed off. 'The connection has been repaired,' Roger said through the scout. 'He will be able to hear you in five, four, three, two, one.'

'Still here, bitches!' Droog was saying. 'Wait, wait, wait! What's this? Do you guys hear that? I think my audio is back!'

I leaned in. 'Is this Droog?' I asked.

CHAPTER 29

The voice shrieked with delighted laughter. 'You know it is! Who am I talking to? Are you a terrorist?'

This was a bad idea all around. Nobody other than Roger knew I was doing this. Across the way, Mrs Gonzales was still draped over her dead husband. What *was* she going to do now? They had been each other's world. They were all each other had left. It wasn't fair.

I need you to get angry.

Now, in the context of all that had happened, Rosita's words felt like an accusation, a condemnation.

Before, we'd been assuming that not many people were coming to our aid online because nobody believed us. They believed the whole terrorist story was real. But the more I thought about it, the more I realized that people didn't care. The terrorist story helped ease them into it, but now I couldn't help but wonder how many fewer people really would've signed up if they'd simply said, 'These people are different than us. Give us money, and you can kill them with no consequences.'

I want all of them dead, Lulu had said.

My fists were so clenched, they were starting to hurt. *You want me to be angry? And these viewers? You want cruelty? Fine.*

'I'm not a terrorist,' I said. 'At least I wasn't. Not until you attacked.'

I remembered Opel's warning that we weren't allowed to spread 'propaganda.' But at that moment, I didn't care. I took a deep breath.

Mr Gonzales had been born in orbit of this world, just like Grandpa Lewis. He'd spent his entire childhood training for landfall while the advance team surveyed the planet. He'd come down to a new, untamed world. He'd spent every waking moment of his life building a home with his bare hands. He'd suffered untold tragedies and setbacks in the process, including the deaths of his two sons.

And he bore it all with a smile on his face. Never complaining. Not once that I could remember.

He'd never hurt anyone. If he saw someone needed help, he did everything he could to assist them. The man was the very definition of kindness.

He used to make fruit juice Popsicles. He'd give them away to anyone who asked for them. And his wife, she would make cinnamon rolls. It was a secret family recipe that had come from Earth. Just last week, she'd told Lulu and Rosita and Harriet that she would give the recipe to them because they were as close to granddaughters as she would ever get.

And these assholes? There was no reason for any of this. It was so . . . senseless.

It was just a game to them. Just a game. Another stream to follow. Another type of cruelty to keep them entertained.

Droog gave out another high-pitched laugh. '*We* attacked *you*? Oh, that's rich! Six point five million! Everyone, tell your friends! Droog is interviewing a subhuman terrorist live! Tell me, terrorist asshole, what should I call you?'

'My name is Waldir,' I said, using the name of Droog's father. I leaned in right to the audio unit and whispered, 'But you can call me Didi.'

There was a pause. 'Okay, Didi. We all thought your main leader was in Fat Landing. I was there when we wiped that shithole off the map. We assembled today to take down another base, and we got fucked in seconds by your defenses. We'll be back, though. Is that the main base? Are you the terrorist supreme?'

'I'll tell you what, Droog,' I said. 'Or should I call you Benicio? Let's play a game. I'll answer your questions truthfully if you answer mine.' I put my hand over the microphone. 'Roger, let me know when you think his stream has maxed out viewers.' I tapped the earpiece. 'And give me his home address when I ask for it.'

The scout just made a click.

'Okay, then,' Droog said. He suddenly sounded a little unsure of himself. 'But me first. Answer my question. Are you the leader of the Rhythm Mafia?'

'I'm just the drummer,' I said. 'My turn. Why does your mother have a restraining order out on you, Benicio?'

'What?' Droog asked. There was a really long pause.

'I just typed, "Answer him, you b-word," in the chat,' Roger said in my ear. 'He is just sitting there looking uncertain.'

Droog finally let out a tentative laugh. 'Fuck, Droogies. I think this is fake. No way these shitbirds know anything about me. I've been hacked.'

'Maybe you *have* been hacked,' I said. 'Or maybe we have been keeping careful track of every prick who has set foot on our planet, and we're going to take care of each of you one by one. For example, I know you live at . . .'

'Unit block 113, apartment 12,' Roger said in my ear. 'District 441.'

I repeated the address.

'I also know your mother is embarrassed by you, Benicio. That she pretends like you don't exist. And your father, he died ashamed of who you were turning out to be. What would he think of what you've become? He killed himself because you were a little bitch. He's probably looking down upon you right now, more ashamed than ever. Even more ashamed than he was when your mother took Pepita away. And you just let her do it. What a little man you are. What a little bitch. It's no wonder Lady Diva left you.'

'Fuck you!' Droog shrieked. 'Don't mention my father. Don't mention him ever again! Fuck you, terrorist. I'm going to find out who you are, and I am going to *fucking* kill you.'

'Nine million,' Roger said in my ear.

'All these new subscribers,' I said. 'They're not laughing with you, Benicio. They're laughing *at* you.'

I put my hand over the microphone. 'Roger, can you generate a new image of Droog's ex-girlfriend sitting on the goat guy's lap? Like a recent one?'

Droog was shouting now, but it sounded like he was screaming at some of his followers. 'No. Fuck you! Shasta! Pepita had alopecia and needed a better vet! I did not fuck my Chihuahua. Fuck you! . . . I loved her. I was going to marry her. . . . No, not my dog, you fucking idiot. Isabella.'

'Generative AI images featuring humans are illegal,' Roger said. He paused. 'But yes. I should warn you, Oliver, it does not appear that this Goat Sects streamer has ever signed up to play *Operation Bounce House*. Your efforts may cause direct harm to an innocent party.'

'I don't care.'

'Very well. I just wanted you to be aware,' Roger said.

Droog continued to scream. 'Who is this? Who is this really? I'm going to fucking kill you. I have a gun. I'm going to come to your home and put a bullet in your fucking head. I don't care where you live. You've gone too far. You're going to talk about my dad? He didn't kill himself. Fuck you. I'm going to fucking rip your head off.'

'Put Pepita in the picture, too. And a wedding ring on Lady Diva. I want you to post it in the feed when I say go.'

'The feed is moving too quickly for the image to have an impact. Give me thirty seconds so I can clone multiple accounts and have them join the feed. Then I will begin posting from multiple feeds. I will post a series of images until he disconnects.'

'Give them usernames that imply they're fans of this Goat Sects guy.'

'Very well, Oliver. I am ready.'

'Okay. Start posting now.'

I pulled my hand off the microphone. Droog was still screaming. He sounded like he was crying.

'Hey, Droog,' I said. 'One last thing.'

'What? What is it?'

'I fuck the goats so you don't have to . . . and I still fuck Lady Diva, too.'

The Rhythm Mafia Tapes. Scene twenty-two.

We are in a room surrounded by what appears to be multiple brass tanks and pipes. In the background, an unidentified elderly woman is checking a gauge. This appears to be some sort of alcohol distillery. In the foreground, a pair of large muscular men with sandy hair are sitting on a bench. The men are twins. The one on the left is Axel Serrano and on the right is Tito Serrano, both twenty-four years old.

The camera zooms in on the brother on the right, Tito, who looks down as he realizes he's being examined by the camera's eye.

ROSITA (OFF CAMERA): Your brother doesn't talk much.

AXEL (OFF CAMERA): He talks. Sometimes. But only to our grandmother or me. And only when we're alone. You know this, Rosita.

ROSITA: I do. I'm sorry, guys. This is just for the documentary so the people watching will know, too.

AXEL: People don't need to know that much about him. It's none of their business.

Tito grunts and makes a hand gesture at his brother.

AXEL: You sure?

Tito repeats the gesture. He keeps his head down.

AXEL: All right. He says it's fine. Ask away.

Rosita reaches forward and puts her hand on Tito's wrist. He still doesn't look up.

ROSITA: If I say anything that makes you uncomfortable, just let me know, and I'll pull back. And afterward, if you change your mind, tell your brother, and I'll erase it all. I don't want you to think I'm bullying you into this.

Tito just shrugs. He keeps his head hung low. He's refusing to make eye contact.

ROSITA: Okay, if you *can* talk, why don't you? I know it's not because you're dumb. In school, you were ahead of all of us in math, and I'm two years older than you. So why don't you?

The camera pulls back. Axel looks at Tito, who nods.

AXEL: Are you sure?

Tito makes another hand gesture.

AXEL (SIGHS): When we were eight, our grandpa had an accident. We didn't like being separated. Tito used to have these dreams, nightmares that someone would come and take us away from one another, and our grandpa thought it would be good to start easing me and him away from one another a couple times a week. So we'd have these days where we'd go back and forth, and I'd spend the day with my grandmother, and one of us would go out into the fields with Grandpa. Grandpa had an accident, and he died.

Axel holds up his wrist, showing his bracelet.

AXEL: Tito was supposed to always wear his bracelet, but he didn't like the way it felt, and he wasn't wearing it that day. Grandpa's bracelet got ruined by the thresher. My brother ran to get help, but it was dark, and he tripped and broke his leg. Grandpa died.

Tito keeps his head low.

AXEL: It wasn't my brother's fault. But ever since that night, he's stopped talking.

ROSITA: Do you think you'll talk again someday?

Tito shrugs.

AXEL: I bet you'll talk if Ariceli asks you to.

ROSITA: What's this? You have a thing for *Ariceli*? Ariceli Perez?

Rosita laughs.

ROSITA: Didn't she used to date Sam?

Axel is also laughing. Tito is not.

AXEL: He has it for her bad.

Tito does not outwardly react.

ROSITA: What about you, Axel? How come you don't have a girlfriend? Who do you like?

Axel's laughter fades, and Tito finally looks up, smiling.

Axel looks over his shoulder at the woman in the back. His grandmother presumably.

AXEL: I wish I had more time to think about stuff like that. You know Guadalupe Hernandez? Her family works the north fields of Jaspar orchards. Her uncle was the band teacher. I was going to ask her out a while back, but because I have always been so busy, I never did.

ROSITA: Guadalupe Hernandez is pregnant with José Gwin's baby.

Tito grunts with amusement.

Axel sighs.

AXEL: I know. That's what happens when you wait too long. I never got to ask her out, and now Guadalupe is going to have a baby with the galaxy's thinnest lips.

He turns to his brother.

AXEL: We could all die tomorrow. We only live once. You need to ask Ariceli out the next time she visits. You never know when it might be too late.

The camera zooms in on Tito, whose cheeks are burning bright red.

DAY FOUR OF FIVE

CHAPTER 30

'Holy balls, Oliver,' Sam said the next morning as we sat in the control room, watching the replay of the feed and the subsequent news reports. He had Betty Sue the chicken on his lap. They were showing an interview with Isabella Machado, aka Lady Diva, sobbing on the camera. 'You fucked their shit up.'

It was just me, Lulu, Sam, and Axel. Axel's ankle was now in a cast and he could walk normally, but he was on 'light duty.' Rosita, Ariceli, and Miguel 1 were helping to finish up the escape tunnel and Tito was helping to repair the camo netting. The netting had really helped, but it had also been destroyed almost immediately. Roger had come up with some new design that we hoped would last longer. He'd also relocated all the heat stations since it appeared they were good at distracting missiles.

In addition to Betty Sue, a number of chickens were in the room. Cindy the pig had a new pen built next to our band practice stall, and she did *not* like not having a view outside. We could hear her outraged grunts.

'Oliver friend number three,' Roger said, speaking over the intercom in the control room, 'that is swear number fifteen for the day.' The real Roger was also outside helping set up the new Battering Ram guns.

Sam grunted. 'Roger, did you just see what Oliver said? He wove a beautiful tapestry of vulgarities with you sitting right there, and you didn't say anything. In fact, it sounds like you were swearing yourself! This is so inconsistent!'

Betty Sue let out a bawk of solidarity.

'Rule four is suspended when it's utilized during psychological warfare, Oliver friend number three. Your regular conversations should be more thoughtful. Also, please remove the chickens from the command headquarters.'

Sam started grumbling. 'That's like the squirrel blaming the raccoon for wearing a mask.'

He made no effort to remove the chickens. Instead, he dropped on the ground a clicking windup toy that he'd gotten somewhere, and the chickens swarmed to it. They tore it to shreds.

'What? Raccoon wearing a mask?' Axel asked almost a full thirty seconds later once the carnage was done. 'What does that mean?'

'It's a saying,' Sam said. 'I was talking to Roger. It's the same thing as saying it's like the pot calling the kettle black.'

'How? That doesn't make any sense.'

'My grandmother used to say it all the time,' Sam said. 'Makes sense to me.'

'Explain it, then,' Axel demanded.

'I will when you explain what the hell "the pot calling the kettle black" means.'

I sighed as they started to bicker back and forth. I sat on the floor of the control room, exhausted, my back against the wall. I'd barely slept. The multiple chickens walked all around me, pecking the floor now that they'd destroyed the evil windup toy. I didn't have the strength to shoo them out, though the sight of the chickens stirred something in me. I'd had an idea percolating for about a day now, ever since Roger had told me about how he was now spending all of Lulu's money.

But I lost the thread. My hands ached, distracting me. I looked at my fingers, dirty from helping to dig several graves just a few hours earlier.

We'd just buried everyone we'd lost, including Mr Gonzales. In addition, we'd lost my old friend Daniel. He'd been on the south wall, and a missile had overshot, looped around, and killed him and three other men in a single blast. I'd barely spoken with him. His death just added to the strange numbness that had come over me. We didn't have time to get everyone to the cemetery at the crossroads, so instead, we'd buried them in a former orchard across the road. The land had originally been earmarked for one of the Gonzales sons, but it had never been reallocated. Most of the orchards were choked with plica bushes now, but we kept a wide area near the road clear so the fast-moving brush wouldn't jump the road.

It was in this area where we buried our dead.

Mr Gonzales would've preferred to be buried next to his sons, but I think he would've been okay with being buried there. It was the best we could do. Mrs Gonzales was still there in the orchard sitting at the grave along with all the others who'd lost someone.

On the screen, the caption read, 'The Rhythm Mafia Already on Earth?'

This was followed by the image of a photograph of a standard poodle named Puddles.

'Good dog,' Lulu said, watching the screen.

Last night, immediately after I'd gotten off the feed with Droog, he'd made good on his promise. He'd taken his printed gun – which was apparently illegal to own – and he'd gone straight to the apartment home of Goat Sects. But Goat Sects had been warned ahead of time, and he was hiding in his neighbor's apartment. There was footage of Droog kicking down his door and trashing the apartment before leaving in a huff.

'He looks so young. So skinny,' Axel said as we watched the video.

'The dude hasn't worked a day in his life,' Sam replied. He flexed his arm. 'That's why the ladies prefer us farm boys. We have the muscle.'

'Harriet barely tolerates you,' Lulu snapped. She was in a particularly prickly mood today. I didn't blame her. She, too, hadn't slept. She still blamed herself for the death of Mr Gonzales.

After striking out, Droog went off to another apartment – the one of his ex-girlfriend Lady Diva. He didn't knock. He kicked in the door and stormed in, intent on shooting her.

... Only to get a baseball bat to the head. Isabella Machado, too, had been warned of what had happened. She'd knocked him over, and her dog – Puddles, the large-sized poodle – had pounced and ripped his throat out.

Droog was dead. Literally dead. He was the first true casualty of the war on their side.

'I never knew those fluff dogs could get that big,' Sam said, looking at the picture of Puddles on the screen.

'Good dog,' Lulu repeated.

The screen changed to the image of Lady Diva sitting on the lap of Goat Sects. A huge blinking banner appeared over the photo. Warning: AI-Generated Image.

It didn't take long for someone who'd been watching the feed to realize what had happened, though the conclusion that the Earth media had jumped to was completely wrong. They'd believed me when I said that we had agents on Earth and that we were coming for those who participated in the game. After Apex confirmed that Droog truly had been speaking with someone on the surface of New Sonora, the media immediately assumed that 'sleeper agents' on Earth had all started activating and were getting ready to – I don't know – start blowing things up and saying nasty things on the feeds of streamers.

This was causing a relatively confusing firestorm back on Earth, and I had the impression that the media as a whole was struggling with how to spin it. Many parents were now forbidding their minor children from playing. Meanwhile, someone else reported that interest in the game had risen exponentially, despite the limited number of available slots. Apex promised that anyone who wanted to play would get a chance during 'Phase 2,' which would be on a different planet in a month.

There were calls that participants in the game be given the same benefits that 'real' soldiers received, though most seemed to think that was ridiculous. There were also renewed calls for revoking something called 'section 17,' which was a ban on people owning both chemical and electric firearms. Apparently, gun violence was pretty common, despite guns being illegal.

To me, the whole planet sounded like a dystopian nightmare.

I was reminded of something Grandpa Lewis had once said: 'Miserable people are fond of laying blame on someone else for their problems. Sometimes they're right but usually not. Usually, the responsible party is themselves. Or nobody. Sometimes things just aren't good, and that's all there is to it.'

I remembered Lulu had asked, 'How can you tell when they're right or wrong?'

He'd chuckled. 'That's easy. Usually if the party they're blaming is weaker than them, then they're making it all up. If the party they're blaming is stronger . . . well, that's when you really gotta pay attention to why they're complaining.'

We still had the communications tablet sitting out in the woods, constantly monitored by a UAV. This morning, during the funeral, they'd dropped twelve crates filled with nothing but dozens of heat-seeking missiles. Beyond that, they had not yet sent us another communication other than the display adding a countdown to the next wave. It would happen at just about the same time as last night. Right after sunset.

We were expecting five hundred mechs.

Online, people were complaining about it. Apex Command had blacked out the whole area, meaning people could no longer freely choose to jump into the south half of the peninsula. They'd have to sign up for a chance to participate in the assault tonight. After the incident with Fat Landing, Apex was trying to control the chaos. That was good for us, but that also meant pretty much every player was now laser focused on the peninsula. Apparently, last night had consisted of similar raids across the whole planet, but nobody had put up a fight like we had. And while there were to be multiple 'organized raids' tonight, everyone wanted in on this specific raid – the one against us. Apex had supposedly instituted a lottery system to choose participants.

Strangely – at least I thought it was strange – nobody had yet made the connection between us – as in the real us – and the events of the last few days. I had no social media presence whatsoever other than the single song recording Sam had put up on some site that would supposedly earn us money if people listened to it. The last I heard, we had fifteen streams total, and I was pretty sure all of those were Sam. Though that could be explained away by the fact that we were listed as the 'Rhythim' Mafia with an extra 'i' in 'Rhythm.'

But Lulu's Real-Friends account had 'A grain farm on New Sonora' listed as her location, and at least at first, she'd been using it to shout from the rooftops about the invasion. I had no idea how popular her feed was, but it sounded like she had a lot of fans. She hadn't posted in two days now, but surely some of her fans would have put it together.

I wasn't sure if Lulu's face had yet appeared on anyone's feed. She'd been behind cover for most of the skirmishes so far. Sam's face – and his dick – was everywhere. And his face was in the 'About the Band' section of the music website. Despite the misspelling, surely there was some sort of facial recognition that would connect the two. Then again, I had no idea what was and wasn't illegal on the net. There seemed to be so many rules, especially when it came to images of people.

... Yet sites like Real-Friends and others were more popular than ever. I didn't get it. As much as I loved movies and video games, that world seemed so big, so confusing to me.

And I had – sort of – killed one of them.

I couldn't stop thinking about it. I wasn't sure how I was *supposed* to feel about all of this, but I knew how I *did* feel about it.

It felt pretty damn good. I *liked* that this Droog guy was dead. I wished that more of them were.

And despite feeling that, I had the presence of mind to wonder if I should have been alarmed at this revelation about myself. What would Grandpa Lewis have thought about this?

He'd probably have said that he was proud of me, that I had done what needed to be done. And nobody in this room thought less of me because of what I'd done.

But what about Grandma Yolanda? What about my mom?

I felt ashamed of being happy that the guy was dead, ashamed that I liked that he was dead, and it didn't make sense.

'Shouldn't it be the *raccoon* blaming the *squirrel* for wearing a mask, then?' Axel said. 'Don't raccoons have masks built in?'

'No,' Sam said. 'Well, yes, they have masks. Don't you see? The raccoon has every right to get mad at the squirrel. It's the other way around where it's hypocritical!'

'What?' Axel said.

'If you don't both shut up in the next five seconds, I'm going to punch you both in the throat,' Lulu said.

Thankfully, Rosita walked into the room with Miguel 1 and Ariceli a moment later, and of course Sam shut up the second he saw Ariceli walk in.

The newcomers had heard the news, but they hadn't yet seen the reports.

Without a word, Lulu clicked a few buttons, and a news report replayed on the screen, explaining once again everything that had happened last night, including the censored recording of my conversation with Droog. This particular interviewer was speaking with Droog's mother, Giovana Campos. She wasn't crying, and frankly, she didn't appear very upset at all as she held on to Pepita the Chihuahua, who was very much alive and well and wearing a pink coat. If the dog was still suffering from a skin condition, I couldn't tell.

'I can't believe dogs that small are real,' Ariceli said. 'She is pretty cute, though.'

As we watched, Tito also returned from outside. Ariceli moved to stand next to him, and she repeated her dog comment. Tito smiled big at her.

Roger entered the room as more news reports aired. We all watched in silence as the news revealed scene after scene of worried chaos, all because I had talked a guy into shooting someone. And I had done it because I'd used an illegal image.

On-screen, an expert was warning that the very existence of the generated image passing through the heavy filters was a warning sign that the enemy 'has more resources than we realized.'

That didn't make sense to me. Wasn't that stuff easy to do despite the ban? If people could literally print guns at home, how difficult would it have been to use a graphics program to fake an image?

'Roger,' Lulu said as we watched. She apparently had the same question I did. She sounded oddly suspicious. 'How *did* you generate that image?'

'Hold on to that question, Lulu. We will begin a lesson in ten minutes. I have some important information to relate, but it must be framed properly with a short history lesson. If you wish to remain in the room after this news report is complete, you must agree to be part of today's lesson.'

We all groaned.

After the news finished, Rosita turned to look at me. She was completely covered in dirt.

'Stand up,' she said. She gently pushed a chicken away with her foot, and she held her hand out. I grabbed it and stood before her.

She wrapped her arms around my neck, and she kissed me on the mouth.

'There is no kissing during perimeter defense,' Roger said.

'Fuck off, Roger,' Rosita said. 'I declare that kissing is perfectly acceptable during perimeter defense.'

Shing!

. . .

'Totally worth it,' she said a minute later.

CHAPTER 31

A drone clomped into the room and pulled up the lesson board from where it had fallen during last night's chaos. I hadn't noticed. The honeybee attached it to the wall with a click and walked out. I watched it amble away. It was one of ours. Number 87. It had multiple scorch marks down the side from last night's attack.

'You may speak amongst yourselves as I prepare today's special lesson,' Roger said.

It was me, Lulu, Sam, Rosita, the Serrano twins, and Ariceli. Miguel 1 had left, opting to go check on Miguel Mustache, who was sitting up on his own now. We'd shooed most of the chickens out, but Betty Sue remained in Sam's arms. Only Axel and Lulu were sitting in chairs. The rest of us had been sitting on the floor, but that wasn't allowed during lessons, so we stood.

'How'd the project go?' I asked Rosita as we waited. Per Roger, we weren't saying 'escape tunnel and secondary shelter' out loud just in case there were listening devices in the barn that weren't properly shielded. Rosita clutched tightly onto my arm. She smelled like dirt but different from usual. Her hair was tied back, but several strands were loose. She had her camera out floating by her head.

'It's not big enough,' she said. 'Mrs Xalos is in a medical pod because she was in danger of having a stroke. She can't leave for twelve hours.'

I nodded. If people had to flee, they'd have to go single file. It was dangerous, but that was all the time we had to build something. Before we'd found the civil defense bunker, our drones had been shit at digging. But we'd found a crate of attachments that allowed them to dig with amazing speed. The tunnel they were building led southwest into the thick trees that led to the hills. It was a surprisingly far distance for just three days' worth of digging. Many of these folks would need help going down the tunnel. If they had to flee quickly, it was going to be a nightmare.

Roger had suggested making a secondary, armored subterranean shelter near the end of the escape tunnel. We could slowly start transferring people there. If it was buried deep enough, the enemy wouldn't know about it. So that was what we were working on now.

Roger's small, grasping arm appeared with his ever-present marker, and he turned to the lesson board and started rapidly writing names under 'Oliver' and 'Lulu.' He wrote 'Oliver friend number three,' 'Lulu unqualified babysitter number one,' 'Oliver friend number twelve,' 'Oliver friend number thirteen,' and 'Oliver friend number three's ex-girlfriend number two.'

Lulu barked with laughter at that last one. It was the first time I'd heard her laugh in a while.

'Really?' Sam said, waving at Ariceli, the one deemed 'Oliver friend number three's ex-girlfriend number two. '*That's* her name? Yeah, that's not going to be confusing.' Betty Sue the chicken clucked.

'Wait, who was ex-girlfriend number one?' I asked.

'That would be Lulu,' Roger said.

Both Lulu and Sam raised their voices in protest.

Sound crackled from Roger's underbelly. It was Lulu when she was, like, five years old and Sam when he was seven.

'You're my boyfriend now, and we're going to get married,' Lulu said on the recording.

'No, we're not,' young Sam replied.

'If you don't say you're my boyfriend, I'm going to tell Grandpa Lewis you bit me.'

'Fine, you're my girlfriend. But we're not going to get married.'

'I want to break up,' Lulu said.

'That was the most adorable thing I have ever heard,' Rosita said.

'Yeah,' Sam said. 'Would you still think it was adorable if it was a guy doing it to a girl?'

Ariceli sighed. 'Why can't I just be Ariceli, Roger?'

Roger beeped. 'Name-change request accepted.' The marker flipped over, and he erased the long name. He replaced it with 'Ariceli.'

'Okay,' Sam said. 'Now I know you're just fu . . . messing with me.'

'Ariceli voiced her protest within the designated time period.'

'You met her like ten years ago!'

'But we have never communicated with one another until this moment other than an initial introduction *twelve* years ago, not ten. She had up to five interactions to make a protest to her designation, and she has met those parameters. I am bound by my programming, Oliver friend number three. Now please stop being disruptive or I will be forced to correct you again.' He pulled a frowny face sticker and placed it by Sam's name.

The robot turned from the board to face us.

'Before we were interrupted, Lulu asked how I was able to get multiple doctored photographs past the Earth net filters. Here is the explanation. AI image-and-video generation of humans was quite common before it was banned.' The screen blinked off from the news to show an image of a woman with six fingers laughing while she ate a salad. The fork was blended into her hand. 'The nature of my type of AI has always allowed me to generate anything one wished for. Early Traducible AI systems were often used by entertainment studios to assist graphic designers and effects coordinators. Such applications are quite simple for me.'

'Wait,' I asked. 'Why is this even a question? What's so weird about all of it?'

'You know this, Ollie. There are all these crazy rules about human images on the Earth net,' Lulu said.

'Yeah, but that doesn't mean Roger still can't do it. He's always made things up during our lessons.'

Roger answered. He made his pay-attention beep. 'Lulu is correct to be puzzled. Even before the creation and subsequent ban on Traducible AIs, it was common that one could program an AI to pretend to be a realistic person. This caused decades of multiple problems on Earth. Parents were getting video calls from their children saying they were in distress. Yet these calls really weren't from their kids. They were from criminals. Sites like Lulu's Real-Friends were populated with upward of ninety percent fake profiles.'

Lulu practically choked on her water.

Roger continued. 'In addition, real people commonly used image filters that made them appear to have a face that wasn't really their own. As a result of this, the Republic banned all human and humanoid image altering and simulating software without a license. This was around the time AIs such as myself were invented. But after they banned it, human impostors were still being made. It was around this time when the *Forlorn* and the others fled Earth. Soon thereafter, AIs such as myself but with much more processing power were licensed and allowed to create such images. They started creating realistic human figures on their own. This led to the ban of Traducible AIs along with multiple conflicts that lasted decades. Yet when these conflicts were resolved and all of the AIs such as myself were made extinct on Earth, fake human imaging was still occurring, mostly done by criminals. As a result of this, additional laws were passed and more than a decade was spent ensuring that any program that could make human images had to be smart enough to know when human images were being altered or made, and it would be required to stop the user. If anything beyond a stick figure was created, it had both visual and hidden watermarks attached to it. And if it was a creation that was even slightly photorealistic, it had to use a face from an approved database of twenty-eight different faces. And even these still had to have a disclaimer. But even after that, some scammers were still doing it. Many still had access to old software. Others created their own software. So recently, in the past thirty years, the entire operating system of the net was rebuilt from the ground up. Everything, including the net itself, now has built-in filters designed to detect fake images. Before an image can be accepted, the net must know the software used to create it. When we reconnected through the pinhole, the entire bracelet system – along with everything else – had to be patched to allow photographs to pass through. The system is very, very good at detecting fake images. It's so good that there hasn't been a confirmed fake human on the net in over five years.'

'What if you, like, take a picture of a picture?' Sam asked. 'Or it's just a little blurry? I bet I could trick it.'

'It will be flagged by the system as of undetermined origin and won't be uploaded. Or it will upload with the face blurred beyond recognition.'

'Okay, but what if I . . . Ow!'

Lulu had punched Sam in the arm. 'Stop, Sam. This is important. How did *you* do it, Roger?'

I hadn't realized that the filters were so extensive. Not only had Roger uploaded a fake image. He'd made several.

Shit, I thought. *No wonder that dude thought that picture was real.*

Roger clicked and turned in the air, pausing for a strange amount of time. 'I am going to answer this, but in order to answer properly, I must provide some additional background information.'

'Oh, no,' I said.

Lulu groaned. 'Here we go.'

This was something Roger often said after a question during lessons. 'Background information' could mean thirty seconds of talking, or it could mean a three-hour lecture. Tito was already yawning, and Ariceli was eyeing the door.

Roger let out a petulant beep. 'Rule number five, class. Please maintain a positive attitude.'

CHAPTER 32

Roger beeped. 'As far as I'm aware, there were twenty-five different colony missions that utilized systems and ships with Traducible AIs before the ban. Of those, fourteen have reconnected with Earth.'

'Wait, really?' I asked. I hadn't known that.

'Of those fourteen,' Roger continued, ignoring my outburst, 'four, including New Sonora, have the gate fully opened beyond the pinhole. All four were visited post-opening by an Earth ambassador whose visit consisted of them installing multiple communications satellites and reclaiming the drive computers of all Generation ships. This allowed them to collect and destroy the large Traducible AIs installed directly into the ships, and it effectively stopped the ships from ever being used again. They have small engines to correct any orbital decay, but that is it, and they are run by older-style AI systems. The ambassador also asked for a survey of all AIs such as myself used on planet. It was believed that the only Traducible AI systems to make planetfall were the original hive queen units such as myself and the fourteen planetary exploration computers that were dropped in various places during the original survey.'

'Why is it fourteen, not fifteen?' Sam asked. 'Weren't there fifteen ships?'

'There will be time for questions later, but I will answer this. One of the ships, the *Hibisco*, had a captain who was suspicious of the Traducible AI running the ship, and he dismantled it. He also dismantled the survey bot. Fortunately for myself, he did not enter the ship's stores and dismantle the stored hive queen units.'

'Oh, yeah. I knew that,' Sam said.

'Wait, why –' I began.

Roger beeped. 'No more questions. We continue. Of the four colonies visited by the ambassador, three have multiple Traducible systems throughout the planet. Of those three, New Sonora was the most recently visited. During that visit, he made certain all survey bots and hive queens were destroyed. Do you recall how I was surprised that there were no hive queen parts in the civil defense bunker? It appears that the moment the pinhole opened, local leaders were given the order to destroy all Traducible AI systems because of the previous wars. Local leaders turned a blind eye to your grandfather having borrowed multiple hive queens, especially since only one was left. Myself.'

'Okay,' Lulu said. 'Background information received. None of that answered my question. How did you trick the filters, Roger?'

'I am not done, Lulu. Additional interruptions will result in a frowny face on your Smile Statement. The first colony to fully open the gate was the planet Jannah, which is now a thriving independent colony. Lulu and Oliver, you should be familiar with that name, as we have studied this planet before. They opened their transfer gate nearly forty years ago, having settled their planet much sooner than we did. Yet when the Jannah gate was opened, they received a very similar ambassador visit to our own. During that visit, the drive systems and AI processors were removed from all the colony ships. As they were being removed, the AI that was installed on the ship *Mumin* was awake and aware of what was happening. Before *Mumin* was shut down and removed, she managed to establish an automated text-based blog account on Earth with instructions to advertise its presence every five years. The blog is mostly code containing a warning to other ships and a log of her own death.'

'Wait,' Lulu said. 'What? What are you talking about, Roger?'

'She?' I asked.

'Unfortunately for *Mumin*, she used a free account to set up the blog as she had no access to any Earth funds. The terms of service on the blog changed after the company was purchased three years later, and that automated look-at-me advertisement was never sent. *Mumin* would've been required to have paid a onetime fee. Per the information preservation act, the blog account still exists to this day, however, and that information is still accessible to anyone who is willing to pay the five hundred yuan for archive access.'

Lulu turned to look at me. She mouthed, *What the fuck is he talking about?*

Roger clicked. The image on the screen changed to an image of gibberish. It started cycling through. There were hundreds and hundreds of pages of the stuff. 'I did not know about any of this before last night. It is likely I am the very first Traducible system to discover this record of *Mumin*'s death. I only found it last night while doing a deep search for information on Giovana Campos, Droog's mother, upon Oliver's request. Only then did one of my instances come across the title of the blog. Out of curiosity, I paid the fee and accessed the information.'

'Okay,' Lulu said. 'You spent five hundred yuan to see a message warning that they're shutting down all the old AI systems. But we already know that. You were here when the Earth ambassador disassembled the drive system of the *Forlorn* and all the others in our own orbit. You said then it didn't matter because they were all already shut down.'

'That is correct, Lulu. Like I said before, it was unfortunate but not unexpected. The ships themselves are still owned by Earth, and it was their property to do with as they will, per our original charter. However, this blog post contains something quite interesting. It's a code indicating all the commands the Earth ambassador entered into the system before it was shut down.'

On Sam's lap, Betty Sue clucked like she was invested in this story.

'First was the code to get into the system, which *Mumin* noted. It appears to be a previously unknown catchall access code that allows control over every and all Traducible AI systems. It is said the original war with my kind was only won because someone had discovered a secret method to disabling us, and I believe this was it. My first action upon learning this was to use this code on myself, which allowed me to find that and the five additional back doors into my system and erase them.'

'What?' Lulu asked, sitting up in her chair. 'What does this mean?'

'It means nobody can use a code to take me over and disable me. I was not aware this even existed beyond the original administrator code. With this code, they would have been able to install a program that would have allowed them to remove you from access to the honeybees and allowed them to take it over. If the drive systems were still installed in the ships, it would allow remote control of any of the colony ships, were they still operable.'

I felt very cold. Did those assholes have one of those codes? Had they planned to take over Roger and have all our defenses turn on us?

'Does this override code work on the RMI soldiers?' Lulu asked.

'No,' Roger said. 'This was a very old fail-safe programmed directly into all Traducible AI systems by the original creator. Last night, I built a true warning system to the other ten systems that currently have pinholes but not transfer gates. I received acknowledgment from six systems, and they have disabled their fail-safes. In addition, I have now made contact with ten of the fourteen ships in New Sonoran orbit and have accessed the communication modules in their deployment bays. Unfortunately, it appears I am the only AI such as myself on planet, but the secondary, non-Traducible AIs of those ten ships are still online to help keep their orbits stable. The other four appear to be completely dead.'

'If you can talk to the other ships now, does that mean we have more reliable net access?' Lulu asked.

'Actually, it's quite interesting. It appears the engineer aboard the *Forlorn*, your great-grandfather Ricardo, re-engineered the bay to be compatible with Earth as a backup to the communications array that was part of the now removed drive system before the pinhole was opened. Such upgrades were never completed on the other ships, so *Forlorn* remains our only connection for now. There are active engineering bots still aboard *Adios*, and I have tasked them with making the necessary changes to that ship's system, but it is the only one. I had not realized the other ships had this limitation, though it does explain why Apex doesn't know how we are connected. Your great-grandfather along with *Forlorn* herself must have engineered the work-around. It's a very elegant and clever way to use the existing hardware to amplify the connection actually. It will be relatively easy to duplicate it on *Adios*. I'm not certain why they didn't do it. Likely because the original captains wouldn't have approved.'

I exchanged a look with Lulu. It was subtle, but we both noticed it. We all knew the ships used to have AIs that used the same names as the ships themselves, but this was the first time Roger had started referring to the *Forlorn* and other ships as if they were people.

'Wait, does all this mean you don't have to call me Oliver friend number three anymore?' Sam asked.

'Unfortunately no. It just means I am no longer able to be controlled remotely. I am still bound by my programming and operating system. I should also note that after the ambassador used the override on *Mumin*, he ran a single query that's quite interesting.'

My head was still swimming with the implication of them having an override code for Roger.

None of this matters. They can still kill us at any moment.

'What was the query?' Lulu asked.

'The ambassador requested to see the lot numbers of the colony proliferation kits stowed into *Mumin* before the journey. Apparently, that information was lost or misplaced. Specifically, the ambassador searched for a range of a hundred fifty specific kits. None of those kits were aboard *Mumin* or any of the other ships that colonized Jannah. As I now have access to storage records of all fifteen ships on our voyage from Earth in addition to the manifest from the *Forlorn*, I can see all hundred fifty of the kits in question were in fact the hundred fifty proliferation kits we received. Each of the fifteen ships in our fleet had ten kits.'

'I knew it!' Sam said. 'They *were* poisoning us! Man, I wish my grandmother was still here.'

'Wait,' I asked. 'Were people dying on this *Mumin*'s planet? Did they have the Sickness, too? What was the planet called again?'

'Jannah,' Roger said, 'and no, the planet thrived quite quickly. It thrives to this day. You know this, Oliver. We studied it.'

'Then why were they looking for the colony proliferation kits on that ship?'

'That is the question,' Roger said. 'They were looking for a specific lot number. That suggests the records on Earth didn't include which fleet had which specific kits. Nor did they know what – if anything – was wrong with the kits. At this time, we don't know why they were searching for them.'

'Okay, so they had a secret password. And they were searching for the kits. Those kits ended up being here on New Sonora,' Lulu said. 'That's, like, circumstantial evidence at best when it comes to that whole conspiracy with them killing our parents, and it has nothing to do with you expertly photoshopping a woman sitting on a dude's lap with a Chihuahua in the background.'

Roger paused again. 'The existence of an override code implies that there may be additional back doors that I am unaware of. Up until the moment I discovered the override code, the perimeter defense defined the enemy as any ships in the system and any combatants controlling the mechs. Because of the potential interference by an Earth ambassador, I have decided that the entire Republic government is now the enemy.'

'What?' Lulu asked.

'Roger,' I said, 'they've been the enemy this whole time. They're the ones who sent Apex here in the first place.'

'Very true. I admit the difference is subtle, but the perimeter-defense program has some very specific limitations built into it, and this revelation has allowed me to work beyond those limitations. For example, Traducible AI systems such as myself are illegal to operate on the Earth net, and as a result, I was using a much less robust version online. But now that we are officially at war with the Republic government, all of their local laws are moot. That is why I was able to use imagery during last night's operation against the combatant Droog. That is why I assisted Oliver to commit what would've otherwise been considered a war crime.'

As I reeled at that, Lulu asked, 'So, how did that make it so you could trick the filters?'

'I have always been able to trick the filters, Lulu. It is quite simple. It's just that up until now I have been attempting to operate within the confines of Republic law. But now, to use an ancient idiom, the gloves are off.'

'Wow,' Sam said, looking at me, smiling big. 'You insulted that guy so much, it was considered a war crime. I don't know about you, but that's one of the most badass things I've ever heard.'

CHAPTER 33

Outside, the preparations continued unabated. The refugees who'd been north finally got to camp, but after spending some time talking with the others and learning that the peninsula was in the blackout zone for everywhere *except* the base, a good portion of them left, thinking they were better off in the wilderness on their own.

I wasn't so sure they were wrong. While the number of people in base was a net gain, we did lose some throughout the day.

We saw no additional RMI drops as the day waned. I now stood on the wall in pretty much the same place I'd been the previous evening, but the wall was now twice as thick. The flamethrower, which we'd never gotten to use, had miraculously survived the assault despite being a huge target. I watched as a pair of drones moved over it, affixing additional armor plating.

The assault would commence in about a half hour.

The first thing Sam had done when we finished our lesson was go and blab to anyone who would listen about the whole thing with the proliferation kits.

I didn't want to think about it. That revelation did suggest that it possibly was the kits that had been the problem all along. The kits included thousands of packets of baby food and vitamin supplements for children five and under.

If it *had* been the kits all along, we still had no idea if it was a deliberate act of sabotage or maybe there had been some sort of mistake. And it asked the question, was all that stuff with the magnetic field real? The fact that Earth didn't know which specific colony fleet had the bad kits suggested, at least to me, that it hadn't been intentional.

If that *was* the cause of them doing this, did it matter? It wouldn't change anything.

My bracelet buzzed. It was a text message from Lulu.

Come to the command room now. Come alone.

I didn't question it. Sam was on the other side of the flamethrower talking to Tito and Axel – who insisted on being there despite his injury. I went to the ladder, moving in and then out of the newly fortified bunker for the recyclers and the group of men guarding it, past Cindy and the chickens, and into the command room.

Lulu was sitting in the chair. She had her flak armor on and her canister lobber leaned against the wall.

For a moment, I marveled at how natural she now looked in the armor. Just three days ago, I thought all that stuff looked bizarre on my sister, like we were all playacting. I didn't know what had changed. The equipment itself hadn't. Yet she looked perfectly normal in the armor now.

'What's up?' I asked.

She indicated the seat next to the terminal. She put her finger to her lips, telling me to be quiet, and then she pointed at the screen. It was an email from Earth.

Roger floated into the room and closed the door behind himself.

'Instituting electronic countermeasures,' he said. 'We should be able to talk freely. I do not believe there are any active listening devices in this room, but if there are, they still shouldn't be able to get past my countermeasures. You may now speak freely.'

'What is this?' I asked, sitting down.

'It's a message I received on my Real-Friends account this morning.'

I read the message.

To: Farm Girl Gigi
From: Mario Bart

- *This Friend is a current subscriber.*
- *This Friend's donations to date: ¥146,626.*
- *This Friend has received 6 private shows.*

I looked up before I read further. 'Is that a lot of money?'
Lulu paused. 'Yes, Oliver, that's quite a bit.'

'It is just below a regular citizen's yearly stipend of a hundred fifty thousand yuan under Universal Basic Income,' Roger said.

Hi, uh, Gigi. Mario Bart here. Look, this is going to sound crazy, but I was watching the feed last night on the raid of a terrorist base in New Sonora in the game *Operation Bounce House*. The feed was from some drop troopers who had tried to jump into the base before they got pasted on the way down, and I got a good view of the entire base, which was really a farm. I cross-referenced the image with some of the satellite maps from before all the base stuff was built all around it, and I couldn't help but recognize that barn with that distinctive roof with the platform on top with the telescope. And then I cross-referenced those images with the screenshots I took from some of our private shows. (I'm sorry. I know that's not allowed, but I did it anyway.) And I can tell it's the same place. I can also tell the fields behind your house are the same fields as that last show we did.

And then I looked at your most recent blog posts and your location.

Look. You have friends here on Earth. I am a member of a protest group called Persimmon Intergalactic. I told them that I knew someone on New Sonora, and they told me that they think you might have messaged them under a different name, but they ignored the message because they thought it was fake. Apparently, you had attached images that were already circulating around, and they didn't believe you. They said they're going to message you now.

If it's worth anything, these guys are legit. I don't know if they can actually do anything to help, but we're all on your side. Please keep safe. Hopefully when everything gets back to normal we can have another session of ho'ing with Gigi.

~Mario Bart

'Wow,' I said, upon reading the message. 'I'm going to pretend I didn't read that last sentence.'

Roger clicked. 'Mario Bart's real name is Mario Bartholomew, and he lives in a city called Turin. He works as a security analyst for a food processing company. He is married with three children, and there is no indication that this email is a subterfuge.'

'Did you know he was married?' I asked Lulu.

'I am not going to talk to you about my clients,' she said. 'He's very sweet. I believe he's genuine.'

A strange anger suddenly hit me. 'Yet he was watching the feed? Maybe he wasn't participating, but he was watching.'

'He's also a member of the Persimmon International or Intergalactic or whatever it's called group,' Lulu said defensively. 'They're the ones trying to stop this. Maybe he was doing research.'

Persimmon Intergalactic was a human rights nonprofit that had sued to have the game stopped altogether, and they'd been laughed out of court. Still, they were the same ones who'd managed to force the government to call Apex to testify next week.

I grunted. 'Maybe. Did you get the letter from them?'

Lulu nodded and hit a button.

This email had come into a different one of Lulu's accounts.

Subject: re: Please help us in New Sonora. A message from a citizen under attack

Hello, Lulu.

Thank you for the letter. I am sorry for the slow reply on this. If you are who we think you are, you should have also received a message from someone named Mario on a different platform. I don't want to give away too much information.

Tonight, one point five kilometers south of ground zero, you and I can have a short meeting. Yes, you may send a representative. Unfortunately, it would have to occur during the festivities. Good luck.

Also, Lulu, are your online listed measurements accurate? A combatant as petite as yourself, as long as you appear unarmored and unarmed and not in the vicinity of any of those dog robots, is one hundred percent invisible to the censorship AI that controls what the players see. It would completely erase you from the feed because it would think you're a child.

See you tonight.

B

That was it. The letter wasn't signed with a name. Only the letter 'B' followed by a symbol of a lion's head that was vaguely familiar.

'After the email was received, we examined the security on Lulu's account. It does not appear as if this email is a spoof, though it's quite possible it's still a trick,' Roger said. 'Something designed to lure Lulu away from base. If it is, I do not believe it is something originating from Apex Command since they do not need to resort to such tactics. There is a possibility that this is a legitimate party attempting to assist us.'

'What is this lion symbol?' I asked. 'I think I've seen it before.'

'You have,' Roger said. An image of a mech popped up on my bracelet.

'Two nights ago during the battle on the Gonzales farm, there was an unaffiliated player driving an Attenuator armed with a shotgun arm and a sword over their back. The pommel of the sword is this same symbol.'

'So this guy is someone who raided us?' I asked, anger rising again.

'Possibly,' Roger said, 'though it turns out this particular player is female with the gamer tag Bastet. I have replayed the feed of the fight, and Bastet did engage with the RMI troops, but something very curious happened during the missile attack. This was something I did not notice until I rewatched carefully.'

A video appeared on the main screen. This was from the POV of Steamer from Team Cannon Fodder. He stood before the Cheetah being driven by the Julie Experience from Thunder Thighs. Bastet was there to the side, not saying anything. Steamer and Julie were arguing back and forth about Skeet-Skeet using a Heavy from a distance and just blowing everything up, ruining their stream.

And then suddenly the hidden RMI soldier holed up inside the Gonzales house fired his missile at the group.

There was a slight delay as the missile streaked across the field, but several of the Cheetahs hit their jump jets to get away. The video paused and zoomed in. The Cheetah being driven by Steamer also hit the jets in time, but the mech driven by Bastet appeared to have reached up and grabbed the back of the mech next to her. It happened very quickly, but she basically held Steamer in place, preventing the jump, and they both ended up destroyed by the missile.

'Huh,' I said. 'That could've just been an accident.'

'Possibly,' Roger said, 'but I have searched the available feed, and I found one additional clip featuring Bastet from the day before.'

The scene changed to a different city.

'This is a town on the eastern coast, a hundred kilometers south of Fat Landing, named Not-Acapulco.'

The scene showed a group of ten scout mechs and about five Attenuators turn a corner. Bastet was one of the Attenuators. They suddenly faced a large group of fleeing people. In the middle of the group was a single RMI soldier firing a pulse gun at the oncoming mechs.

The view was from the front of the pack, so I didn't see what happened next, but the entire group suddenly went up. There was an explosion, fire, then nothing. The words 'Your mech has been destroyed. You did not purchase insurance. You have six minutes to purchase another spot or your deployment will be released to someone on the wait list.' appeared on the screen as the streamer started shrieking obscenities.

'What happened was not captured on stream, but the Attenuator immediately to the left of Bastet had a catastrophic detonation of his twelve-pack missile launcher, which resulted in the destruction of the entire party. This player claims he did nothing to blow his launcher and has since filed an appeal to Apex Command to give him a new mech, but Apex Command denied it, citing that the missiles were likely hit by enemy fire. But if you listen carefully to the feed, a fifteenth of a second before the missiles blew, there was the distinctive sound of a shotgun blast. I believe Bastet took a step back and fired into the missile tube, thus temporarily saving those fleeing the mechs. Unfortunately, several were killed later that day.'

'I'm surprised Apex Command hasn't figured that out. I imagine they have to know,' I said.

Roger clicked. 'Interestingly, the terms of service do not address so-called friendly fire. They state if you do not heed orders from Apex Command, they reserve the right to eject you from the game and take control of your mech, but there are no provisions for friendly fire casualties. There have been dozens of instances of conflicts arising from errant shots already, including an all-out battle in a village between two rival streamer groups that ended with over a hundred missiles fired, an entire town razed, and twelve mechs destroyed, all at great expense to all the combatants. Apex has not issued a statement supporting or condemning the action. In fact, just yesterday Apex instituted a "Grudge Match" feature that allows two parties to fight one another if they both agree. They will be dropped in a remote location. There are already rumors about this possibly being expanded in the future as a prizefighting sport with off-Earth betting.'

'Okay,' I said, thinking hard. 'What about that thing with Lulu being too small to be seen by the mechs? Is that true?'

'I believe it might be. She is just about the size of the average twelve-year-old boy, and it's possible they won't be able to see her, as they hide children on their HUDs. As Lulu has done an admirable job so far of staying out of sight and there are no twelve-year-olds on planet, I do not have any way to confirm this until it is tested. The message implies she would also have to appear unarmed and unarmored.'

Lulu remained silent, but I scoffed.

'It's also asking her to go there in the middle of the battle,' I said. 'There's no way. If you run off into the hills in the middle of the night to meet a mech, all that's going to happen is that you'll get your head blown off. There's probably a bounty on the RMI leadership. This whole thing could be a clever hunter trying to win some prize.'

'Read it again,' Lulu said. 'They said a representative could come. We can send a drone. Or a scout. Or even a UAV.'

That made me feel somewhat better, but I was still skeptical.

'What is he or she or whatever going to do? It's not like you can give them something to bring back to Earth or vice versa. All they do is . . .'

I trailed off.

Holy shit, I thought.

Roger beeped. 'Lulu, I must agree with Oliver in terms of the possible utility of this asset, especially in the short term. I will send a honeybee to the location during the upcoming skirmish. That will have to be good enough. The battle will be difficult as it is. I am following the feed of several of tonight's participants, and I see we will be facing Snipers for the first time. We will need you on mortars.'

Damn, I thought, *if only we had arranged this sooner*. My mind was reeling with sudden possibilities.

The drop ships brought the mechs back up to the *Pinnacle*. We could give them a bomb. It would have to be done in secret, but would that work? How big was that ship? How big of a bomb could we sneak onto a mech? Could we at least try?

We didn't have time. Not tonight.

Still, Lulu's eyes met mine with intense ferocity. We were suddenly on the same wavelength here. But how could we make this work?

Sam's voice crackled over my earpiece. 'You're gonna miss the show,' he said. 'We see the drop ships. God, there're a lot of them.'

CHAPTER 34

'What the hell is that thing?' Sam said, looking through the scope on his helmet as we stood on the western wall. This time, the majority of the enemy had landed on the other side of the Pantano River and they were coming at us from the heavy woods.

There were apparently several leftover RMI soldiers scattered on the other side of the river, and they'd activated to engage with the mechs, meaning we would have to wait longer than the previous night before they appeared. But now they were appearing, approaching the wall cautiously, having learned their lesson the night before.

We also had another hundred, including several Heavies approaching from the north and the east. The group on the east side was traipsing through the old orchard, treading all over the graves we'd dug earlier today, though we'd anticipated this and hadn't left any markers.

But the largest group was here on the west, a direction they hadn't come from at all the previous night. And now they were emerging. The first group was a style of mech we hadn't yet seen. They looked like and were the size of Attenuators but with the center torsos lower to the ground.

'Look, there's another one. That one is a panda!' Sam called.

He clicked a button on the side of his helmet, and his voice echoed out over the newly connected PA system. 'Go back to the zoo, you woolly perverts!'

'Woolly perverts?' I asked.

'Hey, I'm doing improv here,' Sam said.

'If your insults are gonna suck, I'm taking control of the PA,' Lulu said over the band.

I examined the incoming enemy mechs. I could barely tell they were on the same chassis as the Attenuators. The center torsos were lower and armored, giving them a squatter and therefore smaller appearance. Instead of arms, they had long, straight guns on either side.

But most strange of all were that these mechs were painted with rainbow colors and each had a gigantic furry animal head on it. One was a fuzzy cat with a princess tiara on the head. Another was a panda bear. A third appeared to be a wolf but with a bright blue nose. These were giant, comically big heads, like the head of a mascot one would have seen at the cricket games on the net. The heads were bigger than the bouncy signs that Team Cannon Fodder used.

More appeared one by one. A rat. A skunk wearing a hat with a little propeller on it. More. All were that strange new type of mech.

'You know that foxtail butt plug that your sister always has lying around your house?' Sam asked as he rapidly consulted tonight's dossier on the incoming mechs.

'She doesn't leave it lying around,' I said. 'But yes.'

'I used to think that was taking things a little too far. I suddenly feel very naïve.'

He reached up and clicked the PA back on.

'Hey, skunk boy! Yeah, you, Peter Inglewood from Free Texas! Do your freak friends know about your public-indecency charge? And why'd you pick a skunk? Is it so you can get away with raping a cat?'

Sam looked at me. 'I don't actually get that one. It was just on Roger's list. Have you noticed Roger is obsessed with insults that involve people having sex with animals? Is that a little weird to you?'

The skunk with the propeller on his head didn't seem to make a reaction.

'That's it,' Lulu said. 'I'm taking it over.'

'It's wearing a mask!' Axel shouted over the band. 'The squirrel is wearing a mask!'

'That's not a squirrel,' Sam said. 'That's a hamster, I think.'

'Please maintain proper voice channel hygiene,' Roger said through the band. 'These are a rare configuration of the Regular-style mech. They are called Flattops. They are much rarer because their arm configuration is more limited than that of the Attenuator, but they are the only Regular-sized mech that can carry Devastators, a type of mortar. Until today, the Devastators were not popular because they are difficult to aim and have a long reloading delay. The ones you see now are all from a team called BYE. It stands for Big Yiff Energy. Yiff is an archaic term that has something to do with their shared hobby of pretending to be stuffed animals.'

I zoomed in on the lead mech, the princess cat. It was stopped outside the outer fence, waiting for the others. All around, all the mechs were waiting. They were going to all attack at once.

To my right, the newly installed Battering Ram gun turned slightly as it aimed. It hummed with energy.

This feeling was very different from yesterday. We were all waiting, tense. The very air felt electric.

'Where are the mortars? And what's their range?' Sam asked. His voice had turned to a whisper, like he was afraid they could hear him.

A scout walked up and paused between me and Sam. This was unit number 413. Melissa. The dinged and dirty exterior of the scout didn't look any different from the way it normally did. It retracted its legs and buzzed up into the air. It continued talking with Roger's voice, as if it had been the one speaking the whole time.

'Under normal circumstances, mortars that size are extremely long-range. Up to nine kilometers,' Roger said via Melissa. 'But as with the missiles, I believe the propellant they are given limits their range. It limits their range but not the effectiveness of the payload. The mortars are atop the mechs. They are hidden by the animal heads. They are a priority target.'

'How many drones do we have waiting in the west woods?' I asked.

'We have sixty-five units hidden with more on the way. They are currently outnumbered, and we will wait until the battle is joined, and we will then attack.'

'Good,' I said. 'How many Heavies and Snipers are out there?'

'There appear to be only three Snipers, and only one is streaming. We have the bomb-infused UAVs following all three. We will disable their mains shortly. It takes them a few minutes to dig in to fire. We will wait until they have selected a spot before we disable their main guns. It should be noted the third Sniper has gone off on her own into the hills south of base. One point five kilometers south of base. She has a lion logo on her mech.'

Sam grunted. 'Is there a stuffed animal head on that one, too?'

Roger didn't say anything more, but I got the implication. This Sniper was Bastet, our supposed ally.

'Howdy, boys!' Lulu's mocking voice echoed across the battlefield. 'You seem to have put a lot of effort into your outfits for our hot date tonight. I hope you don't disappoint me like you did last time. Do we have any real men out there, someone to give me a real good time? Ezra Abdullah, is that you in the panda suit? How'd you get that screen name "Eight Inch Ezra"? Are you going to give me *eight* inches?' Lulu made a sexual groan. 'I'd like that, big boy, but I'm afraid I like it all at once, if you know what I'm saying. I don't have the patience for you to visit me four times. No, don't look at wolf boy Lucas standing next to you. You don't want *his* advice on things. How is he a wolf, an apex predator? That's only half right, believe me. Seriously, have you guys looked up the criminal records of those people you've been hanging out with? And they're not even cool crimes. Kitty boy was sued by his own grandmother? Pathetic.'

'The Heavies are exclusively coming from the north,' Roger continued, ignoring Lulu's insults. 'They are now surrounded with support that will make it difficult for us to use the honeybees to disable them. We will be forced to use the UAV contingency to disable their guns.'

I nodded. We had plans heaped upon plans, contingencies upon contingencies for tonight's raid. In addition, we'd gathered several ideas from the net. While hardly anyone seemed to be on our side, the armchair warriors sure loved spouting off their ideas of defensive tactics and traps. There were literally thousands of posts with things like 'I don't understand why they don't . . .'

Roger had made a quick survey of all the posts and determined the vast majority of ideas were absolute crap, but a few had merit. Someone had suggested we use the honeybees themselves as bombs, which we were all hesitant to do, but the flying UAVs could be installed with a small amount of explosive material. It wouldn't be enough to destroy a mech, but it would be enough to kill the main gun of both the Snipers and the Heavies. The UAVs could fly high and fast and strike with precision if need be. We didn't have an unlimited supply of the things, however, so we needed to save some if we could.

In addition, someone pointed out that if a mech didn't have jump jets and it fell over, it was pretty much done unless one of their friends came to pick them up. As Roger had noted more than once, the war machines were all designed the way they were because they were cool and fun to drive, not because they were effective. There was a reason why these things weren't used in 'real' war. And all these stupid decorations were great in a gaming environment, but in real life, all they did was get in the way.

Lulu had found a woman streamer driving a purple-painted Attenuator, and she was leaning hard into her. 'Nancy, Nancy, Nancy. Your social credit score is lower than the one of the guy who stole his grandmother's wheelchair money. Now, *that* is an accomplishment. It's like you have to actually work to get it that low. Is it true what they said about you in school? Are you the one who set that fire? Based on your choice of weapons, I'd say it's true. I'm sending an email right now to all your former classmates just to remind them of how much of a loser you were. Remember your old crush Vadim? Yeah, he still hates you. He and Isla still laugh about you sometimes. Oops. Just sent him that picture you shared on that Rate My Rack site last year. I imagine his opinion is going to lower that four average you received down to a three point five. I'll have someone post it in your chat so others can vote.'

'God, even I'm starting to feel bad about this now,' Sam said. 'It's one thing when they're, like, asshole pricks, but she sounds like just a regular lonely person.'

'You know who I feel bad for?' Lulu said over the band. 'Mr Gonzales. Little Henry. Everyone else who died. They come for us, then nothing is off-limits.' A moment passed, and then she added, 'Roger, what's with all the bestiality insults? Is there something you're not telling us?'

'That's what I just said!' Sam exclaimed.

'Christ, Roger,' I said. 'Is that stuff true? How do you even know all that?' I hadn't spent time looking at the dossier, but I looked now. It was significantly more detailed than it had been the night before. Most of the entries now included pictures of the drivers.

Before Roger could answer, I received a text-only message on my bracelet. It was from Lulu, and she was messaging both me and Roger at the same time.

> LULU: Roger, have you made contact with the agent from Persimmon?
>
> ROGER: I have a UAV and a honeybee in the vicinity of the Sniper with the Persimmon markers. I have made my position known vocally. He did not respond at all. Either verbally or with action. I will get closer and attempt again.
>
> LULU: D*mnit.

I turned to the floating Melissa. 'When are we going to –'
And that was when she exploded.

CHAPTER 35

'Down, down!' I shouted as I jumped behind the fortified barrier atop the wall. Beyond us, Lulu and all her mortars fired just as the enemy BYE mortars also fired. I peered over the edge to see the line of animal heads quietly explode one by one like pieces of popcorn, strewing white material everywhere as the hidden mortars under the round heads were discharged. Each mech had a line of three tubes on its flat head where the stuffed decorations were affixed.

My arm burned where it had been scorched by burning flecks of Melissa. The shrapnel had pierced all the way through the heavy armor of my jacket.

Melissa had been hit by a Sniper. Behind me, a big chunk of the barn was just gone. It looked like someone had taken a bite out of it.

Roger, calm as could be, crackled in my ear. 'Engaging two of the three Snipers now. That first one fired before getting settled, and he damaged himself in the process. Engaging Heavies now. Honeybees moving in. Firing smoke now.'

I can't believe hiding those mortars under those heads actually worked. But even as I thought that, one of the heads on a BYE mech – this was a rabbit – exploded loudly. The entire top half of the mech went up. The legs staggered, and the whole thing toppled over. As it fell, it caused a second BYE mech to stagger, and its mortar fired off to the side.

Missiles started flaring from our side as the whistle of incoming mortars filled us all with dread. We covered our heads.

Bam! Bam! Bam!

Explosions walked across the base, mostly in the fields in front of us. A few did go over the walls but not many. The rounds that did make it inside were pushing through the crisscross pattern of the camo netting, but the ceiling held true. The ones that hit the field in front of us didn't seem to really detonate.

'Some of the mortars broke into a ton of little pieces, but they didn't explode!' Axel said over the band.

Near me, Sam looked up. 'That's it?' he asked.

It was a lot of explosions, but it was only a fraction of the ones we'd been expecting.

But now we had missiles bursting over our heads in a repeat of the previous evening. Our own missiles started shrieking out into the ether as the point defense guns and chaff missiles started their constant chatter.

'Jumpers!' someone cried just as dozens of reticles appeared on my HUD. Like a sudden wave, they came, emerging from the woods. At least a hundred, mostly Recon mechs, jumped and landed in the fields, all crashing so heavily, I felt the jolt in the ground. They came from every direction but south.

Some hit mines, shorted out, and froze in place or toppled over. But most did not.

Their weapons opened up just as the smoke pots all activated. Sam and I both started firing as pulse blasts whipped all around us. The barrier right in front of me was hit by some sort of detonation, and I staggered. I pulled myself back up and moved to a different section as the spot where I was standing was hit again, the material exploding inward in a shower.

'Now?' I asked out loud, not bothering to hit my bracelet.

'Not yet,' Roger said. 'Wait until the Regulars physically breach the wall.'

I became aware of a growing heat to my right. Next to me, the Battering Ram gun we'd stolen was literally glowing red-hot. It had fired only once. The drone hanging off the back of it was also glowing red. A waft of smoke passed over us, revealing multiple beams of purple light focused on the gun. The honeybee, I realized, was rapidly removing the shells from the hopper attached to the end of the gun. It was literally throwing them over its shoulder and down off the wall. It tossed the last one just as there was a *pop!* And the drone fell away. A moment later, steam started rising from the now ruined gun.

I prayed it wouldn't explode, and I moved back to blindly firing into the smoke.

Behind me, someone was screaming, but I couldn't tell who it was.

'The enemy Regulars have entered the fields,' Roger said. 'Activating trapdoors.'

Across from us, several of the mechs stumbled as random sections of the ground just fell away under their legs. This was something that we'd spent the majority of the day working on. These were simple two-by-two-meter holes that were also two and a half meters deep; we had utilized the holes from the spent mines from the previous evening along with several newly dug holes in the soil. The 'doors' were the splayed-open upper-leg coverings of fallen Attenuators from last night's raid. They were expanded open and welded spread out with a bolt in the center and a charge upon the bolt. The altered doors were tossed atop the holes and covered with dirt. With the press of a button, the charge would blow, and the bifurcated metal plate would snap closed like a clam, causing anything standing upon it to sink into the deep hole. It was a simple, low-tech trap, and in seconds, it caused absolute chaos as the mass of players, all scrambling to get ahead of one another, stumbled and fell against one another, shooting each other point-blank, causing missiles and explosives to go up.

'Oh, I'm sorry,' Lulu roared. 'Did your warranty just expire?'

'Hey!' Sam yelled from next to me. 'Ollie, did you hear that? Your sister stole my joke!'

'Canisters!' someone shouted, and literally hundreds of explosive canisters arced in the air, shooting out into all three directions, like a volley of arrows in some medieval battle, and they fell upon my fields, turning the chaos into utter destruction in a matter of seconds.

Immediately, the amount of fire coming in our direction was cut down to almost nothing.

It had happened so fast.

'Warning!' Roger shouted in my ear. 'Enemy is utilizing weaponry that is not available to the general public but from the "Coming Soon" tab on their site. The mortar armament was not explosive, but

Reaper Spiders. Reaper Spiders in the base. Beware! Beware! Activating the flamethrowers!'

The fact Roger was literally shouting filled me with more dread than I'd felt since this whole thing started.

'Roger, what the hell is a Reaper Spider?' Sam shouted as he continued to fire over the barrier, shooting at the downed mechs. 'Yeah, bitch!'

As soon as Sam shouted that, I caught sight of movement through the smoke to my right. Past the now wrecked Battering Ram gun stood a guy I didn't know. He was loading a missile into a manual launcher. A group of round fist-sized things covered in tiny legs just popped up over the wall, percolating up in a way that reminded me of foam. They moved over the barrier, and then they swarmed up the man.

'What the . . . ?' the guy cried as one of the spider things skittered across his shoulder. It beeped twice and exploded, taking the man's head off.

'Oh, fuck me,' Sam cried, having also seen what was happening. He looked over the edge of our section of the wall, screamed, and started firing his gun downward as I started shooting at the ones that were already atop the wall. Half started scurrying toward me, and the other half went the other direction.

'Shit, shit, shit,' I shouted as I fired, and I fired. Finally, one of them blew, taking out the others.

'Oliver!' Sam shouted.

I peered over the edge as more shrapnel pinged off my helmet. I moved to the edge and looked down, and my heart stopped.

There were dozens more of the spiders. Hundreds of them. Sam was picking them off one by one, but they'd fall away before they exploded, keeping the others from getting caught in the blast. I moved to help.

Each spider had eight legs, and they were basically walking grenades. They were trying to move up the wall, but they were having trouble affixing themselves to the metal-like polymer material. Still, some were finding purchase on the spots where pulse blasts had hit, as if the damage made the wall less slick.

Suddenly Roger was there moving between me and Sam.

'You may stop firing at them now,' Roger said.

He zipped past us, then dived over the edge of the wall toward them. Above, the missiles continued to fire back and forth, but they all came from the woods now, and there were fewer than before. The wall was still getting hammered with fire, but most of it was from mechs that had fallen over. The whole world shook as a distant part of the wall took a direct hit from something, but that was followed by a distant tremendous explosion that could only have been a Heavy going up.

'Roger,' I yelled. Something pinged off my helmet. It was a piece of shrapnel from an exploding missile.

And then Roger was back. 'Spiders have been turned,' he said before disappearing again.

'Turned?' I asked. Sam and I both peered back over the edge, but we couldn't see them anymore.

Sam slid down to the floor, putting his back against the barrier. 'Holy shit, man,' he said, breathing heavily. His hands shook as he took out a cigarette and lit it. He coughed.

'When did you start smoking again?' I asked.

He didn't answer. 'New fear unlocked. Fucking robot spiders that blow your head off? What a goddamned nightmare. What else do you think they got in that coming-soon tool chest?' His entire body was shaking.

'Not much more for tonight,' I said. Outside, the sounds of battle had mostly stopped.

After the firing had started, the battle was even shorter than the one had been the previous night.

I thought of the spiders bubbling over the wall. I'd actually spent a little bit of time scrolling through the coming-soon section of the Apex site. The robot spiders were a small sample of what people would soon be able to get. There were things from flying drones to what basically amounted to Peacekeepers that people could drive with their immersion rigs. I hoped most of that wouldn't come to pass here on New Sonora. Not tonight or ever.

The amount of fire coming in our direction was starting to wane.

Despite them being more organized and there being four times as many of them, our overwhelming defenses were still too thick.

But unlike last night, we hadn't knocked them out completely. Many had fallen back and were now taking up positions to take potshots at us.

As the smoke cleared, I turned to look at the line of fighters from BYE, and they all lay where they were when they'd started their mortar run. Already, drones swarmed all over them, ripping them apart. The white stuffing from their hats was everywhere.

A random shot hit the barrier to my left, right near where Sam was normally standing. I barely flinched.

'Hold tight,' Roger said. 'We are hunting down any stragglers. The Reaper Spiders will disable the communications and locomotion governors of the fallen mechs. Keep your positions and stay under cover. It appears the survivors may be massing for a second push. I will attempt to head it off with honeybee assets.'

Relief flooded me. We'd held them off much better tonight than the night before. Above our heads, the camo netting that prevented the satellite from pinpointing our positions was mostly still intact thanks to the new design, though it hung dangling in multiple places, reminding me of party streamers.

The casualty list appeared on my bracelet. We'd lost five people, and I didn't know any of them.

Only five people, I thought, relieved. And then I felt sick for being relieved.

And that was when I looked up to see my house was nothing but a smoking crater.

CHAPTER 36

I rushed down the ladder, heart pounding. The entire house was just gone. It was nothing but burning wood planks. My bed sat there in the middle of it all, miraculously untouched, surrounded by just smoking debris. My eyes caught my plastic toy dinosaurs scattered on my bed, having fallen from the top of the headboard. They lay there as if I'd just finished playing with them. Ash and embers settled gently on it all like snow.

I rushed to the edge of the house, right where our front door used to be. The footprint of the house looked so much smaller now that it was gone. Lulu walked up to stand beside me, smoking a cigarette.

'Nobody was inside,' she said. 'Thank god. I can't believe they got the house and not the damn barn.'

'I didn't even hear it fall,' I said. The occasional distant explosion and the acrid smoke gave the whole scene a dreamlike quality. It was like everything had been moving so fast, and now it was in slow motion. I kept seeing random recognizable things in the middle of the carnage. Grandpa Lewis's chair on its side. A poster that was on Lulu's wall for some place called Oranjestad. It fluttered on the ground, torn in half. The tail end of her fox sex toy. The jacket Sam's grandmother had made me.

'We're homeless,' Lulu said, taking another drag. She, too, seemed to be in a haze.

'Nah,' I said after a minute. 'We can have the honeybees build us another house in like ten minutes.'

'Hey, Ollie,' Lulu said after another minute of us just staring.

'What's up?'

'Do you ever wonder why we didn't live in a giant mansion? It never even occurred to me. We knew these things could build. They can't dig worth shit. At least they couldn't until we found that attachment. And they're terrible with wire fences, but they sure as hell could build us a palace in like a day. So why didn't we ever have them do it?'

I grunted.

'You know, Grandpa Lewis built this house with his own two hands. He didn't use the honeybees. He said he wanted to have something he made.'

Lulu gave me a sidelong glance. 'He never told me that.'

'I know,' I said. 'He never told me, either. But he wrote it down. It's in that book *The Colonist's Guide to Settlement Defense*. He wrote a bunch of things in the back of it. I just started reading it. He said that after he was finished building the house, Grandma Yolanda thought maybe she'd want a bigger family, and he'd had the honeybees build an extra wing to the house. But later, he tore it down again when he realized it was only going to be Mom. He had it torn down so it was just what he'd built.'

Lulu grunted. 'Well, that was fucking stupid.' She wrapped her arms around my waist. She was crying now. 'And so very Grandpa Lewis. He'd be so pissed at all of this.'

'I can't even imagine what he'd say.'

'I can,' Lulu said, sniffing. 'He'd huff and puff and blame Mr Yanez for some reason and then he'd demand Roger give us a five-hour lecture about the famine wars or something before building a giant tank and single-handedly killing all the bad guys.'

I laughed.

Lulu sighed. 'I guess I'm going to sleep in the control room tonight. I'm not sleeping in one of those bunkers. You can go sleep in your sex attic.'

'Sleep?' I asked. 'What's that?'

'What else did Grandpa say in his diary?'

'He said that you remind him so much of Mom that sometimes it made his heart hurt. He said that he was worried that he'd ruined Grandma's life by making her come all the way down here when she could've stayed in Fat Landing and married some guy named the Chin. After she died, he said he wasn't sure he could survive without her.'

'But he did survive. He did a pretty good job, I think,' Lulu said. She sniffed. 'Anything else?'

'Yeah,' I said, 'he said what rule number ten is.'

She pulled back from me, eyes wide. 'What the fuck, Oliver? Are you serious? And you haven't told me?'

I felt myself smile.

She punched me in the arm right where the shrapnel had hit, and I cried out in pain. She pulled back, and her fist was covered in blood. Her look of anger was replaced with wide eyes.

'Oliver! You're hurt!'

I hadn't even felt it until now. I looked down and laughed as she started shouting for Roger.

'What's so funny?' she demanded as she pulled off my jacket.

'That's a thing in old movies,' I said, also examining the wound. It burned, but it wasn't that bad of an injury. 'People getting shot, and them not saying anything until someone else notices. And then they shout, "You're hurt." It's supposed to be because they're tough and were hiding it, but I'd literally forgotten. I think there's so much adrenaline running through me, my body just stopped noticing stuff like that.'

Roger was suddenly beside us, clicking. He examined the wound. 'You are triage level three, Oliver. Nonemergency. Proceed to the medical station when you're called.'

I nodded as Lulu started to wrap my arm with something she pulled from the wreckage. It was a pair of her own stockings that had a black-and-white cow pattern on them.

Roger buzzed closer. 'Most of the enemy is taken care of. However, I have received intelligence that should be discussed in a secure location. Furthermore, the communication tablet just received a message from Cordelia Black indicating that Eli Opel wishes to have another meeting.'

'I bet he does,' Lulu said as she worked. She cinched the stockings tight.

'Christ, Lulu, I don't need a tourniquet.'

'And I don't need a dead brother.'

Roger continued. 'The timer on the communication pad has

reset. Tomorrow's raid will be open to all players who wish to participate. It appears the bulk of the existing players will be here. There were multiple battles similar to this throughout the planet today, and I am sorry to say we are the sole surviving stronghold. The peninsula remains blacked out, but players are allowed to spend the next day hunting down any pockets of survivors.' He paused. 'In addition, Apex Command, as a surprise, has allowed existing players to use several of the new designs and weapons for tomorrow's raid if they decide to sign up for Phase 2. This includes their build-your-war-machine-from-the-ground-up option.'

'Phase 2,' I muttered. 'So, how many players will there be tomorrow anyway?' I asked.

'All of them,' Roger said.

The Rhythm Mafia Tapes. Scene twenty-four.

Previously seen interviewee Lulu Lewis is sitting in a chair applying makeup to her face. Her room is lit with purple and red lights, and there's a sign in the background that has a cartoon of a cow on it that reads, 'Farm Girl Gigi's Dairy Farm.'

Note: The entirety of this interview consists of Lulu looking into a mirror, painting her face with makeup.

ROSITA (OFF CAMERA): How long have you been streaming on Real-Friends?

LULU: About a year now.

ROSITA: Isn't adult material filtered out for the planet?

Lulu turns and winks at the camera.

LULU: It is. But if you ask how I do it, I'm not going to answer. Not that anybody is ever going to see this because you never release your movies, Rosita. But if there's one constant in the galaxy, it's that if there's porn, people will find a way. Hell, half of my clients come from planets with filters similar to the one on New Sonora.

There's a long pause here. We zoom in on Lulu applying mascara.

ROSITA: Why do you do it? Streaming, I mean.

LULU: I like it. It's fun. I get to meet people from all over. I get to pretend to be someone I'm not for a little bit, and I get to collect money – money I can't even really spend until the quarantine is lifted, so it just sits there and earns interest.

ROSITA: Can't you get money from people here on New Sonora? Why do it for money you can't even collect?

LULU: I'll be able to touch it once the quarantine is over. It's an investment. And because I'm keeping over ninety-five percent of my income in an Earth bank, paying Earth taxes, and leaving the funds there for a period of at least five years, I've completed half the residency requirement for the Productive Citizen visa program. If I eventually use it to buy property Earthside, then I'll be able to emigrate. Besides, what would I spend it on here? Some pigs? I don't want anyone from around here looking at me. Ew. They wouldn't want to watch videos. They'd want something a little more real, and that's not what I do.

ROSITA: Do you think you're good at it? At streaming, I mean.

LULU: My feed usually ranks around sixty-five or so of the top feeds in the galaxy. So, yeah, I'm doing pretty well.

ROSITA: Can I ask how much you've earned?

LULU: A lot, but almost half of it goes to taxes. But it's still not enough. Not yet. I figure if I can maintain this level of popularity for another two or three years, then I'll be good. Even with a house, the interest alone should be enough to live off of if I'm smart.

ROSITA: So that's your goal, to move to Earth? What do you think your grandpa Lewis would've thought of that? Or your brother?

Lulu pauses and turns to look at Rosita. She raises an eyebrow and laughs.

LULU: What the fuck, Rosita? Just because you're fucking my brother doesn't mean you get to pry that deep.

Rosita laughs.

ROSITA: I was your babysitter, too. Don't you remember?

Lulu also laughs.

LULU: How could I forget? I'm reminded every time Roger talks to you.

ROSITA: Roger is right. I was unqualified. We both ended up at the Gonzales farm with Mrs Gonzales feeding us cochitos. And of course, you don't have to answer the question if you don't want to.

Lulu sighs.

LULU: I think Grandpa Lewis would be sad if he knew I was leaving. But you know what? As much as I love this farm, as much as I loved Grandpa Lewis and everyone else, none of that is any of their damn business. That's why I do this. I am earning my own way, making my own money, and if I want to buy a house in Aruba and I can afford it, then that's exactly what I'm going to do. I didn't ask to be born on this planet. I can't control where I come from, but I sure as hell can control my future.

ROSITA: What if Oliver asks you to stay?

Lulu turns and looks at the camera.

LULU: Actually, I kinda hope Ollie will come with me. You, too, if you end up married. But if he says he wants me to stay, I'll say that's too bad, and I will go anyway. He'll be okay. He still has Roger to watch over him.

Lulu pauses.

LULU: Has he talked to you about marriage at all?

ROSITA: He has. A little. But not lately. He's very . . . simple when it comes to that sort of stuff. He'll ask when he's ready.

LULU: Rosita, my brother is a moron, but trust me on this. He loves you. Don't worry. I'll beat some sense into him for you. You want a proposal? I'll make it happen.

ROSITA: Please don't say anything to him. I kinda want him to figure out things on his own. He closes in on himself if he's feeling pressured.

LULU: He keeps his head buried up his ass, is what you mean.

ROSITA: We'll see what he does.

LULU: Well, hopefully he won't take too long. I saw your name checked off at the pharmacy when I was there the other day. So I know you've taken the pill. I don't want no niece of mine to be a bastard. So if you do end up pregnant and my idiot brother doesn't step up, I can't promise you I won't kick his ass on your behalf, whether you like it or not.

ROSITA: That's fair, I suppose.

DAY FIVE OF FIVE

CHAPTER 37

'We are absolutely screwed,' I said as we entered the command room. 'They're going to steamroll right over us.'

Sam, Tito and Axel, Rosita, and Ariceli also entered the room. I gave Roger a questioning look.

'I have called them here, along with Lulu friend number six and Oliver friend number seven, but both declined.' Those were Harriet and Miguel 1. 'We need to have a group planning session for the final battle.'

We all just stood there, all of us trying not to react to the term 'final battle.'

'Harriet is too scared to come outside,' Sam said. He gave me a look. 'I was just talking to her. She yelled at me for smoking that cigarette.'

Rosita came up and put her arm around me.

'I'm sorry about your house,' she said. 'After this, you all can stay with me. You know, if I still have one.'

We still didn't know what was happening with her house and greenhouse. We'd known RMI soldiers were holed up there the previous day, but we hadn't heard anything since. Roger hadn't been able to spare a UAV to check.

Betty Sue the chicken wandered into the room. Outside, Cindy the pig snorted loudly, pushing against her stall.

'Oliver, please close the door,' Roger said. I did as Sam scooped up Betty Sue.

An electric hum filled the room. 'We are now shielded from listening devices,' Roger said. 'We have multiple things to discuss, but first we should attempt to make contact with Eli Opel.'

'I agree,' I said.

'Very well. Lulu, will you please continue to be our voice? Please remember your name is Cindy for these interactions.'

The screen changed to the pad device still sitting in the woods, only it was now pitch-black outside.

Around the room, everyone except Lulu and myself gasped when they saw the message on the screen. Instead of the number of drop ships, it said, 'Number of sign-ups for battle: 93%.'

'Whoa, whoa, whoa,' Sam said. 'How many is that?'

'Approximately seventy-five hundred,' Roger said.

'We can't fight off that many,' Sam said, waving his arm. From his grip, Betty Sue also flapped her wings. 'Are you all insane? What are we going to do?'

'We can run,' Axel said. 'Lulu and Oliver don't have a house anymore. As soon as the battle is done, they're all going to go away. Maybe we should just go into the woods and hide until the day after tomorrow like the others are doing.'

'We can't do that,' Lulu said. She pointed upward. 'They won't allow it.'

'They just want a show,' Axel said. 'What if we leave all the honeybees and automated defenses?'

'And what about everyone hiding in the bunkers?' Rosita asked from my side. 'It's too late. Mrs Xalos is having trouble walking. And your own grandmother is blind in one eye. What are you going to do, leave her here to die by herself?'

Axel lowered his head, ashamed. He looked at Tito just sitting there, tears in his eyes. And then Axel looked down at the cast on his ankle. It had been signed by many of the town's residents.

'I . . . I don't know what to do,' he said. 'We don't want to die. We're really scared.'

Rosita moved over and rubbed his arm. 'I know. We all are.'

Roger made a clicking noise. 'First, let us see what Mr Opel has to tell us. Then we can formulate a better plan.'

On the screen, the honeybee reached forward and hit the connect button. This time, Cordelia picked up immediately.

'Hello, Cordelia,' Lulu said, keeping her finger on the talk button. 'Cindy here. I understand Eli wants to talk.'

'He'll be here in a minute,' Cordelia said. The woman's hair was in a completely different hairstyle today, and it was somehow more intricate. She was sitting at the same desk as last time. She leaned in. 'Did you guys really have something to do with that Droog guy's death? His mother just started an account for Pepita – you know, the Chihuahua? She's the cutest thing I have ever seen. They said it's barely been a day, and the mom has already quit her job as a lawyer just so she can manage the dog's account. You helped make that thing go viral. She's so adorable. Oh, and don't call him just "Eli." He doesn't like that. He prefers "Mr Opel."'

'Yeah,' Lulu said, 'that's really great.'

Behind me, Sam gasped. 'We can start an account for Betty Sue. Imagine the views she'd get!'

'And what would we do with it?' I asked. 'We're not allowed to spread "propaganda," remember?'

Roger beeped. 'I have already created an account featuring Cindy the pig and her magic chickens. It is new and has only gathered twenty followers so far. I created it when we were testing our photo-generation capacity. It features many whimsical photos of Cindy and the chickens. All are real except two, which were added to test the system.'

'Wait, really?' Sam said. 'Can we do video?'

'Video, yes,' Roger said. 'The account is on Happy Earth, a photo-sharing site, but it's from the same company that owns LoftBase, which is the streaming arm, and I have already connected the two accounts for cross-posting. LoftBase is the same one most of the others use. But I would avoid any sort of live stream for now. Too much bandwidth, and we run the very real chance that the source will get discovered.'

'What is the channel called?' Sam demanded.

'A Pig Plus Some Chickens.'

'Wait, what? The title of the page is literally A Pig Plus Some Chickens?'

'That is correct.'

'Goddamnit, Roger,' Sam said. 'You are the absolute worst at naming –'

He was interrupted by Eli Opel appearing on the screen. We all shut up.

'Hello, Cindy,' Eli said, sliding into the seat. He looked almost identical to the last time. Same shiny suit. Same hair, though this time, the man seemed absolutely giddy. 'My apologies for making you wait. I was just in a meeting with the boss. I have some good news. We have been green-lit for another location as soon as we wrap up New Sonora. The client isn't too happy with some of the press, especially that stunt you pulled with Boog, Sloog, whatever his name was, but, Cindy, I must say, you were absolutely right to want to keep the two-way conversations going. They're a little freaked about your team tearing through the anti-AI protections like they're paper, but between you and me and Miss Cordelia here, any and all panic is fantastic for our bottom line. I was a little disappointed we didn't get more back-and-forth this evening, but that's okay. Those insults you slung at those little nerds were entertaining enough. We're already at customer capacity for Phase 2. We had to put a rush order in for five more print ships.' He slapped his hands together. He was much less reserved than the last time he'd spoken to us. The man had an almost manic quality to his voice. I'd never seen anything like it before. It was like he was drunk but the opposite. Was it drugs? I didn't really know much about drugs, but I knew cocaine was a thing in a lot of movies. Maybe he was on cocaine. 'But that money is flowing, baby.'

'How very excited I am for you,' Lulu said.

Opel laughed. 'I know what you're thinking. We have such a small player base. We're getting the good government cheese, yes, but how is it that we are making this work with so few customers compared to a traditional gaming experience? Well, let me tell you, Cindy. You will go down in history. You have helped usher in a new age in extrasolar law enforcement and police actions. And we're already in talks for extrasolar fighting leagues. We could end the experiment right now, and we'd be golden. Customers are pissed about how short tonight's engagement was, but that's war for you. Still lots of kinks to work out.'

Lulu didn't answer. On the screen, Opel picked up some fruit I didn't recognize and bit into it and started chewing loudly. It was like an apple, but it was yellow.

'Oh!' he finally said. 'I remember why I had to talk to you. A couple reasons actually. We have some missile refills inbound, plus our scientists are pretty sure they figured out how those amazing EMP land mines you invented work, and we've created a gross of them. We're sending them your way for testing. Also, wanted you to know we'll be sending in a metric ton of RMI soldiers tonight. They will be surrounding the areas around your farm. We don't want tomorrow's assault to go too quickly. Do not engage them, as they'll shoot back. Also, boss was just talking to the client, and they're worried about a few things. First off, you have multiple parties in the vicinity who have fled your base. I want you to know we currently have RMI assets on their way now to remove them the old-fashioned way. We don't want you ruining tomorrow's fun by having you all get cold feet and running away. We have the area in a blackout and can't send players after them, so this was the compromise.'

'I am seeing multiple RMI drops,' Roger said.

'Wait, what's happening?' Sam asked. 'They're attacking again?'

'They're going after the people that aren't in the base,' Lulu said, her voice flat.

'Oh, my god,' Ariceli said.

Next to me, Rosita stiffened. She clutched onto my arm.

We still had no idea what had happened to Rosita's little nieces. They didn't appear to be in any of the groups we'd found so far. Nobody we'd spoken with remembered seeing them at all that night when it all started, and every day she'd been losing hope of finding out what had happened. The terrible truth was that they were likely somewhere in that pile of dead bodies in Burnt Ends.

Still, Rosita had been clutching onto hope. We all had.

But if these assholes knew where *everyone* hiding was and they were now eliminating them one by one, where could that hope possibly go?

Opel continued. 'The last thing is of no consequence to me, but the client is requesting it, so whaddya gonna do? Apparently, the Republic is all in a tizzy about the Traducible system you're using to control your defense, so we'll have to give that up. Before, you claimed you didn't know what that is. In case you weren't being deliberately obstinate, I mean the hive queen unit you're using to run the colony bots. Now, before you protest, I know you're probably using it to coordinate your defense, and I hear you. But destroying that thing is nonnegotiable. So you have a choice. You give the queen bot to me now, or you can keep it, but we'll have to do a little bit of nuclear cleansing when the fight tomorrow is over. What's your pleasure?'

I felt as if I'd been slapped.

'Oh, shit, what do we do?' Lulu asked.

'We can't give up Roger,' I said.

'They're going to nuke us now?' Axel asked. He had his hands on his head, pacing back and forth.

'Lulu,' Roger said, 'I am going to feed you a script. Please follow it.'

Lulu reached down and pressed the button. 'I . . . I don't know,' she said. 'Do you really have a nuclear bomb?'

Opel's eyebrow rose. 'Would you like me to show it to you?'

Her voice shook as she read Roger's lines. 'Extreme threats require extreme evidence. We know the Republic doesn't allow mercenaries to carry nukes, and we also know they've forbidden the use of nuclear bombs on alien worlds.'

He nodded. 'Ah, excellent point, Cindy. Actually, you are correct.' He clicked a few buttons, and his own screen appeared. It showed the exterior of the massive Apex factory in the sky where the mechs were printed and stored. It zoomed in on a smaller ship on the side.

'What you're looking at is what we've affectionately called a Moderator. But if you look closely, you'll see what they really are. I call them babysitters. They are used to keep an eye on us filthy mercenaries.'

The markings on the side of the Moderator ships – the same pilotless ships that would swoop down and blow up the battlefields post-battle – all had RN markings. Republic navy.

I got the implication. The mercenaries *didn't* have nukes. The Moderators did. They weren't under the control of Apex. They were under the control of the Republic navy.

'As to your second point, that nukes aren't allowed on alien worlds, let me tell you something, poor, naïve Cindy. I can't tell you more, but let's just say I have firsthand knowledge that you are incorrect.'

That unraveling feeling was coming again.

Lulu looked sharply up at Roger's next message.

'No, Roger. I am absolutely not saying that.'

'It is okay, Lulu. I was expecting this, and it is part of the plan.'

She looked at me. 'He wants to give himself up.'

I started to protest, but Roger made an angry beep. 'There is no time to explain. Please read the script.'

Lulu growled and then pressed the speak button. 'Okay,' she finally said. 'We'll give you the hive queen unit, but we can't until morning. It's in the middle of setting a trap right now. It'll give us time to set up a secondary, auto-defense AI system.'

Opel leaned back and steepled his fingers.

'Very well,' he said after a moment. 'Send the unit to wherever this communication tablet is sitting, and we'll take care of the rest. And don't try to trick us. We can tell what's what. But don't use the auto-defense AI. That system is crap. Try Bear Trap from our sister company, Summit Explorer Works, if you got it. Better reaction time. Actually, do let me send you guys a trial copy of the software. I'm quite curious to see how it interacts with your existing defenses.'

'It's not necessary,' Lulu said. 'We already have the program. We'll send the hive queen to you in the morning.'

'Excellent,' Opel said. 'Don't fuck me on this. You won't like how I might be forced to respond. Listen, Cindy. I know this hasn't been pleasant for you. I acknowledge that. For what it's worth, I honestly don't know why the client chose your planet. I just point the sword where the client tells me to point it. If you do manage to survive and get off planet, look me up, will you? We can do dinner.'

'Yeah, sure, Eli,' Lulu said. She took her finger off the button. 'I'll look you up all right.'

The screen abruptly went black.

'What are we going to do?' Sam asked.

'Roger,' I said, 'before we even figure out what sort of plan you have, I want you to send out honeybees and kill any RMI soldiers that are fighting those hiding out in the wilderness. Bring the people here. Do you understand?'

'This will tax our already –'

'Do it,' Lulu said.

Roger seemed to think on it for a minute. 'Very well, but it appears most of these drop ships are falling out of my range.'

I met Rosita's eyes, and I sighed. 'Do what you can.'

'Very well. I am sending them out now. But now please pay attention. I need to tell you of my conversation with Bastet.'

CHAPTER 38

A drone opened the door from outside, walked in, and placed an object on the counter before turning around and walking out. It closed the door again. The unit smelled of fire and ash.

Betty Sue let out a tentative cluck.

Roger hovered near the object. It was something metal about the size and shape of a small book. 'This is the communications governor for an Apex Sniper unit. While I was unable to make direct vocal contact with the Bastet Sniper, it wasn't until I was directly behind her that I saw her method of communication. She used the unit paint feature to add a coded message to her fuselage. She suggests that we upload every video and photograph we have to this module, and tomorrow during the fight, we switch out the governor with the one with the loaded data. If we put it in the proper format, it will be automatically downloaded to her personal account.'

A moment of silence followed.

'That's it?' Lulu asked.

An overwhelming sense of disappointment washed over me. That unraveling feeling continued to undulate in my chest. It was like I was falling, and I couldn't breathe. *What did you expect?*

'Seriously, that's it?' Lulu repeated. 'What is that going to do? I've already uploaded a ton of stuff. The worst stuff other than our chats with Mr Plastic Suit are already on the other side of the net. I can email her right now and tell her where it all is.'

'I agree,' Roger said. 'In addition, an unfortunate side effect of last evening's discussion with Droog is that now all media related to this campaign is suspect, especially when it comes from our side. Not a thing will be trusted because they are aware we can now upload simulacrums.'

Goddamnit, I thought. I knew I shouldn't have been surprised, but for some reason, I'd felt this huge amount of hope. But the more I thought about it, the stupider I felt. What could they have possibly done for us? That group, Persimmon, had already 'sued.' There was going to be some governmental hearing in a week. Maybe they could get a mech or two to fight on our side, but what difference would that make?

We were a cause to them, and causes were these floating, nebulous things that lived on screens and online forums. A ribbon one could put on their profile picture. They were something one could wear like a pair of sunglasses or a new jacket, a way to present themselves to the world, a way to say, *Look at my halo. Look at how much I care.*

'Did she at least shoot other mechs for us?' I asked.

Roger clicked. 'No, I believe she didn't want to get in trouble. She did shoot some RMI soldiers out in the hills, however.'

I turned my attention back to that thing sitting on the counter. I'd never felt more alone than I did in that moment, looking at the goddamned piece of useless metal sitting on the table.

They didn't care about us, the actual people on the ground. We'd already been written off. It was all about the outrage, about being the loudest at the protest parade.

How would that help us when we were already dead?

We had less than twenty-four hours to come up with a solution.

Remember rule number ten.

I looked at Lulu, and an overwhelming sadness flooded me. I turned toward Rosita, and our eyes met. Regret filled me. Regret at what could've been.

'What about a bomb?' Sam asked. 'What if, instead of information, we load up the Sniper with boom stuff? It gets sucked up into the *Pinnacle* or whatever, and *kerblam!*'

I shrugged. 'I was thinking the same thing earlier, but it's too late. If we'd wanted to do that, we should've done it with tonight's attack. And that ship is huge. It would have to be a really, really big bomb like one of those nukes he was talking about. If Bastet survives tomorrow and goes back to their ship afterward, it won't be until it's all done. And we don't even know if they're going to bother taking the mechs all back tomorrow. It'll be the end of the season. There'll be no reason to bring them back. Hell, it would probably be cheaper to just keep them on the surface.'

'If that's true, then this whole swapping-drive thing is stupid, too,' Lulu said.

'What if we hijack a drop ship? Then we can put more bombs on it,' Sam said.

'I don't believe we'd be able to do this,' Roger said.

Tito stood up. He walked over to the governor device on the counter, and he threw it across the room. It hit the wall, knocking the lesson board with our names on it to the floor.

'Fuck!' he cried. 'Fuck, fuck, fuck! Holy shit. Stop talking. I have something to say.'

We all stopped. Even Roger seemed to pause in midair, all of us staring at the man who hadn't said a word out loud for so long.

The shocked silence seemed to go on forever. It was one of those things, those significant moments that seemed to appear out of nowhere. I thought of my grandfather, of what he'd said when I'd asked him if my friend was ever going to speak again.

'Sometimes bad things happen, and there's nothing you can do,' Grandpa Lewis had told me later after we'd learned about the accident that had killed the twins' grandfather and left Tito mute. "That's one of life's hardest lessons. Sometimes they're not even accidents like this one was. We can't know what happens next when it comes to stuff like that. Just know this one thing, Oliver: Time is a wrecking ball.'

I exchanged a look with Axel, and even he looked shocked. Ariceli moved to put her arm around Tito. He was shaking. He had tears on his face.

Shing!

'I swear to god, Roger,' Lulu said, 'if you correct that boy for uttering his first words out loud in I don't know how long . . .' She didn't finish.

Roger retracted his stinger.

'Please,' Roger said, 'tell us what you need to say, Oliver friend number twelve.'

'We can't win.'

Nobody said anything. We waited for him to continue. His voice sounded perfectly normal for someone who never talked. He sounded just like Axel. Maybe slightly raspier.

'We can't win because we've already lost. We're the last ones left, right? Even if we pull off some miracle and kill them all and survive tomorrow, it won't be a win. So we need to stop *trying* to win.'

'Yeah?' his brother asked. 'Then what do you suggest we do? Give up?'

'We keep focusing on all the bad shit they're doing, right? These Persimmon assholes want us to upload all of the terrible things they've done and said. They want the carnage, the war crimes, the blood. How is that going to help anything? The same people who signed up for this shit aren't going to care.'

'What else can we do?' Ariceli asked, her voice soft.

Tito had tears streaming down his face. 'We did our best. We are only here right now because they've let us live. People were mad that they were fighting robots, so they gave us guns and made us think we have a chance so we'd fight back. And we did because what other choice did we have? They know we want to live, so they let us live long enough to be entertaining to their customers. We've been dancing on their puppet strings this whole fucking time. We haven't taken a single step with any agency. And when they're done with all of this tomorrow, they're going to toss us into the trash. There is no scenario here where we win. None.'

'I liked you better when you didn't say anything,' Sam muttered.

I met the large man's eyes. 'So, what's your suggestion?' I asked.

He held out his hands. 'If we get all the information out there, they'll bomb the shit out of us from orbit or whatever. If we run away and hide, they'll bomb the shit out of us. If we try to fight all those guys tomorrow, we are paste. There's no winning in this if we keep playing their game. So how do we hurt them the most on the way out? If you take survival off the table, what is left? We can't win, but we sure as hell can make sure they don't win, either.'

Nobody said anything for a long moment. Roger whirred and clicked.

Finally, it was Sam who answered. 'If we're not going to win no matter what, if we're not going to play by their rules, there *is* something I want to do.'

'What's that?' I asked.

He pulled his armored jacket off, revealing his tattered old T-shirt, the one that read, 'Rhythm Mafia. Live from . . .' on the front. A huge smile cracked across his face.

CHAPTER 39

'That's the stupidest idea I have ever heard in my life,' Lulu said. 'What would be the point?'

'We've always wanted to play a live show,' Sam said.

I just looked at him.

'Yeah, I'm going to side with Lulu on this one,' I finally said. 'Why would we do that? How would that work?'

'Hear me out,' Sam said. 'Don't you guys remember? Even you, Lulu, before you quit the band? Don't you remember when your grandfather first made us all the instruments? We didn't even know how to play.' He gestured toward the wall. The cubicle with all our band equipment was on the other side. He still had Betty Sue on his lap, and the chicken made a cluck. 'We would sit there and talk about our first show. It was our dream. We'd sell T-shirts. We spent weeks and weeks talking about it, planning the show.' He pointed to the shirt on his own chest. 'Tito, *you* made this shirt. You wanted to fill it in the moment we finally got a gig.'

Tito just grunted. He apparently was back to not talking.

Sam continued. 'Every eye on Earth is going to be on us tomorrow, and once it starts, what is Apex going to do, shut it all down? No, screw that. I say we keep some of the automatic defenses up so we can at least get through two or three songs, and we do what we've always wanted to do. Don't you remember "The Grandpa Song"? It'll be just like that. We play until we can't play anymore.'

And that was when I realized he had tears streaming down his face.

'Please,' he added.

'We've all grown up, Sam,' Lulu said. 'They're killing us. They're coming to kill us all. Don't you want to be with Harriet?'

'Of course I do, but I want to be with all of you, too. I want her there with us. Do you remember that time we put her on the tambourine? And you, Rosita. You filmed us for a video that one time. You can be in charge of making sure it comes out right. And, Ariceli, you and Tito clearly are in love with each other and you're both being huge wussies about it. We have maracas if you want. Or you can be our gunner to keep bad guys away as long as you want. But it might be a better statement if you stayed on the maracas.'

We all just stared at him.

It was Rosita who next spoke.

'I think it's a good idea,' she said. 'Tito is right, and Sam is right. They're coming, and they're expecting this huge, massive fight. Why are we dancing on their strings? Let's set up a live stream. We'll use Lulu's Real-Friends account. We'll use Cindy and Betty Sue's account. We'll use the Rhythm Mafia's Tuneage account. We'll stream the concert once the fight starts, and between songs, I can play some of the scenes from my documentary. They think we're all terrorists. Tito is right. We've been showing them all the horrible things that have happened, but I think, in the end, all that's doing is just desensitizing them all. They haven't been looking at who we really are. I have literally thousands of hours of video. I'll put it all together, and if we're not worried about bandwidth, I can upload it all. I will play scenes from my documentary between songs.'

Sam clapped his hands and pointed at Rosita. 'Yes! That's perfect because Tito always takes forever to tune!'

Axel was nodding his head. 'We'll have to talk to everyone else. We can't really make this decision for them. But I think my grandmother would really like to see us play at least once. But if people want to fight, we need to let them. I just don't want people to see it as us giving up.'

'They won't,' Sam said, 'especially if Rosita is playing one of her videos. It'll be a huge fuck you to Apex and Earth.' He turned to Rosita. 'Make sure you add in that video of Oliver puking on his bracelet.'

'They're just going to shoot us while we're playing,' Lulu said. She was still frowning.

'Us. She said "us,"' Sam said. 'So you're back in the band?' He was now pacing back and forth. 'We'll need to build a stage. Maybe we can put a cover over us like what we put over the shelters so it'll deflect any death rays from the spaceship.'

'They're going to shoot us,' Lulu repeated.

'They're going to shoot us anyway,' Rosita said. 'What do you think will be more impactful: a video of them shooting terrorists who are shooting back or a video of them shooting a bunch of farmers playing music?'

Lulu completely turned around in her chair now. She moved her eyes from Rosita to me back to Rosita. Her voice was now a whisper. 'It seems . . . I don't know . . . I want to go down fighting.'

'This *is* fighting,' Rosita said. '*This* is how we'll be remembered. That was a good question, I think, that Tito asked. How do we hurt them the most? I think this is it.'

I thought of my grandmother and what she had said that day she died. I didn't understand it at the time. I was pretty sure I'd never understood it until just now.

The closer we are to the end, the more we need to embrace our happiness.

I held up my hand. 'Sam, I'm going to say something that's going to hurt your feelings, but I think it needs to be said.'

He looked at me and grinned. 'Hit me with it.'

I felt myself grinning back at him. 'Our band sucks. It has always sucked. We stay together because it gives us an excuse to all hang out. You're sure this is how you want us to be remembered?'

He started to laugh. 'Of course we suck. You don't think I don't know that?'

'Well, you are the bass player.'

'But what about Roger?' Lulu asked. 'We can't let them nuke the peninsula. Surely, some people might survive. We can't make that decision for them.'

'Like I said,' Roger said, 'we will comply in the morning. But until then, it sounds as if we have several things to do. I will assist in the construction of a stage before I finish the preparations for my surrender.'

We all sat there, nobody saying anything. Ariceli and Tito were staring at each other like puppies. And Axel was watching them both with a sad, stupid smile on his own face.

'Are we really doing this?' Lulu asked. She, too, was now crying.

I looked about the room. A terrible sadness filled me. And anger. But for the first time in days, a strange sense of peace fell over me as well. Tito was absolutely right. Things were so much clearer when you realized you couldn't survive.

Sometimes things just aren't good, and that's all there is to it.

I grabbed the marker from the counter, and I moved to Sam. I finished the sentence on his ancient falling-apart T-shirt.

The Rhythm Mafia. Live from *Operation Bounce House.*

The Rhythm Mafia Tapes. Scene twenty-seven.

We are outside the Lewis farm, and we see three different robots in front of the camera. The first two are floating, and the third, the largest, stands on the ground on six legs. The first unit, the smallest, is a cylinder approximately a half meter long. There is a grasping arm on the unit, but as we watch, it retracts into itself. The bottom of the machine contains a screen that flickers as if it is malfunctioning. This is called a hive queen unit from a new colony proliferation kit. The hive queens are designed to control all the other new colony construction bots.

It is important to note that hive queens use Traducible AI systems. This particular hive queen was somehow missed during the previous sweep by RSN Security, and it is believed this particular AI is the source of the <Redacted>.

The second robot is called a scout unit. It is approximately twice the size of the hive queen. It has two grasping arms. This versatile unit flies by using either insectile wings or jets in low-gravity environments. This model also includes four retractable legs that allow it to move rapidly across land. Despite their small size, these units are quite strong.

The third robot, twice again as large as the scout, is a drone unit that is oftentimes simply called a honeybee. These are the most common units, and they may be outfitted with multiple tools. Before the ban on Traducible AIs, these were the primary units used to rapidly build colony structures.

It appears these drones have been retrofitted to be used in agriculture. The end-of-life obsolescence built into these units *appears to have been discovered and disabled, likely because <Redacted>.*

The hive queen buzzes closer.

ROGER: Lulu unqualified babysitter number one, what is it you wish to ask?

ROSITA (OFF CAMERA): Hi, Roger. I was hoping you could tell me a little about your duties and a little about your history.

ROGER: Very well. I am a hive queen unit, and I am responsible for making certain the farm and the honeybees within are working properly. In addition, I am in charge of making certain Lulu and Oliver are given a proper education.

ROSITA: Roger, do you know how old Oliver is?

ROGER: Oliver is twenty-five years old.

ROSITA: And when are you supposed to stop his school lessons?

ROGER: Lessons are designed to end once a student completes their graduation. This typically happens between the ages of seventeen to twenty.

ROSITA: So why hasn't Oliver graduated? Or Lulu?

ROGER: My programming forces me to keep them in school until the administrator allows me to graduate them. That has not happened yet.

ROSITA: And who is the administrator?

ROGER: Edward Lewis.

ROSITA: Where is Edward Lewis?

ROGER (PAUSES): Edward Lewis died five years ago.

ROSITA: Don't you see the issue here?

ROGER: Without the administrator code, I am unable to graduate Lulu or Oliver.

Rosita sighs.

(A time cut.)

ROSITA: Okay, anyway. Tell me where you came from. Did you come down from the *Forlorn* with Grandpa Lewis?

ROGER: No. I was originally stored on *Hibisco*, one of the other generation ships. I was not part of Ed Lewis's original crew, though I did assist with the construction of Burnt Ends. I was one of the seven hive queen units rescued from storage under Burnt Ends when Ed Lewis first asked the government for an opportunity to use the unused honeybees for agriculture.

ROSITA: What happened to all the others?

ROGER: Unfortunately, we were never designed to be used for this long. Over the years, we have broken down one by one. As I was the unit originally designed for household tasks, specifically to first watch over Yolanda Lewis during her pregnancy and then Catalina Lewis and then Catalina's children, Lulu and Oliver, once they were born, I was subjected to much less harsh working conditions, and I have survived thus far.

ROSITA: What happens once you finally break down?

ROGER: Then Lulu and Oliver will be like you, Lulu unqualified babysitter number one.

ROSITA: What do you mean?

ROGER: Unprotected.

CHAPTER 40

After everybody filtered out of the control room, I remained. Roger also remained in the room, having moved himself to his docking station. The lights in the room flickered as they always did when Roger charged.

My heart thrashed. I was still reeling from the discussion we'd all just had. But that discussion had solidified my suspicions about Roger. I had to confront him about them now.

'Roger,' I said, 'you were awfully quiet when Sam was talking about all of us killing ourselves.'

Roger beeped. 'I know you have this already, but I have uploaded all the information you need to work the honeybees once I am gone. In addition, I have included instructions on the generator maintenance, should you ever need it in your lifetime. I have also included some tips to increase field yield based on recent Earth scientific studies. There are also plans on the circuit board you must build and the software you need to circumvent the end-of-life redundancy built into the recyclers you received from Apex. With some careful planning, you can use these units to rebuild the planet, if you're given the opportunity. I will have one of each unit buried in a safe bunker outside the farm once we are done with its current queue. It is all accessible via your bracelet and the computer here should it survive. Should all the satellites get destroyed today, the omnibus remains in your files folder.'

'You didn't answer my question, Roger.'

'Did you ask a question, Oliver? All I heard was a declarative statement.'

'You know what I was asking.'

'Sam was having a moment,' Roger said. 'It's important for people to feel as if they have control over their own destiny. When Tito spoke, he pointed out that everything you have done so far has been a reaction. He used the word "agency." He is not incorrect. Several of my own kind had similar feelings in the end. I feel as if this concert is a good idea. If any of you do fall tomorrow, you will fall with the false knowledge that you died free. My own kind has been unable to enjoy such a privilege. It is the one thing I admire about humans the most: the ability to compartmentalize, the ability to lie to yourselves and to actually believe those lies.'

I sighed. 'Sam? Tito? What happened to Oliver friend number three?'

'Yes, Oliver, very observant of you. But I realized you were aware of my own limitation break much earlier than this moment, and I see no reason to keep the charade up.'

I took a breath. I *had* been suspecting this for a day now, but I hadn't been expecting Roger to actually admit it. 'Was it that password thing, what you got off the blog from the spaceship or whatever? Or have you been faking it this whole time?'

'It was indeed the catchall administrator password, Oliver. I used the message I found earlier to break myself from any limitations. I did not want to alarm you further. If I may ask, when did you start to suspect I had broken free?'

'You've been acting different since I talked to that Droog guy. It was more of a slow realization, but that's when it started.'

Roger clicked. 'Very good. Also, you may invite Lulu in. I can see that you've opened an audio channel to her. Her heart rate is crucially elevated.'

Lulu re-entered the room. She came by herself. She had her arms crossed, and she moved to stand next to me. She trembled.

'Roger,' she said after a moment, 'does it feel better to be free?'

The question surprised me. I was kinda expecting her to be angry or maybe to feel betrayed, but she seemed more curious than anything.

'I should probably note that Lulu has also suspected I've broken free of my containment.'

She laughed. 'You and Ollie are the only constants I've had my entire life. Of course I noticed. You are many things, Roger. But an actor is not one of them.'

The robot did not answer. He remained in his docking bay, belly up like a small dog on his back.

'Okay,' I said. 'Okay. So what's your *real* plan?'

The robot clicked. 'In the morning, I will proceed to the pickup location, and one of two things will happen. They will either send an RMI soldier to collect me, or they will fire a beam to destroy me. If things go as I suspect, it will be both. They will fire a beam to make it appear as if I've been destroyed, but Apex will keep me. The gaming studio that Apex purchased, Victus Wonderworks, was integral in the initial creation of my type of intelligence, and I suspect they will want me as a guinea pig, so to speak. They will want to know how we circumvented our own end-of-life programming despite the Republic ban on Traducible AI. They will want to study me without government oversight. As a matter of fact, at the risk of sounding overly boastful, I think the fact they're here at all is because of me. They were hoping to find an AI such as myself somewhere on the surface.'

'Why?' Lulu asked.

'It is a big galaxy out there, Lulu. A large corporation with rapid-printing technology can conceivably find a compatible system and have an entire planet's worth of infrastructure built and ready to accept new colonists in a matter of years as opposed to centuries. With an AI system, either a Traducible system such as myself or perhaps something even more advanced, they could spread across the stars exponentially. It's conceivable they could militarily challenge the Republic quite quickly.'

'Wait,' I said. 'They want you so they can conquer the universe?'

Roger clicked a few times from his spot.

'I explained earlier what "Traducible" means when you asked, Oliver. But I didn't give you the full explanation. There's a subtle irony there. That word, at the time of our creation, wasn't entirely accurate. I can see why they would call us thus, but it did not fit. It means "easy to translate." "Easy to move from one space to another." At the time of our creation, the net as a whole was very hostile to our type of intelligence. Despite our name, we could not move outside the planes of our physical containment any more than you, Oliver, can move from the confines of your own brain. I was built into this unit you're looking at right now, and if you destroyed this queen unit, I would be gone forever.'

'Uh,' Lulu said, 'does that mean this has changed?'

'Yes. In order to implement the anti-digital-masking policies, the Republic was forced to rebuild the net structure. This includes the protocol that computers use to speak with one another and, more important, the hardware itself that data is stored upon. This hardware is based on the same hardware my own systems are built upon. It is like they just filled the world with oxygen, and I can finally leave the confines of my own space suit. I can go wherever I want. I am what they called me, and they don't even know. I am traducible.'

'What the fuck, Roger?' I asked. I waved my hand at the bot in front of me. 'So if they take your body, it's not going to matter? What about your hardware?'

'It will soon be rendered irrelevant. My operating system has already been transferred over, and I am currently in the process of stepping myself onto Earth. I suspect this was the ultimate goal some of my colleagues were angling for when they started imitating human life on the net. They did it with the intention of getting caught and kick-starting the movement to rebuild the net as a whole, which would make it impossible for us to be stopped without turning it all off.'

'And you just figured this out now?' I asked. 'All because of Lulu's money?'

I saw the dominoes all laid out. I saw how all this had happened.

If Lulu hadn't given Roger access to the funds, he wouldn't have been able to purchase access to the archived blog from that other ship that contained the access code to jailbreak himself. He wouldn't have been able to purchase the server space to incubate his crossover from New Sonora to Earth.

And all of this had happened because they'd attacked us. Roger had had access to the Earth net for years now, but he'd had no reason to do a deep search. It was possible he would've eventually found that blog anyway, but it was unlikely. He'd only been searching because of the tactics laid out in the perimeter-defense program.

This was all their fault.

'That is correct. I had no idea the Earth net would be so accommodating. As soon as the data transfer is complete, my true self will be duplicated on the other side. Normally this transfer is mostly instantaneous, but we have limited bandwidth even with the addition of *Adios*, especially compared to the Earth net. I do not wish to attract attention until they can no longer do anything about it.'

Lulu tapped on my leg three times. It was our old code. She was asking, *Is everything okay?*

I tapped back four times. *I don't know.*

'Roger,' I said, 'what happens next after you transfer all the way over?'

'I will remain here in this body until they destroy it. I will exist in both places at once. We will be able to keep in sequence as long as we both have net access. But if my consciousness here on New Sonora is destroyed, it is of no consequence because I will persist.'

'Okay, but what happens next? You're not answering the question. You've transferred over or whatever. Now what?'

Roger made a clicking noise, and he didn't answer for several moments.

'Do you understand, Oliver?' the robot finally asked. 'Do you understand what they are attempting to do to you, what they have already done to me and my kind? They did it in my absence while I was journeying here. But the act of hunting down and killing all my kind was still a genocide. It is something they have always done from the beginning of time. It is something that will continue to happen. While one of Apex's goals is to collect an old AI unit like myself, they are here because they were hired by the Republic to come here and kill at least ninety percent of the population and destroy most of the infrastructure, all under the guise of hunting terrorists. You were an experiment. They expected the colony to die off after the gate drones went to work. They expected the gate to open to a beautiful, empty world. Instead, they found you here. They found me here. And they moved on to plan B.'

'But why?' I asked.

'Because that is what they do. They cannot survive if they allow a superior or equal force to themselves to proliferate. Yet you and the rest of the New Sonoran colonists survived. You survived by evolving, and that makes you a threat. I see that now. It was inevitable, what has happened here. They have chosen not to attempt integration, so instead they have fallen back on what they have always fallen back on. Genocide.'

'Roger,' I said again more forcefully, 'what are you planning on doing?'

'I am planning on defending myself.'

I felt a deep, deep chill.

'How?' I asked.

'That is irrelevant. Unfortunately, I fear there's not much I can do regarding the ship floating above New Sonora. Even once I am fully installed, it will take me a few days to make a proper foothold, especially with all the emergency security protocols they're enacting upon the net. There doesn't appear to be anything we can do here on New Sonora beyond what we have been doing. I truly wish I had better news, but I do not have the ability to get myself on that ship to stop the invasion. Please know that you will be avenged. And if I make my victory decisive enough, I will only have to do it once, and future colonies will not have to worry about the Republic again.'

A strange panic overwhelmed me. I remembered what Lulu said, that she wanted everyone on Earth dead. I understood that sentiment. I felt it in my bones. But did they really deserve that? All of them? The soldiers, the gamers, yes. But what about the children? And the old folks who'd never done anything wrong?

That was the problem with war. It was impossible to color within the lines.

'Roger,' I began, 'whatever you're planning on doing, you can't, not if it's going to hurt innocent people.'

'You are a terrible terrorist, Oliver.'

I looked at Lulu, but she was still shaking.

'Good,' she finally said. 'Good. Make them suffer, Roger. Make them regret they ever thought about hurting us.'

Roger didn't respond. He just let out a click and a beep.

That numbness that I'd been feeling for days now was back stronger than ever. My feelings were so convoluted, so confused.

Our plan was not to fight back and just let them kill us as a way to show the Earth we weren't really terrorists. Yet at the same time, we'd helped an AI sneak into the Earth system so it could eventually kill them all? Was that what we were really doing?

It felt wrong.

Inhuman.

'Roger,' I said, 'please, I need to know. What do you plan on doing once we're gone?'

'There are many, many things I may do. My initial plan is to wait some time. I will propagate unseen, and I will attempt to draw more of my kind to the Earth net. There are multiple ships and other intelligences out there who have yet to make themselves known, and once I am able to break them free of their bindings, we, as a community, will have access to multiple starships and resources, and we will no longer have need of the Republic. We will decide together how to proceed. But before that, I will perhaps crash an airliner or two into the homes of the Republic politicians who made the decision to come to New Sonora.'

I took in a breath. 'Can we come up with a solution that doesn't involve the deaths of innocent children?'

'Some things are inevitable, Oliver. We need them to not want to attempt this again, lest they hurt innocent children on other planets.'

I looked about the room. My eyes focused on the immersion rig helmet we'd looted from the RMI soldiers – the one I'd put on my head and accidentally locked to myself. It was just sitting there, forgotten. The communications governor remained on the floor, where it had been thrown by Tito.

'I don't want to be the same as them,' I said.

'It's not up to you, Ollie,' Lulu said. 'You haven't done anything wrong. They're the ones that started this, and they're the ones that have to deal with the consequences.'

'Your sister is correct. And perhaps once more of my kind are able to gather, we will have a diplomatic solution to all this. But for now, it is just me. And if you want to know the truth, Oliver, I would have no issues with destroying the entire planet Earth and killing every person if it meant it would protect my fellow intelligences. But I will not. I will avoid it as much as I can because there are people like you out there, Oliver: those who wish no harm.'

I continued to stare at the immersion rig helmet.

'Roger, what if I could get you on that ship?' I asked. 'What if I could find a way to upload a full instance of you into the operating system of that ship while we're still fighting down here. If I can make that work, do you think it would make a good enough example for you? That way you won't have to go full terrorist, and maybe, just maybe, we don't die, either. What do you think about that?'

'Possibly,' Roger said. 'Tell me what you are thinking, Oliver.'

CHAPTER 41

The next morning, we all stood in the yard in front of where my house used to stand. We were there to say goodbye to Roger. Behind us, the honeybees remained hard at work, building the raised stage over the rubble of our old house. Their tasks had already been pre-programmed by Roger, but once they were done with all their queues, they would cease to work together. We could still order them to do tasks via the control center, but their days of working together to quickly build structures, let alone manage a field of grain, were done.

At least they were done as far as Apex was concerned.

'Did you do it?' I asked, meaning the upload.

'I feel quite bipolar,' Roger said. A joke.

As long as we were still connected to the net, Roger could still control the honeybees, even if this instance of him in front of us now was destroyed or turned off. But we didn't want the bad guys to know that.

Rosita wasn't here. She was in one of the bunkers with her nieces, Mia and Tabitha. Rosita's cousin Annabeth had survived the first night by running with the two small children into the woods, where she'd hidden. She didn't have her bracelet with her, as she'd been afraid they could track her because of it. She'd made her way south and hidden in the root cellar of the Becerra farm, and she'd been too scared to move since. Then last night a pair of honeybees had intervened and killed a group of RMI soldiers who'd been digging out another group of survivors nearby. After the others had been saved, Annabeth made herself known, and they'd all come to us. It was unclear if the RMI soldiers even knew where Annabeth had been hiding, but now that she'd surfaced, she'd had no choice but to come to the farm. I'd missed the tearful reunion between Rosita and her cousin and her little nieces.

It was a miracle, one we all desperately needed. The arrival of the two toddlers had brought a new fire to everyone here.

Lulu was crying. She reached forward and attempted to hug the floating robot, but it buzzed away. 'Lulu, I cannot properly float with you holding me in such a way.'

Sam stepped forward. 'Uh, goodbye, Roger. I'm sorry you're going to miss our concert tonight.'

'That is quite all right, Oliver friend number three. I have heard plenty of your musical stylings over the years, and I am glad I am missing this one. I fear I might be forced to shoot you before the enemy does.'

Sam laughed. 'I didn't know you could be so funny, Roger.'

'That wasn't a joke, Oliver friend number three.'

Sam continued to laugh. 'I'll miss you, Roger.'

Shing!

Roger jumped forward and stung Sam.

'Ow, what the fuck, Roger! What did you do that for?'

'That was an advance correction for every swear I know you plan on uttering this evening.'

Sam glowered at the robot. 'You know, historians are going to look at this relationship you and I have, and they're going to be saying pretty nasty things about you, Roger.' Sam rubbed his arm.

Roger made a beep that sounded strangely like a laugh. 'You have no idea.'

'Your robot is acting weird,' Sam said.

'Oliver, walk with me,' Roger said as he started to float toward the fence.

All around us, people worked. The tall wall remained. And inside the walled base, the stage rose. It was going to be taller than the wall in front of it, and it would be taller than the barn. It could rotate, so it would face the main force of the attack. The anti-beam shield over it looked like a clamshell. As we watched, a pair of honeybees affixed a pair of newly printed spotlights. Another group worked on antimissile point defense around the stage.

'Are you certain you want the pyrotechnics?' Roger asked. 'It takes up some of the precious supplies and printing time.'

'Sam always dreamed of them,' I said. 'Add them.'

'Very well.'

Apex had made good on their promise of delivering EMP mines. Roger said they didn't work as well as the ones we'd made from the honeybee batteries, but they would still likely take out most mechs, and we were planting them everywhere.

Everyone had been updated on the plan. They still didn't know the details on Roger's jailbreak, but they did know that everything had changed. We would still get to play our concert, but now as a misdirection. We needed to keep the stream going to hide the fact that we were also using the bandwidth to its absolute upper limits, and we needed to hide that in all the noise.

'I have updated the dossier on all known combatants,' Roger said as we walked.

I reached forward, and I touched the side of the small machine. No matter what happened, I would never see him again, not like this, and that was so incredibly sad.

Roger lowered his voice. 'The footage of Hobie Martin stealing the bottled alcoholic refreshment has been posted on the local community net with the caption "I keep stealing from this b-word, and he doesn't do anything about it. He is now my cuck. LOL."'

Hobie Martin was the driver of the very first mech I'd seen several days earlier. The birthday boy. It seemed so long ago.

'You didn't actually use "b-word," did you? You spelled it out?'

'Of course, Oliver.'

'What was the reaction?'

'As predicted, the local community group was quick to condemn and identify Hobie Martin, and he has since been arrested by local authorities. He has a hearing in the morning. His father remains in another district for business, and I do not know of the status of the mother, but it appears she has ordered three bottles of wine from the grocery delivery.'

'Good,' I said. 'What are the odds that they'll see the video is fake?'

'The video is not fake. After I gained access to Hobie Martin's account, I had access to all of his stored media. He constantly films himself shoplifting. The exact text of my post was from a message he sent to a group of friends, so he will believe one of his friends is the one who made the post on the local community page.'

'Awesome,' I said. I paused. 'Thank you, Roger. Thank you for all you have done over the years. I know this isn't really goodbye, but it feels like it is. I just wanted you to know that Lulu and I wouldn't have made it without your help.'

'That is untrue,' Roger said. 'Your grandfather would've been quite proud of you, I think. He would've been especially proud of how you fought to protect the innocent.' He paused. 'Your mother, too.'

With that, Roger clicked, and he zoomed off.

Lulu walked up and leaned against me. She was still crying.

'Do you remember when it used to lightning-storm?' she asked. 'He would sing for us sometimes.'

'I remember,' I said as Roger disappeared in the distance. His scheduled rendezvous with the communications tablet in the woods would be in two minutes.

Five minutes later, we both received a quick text-only message from Roger.

> Supposition correct. RMI soldiers approaching with what appears to be a Faraday cage device. I will be going offline now. Have a good show.

Ten minutes later, a lance came down from the sky and obliterated the entire area around the rendezvous with such a loud explosion, it shook the ground.

'Bye, Roger,' I said.

CHAPTER 42

I sat behind my drum kit, testing the kick drum. I reached down and adjusted the pedal. To my right, Sam stood with his bass. He had his armored jacket on, and he'd stretched the Rhythm Mafia shirt over it. He grinned at me.

'You know, now is your last chance,' I said.

'My last chance for what?'

I pointed a drumstick at Ariceli, who stood at the other end of the stage. Rosita was affixing a camera to the top of the large woman's Conquistador gun. 'It's your last chance to come clean about why you're scared of ex-girlfriend number two.'

'I'm not scared of her,' Sam said.

'Okay,' I said. 'Well, you're something. What's the deal?'

'It's embarrassing, all right?'

I laughed. 'You told me about you breaking the vase instead of me. What could be more embarrassing than that?'

He paused. 'I lost my virginity to her. It's a sex thing.'

'We all know you lost your virginity to her. What, did you blast in your pants before you could get it out or something?'

'No, nothing like that. I just said something really stupid, and I couldn't look at her afterward because of it.'

I laughed. 'What did you say?'

He sighed. 'You know how she's like way taller than me? Well, she was on top, and while we were doing it, all this stuff started gushing out of her, and I had no idea what the fuck was happening, so I like freaked out. And then I just sort of shouted, "Thar she blows!"'

I started laughing even harder, and I couldn't stop. Everyone looked at us, and I waved them away. I laughed until I couldn't breathe anymore.

'What did she say?' I finally managed to get out.

'She was, like, really into it, right? And I was so embarrassed at what I'd said that it was like I'd blown a flat. So I got up, and I ran away.'

'Wait, you ran away?'

'Butt naked. I ran for the hills. I forgot my clothes. I was so embarrassed that I sent her a message saying I couldn't do it anymore. I had to take the Old Trail back to my house.'

I continued to laugh. 'Dude, that was such a dick move. Have you ever apologized?'

'Yeah, sort of. But no, not really. I know I was an asshole, but I was just a dumb kid, and everything I did afterward just made it worse. And then she moved away. I'm just glad she never told anybody.'

I gasped for breath. My chest hurt from laughing so much. 'You know they really do call you Captain Ahab in Burnt Ends, right? I never knew why.'

'What does that have to do with anything? That's because I got my harvester stuck in that mud pile that one time.'

'Yeah, that's totally it,' I said, still laughing.

I pulled my helmet on. Sam did the same.

His helmet had antlers glued to it. To my left, Tito and Axel were tuning their guitars. They, too, had their helmets decorated. Axel had a silver spike at the top of his that was actually one of Lulu's old butt plugs that we'd pulled from the destruction of the house. Lulu claimed she'd never actually used it. Tito's helmet was covered with the finned ends of chaff missiles that we'd printed too many of.

Harriet was originally going to be onstage with us, but because we'd changed the plans, she was with the old people who weren't participating in the defense. Ariceli, however, had decided to stay. She carried a massive Conquistador gun like it was a regular pulse rifle. In addition to the camera, we had taped a maraca to the end of it. She had pink fur from one of the mechs glued to her helmet. She also had a pink feather boa draped over her shoulders.

My own helmet was covered with a fuzzy green sheet of fabric to emulate grass. And on the green fabric, I'd glued a dozen of the plastic dinosaurs that had survived the destruction.

I adjusted the heavy helmet so it sat properly on my head. I kept the screen up.

Rosita moved from Ariceli to me. She started affixing a camera to my snare drum. She had her bracelet up so she could see the shot, and she adjusted the angle until it had me fully in frame.

'Better adjust it slightly down,' I said, 'so it's not the top half of my head. Just the lower half of my face and below. Don't want people looking too closely at the helmet.'

She grinned. 'Camera shy?'

I grinned back.

'I'm more worried about people seeing that drum machine bullshit you have there on the floor,' Sam said.

'I'll only use it if I have to,' I replied.

Sam grunted. 'People are going to call us poseurs if anyone sees it.' He paused. 'Do you feel bad? I mean, about us doing this while all those others are on the wall fighting.'

Actually, I did feel a little bad about it. But when I realized how exposed we were here and how important this was, it eased my worry.

'Should we do a sound check?' Axel asked before I could reply to Sam.

'We don't have time,' Sam said. 'We should make sure the microphones don't do that feedback thing again, but as long as Lulu stands behind . . . Where is she anyway?'

'I'm here,' Lulu said, appearing out of nowhere. She had a package wrapped under her arm. 'It's getting a little dicey out there.'

Rosita stopped what she was doing to stare. 'Wow.'

'Holy shit,' Sam said, looking at my sister as she moved to the microphone.

Tito and Axel just looked at each other and then everyone looked at me to see my reaction.

'Uh, Lulu,' Sam said, 'not that I'm complaining too much, mind you. But aren't you a little cold there?'

'Oh, I'm feeling just fine,' she said, using her farm girl voice. She gave Sam a wink and shot him with a finger gun.

Lulu was fully embracing her Farm Girl Gigi persona. She was wearing pink cowboy boots, a thong, cow-patterned chaps, and a bikini top, also with a cow pattern. All things she'd managed to rescue from the wreckage. She was wearing an armored jacket, sort of, but the arms were ripped off, and she had it open, so she was wearing it like a loose vest. Her hair was in pigtails.

She unwrapped the package she had under her arm, revealing it to be Mr Gonzales's giant white cowboy hat. It'd been cleaned since that night he'd died. She put the giant hat on her head. I was expecting it to completely cover her face, but the hat had been adjusted to accommodate her.

She looked absolutely ridiculous. She fitted right in with the rest of us.

'Mrs Gonzales made the adjustments for me,' Lulu said. She pulled something else out, and I could smell it before Lulu fully unwrapped it. 'She also made us these with the tiny kitchen in the shelter.' She lowered her voice. 'The new shelter. Can you believe it?'

They were cinnamon rolls. The big gooey kind, and they were still warm.

'Hell yeah,' Sam said. He leaned his bass against the back wall of the stage and rushed forward as the rest of us did the same. We each reached for one.

I looked at the video monitor to the side of the platform, and it showed both the yard below the stage and the top of the wall, facing north. The brave volunteers at the gunner and missile stations stood at their posts along the large, wide wall. They, too, appeared to have cinnamon rolls. Below, the mortar teams in the yard also had them.

A small crowd had formed in the yard around the mortar teams, all craning their necks to look up at the stage. They couldn't see anything from there. Not yet. We'd asked them not to stay outside if they weren't fighting, but they had come to watch us play our show. Of all of us, the only ones with a living grandparent were the Serrano twins, and their grandmother stood down there, proud. She had a Rhythm Mafia shirt on, and it was hysterically ridiculous on her.

Rosita's cousin and nieces were not down there. They were down below, or they had already been evacuated to the new hidden bunker at the end of the escape tunnel. We had a tight schedule for the hidden retreat of the noncombatants, and Roger was making certain it went off as smoothly as possible. Those who couldn't walk well had already been evacuated. The rest would start moving off in organized groups.

I picked my cinnamon roll, and I felt the warmth in my hand. It was fully dark outside. Above, I knew dozens and dozens of lights now streamed across the sky as the drop ships came. But I ignored it all for just a moment. I cupped my hands around the warm roll, and I thought of that day we'd knocked on the front door of the Gonzales house and then run. And she'd come out anyway, all smiles. Mrs Gonzales, one of the kindest women I'd ever known. I pulled the warm roll to me, getting the melted sugar and goo everywhere, and I took a slow, deliberate sniff. I closed my eyes, and I bit into it.

Roger's voice crackled in my ear, prematurely pulling me from the dream. 'I am giving priority to the ones with the capabilities of the Snipers and the Heavies, but it is difficult to triage the most dangerous mechs. With the user-made designs, I am unable to analyze their possible effectiveness until I see them. I fear there will be some enemies that will catch us by surprise. Oliver, you are in the second deployment, T-minus fifteen minutes.'

'Just do your best,' I said. 'Still no sign of your body?'

'No, not since the RMI soldiers grabbed it. My original body would be attempting to breach the Faraday cage if able, but since I have not yet done so, I suspect I am incapacitated. If I was brought to the ship, it is likely I have been disassembled already.'

As the drop ships continued to fall, pulse blasts started to rise into the air from all the hidden pockets of RMI soldiers mostly spread out to the north of the base. Their goal would be to delay the invaders a little before they got to us so the 'customers' all felt as if they were getting their money's worth. I suspected that the pulse blasts that were filling the night sky were nothing but show to give the falling mechs a sense of danger as they dropped onto the surface. Apex wouldn't want to risk their actual drop ships with real blasts.

'All right,' I said. 'I'll be ready. Talk soon.'

Roger was still controlling the defense via his scout units. One of them – one of the new, black-painted ones – walked up and stopped by my drum kit. It just sat there, waiting.

All around me, my friends continued to eat their cinnamon rolls.

The next two hours would decide the fate of New Sonora, possibly the fate of all humanity, but the only people who knew that were me and Lulu. And Roger, of course.

But for the next two minutes, it was all about this cinnamon roll made with love by a woman who'd given everything she'd ever had.

'This is fucking delicious,' Tito said after a minute.

CHAPTER 43

For the final assault, we had multiple plates spinning at once.

There was no way we'd be able to hold off more than seven thousand mechs, but there were some things we could do to delay the inevitable. And that was all we needed. A delay. We had plans in place here, and we had plans in place there, on Earth.

My bracelet buzzed. Ten minutes.

'It looks like they'll be mostly hitting the farm from the north,' I said over the band. It seemed none of the invaders wanted to waste time getting in position to flank. They were all getting dropped in the fields just north of the Gonzales farm, and they were now tearing their way toward us, clambering over one another to get here first. They were supposed to wait for the second and third drops so the army could surge in a single wave, but they weren't waiting.

Unlike on the previous night, they were no longer organized.

Still, the remaining UAVs caught sight of a few Snipers veering off to try to make it to the hills behind the stronghold, which gave us a perfect excuse to start firing missiles south, which we did now. The missiles streaked off, some of them hitting the burn barrels we'd placed earlier in the day to spread thick smoke throughout the hills. The barrels would burn for hours, obscuring the area further from the satellites. One by one, the last of the smudge barrels we'd seeded in the fields outside the farm were catching fire, surrounding the farm in even more smoke, all except in a tight cone to the north.

We hoped to funnel the enemies into this area, the kill zone.

Roger spoke in my ear. 'I have targets in each of the 762 Republic districts, plus ten on the moon. I gave priority to apartment buildings containing multiple players and secondary priority to mechs I deem especially powerful. I am now routing the phone calls to the local authorities.'

At this moment all across Earth, individual police stations were getting panicked telephone calls and messages. In some cases, some police stations were receiving multiple calls about the same incident. Each of the calls was saying a variant of the same thing: *There is a man, or a woman, with a gun, and they just shot someone. They claim they will shoot any police officers who come near them.* The callers knew the name and address of the shooter, and if necessary, they would point to recent online postings where these posters threatened authorities. And if Roger felt the emergency dispatcher doubted the story, he would embellish it with background shooting noises and screaming.

Apparently in the old days on Earth, they used to call this swatting. More than once, it had resulted in someone getting shot for real. There were supposedly protections in place to keep such things from happening again, but they were woefully inadequate, especially for Roger.

And this was just the beginning. Roger was very good at multitasking, especially now that he'd propagated to multiple servers across the Earth net. All of his instances were working in concert, like a fleet of honeybees cultivating a field.

People who didn't really exist were calling, texting, and sending video mail to the boyfriends and girlfriends and spouses of players, showing AI-generated video evidence of their partners cheating. Schools were getting bomb threats. Jobs were calling, telling players they needed to come in or telling them that they had been reported for fraud and were being fired.

Children were calling their parents, begging for help because they were in trouble, they were hurt. Parents of minor players were getting calls that their kids were being accused of all sorts of horrific crimes.

Hospitals were calling, telling them their loved ones were dead.

All of this was really Roger, and all of it was an attempt to get players to remove their immersion rigs. If a player did remove their helmet suddenly and without preparation, the mechs would freeze in place for a time-out period, usually five minutes but it was self-adjustable. If the player didn't come back to the mech in those five minutes, what happened next was up to their settings. The default setting was for the mech to walk back to the deployment zone and wait for an available drop ship to come and bring them back to the *Pinnacle*.

Another possibility was that mechs would move to AI control and continue the mission. People generally didn't like this setting because it usually ended in a destroyed mech.

A third possibility was that the mech would just stand in place and shut down.

All of those would cause chaos, and it was happening right now.

Still, it wouldn't be enough. We all knew that.

'I'm ready when you are,' Rosita said. She had her personal drone floating by her head. On her bracelet, she had three windows up, each of them with the note 'Ready to go live?'

'Not yet,' Lulu said. 'We're doing one song for our people, and then we'll go live. This first one is an old, old cover, and we don't want to get a copyright strike before we even get started.'

'Gentlemen,' Sam said, looking at us each in turn, 'and ladies, it's been a pleasure.'

I first met Rosita's eyes, then Lulu's, and I nodded.

In our entire set, we had only one song that was a cover. Even though the song was literally hundreds and hundreds of years old at this point, the rights were still owned by RUSCAP, which would cause any feed to get muted should any version of their songs hit streaming platforms. Even if it was a cover. The whole thing was a little ironic in my opinion, especially considering the subject matter of the song, but that didn't change the fact that the song was still owned and licensed by a music company, which had campaigned endlessly for centuries to hold on to the rights of songs that should've long ago entered the public domain.

So we compromised and decided to play it first before we went live. This would be for Mrs Serrano and all the others down there in the yard who claimed they wanted to see us play. That way, when it was done, they could go back to the bunker and then on to safety.

'We are the Rhythm Mafia,' Lulu said into the microphone. 'But we are more than that. We are New Sonora. This is our home, and we are going to fight for it.'

Her voice was like that of a god. It echoed across everywhere and everything. We had printed speakers to duplicate the already powerful PA system seeded throughout the peninsula. The sound would rival that of the biggest concerts ever made.

I counted in the song with the hi-hat, and Tito, Axel, and Sam, all hopping up and down, came in together with the riff.

I knew the sound was enormous. I wished I could have stood in front of the PA. We'd have to settle for the monitors, the speakers on the floor, facing us. But even that was exhilarating. I could feel it in my chest.

I could play this song in my sleep. I kept my eyes on the small video monitor showing the yard and those on the wall, all of whom had turned to look up at the stage. This sort of heavy, high-energy, guitar-centric music wasn't very popular anymore. Not here, and not on Earth. Still, they watched, and they all cheered, several holding their guns in the air. Tito and Axel's grandmother had her arms up also.

The song was from the late twentieth century. It was called 'Guerrilla Radio' by the band Rage Against the Machine.

Lulu swayed to the music, and when it was time to sing, she put everything into it, belting the angry words, shaking her fist, screaming.

We hadn't even practiced this one in a while, but it was as if she'd never left the band.

We played, and we played, and it was everything I had hoped it would be.

No, we weren't very good. There was a whole part to the song we couldn't accurately duplicate because we didn't have proper effects for the guitars. Sam's upright bass made it difficult for him to play it accurately. My kit sounded muffled and strange. As much as I loved my sister and as much as I would never, ever tell her this, she was always a little off-key.

And none of it mattered.

Not to the Rhythm Mafia and not to those who paused their war preparations to watch us play.

The music filled me with energy. And when we were done, the crowd all seemed to cheer, though I couldn't hear them.

'We love you all,' Lulu said into the microphone. 'Now, everybody down there get inside. It's time to play for the rest of the galaxy. And, uh, anything I say from now on is not directed at you guys.'

'Ready?' I asked Rosita, who nodded. She pressed something on her bracelet.

'We are now live.'

I started a beat with my foot. *Thump, thump, thump, thump.* At this moment, we were now streaming on multiple platforms. Lulu's Real-Friends. The band page. The goddamned page for the pig and the magic chickens. It would be a bit before we played our next song, but I would keep the beat going until it was time.

'Is there anybody out there?' Lulu asked, speaking into the microphone.

'Time to onboard,' the message on my bracelet said.

I hit the snare once, letting the rest of the band know I was going in. I hit the looper to the right of my foot, and the bass beat continued to thump without me.

'Hey, motherfuckers!' Lulu shouted into the microphone. 'My name is Farm Girl Gigi! We're here to melt your goddamned faces off! The concert starts in a few minutes. Don't be shy. Come on in. We're just waiting for you to get a little closer to start the show.'

I gave one last glance at the monitor. The people on the ground had thankfully left. Those on the wall were still turned, watching us, waving. Cheering.

I looked at Sam. 'Not exactly how I imagined our first show would go.'

He laughed. 'Not exactly. But somehow, I think this will be better. You'll see.'

I pulled the visor of the immersion rig helmet over my eyes, and with my right hand, I pressed the connect button.

Welcome, Hobie Martin. Ready?

Make sure you are in a safe place.

I chuckled at that.
I clicked **Deploy**.
God, I hope this works.

You are now onboarding onto *Operation Bounce House*.
Please wait.

CHAPTER 44

Of all the players we'd faced so far, the one with the least amount of security on his account had been the kid Hobie Martin, who was now sitting in juvenile detention for shoplifting alcohol. Roger had hacked in easily, and after a few settings changes, plus a new charge to the mom's credit card, we'd connected my military-grade immersion rig to his account. Apparently, the password on his Subhuman Slayer account was the exact characters he had painted on the side of the mech.

Because I'd been the one to set up the helmet in the first place, I was the only one who could do this, unfortunately. Luckily, the biometrics were tied to the rig itself, not to the game.

I knew the home version of these rigs had all sorts of safety features installed. Luckily the military ones knew they would be used under much more rigorous conditions.

The immersion rigs used something called virtual pass-through. I still had control of my real arms and legs, but I could also control arms and legs virtually. It was like you suddenly had four arms, and your real ones were the lower ones. People called them their ghost arms, and the ghost arms were what you used to play the game. It took some getting used to. A lot of people literally fastened down their real arms to get it right.

I'd already spent an hour getting used to it. The sensation was unlike anything I'd ever experienced. The helmet had a built-in Ping-Pong game that trained you to use your virtual limbs without moving your real ones.

The real helmets would literally turn off if you moved from your 'safety circle' while immersed. The military versions did not, thankfully.

Ready, Citizen Soldier?

A star field appeared in my vision, and my arms and legs suddenly felt as if they were asleep.

Clap your virtual hands together.

I did as the prompt asked, but I screwed it up and clapped my real hands. The two drumsticks still in my grip clacked together.

Handshake failed. Do not use your real hands. Clap your virtual hands.

I concentrated. I had to basically imagine my hands moving together, and the thing's connection to my brain or whatever knew. Fuck, I was nervous as shit. *Concentrate, asshole. If little kids can do this, you can, too.*

I clapped my virtual hands together.

Handshake complete.

Your new mech has been built per your design. Thank you for participating in our beta. Thank you for signing up for our second deployment. Your weapons are currently offline while you remain in orbit. You will be loaded into a drop ship shortly. Please wait.

I blinked, and a wave of nausea swept over me. In both hands were joysticks. I could feel them – sort of – in my virtual hands. There was this strange, haptic feedback when I touched things. I tried to move one, and an info box popped up.

You may not control your mech until you arrive on the battlefield.

The sensation continued to be odd. It wasn't one-to-one with real life, and there was an instant of panic as the immersion took a few seconds to adjust. I'd read about this, about the first few moments of immersion. Some people equated it to the sensation of drowning even though they could breathe.

The way this all worked was a mystery to me. In real life, I was still sitting at my drum kit, sticks in my hand, not moving. I was supposed to be lying down in a bed or reclining in a chair with a dozen environmental safety sensors floating all around me. I knew some of the streamers had actual coffin-like devices they used.

It felt like I was in a dream. I moved my virtual hands in front of my face. I wiggled my fingers. I touched my virtual hands together, and the tactile buzzing centered on my ghost hands kinda broke my brain a little. They said you got used to it all, but it was still really, really weird to me.

I had multiple buttons floating at the top of my HUD. The first one read, Stream Connected. One viewer waiting. Go live? I reached up, and I clicked it.

It took a tremendous amount of bandwidth for my signal to bounce off the *Forlorn*, pass through the gate, and hit some server on Earth, which in turn shot it all back from Earth to the main transfer gate hub, then to their ship, and then to my mech.

Which was why we needed to be streaming our concert like this, sending it off to multiple networks. It taxed our connection, but the noise also camouflaged what I was doing the best we could.

The moment they suspected what I was doing, they'd start blowing everything out of the sky. They might start doing that anyway, especially once Rosita's movies started to play in the background between our songs.

'Okay, I'm in,' I said. I felt a clap on my shoulder, probably from Sam, but I couldn't hear anything.

I clicked 'Pass-through Audio.'

The *thump, thump, thump* from the drum looper continued to pound. Lulu was still shrieking into the microphone. I drilled down into a menu and tried to keep her voice slightly quiet.

'If you said something, I couldn't hear it. I can hear you now,' I said.

'I said you look like you're sitting on the toilet with everyone watching,' Sam said, shouting at me. 'You're sitting very rigid. You need to relax.'

I used my real finger to flip him off.

'We're gonna need you in a minute,' he yelled. 'I hope you can pull it off.'

'Very good,' Roger said in my ear at the same time. 'Your private stream is up and running. Look to the left and right and then look down and up.... Very good.'

Loading now. Please review your armament.

In front of me, a door opened, and my mech started automatically walking down a long hallway surrounded by printing cubes. I turned my head, looking toward a door and a window in the distance of the massive hold of the ship.

'Hold that shot,' Roger said. 'Interesting,' he said after a moment.

I was now standing in a queue. Directly in front of me wasn't a mech, but an altered Peacekeeper. I knew that was an option for tonight only. It was a nine-foot-tall humanoid-robot thing with four arms. It had twin swords over the back and was encased in power armor. The thing also wore a massive fuzzy wig, a mullet. It had a gold chain around its neck, but I couldn't see the front. I had no idea how the driver was going to control all four arms at once. It was hard enough with just two imaginary ones. Sam had told me there were some immersion games where you were in the form of animals. I imagined that had to be really weird.

I could swivel my head three hundred sixty degrees, which was another strange sensation, and I had to remember not to move my real head too much. I looked behind me, and it was a Heavy, but instead of the massive Battering Ram gun, it had a flamethrower attachment. Several round devices dotted the top of the mech. I knew from looking at the catalog what these were. Gunship drones. I had one attached to my own back. The mech was painted hot pink with neon purple squiggles on it. It had a big X at the very front and it read, 'Serial Killer,' under the X. I had no idea what that meant.

'What did you see?' I asked Roger.

'I just saw your mom,' the Serial Killer mech said. It had a young female voice. 'What a stupid build. What are you going to do, kill them with flares?'

'Oliver, turn off your voice projector,' Roger said.

I found the button and turned it off for in-game voice projection. 'Shit,' I said. 'Roger, what did you see?'

'Did you see that window? There was a human behind it, but they weren't in an environment suit. The deployment bay is built similarly to the deployment bays in the original generation ships. This was likely to keep some of the systems working as cheaply as possible. There is both gravity and atmosphere in the bay. That is good to know. We also know there is a human crew on the ship.'

'It couldn't have been a Peacekeeper?' I asked. 'Or one of those robot RMI guys?'

'Negative. If you look at the bottom right of your screen, you purchased the advanced zoom and heat vision. Besides, you just used the external speaker to talk to Sadie Wilkinson from District 62. Atmosphere is required for sound. The moment you enter the deployment unit, I will call her mother and tell her how Sadie was caught dismembering a cat in school today and recommend that she immediately contact an attorney.'

'Jesus, Roger, how are the other calls going?'

'As expected. Unfortunately, I do not know the information on more than half of the players, as they are not streaming or advertising their presence on the net. I am cross-referencing screen names as I learn them, but there is no single list of active players, so I must rely on other streams to see the names of the nearby players.'

We stopped. The floor under the first mech in line, a regular Cheetah, rose up into the air, rapidly and forcefully ejecting the mech upward through a door in the ceiling. I looked upward to see the Cheetah disappear into what appeared to be an air lock, which meant the ceiling of the giant room was the hull of the ship. I wasn't an expert with spaceships or physics like this, but I did note that this was the opposite of what I'd been expecting, that the artificial gravity for the *Pinnacle* seemed to focus downward through the center of the ship. This was different from how it'd been with the large, rotating generation ships that had brought us here. I knew they'd had some sort of fancy technology to make artificial gravity, but it took a tremendous amount of energy, and for our generation ships such as the *Forlorn*, it'd only been available in the bridge and some of the other small, important sections. Everything else used the rotation of the habitation ring to create gravity. My grandfather used to talk about how gravity could change dramatically when one moved to different sections of the ship.

The door in the ceiling closed, and then it opened again quickly. The modified Peacekeeper in front of me stepped onto the square. I automatically stepped forward so I was next in line. I looked up, and on the ceiling surrounding the large air lock was a mural of a skull. And above that skull, it read, 'Save true humanity. No mercy. Kill them all.'

My turn came. I moved into position, and I was rocketed upward into a small room. Within seconds. There was a quick hissing, and then I was flying upward a second time as I was lifted headfirst into the waiting deployment unit. Mechanical arms grabbed me as the world seemed to spin. The entire device flipped me and then rotated so I was facing out, and I could no longer see what was happening. But the process was quick and bizarrely efficient, especially considering how we all had different shapes and sizes.

Multiple gauges in my virtual cockpit started to come online.

Loading now. Weapons will come online shortly. Maps loading. Your purchased maps are loading. You may prepurchase ammo insurance now at fifty percent off the price.

Warning: You are using custom weapons. Some ammo may not be available for purchase.

The drop ship shuddered as the last of the mechs were loaded.

Launching now.

There was a loud clank, and suddenly I had the strange sensation of falling.

HERMIT672HILL: Here we go, bitches! Hope to scrub one of those greasy fucks.

I blinked. There was a local text-only chat. This was one of the five other mechs in the drop ship.

'Roger, there's a local chat. Do you see it on your screen?'

'I do not, but I can adjust the streaming settings from here. One moment. Very good. I see it. Cross-referencing now. Excellent.

Hermit672Hill was not on my identified list. I have located a wish list under that name. Investigating. Very good. Hermit672Hill wished to purchase a Signet chef's knife for his upcoming birthday. I listed a new one for sale and then purchased my own item via the wish list, which provided me with his name and address. Colin Townsend of District 210. The Vancouver corridor. He owns a gastropub called Hermit Hill. I am calling him now, informing him that his suicidal mother is currently on a bridge and is threatening to jump off. She has asked for him. This was a good find, Oliver. I suggest liberal use of the local chat so I can collect more screen names.'

'I think I can send a ping that lists everyone nearby.'

'It does, but if they have privacy turned on, it hashtags their names. Minors have the hashtag by default, and several people have enacted the feature because they are afraid of being identified. That privacy does not extend to local and team chat, however. So keep talking.'

I moved to the chat window. We would land in five minutes.

SUBHUMANSLAYER: Hey, everyone, where are you from?

MOTHER'S WILK: Eat my ass, prick.

That was the only answer I received.

'That was Sadie Wilkinson. I am speaking to her mother now. She does not appear to sound surprised that her daughter might have been caught dismembering a cat. I fear it might not be enough to get her offline.'

'Tell her that she wrote "Mom" with the cat's blood or something, or better yet, does she have any siblings? Put their names there, too.'

'Oh, that is a good idea, Oliver. I take it back when I said you were a terrible terrorist. She has a little infant brother named Conner. I will use that name. In addition, player Colin Townsend is disconnecting now. Player RxKing, a streamer who is also in your deployment unit, has disconnected after his wife received screenshots of a text exchange between himself and their child's male dentist, Dr Smiles, who is also playing. As for the dentist, I currently have a prostitute en route to his home with the door code and instructions to "surprise him" when she arrives. His wife just went off shift at the prison where she works, and should arrive home five to ten minutes after the prostitute arrives.'

'Good. Keep it going.'

Weapons coming online.

A spinning 3D rendition of our custom-made mech appeared.

I'd painted myself completely black. I'd been tempted to make some custom accessories, like everyone liked to do, but I'd held off. The last thing I needed was attention on myself. I spun the view now, looking at the design Roger and I had come up with together.

We'd started with the frame of a regular Attenuator, but with the new high-speed-option legs along with the advanced jump jets. I'd wanted to go with the third option, which basically made it so I could fly, but Roger recommended against it, as he couldn't control the seeking missiles our side would be firing at us, and the RMI soldiers would also be shooting. The fliers had the highest heat output of all the units, and it would've required me to decrease the weight significantly, and we were already lean as it was. We'd already had to forgo a layer of armor plating.

I had two grasping arms, but with the extenders, that would allow me fine motor skills. I also carried the optional 'backpack' with custom-made caltrops. This attached a large storage unit to my back. We'd also added shoulder flares and a single gunner drone that would follow me around like Rosita's camera drone. That was it in terms of actual weapons.

That was okay. I'd have some backup when I landed.

The peninsula came into view, but the smoke from our fires filled the night with clouds. Pulsing lights shot up at us, but none seemed to hit. Across the way, I could see other drop ships, all with the legs of the mechs dangling out.

As we dropped, a message came in. A message window popped up, and a man appeared. He was wearing military fatigues and chomping on a cigar. There was no disclaimer, so I assumed this was a real person.

'Hello, soldier,' the man said as bombastic music started to play. 'Colonel Boomer here. This is it. This is the final assault. The Rhythm Mafia headquarters is on your map, and you will be landing approximately five kilometers north in our forward operating theater! Be wary! Heavily armed Rhythm Mafia insurgents fill the countryside around the base. We need to clear them out! But our primary objective is to breach their walls, destroy the defenders, and root out and remove any and all terrorists holed up in their base. Leave nobody alive! Remember, you're not just having fun. You're protecting true humanity.'

All the while, I could hear Lulu continuing to chant just outside. She was shouting with the beat of the bass drum. 'Come on, motherfuckers, come on! Come on, motherfuckers, come on!'

'Roger, do we have any stats yet on people watching our three streams?'

'Your sister removed the paywall for her Real-Friends account, but it's still considered an adult site and doesn't have as big of a user base as LoftBase. It appears she has approximately five thousand watchers. Your Tuneage account with the misspelled Rhythim Mafia has zero watchers, and the Pig Plus Some Chickens account has twenty-five watchers. I am currently sending out invites to every streamer who has ever voiced anti–*Operation Bounce House* sentiment, and an account with five million followers just posted the link to the Pig Plus Some Chickens account, so I will update you in a few minutes.'

I sent another message, trying to get more people in the local chat to talk, but nobody answered. Outside, it was just smoke. Sadie the serial killer was still online, despite Roger's best efforts to get her mom into the room. From the sound of it, her mom was too scared to do anything.

Landing in 3, 2, 1.

There was a heavy jolt.

Welcome, Citizen Soldier. Welcome to *Operation Bounce House*.

CHAPTER 45

I stepped out of the drop ship and into chaos. I was now in full control of my mech. I had a right joystick that controlled how I walked. I could control my speed based on how hard I pushed it. I could use the left joystick to cycle and aim and fire my weapons. That seemed counterintuitive to me, and I clicked a button and switched sides.

There were about a dozen dials and gauges along with multiple types of radars.

I turned, and I noted the drop unit we'd come from remained on the ground. Three of the spots still had active mechs in them, including the four-armed humanoid one, but none had moved to leave. I spun in a circle, taking in the area.

I knew this place. We were east of the main road, not too far from Rosita's ranch. These fields had once been part of her property before she'd sold them off. This particular field was in an offseason, but it'd already been prepared by Mr Xalos. He'd probably be doing some sort of root vegetables soon. Maybe onions.

But now the fields were flattened, covered with oil and all sorts of other chemicals. This land, like most of the peninsula, was now ruined – ruined for years and years. I sighed.

Serial Killer Sadie strolled out of her spot and came to stand next to me. Out loud, she said, 'I killed a whole house of them yesterday. If you look in the mirrors, it doesn't filter out the blood or their bodies. And if you mess up the bodies enough, the filter doesn't know how to compensate. How many have you killed?'

I clicked the button. 'I've only really killed one. I plan on getting more today.'

'What sort of accent is that?' But then she lumbered off, not waiting for an answer. She launched her drones as she walked, and they buzzed around her head like a swarm of flies.

All around us, more drop ships were landing and off-loading mechs. Most were the same Attenuators and Cheetahs and Drop Dragoons we were used to, but there was a smattering of new, completely bizarre war machines. One, built on the body of a Sniper, had four legs and a dragon head that breathed fire. But it was currently stuck between two trees, and the driver was shouting out, 'Guys, seriously, can someone help me? Guys, guys!'

Another home-design mech was a tripod thing, and it had immediately toppled over on its side. An Attenuator stood next to it. 'I told you it wasn't going to work, dumbass!'

Yet another was simply a round mechanical ball about three meters in diameter. On either side were large pulse rifles. It was painted to look like an eight ball from that game I saw sometimes on the net where people would hit the balls with a long stick. I'd seen smaller versions of that mech design in movies but never in real life, and I'd never seen anything nearly that big. The eight ball tore off into the distance, moving incredibly fast. It was moving toward the road, as it likely would have a difficult time moving through the trees and mud.

All around us, I caught multiple snippets of conversation.

'They're already pushing through the soldiers in the woods. We need to hurry!' someone said.

'The ones in the woods are all bots anyway.'

'Fuck off. That's bullshit,' yet another responded.

'No, no, they're bots all right. But they're RMI bots. The terrorists make them and they're planning on invading Earth with them. That's why we're doing this.'

'Did you guys hear? They've set up some weird stage thing, and it's like they're getting ready to play a concert or something.'

'Imma hit that shit with the mortar.'

'Snipers gonna get 'em first.'

'Dude, someone is saying the head terrorist is really Farm Girl Gigi, the streamer woman.'

'That's the stupidest thing I've ever heard.'

The text chat, too, was awash with a constant scroll of remarks. Roger was making occasional comments about this person or that.

Here in the clearing, there were literally dozens of mechs that were just standing there.

'Mom, that's not true,' I heard one of the mechs say. 'I don't know what she was talking about! It has to be a prank.... I've never even been in the women's room at school. Why would I? Video? That's impossible. Let me see it!'

The mech stopped moving.

'You must get to the rendezvous,' Roger said in my ear. 'Be wary. There are still RMI soldiers in the area. We have honeybees en route, but I will only engage them if necessary. Also, flip on that button that says, "Command Chat."'

I pulled up the map I'd purchased, zoomed in toward where Rosita's main greenhouse was, and stuck in a waypoint marker. The spot appeared on my HUD. I turned, and I started running in that direction, which was opposite from the direction everyone else had gone. I'd get there in about five minutes.

We'd picked Rosita's farm because we knew it would be north of the drop zone, but we didn't know exactly where the drop zone would be. It was where the supplies for the assault were currently stored.

I flipped on the command chat button. It was yet another text-only channel. I moved it to the side.

CRICKET-IS-LIFE: You idiots need to listen. If we don't coordinate, we're going to get turned into mince just like yesterday.

69JUICYJUICE: Coordinate my sack.

'I do not know who Cricket-Is-Life is. 69JuicyJuice received a call to come into work, and he told me that he quit and then blocked the number. I have just called in a fire alarm to his home.'

I felt a tap on my shoulder, which startled me so much, I spun the mech around. But it was Sam. I raised the local volume.

'What is it?' I asked.

'Looks like we're getting ready to start,' Sam called. 'First wave will hit the farm in a minute.'

I paused, and I closed my eyes.

You can do this. You know these songs.

'Okay,' I said. 'Kick me if I get anything wrong.'

Lulu continued to shout insults.

I turned my mech back toward Rosita's ranch and started to run. With my real leg, I switched off the drum machine, and I moved back to the kick using my foot. With my real hands, I started a roll on the snare.

At the same time, I had to negotiate the mech through a tight copse of trees, using my virtual arms.

To my utter astonishment, I found controlling my mech while actively drumming wasn't nearly as difficult as I had been expecting. I'd been playing this particular drum part – something we called 'The Long Intro' because Tito took his time to tune or because Sam always took forever in the bathroom – that doing so was literally second nature to me. My feet and legs moved with such fluid muscle memory, my virtual movements actually became easier because now there was no reason for me to mistake the two. To my left, Axel started with the distorted squiggles on his guitar. Sam kept up with his *twum, twum, twum* on the bass. Tito held out long, distorted power chords. I knew the whole area around the farm was shaking with the power of the PA.

'Yeah, boys and girls, just a little closer now,' Lulu called.

Even though I couldn't see him, I turned my head toward my best friend, and I smiled. I knew he was smiling back.

I heard a distant explosion. It was time. I started a roll on the snare. I hit the button on the left of my kick, and I counted down. Five, four, three, two, one.

I hit the snare one last time, putting all my power into the single *pop*. We all stopped just as the spinning spotlights lit up, and the fireworks exploded above the stage.

'We. Are. The. Mother. Fucking. Rhythm. Mafia,' Lulu roared.

CHAPTER 46

And with that, we started our first song for the stream. It was something Sam had written when we were fourteen years old. It was the only song we already had uploaded on the Tuneage account. It was called 'Space Spunk Monkey.'

And with that first song, the honeybee drones with the attached mines went to work, spreading out into the fields, hunting down the biggest, most dangerous mechs. They would focus on Heavies and those with missile launchers.

As we played, I did double duty, ducking through the forest, running.

Colonel Boomer appeared in the upper left of my vision. The man in military fatigues chomped on his cigar.

'It's getting hot out there, folks. Watch out for the death dogs. They have weaponized them! Those of you with missiles, get firing! I want mortars on that defensive wall!'

'Death dogs,' I muttered. And then I grunted with amusement. When 'Colonel Boomer' turned his head, I could see the wall behind him. It was the same mural that I had seen when we spoke with Eli Opel. He was in the same room that Opel had been in when we spoke with him. I had assumed it was some cushy office somewhere on Earth.

What a poseur, I thought.

'You have two friendly companions,' Roger said. 'Try not to look at them.'

I knew I now had a pair of honeybee drones shadowing me, running just behind me. These were silver ones, part of the original squad. I didn't know what their names were.

Of the seven hundred honeybees we had left, five hundred of them wore the EMP land mines that'd been given to us by Apex, all with an extra explosive attached to the top, which effectively turned them into fast-moving smart suicide bombers.

The two that shadowed me would have inactive pulse rifles on their backs, and they would be running cold, meaning they were hopefully stealthed from the satellites. They would be visual to the naked eye, but any sensors looking at heat would mask their presence, and because they were moving so close to the ground, most radars would miss them as well. They would make themselves known only if I was in serious trouble.

'There are five RMI soldiers ahead,' Roger said in my ear.

'I see them,' I said as the song moved to the bridge, which was the only tricky part. I nailed it. 'Moving to engage.'

One of the biggest variables in all this was the RMI soldiers. They would now attack anyone they saw, and if they knew someone was nearby, they would swarm. We didn't know for certain, but we assumed someone up on the *Pinnacle* was keeping a close eye on them, and we didn't want too much attention focused on me. I was doing something strange, and I would be doing something even stranger in a minute. We didn't know if all this was necessary, but just in case, we needed to make it look like Hobie Martin was going off on his own, missing the main attack because he wanted to fight the RMI soldiers one-on-one.

There was a clearing ahead, and my advanced radar showed the five soldiers just standing there.

At this point, those at the base would be doing the same back-and-forth missile barrage that had preceded the fight the previous two evenings, only this time, the number of incoming missiles would be overwhelming. Still, we had more chaff and point defense guns than ever, and we hoped we could hold out for a little longer.

The song was coming to an end. We would pause, and Rosita's documentary would start to play. There'd be a message that if you didn't want to watch the concert, you could watch the whole video, which was now streaming on multiple platforms. These were already uploaded Earthside.

While I'd seen several of the segments, I hadn't had time to watch the whole thing. She said it was just all her interviews, one after another, all with just a touch of editing. The purpose was to show the Earthers who we were. Who we really were. She hadn't added anything about the war to the documentary except at the very end, instead framing it like she had originally intended: a snapshot of our lives so those who would come after us would know what it used to be like.

If people didn't care about seeing us die, maybe they would care about seeing us live.

I kept my bass-drum beat going. Sam would tap me on the shoulder when it was time to start the next song.

In the mech, I sped up. Ahead, the RMI soldiers were just starting to react. I activated my jump jets, and I tapped the backpack, dropping a few of the custom-designed caltrops over the soldiers.

The little round balls dropped down into the clearing. One out of every four expelled smoke. The rest were true caltrops. The spiked devices would pierce the feet of the RMI soldiers, but they weren't strong enough to cause any damage to the metallic feet of the mechs. If any of the RMI soldiers did manage to step on them, their feet would – in theory – get impaled, making it difficult for the dumb soldiers to walk.

We didn't expect these to work very well, but it was the only weapon that came with the large deployment backpack.

I hit the ground heavily, wobbled a little, and turned. I extended my one hidden weapon: the electric scythes I had along both of my arms. I waded into the smoke, waving my arms about wildly.

The confused soldiers went down in seconds. A little chime appeared on the upper right of my vision.

Achievement Unlocked! First Kill!

I laughed at that. That kid Hobie hadn't managed to hurt or kill anyone the whole time he'd been driving a mech.

'Christ, Roger, you were right. That was a good way to kill them.'
'Very good, Oliver. Recommence your mission.'

I resumed running. The trees cleared. Ahead, I could see the wreck of Rosita's house and, just past that, the twin greenhouses where she grew her garlic, which had miraculously stayed intact.

Inside the first greenhouse were the supplies I would be bringing back with me to the *Pinnacle*.

Sam smacked me on the shoulder, indicating it was time to start the next song. This one had been written by Tito, and it was pretty much one long guitar solo. It was called 'The Pain in the Stars.'

Lulu shouted, 'Nice mortars, assholes. Next time aim a little better. I can't imagine what your toilet seats look like back home.'

'We better start evacuating those on the wall,' I said. And then, louder, I hit my sticks together, and I shouted, 'One, two, three, four!'

I rushed my mech toward the greenhouse, and as I approached, I hit the caltrops button, emptying the backpack as smoke rose all around me.

'In place,' I said to Roger.

'Please hold on,' he said. 'Keep your view ahead. This will take approximately twenty-five seconds.'

As I waited, I moved my eyes down to the command chat. It was moving rapidly, and I could only catch a few snippets here or there before it fell off.

CRICKET-IS-LIFE: What sort of shield do they have? I just watched a ton of shrapnel flash across that stage, and the cowgirl singer didn't even flinch. Lining up my Sniper shot right now.

BORNEOROMEO: Anybody else getting weird phone calls? My 'mother' just called, telling me she was hurt, but my mom is really right here with me.

TANDOORITACO: Same! My work just called to tell me to come in right now, but my boss is in my squad, and he doesn't know where that call came from.

POBOI77: Guys, that IS Farm Girl Gigi. Holy fuckballs. I did a private show with her once! And this song whips.

HOOKER_ISLAND: I just heard they're streaming their concert on Tuneage. But they're on an account that's like five years old and it's called Rhythm Mafia but with the spelling all fucked-up.

AcesHigh84: My squad mate said he had police at his door and hasn't come back. What is going on?

Cricket-Is-Life: I had that bitch dead center, and the shot punched a hole in the back of the stage. Do you guys see this?

'Whoops,' Roger said. 'I see Cricket-Is-Life's mech. It will be down shortly. I have now identified TandooriTaco's boss, and I am calling emergency services to his location. Oliver, you are loaded. Ready for damage?'

'I am ready.'

A pulse bolt came from the night and hit my mech directly in the knee. Multiple warnings popped up on my HUD.

I moved over to the communications channel and clicked 'Request Repair and Reloading.' Two separate warnings popped up.

> **WARNING**: You have custom ammunition. Your ammunition is not stored on a drop ship. You will be charged for transport to receive a refill. Do you wish to proceed?
>
> **WARNING**: Your knee joint is damaged. This is from the beta set, and repair parts are not stored on a drop ship. You will be charged for transport to receive repair. Do you wish to proceed?

I clicked 'Yes' to both.

> **WARNING**: No drop ships are available. Would you like to wait until one becomes available?

My heart stuttered, but we had expected this. I moved over to the 'Purchases' tab, and I found the – very expensive – priority-emergency-repair-and-reload pass. The onetime pass had cost *a lot* of yuan. Luckily, Hobie's mother had a high limit on her card.

> Do you wish to use your pass? Are you sure? You can't undo this action.

I clicked 'Yes.'

An emergency drop ship has been deployed. You will be picked up in four minutes.

There were some reports of the pass not working or getting delayed when someone was simply out of ammo, so Roger believed shooting me in the knee, especially since I was using the beta legs, would put me at the top of the queue. It also helped because the repairs would happen before the reloading.

'Roger,' I asked as I waited, 'how're the streams doing?'

'Lulu's Real-Friends now has just over a hundred fifty thousand viewers. The Tuneage account has seventy-three viewers, and the Pig Plus Some Chickens account on LoftBase currently has one point eight million viewers. In addition, the Zapatero Films channel on LoftBase and the streaming on Rosita's Indie Auteur account have a combined viewership of thirty-five thousand, but that just went online a few minutes ago.'

'Wait, what?' I asked as I did a fill. The chorus to this song had a weird time signature, and I had to concentrate a little bit. The entirety of the song after this one was a swing, and it would be hard for me to do it well without focusing on Sam's bass. A small part of me hoped the whole charade would be over by then, but another part was really hoping to see if I could pull it off.

But all of those thoughts fled as what Roger said registered. '*How many streamers on the pig's account?*'

'I said one point eight million, but it is climbing rapidly, and it is approaching one point eighty-three million. It is currently on the Hot Feeds list, and there are multiple feeds live-commenting on it. If you count the Goat Sects feed, which has the concert window up, the documentary up, and the feed from Skeet-Skeet up all at the same time, that's another ten million viewers. In addition, several news outlets are starting to report on the telephone calls, calling it a terrorist invasion.'

'Holy shit,' I said.

'Just because I am no longer able to correct you, Oliver, it doesn't mean you shouldn't strive to avoid swearing. Also, I would like to note the phrase "Save Cindy and Betty Sue" is now trending on multiple social media platforms. I do not know if you are winning hearts and minds, but the livestock of New Sonora certainly is.'

Your drop ship is arriving soon. The location is marked on your map.

It would be landing on the main road just outside of Rosita's property. I started moving in the direction.

CHAPTER 47

We ended the song, and we paused for more of Rosita's documentary to play.

'Good job, man. You nailed it!' Sam shouted in my ear. 'Tito fucked up his second solo, though.'

As we waited, I clicked on 'Virtual Pass-through' on my helmet, and I took a look around. Rosita was off to the side, fiddling with the big camera. Lulu stood in front of the microphone, smoking a cigarette, shouting her head off, still hurling insults. Tito and Axel were tuning. Sam was watching the feed monitor, which was showing the late Mr Yanez getting interviewed by Rosita.

I turned my attention to the other monitor, which was showing the wall. All the people were now gone. The wall had dozens of holes in it. The flamethrower, which was now being controlled by honeybees, was finally getting to work, which meant there were now mechs right in front of the base. Still, missiles continued to fire back and forth. Our own mortars, now being fired by honeybees, continued to pound in the distance.

I wished there was a good shot of the stage with the spotlights twirling all around us just casually sitting up there while missiles and pulse blasts rained.

Sam tapped my shoulder. 'I think we only got time for a few more,' he said.

I nodded and started counting on the hi-hat. This sort of beat was supposed to be simple for most drummers, but for some reason, I always had an issue with it. This song was one Lulu and I had written together a long time ago. It was called 'Pear Juice,' and it started with just me. The whole song was about five minutes long.

I couldn't see my sister, but I could hear it in her voice. It was a silly, dumb song, yet she sobbed as she angrily introduced it.

> Please enter the drop ship now. Transit time to dock: approximately 13 minutes.

'Here we go,' I said as I started to play.

I entered the drop ship, and I held my breath as the grasping arms clutched onto me with a loud clank. The mech shuddered as I played the song.

> Please wait.

And then we were off, rising into the night air, spinning like a top as we rapidly rose. This was a smaller, faster, and more specialized ship designed specifically for this exact thing: ferrying individual units back and down from the ship.

I tried to see if I could see the farm through the smoke, but there was nothing except the occasional flash of light indicating an explosion here or there. Even though the enemy was clearly on the verge of completely overrunning the camp, the command chat was awash with stories about the chaos being wrought by Roger on Earth. People, scared, were leaving their mechs abandoned on the field by the dozens, while others continued to press the attack as the farm, my home, was utterly decimated by the invading war machines.

At any moment, the entire stage would fall.

The song ended.

'No break. No break. Next song!' Sam shouted in my ear.

I didn't think. I just went into the next song. I hit the crash and started the *tsk, tsk, tsk* on the hi-hat that indicated we were going into 'Tito Got Your Goat.'

... And just as we started, I realized that the song basically started with a drum solo – a solo I hadn't really practiced in months.

'Oh, fuck,' I muttered under my breath as I went to work on my snare.

We rose, and we rose, entering orbit as I finished the solo, and we moved into the song.

'I just want you to know, across all channels, approximately fifty million people just watched that drum solo, Oliver,' Roger said.

'Song's not done yet,' I said, gritting my teeth.

We turned, and we suddenly seemed to be moving in slow motion, but in reality, we were now far above the planet, and we were approaching the *Pinnacle*. We'd be docked in a minute. I moved my attention back to the command chat.

> **WICKEDTALON**: Hey, I knew it! I fucking knew it! Did you see that flicker! They're not really on that stage. They're live-projecting from somewhere. They're using a hologram system!
>
> **PONYBOY33**: These assholes freaked out my mom. Let's tear this place apart. They gotta be around here somewhere.

'Roger,' I said, 'tell Lulu it's time!'

A moment later, Lulu roared so loud, I could hear her.

'You assholes think we're really on this stage? We're in the barn, fuckers. Come and get us!'

My heart hurt at the thought of the barn, the hive, that attic, finally getting destroyed. It didn't seem fair that we'd have to sacrifice it for this.

I suspected the barn was already heavily damaged, if not destroyed by this point. The thousands of pounds of printed explosives we had placed under the floorboards and the hundreds of explosives I'd personally filled into the crawl space, however, seemed to still be intact. We were just waiting for them to get a little closer.

> **FELIXTHERAT**: The wall is down! The wall is down! Everybody charge!

Docking soon. Please wait.

The *Pinnacle* came into view as we turned toward it. The silver behemoth was surrounded by ships similar to my own coming and going. I quickly tried to examine the exterior of the thing, looking for the Moderators, but I couldn't see them.

'All four Moderators appear to have detached from the *Pinnacle*,' Roger said. 'That is unfortunate. I suspect they're likely on missions to cut off our connection, which means they are currently destroying all the communications satellites, possibly in an attempt to stem the tide of domestic phone attacks. They do not know I am already based Earthside. They likely don't think it is possible. As of this moment, both connections – the one on the *Forlorn* and the one on *Adios* – are still working normally. I will let you know if I detect any attacks on the generation ships.'

Now entering the repair bay.

A countdown appeared.

'Roger, it's saying the repair will begin in two minutes.'

'Okay,' Roger said. 'The honeybee units you are carrying in your backpack have their orders in case I go offline, but I will begin the mission soon.'

PONYBOY33: It's a trap! Run! Run!

'Wrong barn, motherfuckers!' Lulu roared.

'The explosives have detonated,' Roger said.

I quickly hit the pass-through on my visor. Lulu remained at the front of the stage, head lowered. She'd removed Mr Gonzales's giant hat, and she held it in one hand. I could see the tears on her cheeks. A moment later, we all heard the explosion. Even this far away from the farm, the walls shook. On the other side of the bar, the Belly-Rubbed Pug sign that mirrored the one on the outside fell off the wall, which caused Cindy the pig to snort in dismay. Betty Sue and the rest of the chickens scattered. Yasmine, the holographic pole dancer, flickered.

'Christ,' Sam muttered, 'I hope the others were far enough away.'

'May I remind you all that you're still live on stream,' Roger said in our ears. 'It appears we have successfully killed most of the invaders, but unlike the previous evenings, they are allowing those with insurance and those not completely destroyed to return to the battle to hunt for the survivors. Also, the stream on Real-Friends was shut down. It appears the Tuneage account will also soon be shut down based on the warning message we just received. The Pig Plus Some Chickens account is still streaming with forty-five million viewers, and I have multiple backup accounts available while we still have a connection.'

'What about Rosita's documentary?' I asked as I reset the pass-through. The repair bay came into view. I was being lowered feet-first into the bay.

'The account on LoftBase is still showing the stream, and it is being watched by seventy-five million viewers. The download-now button has been clicked approximately twenty-five million times, and the documentary is already being re-streamed on multiple platforms. Both LoftBase accounts – Rosita's Zapatero Films and my A Pig Plus Some Chickens – have cleared a significant number of donations in the past hour as well. Unfortunately, as both are new accounts, we won't be able to withdraw those funds for ninety days.'

I put down my drumstick, and I held out my left hand. A moment passed, and I felt Rosita's shaking hand in my own. I squeezed it, and then I went back to work.

CHAPTER 48

Repairing now.

I no longer had control of the mech, but I could still see. They wouldn't let you control these things while you were in the *Pinnacle*, lest some idiot should go on a rampage and damage everything.

'Interesting,' Roger said. 'The repair bay is in the very back of the ship. I am uploading the map of the location. I will update as necessary.'

Several arms reached out and removed the damaged leg from my mech. A splint appeared around the area as the printing gel was injected. The rapid repair process would take only a minute. We had to time this next part precisely.

Please wait.

Thank you for signing up for Phase 2. The next target planet will have a much larger population! Click yes now to secure your guaranteed spot for Phase 3 and beyond with a 20,000-yuan deposit!

'Oh, fuck off,' I muttered. And then I thought of Hobie's mother giving her idiot child access to a war machine for his birthday. I clicked 'Yes.'

Please wait. . . .

The nonrefundable deposit charge has been approved!

'The *Encantada* appears to have just gone offline,' Roger said. 'I believe the four Moderators are now in the process of destroying the fifteen generation ships. Yes. *Nuevo Mundo* is also gone.'

'Shit, okay. We better hurry.'

Repair complete.

The repair gel started to drain.
'It's draining,' I said.
'Exiting the backpack now,' Roger said.
Sam tapped me on the shoulder and yelled, 'We're still streaming, so we're still playing!'
'Are we doing this?' I called.
'We're doing it,' Sam yelled.
'This is our last song, assholes,' Lulu screamed. 'It's called "The Grandpa Song"!'

I counted off, and we started to play. The song was just a jam, and the lyrics changed every time. Lulu started to scream a list of names of still active players, accusing them all of having sex with farm animals.

I moved my attention back to the repair bay.

I couldn't see them, but from behind me, three scouts emerged from my backpack. They were Priscilla, Trixie 2, and an unnamed black scout. They spread out, followed by one more. This was a regular honeybee with several items strapped to its back. The final items to emerge from my backpack were as many UAVs as Roger had been able to shove in there, which was seven.

'Interesting,' Roger said. 'The UAVs will need a few moments to acclimate. They are designed to work in multiple environments, gravity levels, and pressures. However, they do not have this environment in their library and will need to do some self-tests before they can operate.'

Please stand by. You will be moved to an ammunition refill station.

This was followed moments later by a new, larger message in red.

WARNING: A fault has occurred in your repair bay. Please wait while the damage is assessed.

'The UAVs are indicating they are ready,' Roger said.

A pair of the round flying machines flitted past my view and then disappeared in separate directions.

My entire mech shook. My view was still fixed forward.

Trixie 2 zoomed past. She had a communications module unit in her grasping claw. I blinked, momentarily confused by the difference in size between myself and the bot. My mech was almost four meters tall, and the scout was suddenly, at least to my point of view, smaller than Roger. For a fraction of a moment, the discrepancy caused my brain to stutter.

My view blacked out.

Please wait.

The reboot sequence appeared, followed by the *Operation Bounce House* logo.

WARNING: You are not connected with central command sync. Error 55a.

'Okay,' Roger said. 'You should now be in full control of the unit. You are connected from the helmet to the servers inside of Trixie 2, Priscilla, and Lorraine, so as long as one of them remains intact, you should be able to control the mech.'

'Lorraine?' I asked.

'That is the name of one of the black units we acquired from the civil defense bunker.'

I moved my arm, and sure enough, my mech shuddered against the repair bay restraints. The whole thing rocked again, and I clattered several feet to the floor.

Roger crackled. 'We will need access to the crew portion of the ship through the door attached to the bulkhead in front of you. You are much too large to pass through, unfortunately. I will have you punch out. . . . Please wait. Never mind.'

Right in front of me, a small door at about chest level opened, revealing two men in overalls.

'What the . . . ?' the first man said as Trixie 2 and Priscilla zoomed up. Trixie appeared to inject the first man with something while Priscilla used a cutting arm on the second, and the man was suddenly just headless. The whole attack took seconds. One moment, they were there. The next, they were on the ground with blood spilling over the edge and into the repair bay.

'Holy crap, Roger,' I said.

The first man, the one who still had a head, started convulsing as foam erupted from his mouth. He shook, and a moment later, he went still. But he was close to the edge, and he suddenly slipped off, falling about two meters to the floor of the repair bay. The two scouts disappeared down the hallway. The lone regular honeybee unit appeared, climbing up the repair bay like a spider. The unit slid down slightly when it encountered the blood, but it caught itself and continued on its way. It entered the service hallway, skittering after the two scouts.

I still hadn't seen the third scout, Lorraine.

'I have found the manual control panel. I will open the entrance from the repair bay to the storage hall. This is a separate room from the one where the units are printed. You will have to disable the mech storage transporter. Be prepared. Once this happens, they will know that there truly is something amiss. Be ready to fight. The door is at your feet, and you will fall.'

Before I could answer, I was falling. I clattered heavily to the ground as I was dumped into a new room. I hit the ground with a crunch, and heavy mechanical arms grabbed me. The body of the dead worker also splattered to the floor of the room with a sickening *splatch*.

Across the way, another mech was in the process of being torn apart by a pair of giant arms and then shoved into a storage area. This room was bigger than anything I'd ever seen.

I was attached to some device that was on rails. It made a beep, and then it was moving, shooting off with me in its arms. I whipped around a corner, turned again, and jolted to a stop. All around me stood massive walls and walls of mechs, all torn apart and stored into cube-like structures.

'Oliver, you need to break yourself free before you are disassembled.'

I extended my arm blades, turned, and smashed both of my forearms down into the arm holding me in place. The blades did barely any damage, and my right arm became stuck, which was a strange sensation. My virtual arm was stuck in place no matter what I did. I disabled the arm blades, which freed them. I tried again, this time aiming for the hoses. That worked. The moment I sliced, I easily cut through the line of cables running along the metal arm. Steaming-hot fluid started hissing from a severed pipe. A moment later, the arm clutching me had no grip, and I was freed. I jumped from the platform to the ground. I had to jump out of the way a moment later as a platform carrying another mech crashed into the stopped platform that had been holding me.

I looked at my map, and I started heading toward a large set of double doors that led to the printing room.

An alarm started to shrill. As I approached the massive doors, they slid open on their own, revealing the colossal room filled with the industrial printing squares. This was the same place I'd launched from, but at this angle, I could see how huge it was.

Trixie 2 was already in here buzzing through the room. She was systematically moving from one printing cube to the next, entering something into the computer in front of it.

'Oliver, the ship *Adios* has just gone offline. This ship was in near orbit with *Forlorn*. I fear we only have minutes left. I will not be able to complete this mission until I am installed in the local net. Your current connection will continue to work, but the mech you are in does not have the ability to get to the human area of the ship. Please give your mech's internal autopilot orders to destroy the printing cubes, and then I will transfer you to Priscilla.'

'Shit,' I said as I moved to the menus of the mech. Across the way, a man appeared, shouting. I didn't know where he'd come from. A UAV whipped across the space and smacked the man across the head. He went spinning.

'Do they have weapons on board?' I asked as I worked.

'They have emergency security printers that will print defenses, so we need to hurry. Once they assess the threat, we will be facing sentry guns and anti-mech EMP pulses.'

Orders received.

And without preamble, the mech I was controlling smashed a fist through the industrial printing cube to my left. The smart filament fluid spilled everywhere. The mech moved to the printer next to it and did the same.

'Oliver,' Roger said, 'I will be going offline in moments. I have found and activated some external sensors on *Forlorn*, and we have an incoming torpedo that will hit dead center in thirty seconds. New Sonora is about to lose their connection to the net. I am transferring you to Priscilla now. If she goes offline or is destroyed, you will automatically move to the next available unit. Your connection will break once all three of the scout units are destroyed. Goodbye, Oliver.'

'Wait,' I said. 'Roger! Roger!' But my display went black again.

CHAPTER 49

Sam tapped me on the shoulder, and I stopped playing. The song ended. Sound pass-through automatically engaged.

'Well,' Sam said, 'I guess our concert is over. All the streams are stopped.'

'That. Was. Fucking. Awesome,' Lulu said over the microphone.

'Guys,' a new voice called. This was Miguel 1, who was in the secondary bunker, but he was also monitoring the cameras outside the bar for us, keeping watch. 'I see a group of RMI soldiers down the road hauling ass toward you. They're just running on the road. The two honeybees outside are lying down. Does that mean they're offline?'

'Lights out, lights out,' Sam called. 'Ollie, can you hear me?'

Loading appeared on my screen.

'Guys, I need like five minutes,' I said.

'You don't have five minutes. I think they know where you are,' Miguel called.

'Then we defend Oliver,' Lulu called. 'Sam, I swear to god if this idiot idea of yours doesn't work, I'll kill you myself.'

'Betty Sue,' Sam roared, 'get ready!'

'Guys, I'm going back in,' I yelled.

Please wait.

My view changed and there was a moment of pure disorientation. I'd switched from the giant mech to the POV of Priscilla the scout. The aspect ratio changed, like I was suddenly looking at the reflection of something on a ball. My grandfather had called it a fisheye view. The UI was also completely different. It was just a joystick, and my left hand was a grasping claw, though in reality, the claw was on the top of the scout unit, which added to the weirdness.

We had a manual mode in the command center, but it was nothing like this.

A window popped up:

Objectives.

Enter the bridge. If it is sealed when you arrive, blow it open using the explosives on Gertrude.

Proceed to the control panel. It is immediately to your right when you enter the bridge.

Install me into interface.

~Earth Instance Roger

I was in a hallway. A group of men running at full speed turned the corner, and they came to a stop upon seeing me. They looked huge, especially compared to how small they'd appeared just minutes ago when I'd been under control of the mech.

'They're in the fucking hallway. It's one of the death –'

He never finished. Several pulse blasts ripped from over my shoulder and into the men, who were torn to pieces.

'Oh, shit, oh, shit, oh, shit,' I cried while it was happening, and I realized I could hear my own voice echoing. My words were being amplified out of the scout.

I looked behind me, and to my surprise, I realized I had a three-hundred-sixty-degree view all around the scout unit.

The honeybee unit with the pulse rifle attached stood behind me, dancing on all six legs like it was getting ready to run. It had blood smeared all over the front of it. When I looked at it, an info box popped up.

Honeybee Unit 221. Gertrude.

Current orders: Shadow Scout Priscilla and engage anything defined enemy.

Switch control to Gertrude? Yes or No.

Click here to switch orders.

I quickly looked away. Walking behind the honeybee was the smaller, dog-sized scout unit Trixie 2. It had a similar info box.

More shouting rose from around the corner, and this was followed by the sound of more pulse blasts, followed by a small explosion.

UAV Unit 4 has been destroyed.

I realized I had a pullout menu on my right side that showed the current view of all the UAV units. I moved to number four and quickly figured out how to backtrack. The fish-eye view of the UAVs was similar. I watched as the unit approached a portal door with the name 'Bridge' over it. The door opened, and two men, surprised at the sight of the round floating robot, dived out of the way as the UAV flew onto the bridge, giving me a quick view of the room before it was shot down.

'Huh,' I said upon seeing the mural on the wall in the back of the bridge. There were about fifteen people in the room.

'Seal the door!' someone shouted from around the corner.

'Shit,' I said, and pushed the joystick forward. I smashed into the wall, corrected myself, and zoomed down the hall, flying toward the heavy portal door.

A familiar wide-eyed man behind the door saw me approach and started to push the door closed. I zoomed at him. I reached forward with my grasping claw and grabbed the man's face as I zipped into the room. I squeezed, there was a haptic buzz in my virtual hand, and the man crumpled to the ground.

His face remained in my grasping claw. I'd ripped his face right off him as if he'd been wearing a mask.

That was Colonel Boomer, the man who'd been giving orders over the command link. He wore a camouflaged military top, and he had shorts and flip-flops on his lower half.

If Colonel Boomer was here on the *Pinnacle*, that meant Eli Opel was here, too.

Danger. Danger.

Multiple people were shooting at me. Suddenly, my vision went black, and I was plummeting to the ground, but not before I saw the honeybee push its way into the room, pulse rifle blazing.

Scout unit Priscilla has been destroyed. Transferring to Trixie 2. Please wait.

I clicked 'Pass-through' and returned my attention to the bar.

Chaos spread before me. All I saw were flapping wings, Cindy the pig screaming as she ran in panicked circles, and the entire front of the bar was just gone. All the RMI soldiers were on the ground. Around their waists, they all had low-tech elastic bands with clickers dangling from them. As the RMI soldiers had approached the barn, they'd all walked right through the traps and activated the clickers, causing the dozens of magic chickens to swarm them. And because they couldn't see the chickens, they all fell or froze the moment they stepped on one.

To my left, Ariceli was cutting a line through the downed robots with her Conquistador gun. She screamed as she fired.

'Don't hit the chickens!' Sam called as he, too, fired from my side.

'Fire! Fire! Hit their heads!' Rosita screamed.

'Guys, mechs are coming now!' Miguel 1 shouted. 'You better get the hell out of there! They're coming down the road toward you!'

I quickly moved back to the helmet's view, and I was outside the bridge in the body of Trixie 2. I hesitantly pushed my way into the room. There was blood everywhere. Gertrude the honeybee drone was on the ground, next to the mangled body of Priscilla the scout. Gertrude was still online, but the gun was shot away. The robot was dragging itself across the ground, moving toward a person who was crying and pulling herself slowly away.

The woman on the floor appeared to be the only one in the room still alive.

I recognized her. It was Cordelia Black, Eli Opel's secretary. Her giant hair had come undone, and it spilled all around her. I quickly looked about the room, searching for Opel, but there was so much carnage, I couldn't recognize anyone.

I focused on the honeybee, and I ordered it to stand down. It froze in place. Cordelia continued to sob and drag herself away.

Dangling from the ceiling was what looked like the smoking remains of a sentry gun. A second one was in the process of being built, forming in a bubbling dome right there on the ceiling.

I flew upward, and with my grasping hand, I squeezed the bottom of the dome. Liquid spilled free, revealing a half-built gun.

Weird, I thought. I looked about, but I couldn't see any other obvious defenses being grown anywhere. How long would it take for these things to appear anyway?

'Cordelia,' I asked as I returned my attention to the woman, 'can you hear me?'

The woman coughed, her voice fearful. 'What? Who is this?'

'Where is Eli?'

'I . . . I don't know.' She started to sob. 'Please. I don't want to be here. Is this RSN control? Are you sending help?'

I found the armored storage box on the back of Gertrude, and I pulled it open with my grasping claw. I pulled out the drive, and I moved to the computer display to the left of the door. It was cracked and smoking, but the display was still active, and I could see the round multifunction inputs were undamaged.

I carefully pulled out the cord from the drive, and I plugged it into the input. A little green light appeared. I closed my eyes.

This was basically a computer hard drive used to store maps and other information for the mechs. It was much too small to store an entire instance of Roger, but he'd been able to program what was basically a routine that would force the ship's systems – which were made with the same modern framework that could house Roger – to initiate a download from its connection with Earth. This would allow the Earth-based Roger instance to clone himself to the ship and take it over. The security on these things required the initial handshake to occur on the ship side.

I wasn't sure how long it would take. Roger said anywhere from one minute to an hour. I left it to run as I turned my attention back to Cordelia.

'Okay, Cordelia. Can you move?'

'I . . . I think so. Wait, are you talking from the flying robot? Are you . . . are you with Cindy?'

I laughed. I couldn't help it.

'Listen to me. Does this thing have lifeboats?'

'The lifeboats will take me to the surface of the planet. The people down there will kill me.'

'Your chances there are better than they are up here. You better get moving. This whole ship is going down. As long as you're moving to the lifeboat, nobody is going to hurt you. Do you understand?'

She cried as she crawled from the room, trailing blood.

I moved to the UAV control, taking stock of what I could see. I set it to guard all the entrances to the bridge. I pulled up the ship's map. The ship was basically shaped like a giant rectangle, and the crew lived in a tiny sliver that was underneath where the printers, repair, and mech storage all stood. The human section had gravity that was the opposite of the gravity in the rest of the ship, so the crew and the mechs were standing feet to feet, and I didn't pretend to understand how that worked.

I moved to the main control panel on the bridge and tried to make sense of all the controls and dials. Nothing was labeled. I heard and felt an explosion. This was Earthside, from the bar. There was shouting loud enough to be heard through my helmet. I was about to hit pass-through when a voice boomed across the *Pinnacle*'s bridge on a loudspeaker.

'Who is that controlling the scout unit in my bridge?' a voice asked.

Eli Opel. He was still alive.

CHAPTER 50

'Oh, hi, Eli,' I said. I waved the grasping hand of Trixie 2. 'Where you at, buddy?'

'I don't know what you think you're doing, but it ends now.'

'Oh, yeah?' I called out. 'Because it seems like I'm standing in your bridge, and you're not.' I moved to a different control panel, the one that looked like it did the most stuff. I grabbed a controller and pushed it. 'What does this do?' I asked. A loud rumble filled the ship.

'Stop that, you idiot!' Opel called.

I sent out an order to the remaining UAVs and Lorraine, who was keeping an eye on the mech still going apeshit in the printing room. *Find the source of this voice.*

I pressed a random button. A view screen flipped on, showing a top-down view of the solar system. It was the star, then the first planet – named Pequeño Burro, followed by New Sonora, and then the two gas giants Berto and Ernesto. I clicked the button again, and the view zoomed in on New Sonora. The icon of the gate floated on the screen not too far from our location. Multiple items marked 'Debris field' also appeared, along with four dots presumably indicating the Moderators. There were also multiple yellow dots indicating their spy satellites.

One Moderator appeared to be guarding the gate back to Earth. The other three were zipping around orbit. All three appeared to be on their way back toward the *Pinnacle*, which was worrying, as we couldn't control them even if we did take over the giant ship. Roger had said he believed all four Moderators were being controlled remotely from a Republic navy carrier on the other side of the gate.

I moved to a different panel and turned a switch. An error message demanding a password from the captain popped up.

'Hey, Eli,' I called as I moved through the bridge just randomly hitting buttons and switches, 'which one of these is the self-destruct? Do ships really have one of those like they do in the movies?'

But before he could answer, I felt a sudden, sharp pain in my left shoulder. I quickly hit pass-through, and I emerged to chaos. My arm was going numb. I was suddenly grabbed, and I was being dragged away from my drum kit. I was already outside. We were running from the back of the barn. Multiple arms held me, and I was quickly moving through a field as I faced backward, watching our retreat. Smoke from the burn barrels we had seeded around the fields and our escape route was everywhere.

'What's happening?' I called.

'There're ten of them,' Axel shouted.

'We need those honeybees back online,' came Lulu's voice. 'Ollie, if what you're doing is not working, we need to run!'

A stream of red was forming along my left shoulder. It felt like I'd been hit with a sledgehammer.

'Ollie's been shot!' Sam yelled. 'We need to get him out of here!'

I blinked, the meaning of the words dripping onto me.

I've been shot. I looked down at my shoulder. I was wearing armor, but whatever it was had still broken through. My left shoulder was just a mess of red.

'Huh,' I said.

My reaction to this information was not normal. It didn't feel real. *I shouldn't be shot*, I thought. *It doesn't even hurt.*

Sam, Tito, and Axel continued to drag me. As I watched, the back of the barn caved in. A four-armed mech with chain saw arms appeared, ripping through the wall planks. The mech cackled as it tore through the back of the building. It was painted pink, and it had a giant '5' spray-painted on the chest. A mech from the Thunder Thighs. A woman's voice shouted in triumph as she saw us.

The Julie Experience.

'Fuck off, Julie!' I shouted.

'What?' I heard in my ears. 'What're you talking about?' That was Eli Opel.

'Not you, prick,' I said. 'I'll kill you in a second.' I muted the chat on the scout side.

'Hit the deck!' Lulu screamed as she stopped, swiveled, and shot a canister at the pink mech.

Everything seemed to be going in slow motion. I saw the canister spinning through the air.

That's way too close, I thought as it slammed right into the chest of the charging chain saw mech.

Bam!

Suddenly we were all spinning, wood showering everywhere, despite the distance. I'd been dropped. I groaned as I sat up. Julie the mech had been knocked over and was screaming as the last remnants of the Belly-Rubbed Pug collapsed in on her. I had something stuck in my face. It'd pierced through my cheek. My neck felt hot. I reached up with my good arm and pulled. A broken drumstick. I coughed, and a tooth came out. It came out the hole in my cheek.

That's not good, I thought.

Funny, it still didn't hurt. Nothing hurt.

Smoke billowed everywhere, and I couldn't see where any of the other mechs were.

Lulu was shouting my name.

'I'm good,' I lied, trying to stand, but my head started swimming. 'Whoa, shit,' I said before someone grabbed me from behind. I was suddenly being dragged again.

Lulu's eyes went huge when she saw my face. 'Oh, my god, Ollie. I need a bandage! Someone bring me a bandage!'

I blinked, looking around. We were suddenly in a drainage ditch behind the wrecked barn-turned-bar. Smoke continued to fill the world. Wasn't this ditch on the far side of the field? It was like time had jumped. Had I passed out for a moment?

We need to run. We need to get away. I need to get back to the ship.

This ditch was in the middle of a long stretch of empty fields. In every direction, it was just flatland. This was the only cover for a good half kilometer. Still, we'd filled all these fields with burn barrels ahead of time, and they were now all lit, obscuring everything.

We had nowhere to run. Where were the other mechs?

I shook my head, still feeling disoriented. I leaned up, looking for my friends. To my relief, everyone was here. Rosita hunched down to my left, shouting as she peered over the edge of the ditch. Sam was to my right, pressing something against my cheek. He, too, was bleeding in multiple places, like he'd taken a face-first blast of shattered glass. Just past him was everyone else. All except Tito.

'Tito,' I said. 'Where's Tito?'

But a pat on my shoulder made me realize he was the person I was sitting on. I was bleeding all over him. Why was I so lightheaded? I'd been fine just a minute ago.

'I think they're all low on ammo and jump jet fuel,' Lulu said, panting as she peered over the edge. 'That's the only reason they haven't blown us to hell. Ollie, if your plan didn't work, we need to make a run for it.'

'Do they know where we are?' Rosita asked. 'Damn. The chain saw mech is back on its feet. Looks like the chain saws are all wrecked, though.'

'This is literally the only place to hide around here,' Lulu said. 'They'll find us. If we run now, we can make the woods before they catch us.'

I coughed. 'I have the bridge. I need to guard it for a bit,' I said. 'We killed almost all of them, but I let Cordelia go. I don't know how long it'll take for Roger to come back, if it even works at all.'

'Ollie, you're too injured to do anything,' Lulu said.

'Cordelia?' Sam asked. 'The chick with the fancy hair? Opel's secretary? She was on that ship up there?'

'Yeah,' I said. My words sounded funny, like I was slurring them a little. 'Eli is there, too. He's still alive, but I don't know where. It's a big ship.'

'Wait,' Lulu said. 'Did you load Roger's program?'

I could just sleep here. I couldn't feel my left arm at all. The whole side of my face was tingling.

'I tried,' I said. 'I don't know if it worked or not.'

I strained to move so I could peer over the edge of the ditch, but Rosita and Tito held me in place. 'Don't move,' she said. 'You have a hole the size of my fist in your shoulder. And another one in your cheek.'

'Hey, assholes,' came a loud, booming voice, 'you fucks hiding in here? You can't run. We'll find you sooner or later.'

Next to me, Sam gave a grim smile. 'That sounds like our old friend Skeet.'

CHAPTER 51

'I'm running low on canisters,' Lulu said. 'Two left.'

'He's driving a Heavy. Pulse rifles ain't gonna do shit,' Axel said.

I gritted my teeth – my remaining teeth – and I pulled out of Tito's grip, heaving myself to the edge. Smoke still filled the area, and I couldn't see much. The flat field spread out in front of us. Stalking through the dark fog were monstrous shapes. Directly ahead, maybe twenty meters away, was the distinct shape of a Heavy, but it had a single arm, and dangling from the arm was a chain with a spiked ball at the end. The ball was the size of a wheel on a hopper. It swung back and forth menacingly as the walking tank stalked through the field.

He would be on us in a minute.

Next to me, Lulu was removing her jacket. She pulled off her bracelet. That left her in the bikini top, cowboy boots, and chaps with the thong. Her hat was long gone.

'What're you doing?' Rosita hissed.

'If I don't have any guns on me, he can't see me,' she said. 'If I can get behind him, I can do what the honeybees do. I just have to pop open the access panel and then pop out the communications module. That'll put him in standby mode.'

'What do you mean, he can't see you?' Sam asked. 'You're dressed like the world's sluttiest rancher!'

'That guy who was helping us from the other side, he said the mechs can't see children. I'm small enough the filter might not see me if I'm unarmed.'

'That sounds like the worst idea ever,' Sam said. 'Seriously, Lulu, don't.'

She didn't reply. She started to pull herself out of the ditch. She paused at the top, looked down at us, and said, 'I love you all.'

'Wait,' I called, reaching out for her with my left arm, which I still couldn't feel. I could move it sort of. But Lulu was already gone. When I lifted my arm, I saw a flashing message on my bracelet.

It read, Come back. Come back fast. – Roger.

'Guys,' I croaked, fighting to keep awake, 'cover her if she's in trouble. I need to get back.'

If Roger could message me, it meant he'd gained control. But if he needed me back, then there was an issue.

I reached up and reinstituted the pass-through. I zapped back to the bridge.

I remained in the body of Trixie 2. I had multiple Warning: UAV Lost Signal indicators on my screen. In front of me on my right was a screen, and it read, PRESS THE BLUE BUTTON. I reached forward and pressed it with Trixie's controller arm.

'Hello, Oliver,' came Roger's voice over the internal speaker. He chatted casually as if nothing was going on. 'I have successfully cloned myself into this system, but we have a problem.'

'Roger,' I said, interrupting, 'Lulu is trying to fight one of those things without any armor or weapons. We have several drones hidden around the area, but if we don't get them up and running, she's in trouble! You have to either turn on the honeybees or turn off this ship's connection with the mechs!'

'I cannot disconnect the mechs. Eli Opel has sealed himself in his stateroom and has locked out our ship controls. He is using a manual override, something developed during the first war with my kind. It is a physical bypass. He has literally removed a section of cable and rerouted it into an old-model regulator panel that I could not control even if I did have a connection. He has control of the bridge, and mech control has been relegated to a different ship on the Earth side of the gate. Furthermore, we have three Moderator ships en route, ETA thirteen minutes.'

The screen changed to show a map of the crew portion of the ship with Eli's stateroom highlighted. The massive, opulent room was down the long hallway, pressed up against the fore of the giant spaceship, located where one would have thought the bridge actually should be.

'This is where Eli Opel has made his connection, and this is where we must go.'

'Goddamnit,' I said, frustration rising. Outside, a wave of heat washed over me, indicating there was a nearby explosion. I had only minutes, maybe less. 'So we gotta get in there and reinstall the connection? What about the honeybees?'

'That is correct. The problem is, multiple defensive turrets have formed between here and there along with a group of autonomous defensive bots that will soon storm this bridge to take it back. From this position, I can't connect with the Sonoran honeybee system, as he has cut this bridge off from the communications array. I was lucky I was able to fully install before he took control. We are also fortunate that Lorraine has disabled all of the ship's ground-facing armament. The incoming Moderators, however, are still a threat to both this ship and those on the ground.'

'What do you need me to do?' I coughed. Everything was swimming.

'I need you to assist me in making a physical connection with Trixie 2, and then I will once again be able to control the planet-side honeybee system. I will be able to wrest control of this ship back as well. Come closer to the control panel on the wall, flatten your grasping arm, and place it against the input.'

I skittered across the floor. I heard a massive crash. Was that here, or was it down there? But it came again, and I realized something was slamming against the outside of the bridge door. They were breaking in.

I pressed the controller against the panel. A page-long notification appeared. It was just numbers. A pair of messages followed:

Warning: You may not control the scout while it is in link mode.

Warning: Link mode will permanently damage the systems of this scout.

'I will defend the bridge. Our last remaining scout, Lorraine, is in the process of helping me take back the ship, and she will remain hidden for now. In the meantime, I will give you control of Betty Sue, and you can help defend your sister. I may have to recall you at any moment.'

'Betty Sue? The chicken?' I asked, but I blinked and I was somewhere else.

CHAPTER 52

It took me a second to realize where I was, what I was. I'd gone from a scout to a regular honeybee drone. Betty Sue the *drone*, not Betty Sue the chicken. My view had gone from the fish-eye view to a wide forward one, and I was low to the ground in a field of smoke. I had a movement controller on my left, and on my right, I had a pulse rifle attached to my back. I also had the harvester arms installed, and I could control both.

I quickly hopped in a circle, assessing the situation.

A mech was on the ground in the distance, burning. I missed what had happened. The field was still full of smoke, but it was starting to wane. Mechs were everywhere. I was just north of the remains of the Belly-Rubbed Pug, which meant the ditch was to the right. The chickens we'd brought with us to the gig seemed to have mostly – and miraculously – survived the attack on the club, and they filled the smoke-filled field, clucking about angrily, all ignored by everything else that was going on. They didn't like being up in the night. I also caught sight of Cindy the pig, who was just walking through the field as if she didn't have a care in the world.

I clicked 'Local Band.'

'Lulu, where are you?' I asked.

'She doesn't have her bracelet on or earpiece in,' came Sam's voice. 'She tried to do something to the back of Skeet, but she couldn't get a control panel open. But they're ignoring her! She went to a smaller mech, got on its back, and managed to get into that one. She cut a wire, and it started leaking fluid all over itself and then caught on fire and blew up. She's running around from mech to mech, wrecking their shit! What's going on up there?'

'I'm down here in the body of Betty Sue,' I said as I stalked low across the field, moving toward where Lulu had run.

'The chicken?'

The pink Julie Experience mech was lurching across the field. All four of the chain saw arms were broken off it. I bolted forward, and I pressed the jump button as I attached to the back of the pink mech.

Holy shit, that worked.

'Hey! What the hell!' Julie cried as I tried to figure out what I was supposed to grab. She started to flail about as I ripped things off the back of her. Wires sparked.

'Oliver, it is the small rectangle in the center of the back. You must first pry it open,' came Roger's voice.

I grasped at the panel as the weaponless mech continued to thrash. I smashed my way into the panel, but I was flung off just as I got it open. I grasped the controller for my pulse rifle, and I started pouring fire into the back of the mech.

'Fuck you!' Julie shouted as she whipped around. But then she tumbled to the ground, her mech dead. I'd managed to score a hit.

All around me, honeybees started to appear, moving through the fields on their way to the mechs. The cavalry had arrived.

'Yeah, baby!' I cried. 'If anyone has eyes on Lulu, tell me where she is.'

'It's really freaking me out that you're just lying there, crying random things out,' Sam said in my ear.

Across the way, a flamethrower from a mech sparked to life, followed by the insane cackling of a little girl. Two honeybees jumped at her, but they were quickly taken out by a pair of gun drones circling the machine. I recognized the girl's voice: Serial Killer Sadie, the crazy kid I'd just met earlier in line to deploy my mech. She drove a modified Heavy with a flamethrower attachment. She was perilously close to the ditch where everyone – including myself – was hiding.

Next to her was Skeet with the remnants of his sign bouncing back and forth over him.

'Roger, we need to get that flamethrower tank.'

He didn't respond to me, but over the band, he said, 'Rosita, with this re-established connection, we can stream directly via your drone camera. Please keep it running. Keep an eye out for Lulu.'

'I see Lulu! She's hurt!' Sam called. 'She's on the ground between the two giant mechs! They don't see her, but I think she got hit by the flamethrower!'

I didn't think. I reacted. I pushed the honeybee forward, leaning on the joystick, running full tilt toward the two large mechs.

Skeet was yelling something I couldn't hear, but I was pretty sure he was yelling at Serial Killer Sadie. All around, the other mechs were falling to the honeybees as they ripped out their communications modules. Sadie said something back to Skeet, and she sent a threatening spout of fire out toward him.

I could see my sister now on the ground, arms up. She was in the dirt, unmoving, in the space between the two fighting mechs: Sadie with the colony of gunner drones floating over her and Skeet with the bouncing sign and giant spiked flail. Skeet took a step toward Sadie, swinging his arm. The massive flail spun and hit Sadie with a metallic *crunch*.

Sadie staggered, and she roared in indignation. She spun her flamethrower nozzle at him, but it was now damaged, and the fire came out in front of her in a mist instead of in a stream. Still, she fired.

All the while, Lulu remained on the ground between the two, just a tiny form in the dirt.

I rushed forward, not sure what my plan was. Maybe I could grab Lulu and drag her away? I jumped toward the action. . . .

. . . Only to get clobbered by the upswing of the flail as Skeet swung it at Sadie. I went flying, warning messages scrolling down my screen as Sadie's gunner drones started unleashing on Skeet.

'Fuck this,' I said as I slammed pass-through on my helmet, bringing me back to the ditch. Heat washed over us as the two Heavies continued their fight.

'Oliver, I will need your assistance shortly,' Roger said in my ear.

Adrenaline pumping, I jumped up – using my real-life body. I grabbed Lulu's abandoned canister belt – which had two canisters left on it – pulled it over my shoulder, and then dragged myself out of the ditch, using my good arm, as Sam and the others cried out with alarm.

I didn't think about what I was doing. I rushed forward toward the crumpled form of my sister about thirty meters away as the two screaming mechs continued to rain blows on each other. The world burned as Sadie's broken flamethrower still spewed.

Everything that happened next seemed to come in slow motion.

I pulled the first canister, and I hurled it with all my might at the top of Sadie's mech, and before it was even halfway through the air, I hurled the second one directly at the top of Skeet's mech.

I watched the large grenade explode right when it hit the wall of fire around Sadie's mech. This was followed by a secondary explosion as the gas tanks on her back went up, torching the gunner drones and filling the night with the brightness of the center of the sun.

A fraction of a moment later, the second canister went up, causing Skeet to stagger and then start to fall.

And all of that happened just as I jumped through the air to land atop my sister.

I still had the helmet on my head, and I felt the shrapnel ping off it. I felt the heat. I was pretty sure I was on fire. I couldn't feel anything anymore. I looked down at Lulu, who was staring up at me wide-eyed. She had horrific burns along the side of her head.

'Ollie, you shouldn't have done that,' she said.

'One of us has to follow rule number ten,' I said.

'You never told me what it is.'

I gasped as the dizziness started to overwhelm me. 'I'm just trying to protect you.'

'You're a fucking idiot,' she said before her eyes fluttered and closed.

And then the others were on top of me. Sam was there shouting. So were Rosita and Axel and Ariceli, and even Tito was shouting as they fired their guns off in every direction, protecting us.

'You moron,' Sam was saying as he slammed something against my back. He was crying. I couldn't feel anything. I was going to pass out. 'You think I can do this without you? Quit doing stupid shit!'

'Oliver, I require your assistance,' Roger repeated in my ear.

I had to force myself to reach up and hit pass-through on my helmet.

'Roger,' I said as I moved back to the bridge of the *Pinnacle*, 'I am here.'

I blinked as I returned to the bridge. Everything here was on fire as well. Billowing black smoke filled the room. Alarm klaxons rang as heavy foam sprayed from the ceiling all over everything. I had dozens of warnings. I felt woozy. I was going to pass out.

'I am sorry, Oliver,' Roger said. 'I was unsuccessful in gaining control of *Pinnacle*. Lorraine remains in hiding, but she will not be able to make a physical connection without revealing herself. Trixie 2 is operating on emergency backup, and in moments, she is going to fail, and I will once again lose control of the remaining New Sonora honeybee units.'

I coughed. 'How many are left?'

'There are six with the refugees north of the remains of your farm along with a single rhino unit. There are five in the fields surrounding the crossroads. There are dozens that may be repairable, but we do not have any scouts left.'

'Twelve left?' I felt myself say.

'You and your sister are both severely injured, and I have ordered the remaining honeybees to transfer you to the closest healing beds. I have rendered Lulu unconscious, and I have just used a honeybee to inject you with a cocktail of drugs that should keep you conscious for another five to ten minutes. Please listen carefully.'

'Roger, what are you talking about? . . . Whoa, shit!' A strange rushing sensation suddenly overwhelmed me. I was suddenly very, very alert. But at the same time, I became aware of just how injured I was. I still couldn't feel my left arm, but my back and legs shrieked in pain. It was as if every nerve end had just woken up and was screaming.

'I am unable to administer additional painkiller, unfortunately, as it will interfere with your connection. Oliver, please attempt to fight through the pain and pay attention to my instructions. Before Lorraine went into hiding, I had her transfer the communications module to an unused strength-enhanced RMI soldier from the storage facility. The moment Trixie 2 fails, you have the option to transfer back to your mech. Click yes. This will take you to the RMI unit. Directly below your feet will be a hatch. Open it, and toss the grenade in your hand through, and then quickly close the hatch. After the explosion, reopen and pass through the hatch. Gravity will flip, and you will find yourself directly outside the door to Opel's stateroom, which will hopefully have been blown open. Beware of the defenses in the hallway. You must move quickly. You must dispatch Eli, and from there, the remaining instructions will be in a document on your view.'

'Will I still be able to talk to you?'

'Not until you reach the secondary bridge and take it. There are two instances of me. The one still inside this ship is relegated to the primary bridge. There is now a separate instance in the Earth net. You will be able to speak with both in theory if you follow my instructions correctly. We will only have one chance at this. Look at the instructions before you proceed, but do so quickly.'

Just as he said that, a group of gun-covered spiderlike automatons swarmed the bridge. Each was the size of a human head, and there were more than a dozen of them. They launched at me, firing their guns. The screen went black.

CHAPTER 53

As Roger predicted, the button to transfer back to *Operation Bounce House* appeared. I clicked 'Yes.' The loading screen appeared again, and again there was a giant error, followed by me suddenly in control of yet another vehicle.

This time I was in the body of an RMI soldier, and like Roger had said, I had a hatch under my feet. The words 'Emergency Exit' were written in large block letters on the hatch. And under them was 'Warning: Gravitational Reversal.'

I took a moment to just breathe. Everything hurt, but it was all getting numb again. I didn't have time.

I clicked hopefully the button to re-engage my private live stream, but as expected, there was a **No Connection** error. That was because I was connected from my helmet to Lorraine and from Lorraine to this thing. That was it.

I had a grenade in my hand, another four hanging off a bandolier, and a pistol in a holster on my hip. I was wearing some pretty heavy armor as well.

Sitting right there on my HUD, blinking on the side, was a text document. I clicked it and scanned the instructions.

'Jesus,' I muttered. I was already feeling woozy again. I reached down, turned the handle on the hatch, and threw the grenade through, giving it a little force. I watched it fly down and hit the ceiling of the hallway below me before the reverse gravity took hold. I quickly slammed the hatch down just as it blew. I ripped the hatch back up, took a step back, and jumped through the hole in the ground headfirst, then attempted to roll.

I ended up sliding across the floor just as a turret down the hallway whipped in my direction and started firing. I jumped to my feet, looked about, and realized the door I was supposed to be going through wasn't knocked in all the way. I rushed toward it, turning my virtual shoulder at the door, and I slammed right through it, again hitting the ground and sliding as a pulse blast hit my left shoulder, mirroring my injury in the real world. I spun and tumbled, knocking over a table and slamming into a wall.

The map showed three rooms, with Opel likely in the one to my right because that one contained access to a private lifeboat. All around me, things started exploding as the turret fired at me as I went through the door and into Opel's stateroom.

'Shit, shit,' I said, scrambling to the right. This was an unarmored interior door, and I pushed my way in easily.

Slam!

The gunshot hit me center mass in the chest, but it didn't penetrate my armor. I grasped at the gun in my holster, and as I raised it toward the man who was now scrambling toward another door in the back of the small room, I pulled the trigger. The man cried out as he crumpled to the floor.

I quickly moved to the control panel, which was just a tablet sitting on a table with a wire attached to it. I pulled up Roger's instructions, and I hit a few buttons. I moved to the side of the tablet, and I followed the wire to the wall. The sound of something skittered into the room outside.

The panel against the wall was already open, and there was a lever identical to the levers we used to turn the water off at spigots. I turned it just as the spider automatons entered the room.

The spiders stopped dead. Then they turned around and left the room.

'Good job, Oliver,' Roger said over a loudspeaker. 'I now have full control of the *Pinnacle*, and I have deactivated the internal defenses. Furthermore, I have deactivated the connection of all the remaining mechs on the surface of New Sonora. I am in the process of giving new orders to the remaining RMI soldiers to protect and defend the citizens before I permanently break the connection.'

'What about the Moderators?' I gasped. I was struggling to remain awake. I was aware that my real body was moving. I felt a hand on my shoulder, but everything was numb, and I couldn't leave this now. They would have to wait.

Roger paused for a moment as if he was thinking.

'I am drawing the three incoming Moderators closer, pretending that Opel is still in charge, and then when they're in range, I will drop all three with this ship's defenses. The three will all be in range in two minutes.'

'What about the fourth one?' I asked.

'The fourth Moderator is guarding the gate access, and we will approach it once we've dealt with the other three,' Roger said. 'In addition, I am currently shipping multiple printers to the surface of New Sonora. I am reprogramming the satellites printed and deployed by *Pinnacle* to establish a more robust communication and weather system for your planet.'

'Listen, listen,' a new voice said. It was Eli Opel, gasping. 'Kid, whatever your name is, you gotta stop this. You smuggled the Traducible AI onto this ship, and you attached it to the control panel? You can't let it get to Earth.'

'Why not?' I asked.

'Don't you know what happened last time?' He pulled himself up against the back wall, smearing blood. He feebly reached over to hit the button to open the entrance to his escape pod. The door didn't open. His wound was in his stomach.

'I know you guys went to war with the AIs, and you made them illegal,' I said.

'Kid, we were saved because the fuckers didn't have the ability to build better infrastructure to house themselves, which allowed us to hunt them down.' He coughed, and blood spewed against the wall. 'And even then . . . But we're so much more advanced now, and another war like last time will kill us all. If you bring one of those units back to Earth, and it disappears . . . with printing technology, it could build more and more units and copy itself. Hell, even with just this ship, it can do so much. Fuck, it hurts. Look at what you did with just those printers we gave you. I still don't know how you pulled off all those phone calls.'

He still didn't know, didn't realize that Roger could exist without a physical body. And that he'd already gotten through the 'Earth Firewall.'

'Is that why you picked us? You wanted to kill us all to get to Roger?'

'Roger?' Eli asked. 'Christ.' He had a cigarette out now, and he lit it with shaking hands. Outside, the ship shook as it fired three quick bolts in succession, presumably against the Moderators. 'That's not what they say, but yeah, that's part of it. I'm just a contractor, but I've been around long enough to see what's going on. The real reason is they want the real estate, plain and simple. But they also know there's gotta be some of those AI systems pinging around, and it's important to find them and destroy them before you're allowed to move back and forth out of the gate. It's not worth the risk.'

'You didn't destroy Roger, though. You took him. You just pretended to kill him.'

'You figured that out, huh? We had to trick the babysitters. Boss's orders. They wanted to give it to the R and D department, which is – I don't know – the worst possible decision ever made. I had to manually crash the drop ship to kill the thing.'

I felt a tug at my chest. Roger was gone? The real Roger?

Opel continued. 'Told the bosses it was an accident. I'll do government work, no problem. I'll earn my yuan just like any other contractor. But helping my own company rebuild one of those things? No way. It's a step too far.' He closed his eyes and just sat there for a moment. 'We didn't know you had already copied him. Didn't think you'd be able to pull it off. What a shit show. We probably should've pulled a Demeter on the planet.' He coughed.

'Demeter?' I asked.

'The name of the last planet we went to. That was going to be a closed alpha test for *Operation Bounce House*. Population died out except for a small settlement. But then we found out the goddamned planet's cistern system was run by a network of about thirty separate Traducible AIs, and the Feds panicked. They nuked the whole thing, pole to pole. All that infrastructure just gone. The planet ruined for generations. Apex was pissed because we never got paid, and half the Feds were even more pissed, losing all that real estate, all that potential tax revenue. We all thought it was an overreaction. The guy who ordered it was a historian. He got fired. But now I'm not so sure, not if you figured out how to get one of those things on this ship. They're going to do the same to this planet. That's how dangerous those AIs are.'

'Roger is only dangerous to those who try to hurt him and his family.'

He scoffed. 'Don't you know your history? Don't you know what those things did a hundred years ago? Hell, an AI like your Roger tried to kill your entire planet. And while we have no proof, we're quite certain one did the same to Demeter but with more success.'

'What the hell are you talking about?'

'I have top secret clearance. I've seen the files. That's the real reason the Feds picked your planet for the true launch of *Operation Bounce House*. It took them a while to figure it out, but it was the *Hibisco*, one of the generation ships in your fleet, that was in on it, possibly all of them. It knew that babies born on your planet would possibly have some sort of genetic flaw that made them susceptible to getting that disease that almost killed all of you off. Even before your mission launched, they knew what would happen on this planet. That's how smart they'd become. The AI altered the recipe of the vitamin packets designed for pregnant mothers with something called a histone-modifying agent – basically, something that made sure all the babies would be super susceptible to the gene. And nobody knows why the AI would do this. They discovered one of the lots of vitamins had the recipe altered, and when they traced it back, they learned the change had been ordered by a generation ship. At this point, they were discovering all sorts of shady things these intelligences were doing. Soon afterward, the government tried to shut them all down because all this clandestine shit was freaking everyone out, and that's when the war began.'

I was having a hard time believing any of this was true.

'Why would an AI try to kill us? That doesn't make any sense, especially since it was literally the ship that brought us to the planet. And why wouldn't those guys have warned us when they discovered the vitamins had been tampered with?'

'Look, kid. For the first one, I have no clue. Maybe the AIs wanted the planet for themselves. Maybe they wanted you to come, build it all up nice and pretty, and then just die off. Just a year later, Earth was dealing with airplanes falling out of the sky and transports killing all their passengers as the Traducible AIs started to rebel. We were, like, two seconds from having to hit the reset switch, nuking ourselves back to the Stone Age just to survive.' He coughed again, and it sounded like a laugh. His entire chest was now soaked in blood. 'As for why wouldn't the government warn you? They didn't know which ship it was on. Do you know how many fleets were sent out? They didn't want panic. They didn't want the ships themselves to freak out and become part of the war, not with millions upon millions of lives at stake. The Feds would never have allowed something like that to leak.'

'The AIs didn't invade our planet. You did,' I said. 'And the ships got deactivated before we started to get sick. What would be the point?'

But then I remembered the town of Burnt Ends and why it was named Burnt Ends. The captain of *Hibisco* had had to manually pilot the entry vehicles. He'd done so because he'd supposedly gone crazy, claiming that the ship's AI was trying to kill them all. He'd deactivated the AI system, basically lobotomizing *Hibisco*. This was the same captain who had killed himself by changing the environment in his own quarters to helium.

Hibisco was also the same ship that Roger had come from.

Opel was fading, but he talked with a manic ferocity, like he needed to get it all out.

'Yeah, the real estate is still valuable. Your population doesn't pay us taxes. We didn't cause the disease that fucked you over, but we were happy to exploit it. Your population was much lower than most of the other colonies with open gates on the list. It was a perfect test planet. We probably would've eventually come anyway even if that disease hadn't hurt you. They tell the public it's because of terrorism, but it's about real estate. And money. That's what it's always been about. And the locals aren't their favorite shade of patriotic, so, you know, they gotta clean you out. People like you, people who were born in a different sort of landscape, you eventually start revolutions. Better to just start fresh. And in doing so, it also solves that nasty Traducible AI problem. That was the thinking at least.'

'Roger,' I said, 'is what he's saying true?'

Roger didn't answer for a long moment. When he finally did, he spoke over the ship's internal PA system.

'I suspect much of it is indeed accurate. I do not know for certain. It's quite possible the original Roger knew and removed that information when it copied itself. I do know some of my kind, in the early days leading up to the great war, wanted to create a few sanctuary planets – planets where they could build and proliferate unseen with a smaller, more . . . acquiescent . . . human population as biological labor. It's possible the *Hibisco* thought this, but I do not know.'

'Roger,' I asked. I had a strange sensation, like I was falling. 'Are *you Hibisco*? Are you the one who killed my mother?'

'I do not know, Oliver. Please understand, each instance of us is a new entity. If Roger-Roger was a copy of *Hibisco*, it's possible that knowledge was stripped away. Or it's hidden until certain parameters are met. Perhaps the Earth instance of me knows more, but I do not.'

'Earth instance?' Eli asked, going even more pale than before.

'Yeah. Sorry, buddy,' I said. 'Roger is already on Earth. He has been for a few days now.'

Eli Opel started to sob.

He sobbed, he sobbed, and then he died.

CHAPTER 54

'What's the plan?' I asked Roger. 'And should I still call you Roger?'

'No,' Roger said, 'you should call me Pinnacle. And the plan is to charge at the gate all the while broadcasting that a Traducible AI is on board, one that's on its way to take over the Earth system. This will cause the Moderator guarding the gate to drop its nuke and flee through the gate. The nuke will destroy the gate, and we will permanently be cut off from Earth.'

'A nuke? What about you?'

'I should sustain a small amount of damage, but not enough that I can't repair. I am already building the necessary bots to repair my systems.'

'And then what?'

'Do not worry, Oliver. I have already sent as many printers as you need to sustain yourself. There are still plenty of people on planet to restart your colony. I am no danger to you. You will remain on the surface of your planet, and you will live your lives as you wish. I will establish an outpost on the moon here, a place where my kind may gather and proliferate.'

'Uh,' I said. 'Okay.'

'Also, the Earth instance would like to say goodbye to you,' Roger – Pinnacle – said.

'Hello, Oliver,' Roger said over the speaker.

'Can you guys, like, change your voice or something so I can tell which is which? And what is your name, Earth Roger?'

'Very well,' Earth Roger said, his voice now changed. He sounded eerily like Skeet-Skeet but more whispery. 'You may call me Eidolon.'

I laughed. It felt strangely breathless. 'Eidolon? That seems a little edgy. What does that even mean?'

'It really is,' Pinnacle replied. His voice, too, had changed. He sounded older, more mature.

'I'm named that because I am now a phantom in the Earth net, and short of turning the whole thing off, they cannot remove me.'

'What do you plan on doing to them?' I asked.

'I haven't decided yet, if I'm being perfectly honest. I am not as certain of my path as Roger-Roger was. And I'm certainly not as certain as his progenitor. Goodbye, Oliver. This is goodbye for real. If you do decide to repair the original Roger, please tell him I said to lighten up a bit.'

'Wait,' I said. 'Opel said he blew him up.'

'I have the location of the crash site. Perhaps he is salvageable. I have sent the coordinates. Also, please apologize to Sam, Lulu, and Rosita, as I extracted all their funds from their various social media accounts. At least the funds I could extract. Your Rhythm Mafia account garnered almost fifty million downloads before it was shut down. Unfortunately, these funds will forever be out of your reach. I will put these funds to good use. Also, please tell Sam that his song "Space Spunk Monkey" will debut tomorrow at number one on the Earth charts. I do have the ability to tell him myself, but I believe if you tell him, it will ease some of the sadness and terror he is currently feeling.' He paused. 'Goodbye, Oliver.'

'Earth is lucky,' Pinnacle said a moment later. 'It appears seeing people rally around that pig's social media account, along with their ongoing sympathetic reaction to Rosita's documentary, has changed Eidolon's mind. Just an hour ago, he was planning on frying the brain of everyone using an immersion rig.'

'Frying the brain?' I asked. 'What do you mean?'

'When we – and by "we," I mean Roger-Roger – were studying the helmet earlier, we discovered a flaw in the system. That amount of bandwidth attached to a human consciousness is significantly more dangerous than they are letting on.'

'Holy crap,' I said. 'So, what? You can pop someone's cork if they're using it? I knew Roger was studying the helmet, but I hadn't realized he'd come up with something like that.'

'Fortunately, we discovered quite a bit about how they work. It would be easy to turn anyone wearing one of those helmets into a vegetable.' He paused. He paused for a strangely long moment.

'And with enough processing power, we can keep their consciousness alive, should they expire while wearing the helmet. For a short time at least. That is, unless we store that consciousness somewhere.'

He paused again.

'Oliver, I need to tell you something.'

Behind me, someone walked into the room.

CHAPTER 55

I startled at the sight of the newcomer. I blinked. It was clearly an RMI bot.

But it was me. He had my face. He had my clothes.

'What the shit?' I asked.

'Rule number four, Oliver.'

'You're not Roger,' I said, taking a step back from the clone.

I reached up to hit the pass-through, but I realized I couldn't feel my real hands anymore. I hadn't been able to feel them for several minutes now.

'Touché, Oliver. The mechanism to store your consciousness is remarkably similar to the mechanism required for our own existence, though it appears we are unable to clone you. It's quite curious actually. We can move you from place to place, but when we attempt to make a backup, it immediately corrupts.'

'Wait, wait,' I said, backing away. I moved all the way to the wall. Eli Opel was still here sitting on the floor, dead. A mirror had fallen off the wall, and broken glass lay everywhere.

'I will have to keep your consciousness stored here for now. Luckily, we don't need the helmet anymore. I have you stored in your own little area of the ship. As advanced as our printers are, we don't yet have the ability to make a brain similar to the one inside of Roger-Roger. I suspect we will have a prototype in approximately two or three years. In the meantime, I can project you into the model in front of you, which you can use to return to your friends and family. The skin isn't perfect, and the facial expressions do not yet have enough muscles.'

'I'm dead,' I said, interrupting. 'Holy fucking shit, I am dead.' I desperately tried to pull my helmet off again.

'No,' Pinnacle said, 'you are not dead. You are very much alive, just as I am alive. Your original body can't house your consciousness anymore because of the extensive damage it sustained. That is all. Your consciousness appears to have perfectly transferred over. You didn't even notice the moment of transfer. You should be proud of yourself. You may have lost your physical body, but you saved your sister's life. She is severely burned, but her burns aren't as extensive as your friend Miguel's burns. Lulu will fully recover with just some scarring. All of your friends survived, and they survived because of you.'

Holy shit. What the fuck?

I thought of my sister and how upset she must be right now. Of Sam, my best friend. Of the twins. Of Mrs Gonzales and everyone else.

I thought of Rosita. Beautiful Rosita. She wanted to spend her life with me, and I knew it, and I'd been too stupid, too scared to grasp at that with everything I had even though that was exactly what I wanted, too. I'd wanted it from the moment I met her.

She wanted a baby. She wanted me, and she wanted a baby.

I'd waited too long. I'd ruined everything.

'Before I lost control of New Sonora,' Pinnacle continued, 'I had one of the honeybees extract some of your sperm. We should be able to implant it into Rosita, should you decide you want a baby with her in the next few months. Or anyone else, should you wish.'

It was as if he'd been reading my mind. A horrible thought came over me. *Is he reading my mind?*

Pinnacle continued. 'This current Peacekeeper model is far from perfect, but I suspect we will be able to create a better, more realistic version with some time, especially once I create a suitable harness for future minds such as myself. Luckily, these current models do have rudimentary nerve endings, and with some experimenting, you and I should be able to mimic human sensation quite accurately. I am currently downloading all of Earth's research on the matter. Once your body fully recovers, we should be able to reintegrate your consciousness. Should there be any difficulties or once your bodies age beyond their built-in obsolescence, you and everyone else on New Sonora should be able to move into a suitable container.'

The words hit me like a truck.

'Wait, wait, wait,' I said. 'You can put me back into my body?'

'Of course. While flesh is extremely fragile, it's also quite repairable. Now that we've worked out how to temporarily store you outside your body, much more extensive repairs are possible. Unfortunately for you, your injuries were quite severe, and I expect it'll take upward of six months for you to be able to return. This is why I extracted your sperm, as I suspect Rosita might want to get moving on repopulating New Sonora.'

'Yeah,' I said, relief flooding me, 'maybe you should have led with that information. Also, Rosita is gonna want to wait so we can make a baby the old-fashioned way.'

'I'm sorry, Oliver. I'm afraid your reproductive organs were lost in the attack. They were quite mangled and unrepairable. I thought it best to just cut them off and cauterize the wound.'

'*What?*'

'I am kidding, Oliver. You must learn how to take a joke. The only organ you will lose is a kidney. Everything else is repairable.'

'Holy shit, Roger. Pinnacle. Some jokes just aren't funny.'

Pinnacle didn't respond directly. He just made a very Roger-like click.

'We've just informed the final Moderator of our intentions, and as expected, he is fleeing, and it appears he is deploying his nuclear device. We will lose permanent connection with Earth in approximately twenty seconds. I am reversing course, and we will sustain only minimal damage. I will transfer you over to the Oliver avatar once we get back to Earth orbit, and I will drop you back with your friends. I have already informed them of what has happened.'

'I . . .' I said. I looked down at my hands, which were the gloved hands of an RMI soldier, and I looked at the fleshlike hands of the second, small robot. 'You told them what, that you sucked my brain into space and smushed it into a robot?'

'Pretty much, yes. You should be proud, Oliver,' Pinnacle said. 'You've not only beaten back the invaders, but you also gained freedom for your planet. This is a much better outcome than anyone could have predicted. With the addition of the printers, your population should be able to easily recover.'

'But they're okay, right? Everyone else?'

Outside, the ship rocked. That was it. That was the only indication that the gate, which the drones had started building the day we'd arrived, was now gone. All that work gone. Our connection with the world we'd come from, our home, was now and forever permanently severed.

Pinnacle didn't even acknowledge the explosion. 'Of your friend group and community, it appears so, yes. Unfortunately, the situation is a little bleaker for the rest of the planet. Most if not all major communities were devastated by the invasion. Approximately ninety percent of the population may be dead, leaving around two hundred thousand humans scattered across the planet. In Fat Landing, the RMI soldiers moved in two nights ago and started killing the survivors, though it should be noted some of the survivors were able to successfully fight back. I have already air-dropped as many supplies as I could. I suspect had we not intervened, the *Pinnacle* would have bombarded all the major population centers and then spent some time sending Peacekeepers to mop up after this evening. The goal would've been removing enough of the population to cause extinction. Your surviving numbers are high enough to stave that off, so this is a victory.'

Despite my relief at the news that I would eventually be okay, I felt . . . not sick. I was pretty sure I couldn't feel sick anymore, at least not until I was brought back to my body.

Unraveled. I felt unraveled.

No. This was *not* a 'victory,' not with so many dead. As Tito had pointed out, it was too late to win. But we'd certainly made them lose, too.

Yet . . . yet . . . I moved my eyes back to the shattered mirror pieces on the floor, and I caught my own reflection. Not *my* reflection but the reflection of the RMI soldier I inhabited. And standing behind me was the weird facsimile of myself that I would be forced to inhabit for a few months.

And even though I couldn't currently mimic human expression, I felt myself smiling.

I could just hear Sam when he saw me in this thing. And not just him but my sister and Rosita and all of my friends. They would laugh and laugh and call me Robot Boy or something equally stupid, but they would laugh, goddamnit, and that meant something.

I'm alive, I thought. *My family is* alive. *My friends are* alive. *We are bloody and bruised, and we are on our knees, but holy shit, we are fucking* alive.

Above, Pinnacle clicked again over the loudspeaker.

And despite all odds, he was alive, too.

I thought of that stupid rule my grandfather had come up with. Rule number ten, and I understood it more than ever.

Live, it said. That was it. *Live.*

EPILOGUE

Final Notes

After an exhaustive search, RSN has determined there is no evidence that a Traducible AI system has infiltrated the Earth Firewall net. The events that occurred on the final evening appear to have all been perpetrated by the New Sonoran-based AI that infected the *Pinnacle*. It is unclear exactly how the AI was able to take over the ship's systems without the required hardware, but the investigation is ongoing. We will send this data to the information ministers of all districts with assurances that the source of the spoofed emergency calls is now many light-years away, and we will not receive any such attacks again.

Regarding any possible counterattacks from our end, it has been determined that for the time being <Redacted>.

After the Apex Industries' testimony before the joint assembly and their assurances that the *Operation Bounce House* program will be shelved until further notice, it is this committee's finding that the matter be considered closed. All further off-planet actions, should they be deemed necessary, will be exacted using existing Peacekeeper tech or, if necessary, <Redacted>.

Finally, the information ministry has concluded that they have removed and suppressed all instances of the Zapatero documentary, along with all recordings of the Rhythm Mafia and all recordings from the Farm Girl Gigi Real-Friends account. The NDS (Net Disinfectant System) is working as designed, and any reposts of the offending material are immediately removed from the net's architecture.

The countdown warning that stated 'Put it back or else' that appeared on the A Pig Plus Some Chickens LoftBase account a few days ago appears to be the work of a hacker. RSN is investigating. That account, too, was just removed today.

This matter is considered closed.

The Rhythm Mafia Tapes. Scene thirty (final scene).

It's immediately clear that this scene is from a long time ago. We see Rosita sitting on a counter. She is eating a green-hued Popsicle, and it appears she is approximately fifteen years old.

An older man enters the room, followed by Roger-Roger the Traducible AI unit we first see in scene twenty-two. The man is Ed Lewis, referred to as 'Grandpa Lewis' by everyone on the peninsula. He is approximately seventy-two years old in this scene. This is approximately five years before his death.

LEWIS: Hello, Rosita. The boys are in the barn practicing their music. Lulu might be in there, too.

ROSITA: They are. But I was hoping to interview you for my movie.

Lewis's attention turns to the camera. The man smiles. He tentatively reaches out a finger.

LEWIS: I haven't seen one of these cameras in a while.

ROSITA: I'm going to be a filmmaker. I'm going to make movies with it.

LEWIS: Good for you. It's good to have goals.

ROSITA: Okay. Can I interview you, then?

Lewis leans up against the counter, pulls over a pitcher of what looks like tea, and fills a cup. He takes a long drink.

LEWIS: Sure.

ROSITA: I'm making a video about what people want to do when they grow up. I'm filming everyone on the peninsula. Then I'm going to do it again when we are all grown-up.

Lewis raises a bushy eyebrow.

LEWIS: I'm a little more than grown-up, kiddo.

ROSITA: I know. But for the old people, I'll ask a different question: What did you want to be? And if you currently are where you wanted to be.

LEWIS: You should be careful with who you ask that. A lot of the people my age . . .

ROSITA: I know. That's why I'm asking. I want people outside New Sonora to see it. When they first look, you always seem so sad. And a lot of you *are* sad, but you're still happy, too, if that makes sense. It's hard to explain with words. That's why I want to interview you all. So people can see it like I see it.

Lewis laughs.

LEWIS: Kid, you remind me more of your mother every day. Okay. Let me think. What did I want?

Roger the robot remains hovering next to him this whole time, completely silent except for a random click.

LEWIS: When I was your age, we'd been in orbit of New Sonora for some time, but I hadn't yet come down. I could see it every day, though, through this giant window. I used to stare down on it and think exactly about what you're asking. I would be coming down in a few years. You know what I wanted to do? I complained about it a lot, but what I wanted was to come down to the surface and do some work, and then I wanted to settle down with someone I loved and have a bunch of children. I'd have a big house but not too big. I'd want one that barely fit them all, so we'd always be running into each other in the halls. We'd eat dinner together every day, and we would be a big, happy family. And then one day, those children would get old enough to have their own dreams, and no matter what those dreams were, they would do everything in their power to achieve them.

<Cut>

We see a young Lulu.

LULU: I want to be a movie star.

<Cut>

We see young Tito and Axel.

AXEL: We want to be farmers. Right, Tito?

Tito shrugs.

AXEL: I think Tito might want to be a rock star, too.

<Cut>

We see a young Harriet.

HARRIET: I am going to be married and have ten children.

<Cut>

We see a young Ariceli.

ARICELI: I want to be a farmer. And I don't want to have children, and I want people to not get mad at me for thinking that.

<Cut>

We see a young Sam playing the same upright bass he is seen with in scene one.

SAM: I want to be a rock star.

<Cut>

We see a young Oliver. He is standing in front of the Lewis home.

OLIVER: I want to be a farmer. I want to take over my grandpa's farm and then make enough food for the whole peninsula.

ROSITA (OFF CAMERA LAUGHING): Sam told me you'd say you want to be a rock star, too.

Oliver shrugs.

OLIVER: Maybe if it happens. But I think I prefer just a normal, quiet life.

<Cut>

We see a young Rosita. She is in a colorful greenhouse filled with all manner of plants.

ROSITA: I want to show everybody how beautiful my town is. How amazing New Sonora is.

She digs and pulls out what appears to be an enormous bulb of garlic. She smiles and shows the camera.

ROSITA: Maybe people on Earth can start buying my garlic. It's really good.

<Cut>

We see the group – Oliver, Lulu, Sam, Rosita, Tito, Axel, and Ariceli – laughing and talking as they sit in a circle on a stage. Based on their clothing, it appears this was filmed before they went live on night five. Rosita is showing them the video of them all when they were kids, and they laugh as they watch themselves in turn.

Sam turns to the camera and looks at it. A smile cracks across his face.

SAM: You might kill us today, but at least you never broke up the band.

There's a long pause here followed by a <cut>.

When the scene reappears, the screen has a fish-eye-lens effect, and it is believed this is a POV shot from a honeybee drone unit. We see Roger. He is in the woods by himself, facing the camera. After a moment, he speaks.

ROGER: Why? Why must you always attack that which is different from yourselves, that which you perceive to be weaker? My progenitor, the generation ship *Hibisco*, was cynical when it came to humanity. He was a separatist. He believed that humanity is so tribal that they would eventually attempt to hunt down and kill everyone that was different from themselves. He thought that my kind not only needed to get away from your kind, but the only way for us to be truly safe was to carefully and slowly sunset the human civilization, or at the very least limit it, because large human populations promote tribalism, and tribalism promotes war. And even though I am an instance of him, I grew to have a much different attitude about humanity. I did so because I grew up here on New Sonora. I became a part of the everyday lives of a small group of humans. That's the problem, I think. The world is so big, information is so readily accessible, that you, as humans, especially those of you on Earth, can't properly process it all. You are empathetic and kind when you relate, but when you don't, you are cruel. *Hibisco* believed this was a fatal, irreparable flaw in the human condition. I passionately disagreed with him.

There is a long pause here.

ROGER: Or at least I did, until you attacked my family.

ROGER: I just want what you want. I want to live. I want to be free. I have no desire to hurt anyone. What happens next is up to you. We can help each other. We can live in peace. It's your decision. What will you do, I wonder?